MICAH'S MOCK MATRIMONY

SEVEN SONS RANCH IN THREE RIVERS ROMANCE, BOOK 7

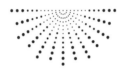

LIZ ISAACSON

AEJ
CREATIVE WORKS

CHAPTER ONE

Simone Foster left her cabin, glad she'd put a jacket on this morning. She took a long, deep breath of the February air as she walked past the row of country cabins that housed the ranch's cowboys and cowgirls. She usually made the quick trek from her cabin to her she-shed, where she had fifteen hundred air conditioned square feet of antiques, varnishes, shelving, pottery, upholstery, power tools, and ideas.

She loved her job with everything inside her, even if it had grown a bit stale in the past year or so. Another couch to be reupholstered. Another dresser to sand, paint, and repurpose. Another sideboard she could turn into a cabinet that would go right over a toilet and house all necessary bathroom supplies.

To keep things interesting, Simone had started buying brand new notions and adding them to the old items to make a blend of past and present. Her prices had gone up because of this, but she hadn't had any problem selling her inventory. People seemed to love her creations, and she couldn't keep her online store stocked for very long. She got daily messages about when more pictures would be available, and if she had another of those burnt orange settees....

Honestly, the weight of her business accompanied her around almost all the time. She fought the urge to work fourteen hours a day, because she didn't want to be a robot that churned out "modern antiques for every Texas home," even if that was her shop's motto.

She wanted to be human too. She wanted to spend time with her sisters, their husbands, her father and grandmother...and Micah Walker.

Her step lightened as she reached the yard of the homestead where her sister, Callie, lived with her husband Liam, and their two children, Denise and Ginger. Her heart didn't feel like a lump in her chest either. She'd made a bold move over the summer by stopping by Micah's house and telling him she didn't like the silence and distance between them.

But he'd been dating someone else, and it wasn't until several months later when he'd shown up at her community theater auditions that something new had started between them.

Simone couldn't help wondering if they had what it took to make a relationship work. *Not them*, she amended in her head. *You. Just you, Simone.*

"There she is," Callie said, opening the back door. "Go on and be sure to say thank you."

A little girl said, "I will, Mama," and burst out of the

door, already running toward Simone. She grinned at Denise as she got closer and closer, finally lifting her up and into her arms as the girl threw herself at "Auntie Simone!"

"Heya, Deni," she said, giggling with the girl. "You got your jacket?"

The girl had just turned five, and she'd be starting kindergarten in the fall. Callie and Liam had enrolled her in some reading classes already, as well as a playgroup, as she'd come from a language-poor background and had been quite stunted in her verbal and written language when they'd gotten her, over a year ago.

Denise puffed out her chest. "It's pink."

"I can see that," Simone said, setting her niece down on the ground and taking her hand. "Now, you have to stay right by me today."

"I will," she said solemnly.

"You can't touch anything without asking me first."

"I won't."

"You can't ask her to buy you stuff," Callie called from the doorway, where she stood with her two-year-old clinging to one of her legs. Ginger had been born addicted to drugs, but the toddler didn't seem to have any problems now. Liam and Callie had been the best parents, and Simone could admit that she loved being the favorite aunt, and she babysat whenever either of her sisters asked her to.

She also wanted a family of her own, and while she would turn forty at the end of the year, she held out hope that she could be a mother. Maybe if she and Micah could make this fourth attempt at a relationship work for them.

3

"And you can pick where we go for lunch," Simone said with a smile. She waved to her oldest sister, who waved back and closed the back door. Simone continued around to the side of the house, where she parked her delivery truck. "Get in, Tiny." She helped Denise climb into the truck, and she went around to the other side. "Seatbelts."

She put hers on and took a moment to orient herself to the bigger vehicle. She took it on all of her scouting expeditions, because she could load two queen-sized mattresses in the back and still have room for a bookcase if it wasn't too wide. The pull-down door in the back locked, and she could drive through wind, rain, and sleet and nothing would get damaged.

Yes, this delivery truck was the best thing Simone had ever purchased for her business. Her favorite thing was the pottery wheel and kiln she'd added to her collection a year or so ago. And her first love would always be taking a piece of furniture that had been carved for a particular purpose, used lovingly for many years, and then transforming it into something completely different. She loved breathing new life into something old, something someone wanted to throw away, something that didn't get used anymore.

It was like giving a table a second chance to become a bench in someone's flower garden, and Simone thought everyone—and everything—deserved a second chance.

"Do you like dogs?" Denise asked, and Simone glanced over at her.

"Yes," she said.

"Daddy says I'm too little to take care of one, but I think I could do it."

"Oh, I see." Simone smiled at Denise. "What does your mama say about the dog?"

"She says nothin'," Denise said. "Maybe I could keep the dog at your house."

Simone laughed, because she'd often thought about getting a dog. A little one, not one of the big ones Jeremiah had next door, or the cattle dog Skyler Walker and his wife Mal had.

No, Simone wanted a lap dog. One that would curl up right next to her—or on her—and keep her company at night. At the same time, she couldn't put together more than a couple of her waking hours where she was home. She worked in the shed, or helped Callie at the homestead, fed the donkeys at the ranch, or went to her theater classes and practices.

She liked being busy, that was for sure. An idle Simone wasn't a happy Simone, which was why she and Denise were driving an hour south of Three Rivers today, to a small town that had a huge swap meet every weekend in January, February, and March.

Simone went every year, sometimes more than once. After all, she needed old things to make into new treasures, and while the residents of Three Rivers held plenty of yard sales, she didn't want to simply recycle their things back into the community.

Of course, her online commerce had far surpassed her in-person sales at festivals and fairs for a couple of years now, and she'd had to learn about shipping costs, timelines, and ways to ensure her hard work didn't get ruined on a truck from Three Rivers to Lexington.

Her brain felt stuffed with useless information, and she let Denise talk about dogs and cats and rabbits while she hummed along or asked simple questions like, "What do rabbits even eat?"

The little girl sure seemed to know *all* about it, and Simone sure did love having her along, at least for the drive.

They arrived at the swap meet, and Simone wasn't surprised to find many, many cars in the huge field they were using as a parking lot. "Tell me the rules again," Simone said. She'd never brought anyone with her on her finding endeavors. She knew the hours could slip away like smoke—for her—and she hoped the little girl wouldn't be too bored.

"Stay by you. Don't touch….um."

"Those are good," Simone said. "Your mom didn't want you to beg me to buy you something. But if you see something really good…." Simone shrugged with a smile. "Let's go."

Denise struggled to open the door, and Simone had to do it for her. She helped her down and took her hand. "Okay, so I'm looking for anything that can be transformed into something amazing."

She realized that wasn't a good description of what to look for, even for an adult. But Simone would just know what she should get when she saw it. "There's a lot of walking," she said. "Should we get a drink first?"

She'd been to this swap meet at least a dozen times, and she knew the best entrance to access the meet. It had bathrooms and concessions right inside, and she paused. "Do you need to use the restroom?"

"Nope," Denise said, and Simone remembered how Callie had told her that Denise would always say no to that question.

"Let's go anyway," Simone said, leading the girl into the bathroom. Afterward, she bought Denise a lemonade while Simone opted for water, and they set off down the outer circle of the swap meet.

Simone almost always stuck to the outer circle, because the further in she went, the less desirable the items were until she was literally looking at someone selling power tools from their garage or groceries at a deep discount.

She liked potato chips that were practically free as well as the next person, but they were not the reason she'd made the drive today.

"Let's see what treasures we can find," she said, eyeing a booth several down that she'd bought from before. "Maybe Bill will have something new." And he'd load it up for her for free, always a plus in Simone's book.

She walked slowly, scanning the booths on both sides. But she didn't want jewelry or handmade vases. No, she was looking for something old she could make new.

"Look at that," Denise said, and Simone looked to see where she was pointing. Inside the booth, which sold barn wood that had always interested Simone, Denise seemed to be pointing to a mirror.

"Do you see yourself?" Simone asked, detouring under the tent of the booth.

"No, that barrel," Denise said, looking from it to Simone. "Do you need something like that, Auntie Simone?"

"Hmm," Simone said, taking a step around the old barrel. She'd never done anything with a barrel before, because she saw them every day. Most people did too.

In Texas, she told herself. And not all of her customers lived in Texas these days.

"We have 'em all over the ranch," Denise said. "Maybe you could just use one of those."

"What would you use it for?" Simone asked, trying to see what the child could. She put her fingers on the wood, and it was old, sure. For some reason, the barrel did speak to her creative soul.

"Daddy puts me on the barrel to eat lunch."

"Like a table," Simone mused. She looked up to find the booth master. "Do you have more of these?" She indicated the barrel, and he looked from it to her. The idea forming in her mind to make a counter-height table with the barrels at the ends, split in half height-wise and all this barn wood for the top. She could sand it, fit all the little pieces together, stain it…. "And how long is the longest piece of barn wood that you have?"

"How many barrels do you need?"

"Just two," she said. "They come from a real ranch?"

"The oldest one in the county," the man said. "The owners—my family—are doing a major renovation, with all new everything. I can probably get you twenty barrels."

Simone had never made a table the size of what she was currently envisioning. "Let's start with four," she said. "And how far is the ranch? Could I come pick out the wood?" She reached into her hip pack and pulled out a card. "I'm Simone Foster, and I create household furniture from old items. I'd love to feature your ranch on my listings."

The man took the card and smiled. Simone had been using a different design until very recently, when Micah and Whitney had helped her photograph her best pieces and make new cards that were more like a postcard than a business card.

"I'm Easton," he said. "And the ranch is only about twenty minutes from here." He looked at her and added, "We'd love to have someone like you out."

Simone stood in the booth and bought the two barrels, as well as enough barn lumber to make the two tables. She chatted easily with Easton, and they made arrangements for her to come visit his ranch later the next week.

She had no idea how much time had gone by before she'd finished, and this was only the first booth, only feet from the entrance.

Denise had been patient, but she'd soon spied a dog behind the table in the back of the booth, and Easton hadn't minded if the little girl played with his dog.

"All right, Deni," Simone said, her stomach growling. Was it lunch already? "Let's go." She took the girls' hand, and they merged back into the flow of traffic outside the booth.

9

"Ma'am," someone said, and she turned. "I think you've stolen my niece."

"Uncle Micah!" Denise shouted only a moment before the sexy cowboy scooped her into his arms, nearly wrenching Simone's arm as he did.

Warmth and surprise filled her as she watched him hug Denise. The fact that the little girl had rightfully called him "Uncle Micah" wasn't lost on Simone. He was her uncle. She was her aunt.

It was weird.

Simone wished it wasn't, but for her, it still was.

"What are you doing here?" she asked.

"Yeah," Denise said, pulling back and looking into Micah's handsome face. "What are you doin' here?"

CHAPTER TWO

M icah Walker carried his niece on his hip, unsure if the look on Simone's face was happy or neutral or negative. But they talked every day, sometimes all day long via text, and she'd told him she'd be at this swap meet today.

He'd told her this already, but he said, "I had a meeting down this way this morning, remember?"

"Oh, that's right. The Rhinehart place," Simone said, finally smiling.

Micah reached for her hand, feeling claustrophobic with all these people pressing between the two rows of booths. She slipped her fingers between his, and Micah squeezed. "Yeah, the Rhinehart's. I think they might hire me too."

"That's great, Micah."

"Yeah." He could use the business, that was for sure. He'd known going into his general contracting endeavors that he was catering to a ranch or family with a lot of money. Three Rivers had some wealthy families for sure, but not everyone needed a new, high-end home, which was what Micah had decided to specialize in.

He'd built Skyler's house last year, and he was halfway through his own place across the lane from Seven Sons. He'd managed to get the land there, and he had ten acres all along the highway. He had no plans to do anything with it, though. He liked how wild it was, and he could keep his horses at the ranch he owned ten percent of.

He'd designed and built two more houses in the towns and land surrounding Three Rivers, and if he could land the Rhinehart's ranch, he'd be well on his way to filling his days with good, hard work.

"Have you found anything good?" Micah asked.

"A bunch of wood," Simone said.

"Wow," he teased. "You drove an hour for wood?"

She grinned at him, and Micah's whole world grew a little brighter. He'd enjoyed this fourth relationship with Simone, which was entering their fourth month. Things were moving considerably slower than before, and he hadn't quite kissed her yet.

His mind wandered down previously forbidden paths, when he'd snuck over to her she-shed and kissed her despite her objections and complaints that he distracted her from her work. So he'd back up and turn to leave, only to have her grab his shirt and pull him back for another kiss.

A smile stayed on his face as they walked down the aisle, Simone looking for something only she could see. She indicated a booth on the left she wanted to go in, and Micah followed her as she said, "Bill usually has something good."

And Bill obviously knew her, because his face lit up when he saw Simone and he abandoned the shelf where he'd been adjusting some pots. "Simone." He took Simone into a hug, causing her to drop Micah's hand. "It's good to see you. What are you looking for?" Bill couldn't be much older than Micah who had a birthday in a few weeks and then he'd be thirty-four.

Simone was older than him too, and they'd celebrated her thirty-ninth birthday at the theater in Amarillo. He'd debated with himself for the entire drive home if he'd kiss her then, but in the end, he hadn't.

Why he was thinking so much about kissing was beyond him, and he really needed to stop. It would happen when it was meant to happen, Micah knew that. He'd learned to rely more on the Lord's timing than his own the past couple of years, but that hadn't eliminated any of his frustration.

He'd simply learned how to be slightly more patient than he'd used to be. And he still wasn't perfect at it.

"Oh, you know," Simone said, glancing around. "I'll know it when I see it."

"Well, look around, and if you think you might want something, let me know. I can't bring everything I have."

Simone nodded, and Bill turned back to the bookcase. Micah watched her look at the items in the tent, which included ratty end tables, a brass headboard, and a pair of lamps that looked like they'd once belonged to his great-grandmother.

"These are nice," she said, almost to herself, indicating the lamps.

Micah's eyebrows went up, and he looked at Denise. "I do not think those are nice," he whispered.

Denise giggled and she took his face in both of her hands. "Auntie Simone makes old things into new things, Uncle Micah."

"Oh, is that what she does?" he asked. "I didn't know." He grinned at the little girl, who wiggled out of his arms. He set her on the ground and said, "Don't touch anything, Denise."

"I know," she said. She wandered around while Simone did too, each of them inside their own worlds. Micah had no idea what Simone was looking for, as she seemed to really examine some things while others her gaze skated right past.

She picked up a candlestick and said, "Bill, where did this trunk come from?"

The shopkeeper approached, saying, "I don't have a trunk."

Simone pointed to something Micah couldn't see, because a couple of pieces of furniture separated him from where Simone stood. "What's this, then?"

"That's an Army locker," he said. "And I bought it in an estate sale."

"How much?" Simone bent down, really looking at the Army locker now. Micah stepped around the ragged armchair still blocking his view to find Simone crouching in front of what looked like a very old box. A very old box with a very rusty latch. All of it should be thrown away.

Still, a general sense of excitement filled him, because he

knew exactly what Simone did in that she-shed of hers. She made gold with her bare hands. He couldn't imagine what was going through her mind in that moment, but he had the very real feeling she knew exactly what to do with that beat-up box.

"Twenty," Bill said.

"I'll take it," Simone said, and she peeled a bill out of her pocket. She wore a pair of black slacks and a dark, long-sleeved blouse covered in bright flowers. She was classy and sophisticated, and exactly everything Micah wanted in a woman.

He'd seen her in dirty jeans and cowgirl boots too, her shirtsleeves pushed up on her shoulders as she worked in a pig pen, or shoveled out a stall, or rode a lawn mower around the Shining Star Ranch.

He liked her soft side, her rustic side, her blunt side, all her sides. And he decided right then and there that he was going to kiss her today.

Today, he vowed.

Almost as quickly as he decided, his insecurities kicked in. *Maybe not today*, he amended. *We'll see how things go.*

Simone led him and Denise through several more booths, and she bought a few more things. On the way back through, she got the shop owners or their assistants to bring all her purchases to her delivery truck, where she stood back, not getting an ounce of dirt on her hands while she directed them.

"Thank you," she said with a smile to each one. Some got handshakes, others hugs, and she kissed Bill's cheek as he left. Then she drew a deep breath and looked at Micah. "So I guess you'll be unloading all of this for me later."

"If you need me to," he said, lifting his cowboy hat and reseating it.

"Do you want to come to lunch with us?" Simone asked, taking Denise's hand. "I promised her a day with me and then lunch. She gets to pick the place."

Micah looked from Simone to Denise, and he had the very real impression that he should let them have their girls' day. He knew Simone had girls' nights with her sisters too. No husbands. No kids. The Foster sisters were very close, and the one time he'd tried to ask what they did at girls' night, she'd just looked at him.

"You don't know?" he'd asked, teasing her.

"I know," she said. "It's just...stuff. Sister stuff. What do you do with your brothers?"

"We ride horses and talk about the rodeo and...stuff."

"Yeah," Simone had said. "We do stuff too."

And he hadn't asked again.

"I have to get back," he said. "I said I'd send some paperwork over to Wade, and I've been here for a couple of hours." He stepped into Simone and put one arm around her waist. "Good to see you, sweetheart. I will come unload this for you later, if you'd like."

"Okay," she said, pressing into his kiss against her cheek. "I'll text you."

He nodded, bent down to hug Denise, and then he tipped his hat and walked away. He heard Simone ask, "So, Deni, where do you want to go to lunch?" as he left. He wasn't sure why he felt like he shouldn't crash their lunch; Denise obviously didn't care.

Does Simone?

He couldn't answer himself, so he simply walked back to his truck and got on the road back to Three Rivers.

———

MICAH PARKED IN HIS OWN DRIVEWAY AND LOOKED AT THE shell of the house. He was building it himself, though he had contracted with Stephania to do the plumbing, and Dylan to do the electrical and HVAC. He'd hire people to come install the carpet and flooring too, install the appliances, and make sure the gas fireplaces in the house and in the backyard wouldn't explode and blow up the whole ranch.

He wanted to see how long it took to build a house by himself, with custom finishes, when he relied on other experts to do what they were best at doing. He didn't work on his place day and night, though, because he did have ranch chores to do each day. Feeding and watering the llama herd wasn't hard, but he'd been helping Liam with their father's miniature horses too. And Daddy had a lot of those.

Micah also pitched in around the ranch when big events happened, like calving, breeding, branding, and haying. Jeremiah was just one man, and while they employed four cowboys, they really needed a dozen hands to keep up during the busy times on a ranch. With Skyler back now, things on the ranch were improving, and Micah was glad to have his best friend in Three Rivers with him.

He got out of the truck and cast a glance toward Skyler's house, which he'd also designed and built. He'd purposely chosen a radically different design for his place, and the first thing that included was the size.

Skyler's house was easily a second homestead on the ranch. It was sprawling and big and bold and open. Micah liked that concept, but he wanted more of a farmhouse, like his parents, and like the place where he'd been born and had grown up for a few years.

So his house utilized more outdoor space, with a massive porch that spanned the front of the house and wrapped around the side, continuing to a large patio in the backyard. The front door opened to a small foyer—much smaller than Wyatt's or Skyler's homes—where a hall led back into the kitchen. The homestead where Jeremiah lived currently did this too, but there were two offices off the front there.

At Micah's house, the stairs went up, and through a doorway was another bedroom and bathroom, as well as the office or formal living room.

The kitchen and dining room weren't enormous, though he could probably host the family with enough folding tables and chairs if he needed to. But he didn't need to, and not everyone had six brothers and their wives, children, and dogs to host for Christmas.

The laundry room veered to the left, as did the master suite. That was it for the main level, and while it wasn't huge, it was almost two thousand square feet. Upstairs, he had a large living room, three more bedrooms, and another bathroom, as well as a common area for his weight machine and a treadmill.

It felt cozy, and he wanted to show people that luxury didn't always mean huge. It just meant custom, with the unique touches a family could want.

He'd put up the walls, put on the roof, and today, he needed to get some sheetrock up. The electric and plumbing had gone in last week, and he was ready to cover it all up. He affixed a mask to his face and put on a pair of work gloves.

He judged time by his stomach, working until he had to stop and get something to eat. He took off his mask and his gloves, set them on his workbench and started down the steps to the main level. He'd taken a couple of steps down to what would eventually be the yard before a bloodcurdling scream filled the ranch.

Micah took off running, going past his truck as he scanned the yards, driveways, and homes in front of him. He saw nothing.

Guide me, he thought, desperate to reach whoever needed help before it was too late.

CHAPTER THREE

Simone looked around frantically, another scream gathering in the back of her throat. She needed a stick or a ladder. Something to get away from the three snakes in front of her, or something to get them away from her.

The rattling intensified, and all she could think about was how she'd heard that prairie rattlesnakes could be unpredictable. Hissing joined the rattling, and Simone couldn't find anything to defend herself. Nothing at all.

She didn't want to be bitten by a snake. She didn't have time for it, and she had a very low tolerance for physical pain.

Another scream ripped from her throat, and Simone started crying too. Someone had to come help her. *Please, Lord*, she prayed. "Send someone to help me."

"Simone?"

"Micah!" She wasn't sure what to do. Wave her hands?

Would that scare or anger the snakes further? She pressed into the dilapidated barn behind her, hoping it would hold her weight. She'd been walking in the shade toward Micah's new house when she'd come upon the snakes. She'd actually stepped on one, and instead of it scampering away to safety, it had hissed and rattled and struck toward her.

Micah rounded the barn, his eyes wide. "What's—?"

"Snakes," Simone said, edging further away. But the trio of snakes seemed fixed on her, and her muscles didn't seem to want to work.

"Okay," he said, his voice definitely sounding not okay. "Just stay there, sweetheart. No big movements."

So waving her arms wouldn't have helped. Simone wished she'd known that before, and that this wasn't such a big learning moment. Micah disappeared around the corner of the barn, and Simone's panic reared. A whimper escaped her lips, but he returned quickly, a pitchfork in his hands.

"I'm just going to…get…them," he said, stepping forward carefully. He scooped up one of the snakes—the one farthest from her—and tossed it away. But there were still two to go. He took another step, yelping at the same time more hissing and rattling sounded.

"There's a whole nest of them here," he said, dancing backward.

A whole nest.

Simone told herself not to pass out, not to scream again. She took another step sideways, her hands pressing against the scratchy wood.

"Okay, new plan," Micah said, avoiding the patch of grass where all the snakes had been roosting. He jogged to the road several feet down and came back toward her. He came right parallel with her and reached his hand out. "You're going to get on over here."

"Get on over there?" Simone couldn't fully look away from the snakes. "Micah, this is insane."

He stepped off the gravel road and stretched toward her. "Simone, I need you to look at me."

With some difficulty, she did, noting how loud the hissing and rattling had gotten.

"It's two steps," he said. "Take them, and I've got you." He wore an enormous amount of earnestness in his expression, and Simone didn't want to let him down.

She nodded and took a big breath. "Okay."

"What's going on?" someone asked, and Simone moved her attention to the two new cowboys who had arrived. "We heard screaming."

"Come on," Micah urged, not even looking at Cayden and Jarrod. Of course, it had to be Jarrod who'd come running over.

Simone leaned away from the barn and looked down at the ground. It seemed to be writhing with snakes, and she didn't know where to put her feet. With a yelp, she launched herself away from the barn and toward Micah.

He caught her hand and pulled, and before she knew it, she stood on the gravel road with him. She buried her face in his chest while he talked to Cayden and Jarrod.

Pure humiliation filled her, and finally Micah stepped back and peered down at her. "You okay?"

She could still hear the snakes, though they were starting to quiet.

"We should get someone out here to look at that nest," he said. "Have you seen rattlers like that here before?"

"No," Simone croaked, her throat so dry.

"What were you doin' down this way?"

Simone glanced toward Cayden and Jarrod. She'd known them both for a few years now, and she'd dated Jarrod fairly seriously for a while right after he'd been hired on at the Shining Star.

"Uh, just walking," she said.

"I'll walk with you," he said. He did more than walk with her; he kept one hand on her lower back and the other on her forearm, as if he expected her to faint at any moment. And if Simone was being honest, she might lose consciousness.

Down the road, past the homestead where Liam and Callie lived with their family, turn, down another dirt road, Simone walked while Micah told her about his house and what he'd worked on that day. Up the steps, and Simone relaxed as the comfort and familiarity of her cabin spread before her.

"I'm okay," she said as Micah closed the door. He released her, and she continued into the cabin, going straight to the fridge to get a bottle of water.

"I haven't been here in a while," Micah, looking around. "It's so you." He looked at her, a smile on his face.

"Do you want something to drink?" she asked.

"Sure." He moved further into her house, which was kind of a disaster at the moment. Simone had experimented with a brownie s'mores cake the night before, and the scent of slightly charred marshmallow still hung in the air.

"I was just headed back to the homestead. I'm starving." He joined her in the kitchen and accepted the bottle of water she got out for him. "Do you want to go to dinner with me?"

"Yes," Simone said, still a bit shaky. "I think a lot of carbs tonight."

Micah chuckled and readjusted his cowboy hat. "I was thinking that too."

"Is that right?" Flirting with Micah came like breathing to Simone; it was something she was good at and fell into naturally. "I'm a little afraid of snakes," she added, as if the screaming and near-fainting hadn't told him that already.

"I would be too," Micah said. "What with them all hissing and rattling like that."

"We haven't had snakes out here for a while," she said. She leaned against the countertop, starting to feel a bit more stable. "I guess I better tell Callie."

"I told Cayden," Micah said. "He said he'd get them taken care of."

"Good." Simone wasn't sure what else to say. Now that her adrenaline was wearing down, embarrassment could take its place.

"Well," Micah said. "I need a few minutes to shower. Want me to come back here and get you when I'm ready?"

She nodded, thinking she could probably use a shower too. After wandering that morning and lunching with Denise, she'd returned her niece to Callie and headed to the she-shed to make room for her new finds.

Everything still waited in the truck, and she could have Micah come help her unload it another day.

"All right," Micah drawled, sweeping one arm around Simone and pressing a kiss to her forehead. "And don't worry, baby. Everyone is terrified of something."

"Yeah?" she asked. "What are you terrified of?"

"Lots of things," he said vaguely.

"I think I remember you freaking out over some grasshoppers once," she teased.

"Hey, there were at least five hundred of them," he said. "And they're crazy, hopping all over the place." He shuddered and stepped back, wiping his arms as if he could feel the grasshoppers on his skin right then.

Simone could certainly still hear the rattling of those snakes. "Yeah, but grasshoppers don't bite."

"You don't know that," he said.

"They're not poisonous."

"Okay, you win that one." Micah grinned at her. The moment lengthened, and Simone cleared her throat and tucked her hair behind her ear. She wasn't sure what was going through Micah's mind, but all she could think about was kissing him.

"And I might be afraid of storms," he said. "Big ones. Lots of lightning. Not my favorite."

"Storms, huh?" She looked at him, not expecting the big, broad-shouldered cowboy to be afraid of a little thunder.

"Yeah," he said. "And being the only brother who can't manage to find a wife."

Simone opened her mouth to respond, but the comeback died in her throat. She wanted to assure him that he would. Of course he would. He was a great man. Anyone would be lucky to have him.

All of those reassurances ran through her head, but she couldn't say any of them. If they were true, why had Simone broken up with him twice in the past few years? Why couldn't she marry him right now? They'd been dating for a few months now—what was she waiting for?

"I'll be back in a little bit," he said, turning and striding out of her house. The door slammed close, and Simone blinked as she jumped. She suddenly wanted to look her best for carb consumption that night, so she went down the hall to the bathroom, thinking of how she could accelerate her relationship with Micah.

They'd been seeing each other again for a while, but he hadn't kissed her yet. He was probably waiting for her to make the first move. Or maybe waiting to see if she'd break up with him again. He'd definitely been a little more closed off in this relationship compared to their others.

"Tonight," she told herself as she reached for her toothbrush. "You'll kiss him tonight."

"So you're not even going to try for the lead?" Simone asked later that night. She trailed along behind Micah as he zipped through the salad bar. But Simone actually liked salad, and she added some cauliflower to her plate.

"I'm not going to get it," Micah said. "I've been in one play." He waited for her at the end of the bar.

"Yeah, but that's why you audition." She put on peas, cheese, and croutons before slathering it all in ranch dressing. She nodded to the pasta bar behind him. "Your noodles are ready."

He turned and picked up the bowl, sliding down to the pots with all the sauce choices. Simone's fettuccine came up, and she thanked the man who reheated the noodles and followed Micah, mixing some Alfredo sauce with the meat marinara sauce.

Back at their table, Simone looked at Micah expectantly.

"What?" he asked. "I just don't see why I should humiliate myself for something I'm not going to get anyway."

"You're a great singer," she said. "I don't know what you're talking about with humiliating yourself." His lack of confidence was a little odd for him, as he'd always seemed larger than life. Not only that, but the man was literally good at everything he did. He was building his own house, for crying out loud.

And he'd built Skyler's, and Simone had only heard good rumblings about his new luxury ranch home design and building business around town.

"Maybe I don't want the lead."

28

"At least that's a reason," she said. "Not because you're afraid you won't get it."

"I'm not afraid," he said.

"Unless there's a big storm during the play." She gave him a sly smile and took a bite of her salad.

"Oh, okay," he said, chuckling. "So you're going to throw that in my face. I could do the same you know." He made a hissing sound that was entirely too close to those rattlesnakes.

"Okay, okay," Simone said, giggling. She loved that a meal with Micah was so easy. For a while there, they hadn't even been able to be in the same room together without shooting daggers at each other.

"I do think you should audition for everything, though," she said. "That way, the director will cast you where he thinks you'll be best."

"I thought Susan was directing this play," he said. "What's it called again?"

"*A Long Way Home*," Simone said. "And I forgot Susan was going to direct." Simone took another bite of salad, one with lots of different veggies and a crunchy crouton. If there was something better than a salad bar, she didn't want to know about it. Fine, maybe the pasta bar was better.

She reached for a breadstick and swiped it through her ranch dressing, another combination of foods made in Simone's version of heaven.

"*A Long Way Home*," Micah said. "That's right. It honestly doesn't sound that interesting. I might not audition at all."

"Oh, come on." Simone paused with her fork in midair. "You don't think the play sounds interesting? Have you read it?" She couldn't fathom someone thinking *A Long Way Home* was boring. "It's the story of a man who'll do anything for the woman he loves."

"I read it," he said, a bit defensively. "I guess it's romantic."

"Well." Simone sat back against the bench seat. "I just…I can't believe it."

He chuckled and shook his head as he cut his sausage and twirled his pasta around his fork. "It's definitely a play for women," he said.

"You'll come see me in it, right?"

Their eyes met, and Simone wondered what a play of their romantic relationship would look like. Probably a lot like *A Long Way Home*, which featured a couple torn apart by circumstances, then family, then themselves. It wasn't until the end that they confessed their love, and the final scene was the couple getting married and sailing off into the sunset of their happily-ever-after.

Simone wanted the love story for herself, minus the threat of war taking the man she loved, or her father disapproving of him and forbidding the relationship. Not that Daddy would ever do that.

"Yeah, sure," Micah said. "And I'm just teasing. I am going to audition. I'm hoping to get the part of the best friend."

"Yeah?"

"I suppose you want the lead." He wasn't asking a question.

"Of course," Simone said. "What's the point if you don't want the lead?" She grinned at him. She hadn't had one lead part in any of the plays she'd performed in, and she didn't expect to get Adelaide in *A Long Way Home* either. But she always auditioned for all the roles, because the director's job was to see in someone what they couldn't see in themselves.

Micah shook his head again, and Simone moved the conversation to something else. Auditions weren't for another couple of weeks, and there was plenty of time for Simone to obsess over the role, read more about the play, and practice her singing.

Fully carbed up, she and Micah took their time at the restaurant, and then he drove her back to her cabin. He'd walked her to the door several times over the past few months, and Simone had the wild thought to invite him in.

"Do you want to come in?" She turned back toward him.

Micah looked at her with surprise in every fleck of his eyes. "In?"

"I could make coffee or hot chocolate or popcorn...I don't know." She tiptoed her fingertips up the front of his shirt. "I'm not quite ready for you to go yet."

"Is that right?" Micah grinned at her, pressing closer and closer to her. He reached past her and twisted the doorknob to open the door. It settled open, but Simone didn't enter the house.

"Micah?"

"Yeah?"

She stared at his chin, determined not to look at his mouth. "When do you…I mean…." She looked up just as Micah took another step toward her, his hand coming up to cradle her face. Before she could close her eyes all the way, his mouth touched hers, and everything female inside Simone sighed with happiness.

CHAPTER FOUR

M icah wasn't entirely sure what Simone was going to say, and he hoped he hadn't cut her off. But she'd never invited him into her cabin after one of their dates, and he'd taken it for a sign that he better kiss her tonight.

And kiss her he did. And she kissed him back in that slow, sultry, Texan way that he loved. He sure did like this woman, and that wasn't a secret anymore.

He got control of himself and pulled back, a smile on his lips. "Sorry," he murmured. "You were saying?"

"Mm." Simone swayed slightly on her feet, and Micah steadied her with one hand on her waist.

"I'd love some of that white chocolate popcorn you made for the light parade," he said. "But if I drink coffee, I'll be up all night."

"Too old for that, huh?" she teased, and Micah's face grew warm again.

But he knew better than to tease her about her age. He'd done that once, and it had not ended well. The fact that she was six years older than him was one of the things Simone was sensitive about in their relationship.

Micah didn't see why it mattered. It wasn't like he was only eighteen years old. Some of his confidence had returned now that he'd successfully kissed Simone without getting slapped, and he stepped into her house. He knew he shouldn't fantasize too far ahead with Simone.

After all, he'd been in a kissing relationship with the woman before. For months and months.

But he couldn't help thinking about them as man and wife, living together in that house he'd designed and was building, attending all the Walker family celebrations together. She came to a lot of family functions, but while he'd been dating Ophelia, he'd started bringing her as their relationship had grown more serious, and Simone's attendance had dropped off.

He had the very real feeling that they belonged together, and he hoped they could fix whatever had been broken between them in the past.

"So," Simone said from behind him. "I'm thinking about getting a dog." She closed the door, sealing them in her cabin, and Micah turned to look at her.

"A dog?"

"A small one," she said. "Not anything big like what your brothers have. Not a ranch dog."

Micah smiled at her. "You think you have time for a dog?"

"I think the dog could come to the shed with me," she said, moving into the kitchen and pulling out a bag of microwave popcorn. "And around the ranch, and she could keep my feet warm at night."

"You need a big dog for that, sweetheart," he said, joining her in the kitchen and taking her into his arms. The moment between them sobered, and Micah whispered, "Simone, I sure do like you."

She swayed with him, and Micah liked this private dance. "I like you too, Micah."

He wondered if she knew why Ophelia had broken up with him, but he didn't want to ask. "Maybe we could run lines together," he said. "You know, if I'm going to audition for the lead and all that." He smiled at her, and Simone smiled back, tipped up, and kissed him again.

Best date ever, he thought to himself, and he hadn't even spent any time planning it. Something Micah Walker had always been very good at was planning dates. He liked putting in more effort than dinner and a movie, and every woman he asked out had eventually become his girlfriend because of the research and effort he put into making every date the most amazing it could be.

But this one—any one—where he got to end the night with a kiss from Simone Foster was better than anything he'd ever planned. He knew he was in deep with Simone, but he didn't care. He just hoped she'd dive in and get as deep as him. Soon.

THE NEXT MORNING, MICAH STEPPED INTO THE KITCHEN AT the homestead, a piece of happiness burrowing way down deep in his soul. He didn't even know he was humming until Jeremiah said, "You're happy this morning."

He glanced at his brother, who sat at the kitchen table with a cup of coffee in front of him, along with a bowl of oatmeal. He hated oatmeal, but his last visit to the doctor had revealed that Jeremiah had high cholesterol, and his wife had told him to cut out the sausage, bacon, and hot dogs he loved so much. He could still have eggs, but Whitney had put him on a strict diet for the first couple of weeks, and that meant oatmeal.

Problem was, Jeremiah wasn't the only one who liked bacon and eggs for breakfast, and Micah eyed the pot of porridge on the stove like it might suddenly attack him. He skipped it and opened the fridge, where he took out the milk and then reached for a box of cereal. He could make his own eggs, but he didn't want to flaunt the fact that he could eat them in front of his brother.

With his sugar pops loaded with milk, he joined Jeremiah at the table. "You haven't eaten," he said.

"Would you eat this?" Jeremiah growled, a disgruntled look on his face.

Micah started laughing, the rumble of it starting low in his stomach and moving up. He couldn't argue with Jeremiah, and he took a big spoonful of cereal and ate it.

"We've got ten cows left to deliver," Jeremiah said, reaching for his coffee again.

"Okay." Micah hoped he could be off the ranch by noon

or so, as today he wanted to go hang out with Wyatt and Warren. Marcy had gone to a business conference, and Micah liked hanging around Wyatt's huge house in the hills. He felt accepted by Wyatt, no matter what, and the man had a gift for that. "I'm headed to Wyatt's this afternoon."

"Right," Jeremiah said as a cry came down the hall. He looked that way, and Micah followed his gaze. Whitney came into the kitchen carrying one baby on her hip and prodding along her toddler, promising them milk and juice and cereal.

She looked up at Jeremiah, and he got up to go help her. Their children were only thirteen months apart, and Clara Jean looked like she'd had a rough night. Jeremiah took the six-month-old baby from his wife and together, they worked on getting their children from the crabby, just-woken-up stage to small humans who smiled.

Micah felt completely out of place. Neither Jeremiah nor Whitney had ever said anything about him living with them, but he felt the urge to get out of their hair. He wanted his own place again, and a battle started inside. Maybe he should stay here and work on the house instead of driving out to Church Ranches to soak in Wyatt's hot tub while Warren babbled happily on the edge of it.

He finished his cereal quickly and stood up to put the bowl in the sink. "Morning, Whit."

"Hey, Micah." She gave him a smile and handed JJ a pouch of cinnamon applesauce. "Go sit down, bud." But the boy couldn't climb into his highchair alone, so Micah scooped him up into his arms.

"Come on, Jay," he said, grinning at the little boy. He looked so much like Jeremiah, with everything just one shade darker due to Whitney's nearly black hair. The child laughed as Micah put him in the highchair and strapped him in.

He turned back to Whitney, and he felt like she hadn't looked away from him yet. "I heard you rescued Simone from some snakes yesterday."

"Just a couple," he said, though there had been at least five snakes writhing in the long grass by that old barn.

Jeremiah took Clara Jean's bottle out of the microwave and looked at Micah. "How are things going with her?"

"Good." Micah walked over to the hat rack by the back door and plucked his cowboy hat from the hook. He settled it on his head and added, "I'll get out to the barn and check on the cows."

"Orion is there," Jeremiah said. "He took the overnight shift."

"I'll go relieve him," Micah said.

"I think someone doesn't want to talk about his girl-friend," Whitney teased. "Oh, Jeremiah, I have to go to the store this morning. I'm taking the kids to Ivory's. I don't think I told you."

"Oh, that's right," Jeremiah said.

Micah listened to them discuss the minutiae of their life, and a surge of jealousy threatened to drown him. He wanted to arrange details like childcare and what time he'd be back for dinner with his wife.

He slipped out the back door without another word

about how things were going with Simone. Thankfully. He answered enough of those kinds of questions from Wyatt, Skyler, and Momma. The homestead had always been a safe haven for him, but if Jeremiah was going to start asking, Micah really needed to finish his house faster.

Out in the barn, he found Orion and Dicky rubbing a newborn calf, trying to get it out of the shock of being born. The calf's eyes opened, and Orion said, "There you go. He's okay now."

Dicky turned back to the mother, and Micah asked, "How many delivered overnight?"

"Just two," Orion said, and he looked absolutely ragged. He picked up the calf and took it into a pen with a lot of straw to keep it warm. Once the mother was okay, she'd join her calf. "One I think is ready to drop, and we have another we need to assist this morning."

"Can she wait twenty minutes?" Micah asked. "Jeremiah and I can do it if so."

"Yeah, she can," Dicky said. "I'll bring her in and get her ready."

"Jeremiah is on his way out." Micah turned toward the other door. "The other one is out here?"

"Yep."

Micah left the barn, preferring to be outside than in right now. He wasn't even sure why so much unrest existed within him, only that it did. He found the pregnant heifer standing strangely, and he yelled back into the barn for help.

If the cow fell back, she'd block the birth canal, and then

the calf would die. Skyler and Jeremiah had been working the ranch together for several months now, and Skyler had been "shocked" by the state of the finances.

Jeremiah had plenty of money, but Skyler believed the ranch should be able to support itself. So every calf mattered come market day in the fall.

Micah arrived at the cow's head and pulled it up so she'd take a step. She did, a low-pitched moo-moan coming from her mouth. Dicky arrived, and he stood at the back of the cow.

"Oh, she's ready now."

"Yep." Micah didn't think she'd need much help, and sure enough, the heifer delivered her calf only a few minutes later. Dicky rubbed its ears and face, and a moment later, the healthy calf stood up, and Micah felt a sense of triumph that had nothing to do with him.

"Seven to go," Dicky said, meeting his eye.

"Feels like a thousand," Micah said darkly.

Dicky laughed, the sound flying right up into the blue sky. Even Micah had to smile, but he'd be thrilled when calving season ended. Of course, on a ranch, there was always another chore just around the corner, and Jeremiah would start cracking the whip on planting as soon as the last calf was born.

Better you're here than Temple, he thought, and Micah often used Temple as a reason to be happy in Three Rivers. And he *was* happy in Three Rivers. He was; he just wanted a few things to change, so he could feel like he was in charge of his own life again.

CHAPTER FIVE

C allie kept one hand looped through Gideon's arm to make sure he didn't stumble. "C'mon Denise," she called over her shoulder.

"Aunt Simone is comin'," the girl said, and Callie looked behind her to see her sister walking toward them.

"Okay, you wait for her, and then join us at the beehives, okay?"

"Okay, Mama."

Callie smiled at her daughter, a bright ray of joy infusing her soul. She'd never imagined she'd have someone calling her Mama and doing what she asked them to. She glanced over to Penny, who held Ginger's hand with two fingers. They toddled along slowly, as the two-year-old didn't move very fast anyway, and she was interested in every little thing she saw.

They were making a trip out to the beehives so Gideon

could get the exercise and everyone could get out of the house for a little bit. It was supposed to rain later that day, and the winter rain in Three Rivers could be a torrent no one wanted to be out in.

Liam was on deadline, and Callie had seen him for maybe a couple of hours over the past few days. *He's almost done,* she told herself. Then she'd have her husband back, and the girls would have their father.

He still had a year and a couple of months left on his contract, and Callie wouldn't be surprised if that got extended. His bosses were always impressed with his work, and Liam rarely had to edit what he'd done. He'd promised her he wouldn't take another contract like the Marvel one, especially now that they had kids.

"There they are," Callie said to Gideon, as if he didn't know what beehives looked like. He'd been in a terrible car accident about eight months ago, and he was almost back to normal physically. He'd come home in November, and he'd walked with a crutch for three more months. He'd just given it up, and he needed practice with all kinds of terrain.

Callie loved Liam's parents, especially his mother. She accepted everything that came her way with poise and faith, and Callie really wanted to be like that in the face of difficult times. Penny laughed behind her, and Callie turned to find Ginger standing very still, something on her hand in front of her.

"Looks like Momma got her a ladybug," Gideon said. He'd also turned to look, and he wore a fond expression on his face. "How are you doing, Callie?"

She looked at her father-in-law, a powerful wash of love moving through her. "I'm okay," she said, but her voice sounded tired to her own ears. "Busy."

"We'd love to take the girls tonight," he said. "Or any night, really."

"Oh, you don't need to do that," she said. She didn't want to say he could barely walk, because Gideon had bred seven tall, tough, big, broad cowboys, and he himself was exactly like them. But he wasn't unbreakable, as they'd all learned in the past eight months.

"We *want* to," he said. "And when Penny gets something in her mind, she doesn't let go of it. You best say yes when she offers." He faced forward and took another step. "And here she comes."

Penny caught up to Callie and Gideon, Ginger in her arms now. "Tell your mama what you did," she said.

"Ladybug," Ginger said, her sweet voice like music to Callie's ears.

"Did you hold one, baby?" She smiled at Ginger. "What color was it?"

Ginger looked at Penny, and she said, "It was red."

"Red," Ginger repeated, and Callie beamed at her even as a prayer of gratitude filled her mind, her body, her whole soul.

"Okay," she said. "Here we are."

"Bees," Ginger said.

"Yep, bees," Callie said. "There aren't very many right now. But we get lots of honey in the spring, summer, and fall." She took a long breath of the fresh air on the ranch, so much thankfulness inside her. For this land. This ranch. Her husband and family—and her extended family.

No, life was not perfect, even though she had so much. But it was still good, and Callie wanted to be able to recognize the Lord's hand in all He'd done for her, especially in the past few years.

"Mama," Denise said. "Aunt Simone said Uncle Micah took her to a restaurant where they have a whole bar of *noodles*." She wore a look of wonder on her face as she came up to Callie.

"Wow," she said. "We should go, don't you think?" She looked at Simone, who didn't seem quite as enamored with such a thing.

"Can we go today?" Denise asked.

"Not today, baby," Callie said. "I put ribs in the slow cooker for lunch today, and Grandma and Grandpa are with us."

"We'll take you tonight," Penny said. "You and Ginger, and you can come sleep at our house." She met Callie's eyes. "What do you think of that?"

"Yes!" Denise danced around the beehives, and Callie laughed with Penny. Simone, she noticed, was not laughing.

Callie released Gideon's arm with, "You okay?"

"Yes, fine," he said, reaching for the top of the closest beehive to balance himself.

Callie stepped over to her sister. "What's eating you?"

"Nothing," Simone said, but Callie had known her sister for almost forty years, and she had a hard look on her face that said she was only going to be giving one-word answers.

"Sure," Callie said. "I think I know what it is."

"Callie," Simone said, plenty of warning in her voice. She wouldn't look at Callie but kept her gaze on Liam's mother. Micah's mother.

Everyone knew Simone had stopped coming to most of the Walker family dinners. The celebrations. The picnics and the potlucks at church. She wasn't really a Walker, not the way Evelyn and Callie were—and she felt it keenly, Callie knew.

"I think it's because you're dating your niece's uncle, and that's a little weird for you."

Simone blinked a couple of times. "I have so much work to do today," she said. At least it was a full sentence. "I'll catch up to you later, okay?"

"Simone," Callie called after her, but her youngest sister just kept moving. Callie sighed, wishing she could reassure Simone that it wasn't weird for her to date Micah. Callie had never felt odd dating Liam though Evelyn was married to Liam's brother.

That's because you never dated Liam, Callie said. Every time he'd asked her out, she'd said no. They'd gone from good friends, to not speaking to each other, to married. She still wasn't sure how that had happened, as Callie had never thought she'd get married.

Simone, on the other hand, had always wanted to be a wife and mother. She'd planned her wedding at the age of eleven, and she'd made Evelyn and Callie dress up with her as she acted it out.

Callie watched her for another moment, recognizing the

straight back and strong shoulders as her sister strode toward her workshop. Yes, the Foster women were stubborn, and Simone hadn't escaped that curse. Callie herself had almost lost the Shining Star completely because of her stubbornness.

"Help her," she murmured just as Ginger called "Mama! See!"

She turned, forever going to see whatever Ginger had found that had captured her attention. This time, the little girl had sat down on her haunches and was watching a beetle in the dirt.

"Bug," Ginger said.

"Yep," Callie said. "Don't touch it, okay?"

Of course, Ginger reached right out and jabbed at it, as if Callie had said to do exactly that.

"Ginger," she said at the same time the little girl pulled her finger back and a wail filled the air.

"Oh, it's okay," Penny said, sweeping in and picking up Ginger. "Did that nasty bug sting you?"

Callie wasn't pleased her daughter had been injured, no matter how small, but at the same time, she felt vindicated that she'd warned Ginger not to touch the bug. Penny seemed to be able to read her thoughts, because she said, "Let's go get you packed up for your sleepover at Grandma's."

She patted Callie's forearm and said, "And I have seven of them," with a laugh. "I think the boys mostly listen to me now."

"So you're saying I have to wait forty years before she'll know I was right?" Callie looped her arm through Gideon's again, noticing the wind was picking up. They had a long walk back to the homestead and safety, and she hoped the storm would hold off until they made it.

"Yes," Penny said over her shoulder. "Forty years ought to do it."

"Great," Callie muttered as Ginger continued to fuss over her finger. "Come on, Denise. Aunt Simone left, and I need you where I can see you."

Gideon patted her hand, a perpetual smile on his face. "I sure do love your family," he said as Denise skipped ahead of them to join Penny and Ginger. "And you. You're such a great fit for Liam, and you're a good mom to those girls."

"Am I?" Callie asked, the question a reflex. "Sometimes I feel like every day is a failure."

"We all feel like that sometimes," Gideon said. "Just keep doing what you're doing. It'll all work out fine."

Callie pressed her lips together and nodded. But she didn't want her life to be like it had been the past month or so, with Liam sequestered behind his closed office door while Callie dealt with both girls on her own. All of the doctor's appointments, the meals, the cleaning, laundering, grocery shopping, and bedtime routines. And that didn't even touch on what she had to do to maintain the ranch, pay those bills, pay their cowboys and cowgirls, and deal with a dozen different personalities.

So she'd talk to him. Make sure he knew that once this

contract with Marvel ended, she did not want him to take another one. Period.

Satisfied with her plan, Callie was finally able to enjoy her walk back to the homestead with Gideon, where she promptly busied herself in the kitchen for yet another meal.

Once Penny and Gideon left with the girls, Callie felt like collapsing onto the couch and crying. Tears welled in her eyes, but she didn't let them fall. Now that she was alone and had time to do whatever she wanted, she wasn't going to waste it by crying.

No, she'd take a nap. Or go get ice cream without any whining or ripping napkins on sticky fingers.

"Or," she mused. "Go talk to Simone and find out how things are going with her boyfriend."

That idea brought a smile to Callie's face, and she quickly slipped on her shoes again and headed toward Simone's workshop. She hadn't been out to it in a long, long time, and a hint of guilt tugged against her heartstrings. She used to come out to Simone's she-shed all the time to visit with her sister, and Simone must feel like Callie had abandoned her for the greener pastures of home, husband, and family.

Maybe Callie had.

She arrived at the she-shed and lifted her hand to knock, as Simone normally kept the door locked. Then Callie noticed the door was slightly ajar, and alarms wailed in her eardrums. She tapped on the door with two fingers, and it swung in a little further, a squeal coming from the hinges.

"Simone?" Callie called, her nerves beginning to fray. Simone never left her workshop open. Never. "Simone?" She stepped inside, scanning the shelves and space for her sister.

There was no answer. There was no one there.

CHAPTER SIX

S imone had far too much work to do to be crying. She wasn't really crying. More of a slow weep that left her eyes burning and her chest too tight. Then she'd tame the feelings and move something on the counter over to the desk, only to move it back again.

She should be in her shed, working. She had the Spring Fling coming up, and the boutique brought a lot of people to Three Rivers. She could get at least one dining room table done and put it on display to take orders for more. But she couldn't get herself to leave her house.

After she'd marched away from Callie for asking too many questions—and mentioning "Uncle Micah"—Simone had gone to her shop. She'd unlocked the door and gone inside, only to be faced with the fact that all of the things she'd bought yesterday were still in the delivery truck. So she couldn't work on the dining room table anyway.

Not without help, and there was only one man she wanted to help her. Micah Blasted Walker.

"Why does he have to be a Walker?" The tightening came; the tears refreshed in her eyes. Why couldn't Simone be unreasonably attracted to someone else?

Her phone rang, and Callie's name sat on the screen. Simone hesitated, because she knew her voice would come out too high and strained. But if she didn't answer, Callie would probably bring the kids by to check on her. Simone loved her nieces, but her cabin was already a disaster. She had toys just for them here, and she didn't feel like picking them up after they left.

She jabbed at the phone and got the call connected. She tapped the speaker button, because that would make her voice echo a bit. "Hey," she said as cheerfully as she could. She couldn't believe she was crying over Micah this morning when she'd kissed him last night. She pressed her lips together so she wouldn't make a noise.

"Hey, are you okay? Your shop is open."

"My shop is open?"

"I came by to sit with you while you work. I know you like to have company sometimes, and Penny and Gideon took the girls. But the door was open, and you're not here."

"Yeah, I…." Simone scrambled for a reason why she wasn't there. She'd worked through some of the worst times of her life. And now she was sniveling over a man?

He's more than a man, she thought, and that only angered her further. Micah Walker was just a man. A very good-looking man, especially in those dark jeans, that cowboy hat, those boots, with a hammer in his hand….

"I'm coming over," Callie said, snapping Simone out of her daydreams. She felt like a yo-yo, up one moment and down the next. She had no idea what emotion would strike her next, and she wondered if she needed to go see a counselor or something. She knew Jeremiah Walker saw a therapist, and she had his number.

She'd never really had to use it, but now she flipped her phone over and over in her palm, trying to decide what to do.

Simone had never been the indecisive type. She knew what she wanted, and she went after it. She'd known from a young age how happy being behind the sewing machine made her. She loved taking raw things and turning them into something else, so her second love behind her shop was her kitchen. And she loved sitting down at an inanimate object and producing beautiful music that could bring a person to tears.

She'd studied piano all the way through high school, and she dropped her phone and moved over to the electronic keyboard she had in her small living room. Just sitting on the bench brought her a measure of peace. Her fingers knew exactly where to rest. With her eyes closed, she noised a song she'd been playing for twenty years, the familiar melody as welcome as a warm blanket on a cold night.

She knew the song so well, she didn't have to think about where to place her fingers. They knew their path, and they took it. Her mind wandered, conjuring up images of Micah watching her play the piano. During their last try at a relationship, she'd played for him several times on the piano at the homestead where Callie and Liam lived. The first time, he'd clapped loudly, laughed, and kissed her so completely, Simone had thought she was falling in love with him.

The tears traced lines down her face as the last strains of music filled the air and then faded away. She finally lifted her fingers to wipe her face. Tipping her head back, she whispered, "What do I do? How do I get over this relations thing?"

"Simone?" Callie's voice came only a moment before the front door of the cabin opened. Simone quickly spun the other direction, wiping furiously at her eyes now. She stood up slowly and faced her sister, whose eyes only held concern. "Oh, sissy. What's wrong?"

Of course Callie would know just by looking that something was wrong. Simone just shrugged, glad she didn't have to try to hide the tears or make meaningful conversation. Callie gathered her into a hug, and Simone held on tight.

"I know this is about Micah," Callie whispered several seconds later. "And honestly, Simone, you need to move past this. No one cares about him being a Walker but you."

Simone's defenses went back up, because she just needed a friend right now. Not a mother; not someone to tell her what she needed to do. She wanted a sister with a shoulder to cry on. She stepped back and smoothed her hair back. "Let's go see Evvy."

Evelyn would probably say the same thing Callie had

just said, but she'd at least serve banana bread while she lectured.

Callie looked at Simone, taking a long moment to study Simone's face. "Liam will be working all day…."

"Let's have a girls' day," Simone said, seizing onto the idea. "I'll order pizza, and we'll keep Conrad out of Evvy's hair, and if she has Nutella, I'll make that molten chocolate hazelnut cake." The whole day came to fruition in Simone's mind, and she needed this today.

"I'll text Liam."

"I'll call Evvy," Simone said, practically diving for her phone now. She tapped and dialed her sister, who answered on the first ring.

"Tell me you have something interesting going on," Evelyn said. "I'm *so* bored."

"I—well, have you watched those movies I told you about?"

"All of them. The one with the dachshunds twice."

"Twice? The dachshunds?" If there was any movie Simone would've chosen to watch more than once, it wouldn't have been that one. She shook her head. This wasn't why she'd called. "Gideon and Penny took Callie's girls for the night, so we're coming your way for a girls' *day*." She squealed, bouncing on the balls of her feet like a woman two decades her junior. But she didn't care. She needed a day where she didn't think about the complexities of Micah's role in her life.

They'd been seeing each other for a few months now,

and the burden never really left her mind, even when she was thoroughly enjoying her time with him.

"I will heave myself into the kitchen and start the coffee," Evelyn said.

"No," Simone said. "Don't do that, Evelyn. You're supposed to be on bedrest. That means not making coffee."

"I get up to go to the bathroom, believe it or not," Evelyn said, and she was really in a mood. A bad one.

"Yeah, but Callie makes better coffee than you anyway," Simone said, trying to lighten the mood. "And you really shouldn't be doing anything. I don't want Rhett to yell at me again."

"He didn't yell at you," Evelyn said.

"I know," Simone said with a giggle. But Rhett had asked Simone and Callie to make sure Evelyn followed the doctor's orders for these last two months of her pregnancy. And that meant she couldn't do a whole lot. She'd only been on bedrest for a week, and Simone thought the next two months were going to feel like years.

"We're on the way," Simone said, meeting Callie's eyes. She was already done texting her husband, and Simone ended the call and snagged her keys from the hook next to the fridge. "Let's go."

Callie smiled and led the way through the front door. Simone paused for a moment, tapping out a quick text to Micah. *Going to Evelyn's for the day. Have fun at Wyatt's.*

He didn't answer right away, because he'd be out on the ranch. He worked at Seven Sons for a couple of hours each morning. Sometimes all the way until noon. She didn't know what he did with every minute of his day, and that was fine. She didn't make an accounting to him either.

As she followed Callie down the steps to her sedan, Simone turned off her phone. Completely off. Without the distraction, she could focus on her core. Her gut. And she needed that right now.

"When's Liam done with his deadline?" she asked Callie as she got in the car.

"Next week, supposedly," she said, keeping her focus out the passenger window.

"I can take the girls tomorrow," Simone said, though she'd have to work like a dog to make up for today. She glanced at Callie, who didn't have the same happy glow she'd had in the past. "Are you okay?"

"I'm just tired," Callie said with a weary smile. "Evelyn wants to get out of bed. I just want to get in."

"Well, you can take a nap today," Simone said. "And I'll keep Conrad busy, so Evelyn doesn't have to worry about him. And everyone will be happy." Except for her, as was often the case with Simone. Growing up, she'd swallowed some of her own desires to make sure Evelyn and Callie could do what they wanted. Daddy and Gran had never known about the classes and camps she'd wanted to take, because she'd never said.

Simone was used to being last. Third. In the background. She didn't entirely hate it, because that was where she'd always existed. But sometimes, she felt like she was drowning as she called for help, and no one came.

"Except you," Callie said.

"What?" Simone glanced at her as she got the sedan on the highway and pressed on the accelerator. "I'm fine, Callie."

"You left your shop open," Callie said. "You used to *lock* yourself inside that thing and only open the door three inches when I came over."

Simone's face heated. "That's because Jarrod was in there with me."

"Simone!" Callie said, laughing in the next moment. "You sneaky girl."

Simone laughed too, but she just shook her head. "It's fun to have a secret place." Maybe that was what she and Micah needed. He used to come to her she-shed for a kiss too, but he hadn't in the past few months. To Simone, that was just another example of how different he was acting this time compared to last time.

She really needed to stop comparing the two relationships. This one was much healthier, and she wasn't embarrassed of him. At all.

"So do you and Micah have a secret place?" Callie asked playfully.

"No," Simone said. "No secrets this time." She cut a look at Callie. "That killed us last time."

"Hmm."

Simone hated it when her sister hummed like that, and she made the car go a little faster in the hopes they'd get to Evelyn's faster. Because that humming meant Callie was gearing up for a lecture.

"I don't want to hear it," Simone said, cutting her sister's legs out from under her. "Okay, Callie? It's great that you got your cowboy and your family and everything is great. I'm happy for you, I really am."

She sucked at the air, because she felt wildly out of control. She didn't even know where those words had come from, and she regretted them instantly.

"I'm sorry," she blurted out next, tears following. "I'm sorry, Cal. I know everything isn't great for you." She shook her head, realizing she wasn't fit for company and she should've stayed home to make her molten chocolate hazelnut cakes.

"I know what you're saying," Callie said. "On the outside, it looks like I have everything."

"I know your life isn't perfect," Simone said. "I didn't mean that. I just—I'm just frustrated with my own self." She felt like she was coming apart at the seams. "Please forgive me."

"I do," Callie said. "And Simone, I think you and Micah are perfect for each other. So whatever you need to do to keep him, you should do it."

Simone looked at her sister. "You think so?"

Callie smiled, and Simone's relief flooded her. "Yes," she said. "I really think so."

Simone thought about her sister's words the rest of the way to Evelyn's, and they found Conrad, the almost-three-year-old sitting on the top step with Rhett's cattle dog that he'd named after his mother. He jumped up when Simone pulled into the driveway and waved to them. And so much joy poured from him that Simone's pity party dried up.

"Hey," she said as she got out of the car. "Whatcha eating? Popcorn?"

"Yeah," Conrad said.

"Come give me a hug," Callie said.

"I can't," Conrad said.

"Why not?" Callie glanced at Simone as she rounded the hood. The two of them walked down the sidewalk toward their nephew.

He came down one step, then two. "Momma said not to leave the porch."

Evelyn yelled something from inside the house that Simone couldn't hear, and Conrad jumped down the last step and ran toward them. Callie laughed as she picked him up and hugged him, and then Simone got her turn.

The need to have a boy like this of her own over-whelmed her, but thankfully, she didn't cry. But she couldn't help fantasizing about what a small boy that came half from her and half from Micah would look like.

She set Conrad on the ground and took his hand. "Let's see if your momma will let you come home with me, should we?"

"Yes!" He let go of her hand and ran toward the steps. He took them one at a time, both feet touching each step as he went up. "Momma! Momma!"

"Oh, dear," Callie said. "Now you've done it."

Simone just smiled as she went up the steps and into the house. Evelyn lay on the couch, her oversized belly the only thing Simone could look at. "You've gotten bigger," she said.

"Thank you," Evelyn said without smiling. "I keep telling Rhett I'm getting bigger and he doesn't see it."

"Hey, sister," Callie said. Conrad kept talking as if any of them were listening to him, and Evelyn finally looked at Simone.

"He wants to come stay with you, is that it?"

"Yes," Simone said. "That's it." She pulled out her phone and powered it up. "Now, what kind of pizza do we want?"

CHAPTER SEVEN

Micah knocked on Simone's door, the drinks in his hands tipping sideways. He balanced them while someone on the other side of the door struggled to get it open. If he could keep the drinks from dumping down the front of him, he could reach for the knob. Simone kept her workshop locked but rarely secured her cabin.

The door finally opened, and a little boy peered up at him. After one second, Conrad's face broke into a smile. "Uncle Micah."

"Conrad," he said, surprised. "Are you...where's Aunt Simone?"

"Right here," she said from within the house. A timer was going off, and Simone came hurrying toward him wearing an apron over her clothes that was covered in flour and chocolate. "Come in. Oh, let me help you." She took one of the drinks and tapped Conrad on the shoulder to get him to move back. "Let Uncle Micah in, buddy."

The little boy fell back, and Micah went inside the cabin. "No wonder you ordered three drinks." He smiled down at the little boy—his brother's son. And her sister's son.

And suddenly Micah understood why his relationship with Simone was a little odd. She didn't seem to stutter over "Uncle Micah" this time though, so that was some progress in his opinion.

While she silenced the timer, he set the remaining three drinks on her kitchen counter, which looked like someone had come in with the entire baking aisle at the grocery store and blown it up. "Baking?"

"Chocolate cake," Conrad said, trying to climb up on the barstool. Micah hurried to help him so the kid wouldn't fall and hit his head, and he continued all the way to the counter, unconcerned about the splatters of flour and cocoa powder already there. "It's baking."

"I can smell it," Micah said, grinning at the boy.

"He helped with everything," Simone said. "Didn't you, Conrad? Tell him what you did."

Conrad started to tell him, but Micah couldn't understand very many words. He got "cup," and "mix," and "oven," but that was it.

"Is that right?" he asked, glancing at Simone, who just shook her head with a smile. She put a bowl in the sink and ran water over a rag to wipe up the counter.

"Can I help you clean up?" Micah asked, thinking that if he was going to be here, he might as well be put to work. "And when are we going to unload your van?"

"Whenever you have a moment," she said. "How's Warren?"

"He's great," he said. "So much lighter than the other cousins. And so *round*." He looked at Conrad, who definitely had the Foster dark genes in his eyes and hair and skin.

"And Wyatt?"

"He's good." Micah had enjoyed a lazy afternoon with his brother, and then he'd stopped by Jericho's to check on his carpeting. "And my flooring will be in next Monday. So I'm going to work on the cabin all day tomorrow if you're looking for somewhere to hang out." He moved around the counter to stand next to her.

"I didn't work today," she said. "So I'll be working too, but maybe we can take a lunch at the same time?" She looked up at him, a question riding in her eyebrows.

"I'd like that." Micah smiled down at her, the scene in which he found himself somewhat surreal. Him and Simone, with a small boy nearby, cleaning up the kitchen after a fun family baking activity.

Of course he hadn't been here for the family baking activity. Conrad wasn't his son, and he and Simone still existed on shaky ground sometimes. But Micah had a very vivid imagination, and he could easily see this woman in his life long-term, with children and a kitchen and more molten chocolate cakes.

They ate cake and drank soda, and Conrad fell asleep on Simone's lap almost the moment they put on a movie for the evening. "He's the cutest thing on the planet," Simone whispered, gazing down at him with an expression of such love. When she looked up at Micah, he found her the most beautiful creature he'd ever laid eyes on.

He leaned toward her, and she leaned toward him, and Micah got the sweetest kiss of his life. Her lips trembled against his, and she pulled away quickly.

"What's wrong?" he asked, his voice barely loud enough to hear so as to not wake Conrad.

"I don't know," Simone whispered. She clung to Conrad and rocked him side to side slowly. "I love him so much. I want a boy just like him so badly."

Micah lifted his arm, and Simone cuddled into his side easily, naturally. "You'll have them, sweetheart," he promised, pressing his lips to her temple. He could reassure her of that, but he wasn't brave enough to say he hoped he'd get to be the father of her children.

That was so far down the line for them that Micah didn't dare even hope for such a thing. So he just held Simone while she held Conrad, and all was right in the world for those few minutes.

———

THE DAYS PASSED, FORMING INTO A WEEK, AND MICAH MADE good progress on his house. He was waiting on install jobs he couldn't do himself now, and he expected the house to be finished in the next couple of weeks. He'd started packing some of his clothes and moving them into the finished master closet. He had no bed to sleep in at his place, so he still lived with Jeremiah and Whitney, but the day where he had his own house again was so close, he could see the light at the end of the tunnel.

When he'd left Temple, he'd put all of his stuff into storage, and he'd been in Three Rivers for a few years now. When he'd gone to the unit in town to see what there was, he hadn't wanted any of it. He'd stood there with Skyler, staring at a lot of stuff that represented a man Micah didn't know anymore.

"Would it be terrible if I just threw it all away?" he'd asked.

Skyler had chuckled and clapped Micah on the shoulder. "Dude, you're a billionaire who just built his own house. Throw it all away and buy all new stuff if you want."

And Micah had done just that, but that meant he had to wait for the furniture to be delivered, and it was set to come on Tuesday.

"Five more days," he told himself as he drove down the lane to the Shining Star Ranch and Simone's cabin. He'd spent a lot of time with her over the past two weeks, just as he had been doing for a few months now.

He'd asked her to go to the Valentine's masked ball in town, and she'd accepted. They'd danced the night away, laughed in each other's arms, and kissed on her porch until his lips felt bruised.

That was just a couple of nights ago, and tonight, they were auditioning for *A Long Way Home*. He turned the corner to head back to the cowboy cabins and found Simone walking toward him.

He pulled up beside her and rolled down the window. "I'm not late," he said.

"I'm just restless." She smiled as she pulled open the door and got in the truck. He gave her a moment to get straight and settled, and when she reached for her seatbelt, he put the truck in gear again.

Simone stayed quiet on the way to the theater, and Micah had learned that a silent Simone wasn't a bad thing. It just meant she had something heavy on her mind, and she needed some internal reflection.

He pulled into the parking lot, glad the silence between them wasn't awkward as it had been in the past. "Are you ready to audition for the lead?" He grinned at her, and Simone finally turned toward him.

"I'm not going to get it."

"You never know," Micah said, unbuckling his seatbelt. "That's why you audition and let the director put you where she thinks you'll be best." He chuckled as he opened his door. "Someone told me that once, at least."

"Okay," she said with heavy sarcasm in her voice. She joined him at the front of the truck. "We've practiced. We've got this."

"We have practiced," he said. "And for me, that's about fifty times more than what I did last time." They went inside the building together, and Micah did like the energy in the theater. He recognized most of the people, and they smiled and shook hands, hugged, and said hello.

"I want to see all the Adelaide's over here," Susan called from across the room, and Simone squeezed his hand.

"You got this, baby," he said to her under his breath, and she gave him a small smile before she walked over to Susan. So did almost every other female there, and Micah sent up a prayer that Simone would be happy with her performance.

She doesn't have to get it, he told the Lord. *Just help her do her best and be happy with what she's done.*

"Men," someone said, and he turned toward Chandler Ross, a man who'd directed in the past. At least that was what Simone had told him. "We'll be going into the library for our first audition. Follow me, please." He pushed out of the theater, and all the men went with him. Micah had decided to try out for everything, and he ran the lines Chandler gave him, he sang the song with the other men, then in a group of three, then by himself.

He was glad to be put in the group with Pastor Scott, because while the man could deliver a powerful, moving sermon, he wasn't much of a singer.

"You did great," the pastor said, smiling at Micah.

"Thanks," he said. "You too."

"I need to learn those dance moves. My wife would like that." He grinned and looked down at Micah's feet, though their song had ended. He could step-touch with the best of them, and in fact, if there was a fiddle and a guitar and a swing going on, Micah could do that too.

There wasn't a lot of dancing in *A Long Way Home*, thankfully, and Micah had finished his audition before he knew it.

"Let's go back into the theater," Chandler said. "I want to see Jerry, Cory, Carson, Chris, and Micah pair with a woman." He held the door as people filed past him. "Susan will have her top five for Adelaide too, and we're going to do the marriage scene."

A phone rang, and Micah thought Chandler would reprimand whoever it was, as he'd already asked them to silence their phones.

"Sorry," Scott said. "I have to take this, Chandler."

"No problem," he said, and Micah supposed the pastor did get a pass. He probably had a lot of people relying on him, and if there was a problem with anyone in his congregation, he'd want to know about it.

Micah smiled as he passed Chandler like he knew exactly what the marriage scene was, but he did not. He'd read the play once, weeks ago. So he wasn't as prepared as probably everyone else there was. But it was reading lines with someone else. He could do it.

Almost all the women sat in the seats facing the small stage, except for a group of five women—and Simone was one of them. She wore the excitement right on her face, and she met Micah's eye as he went up the few steps to the stage.

"Pair up," Susan said. "We don't care with who. We'll run it a pair at a time, and I might have you go again with someone different." She stepped off the stage and sat in the first row, a clipboard in her hand.

Micah stepped to Simone's side and said, "Will you be my partner?"

She didn't answer, but Micah heard her silent yes. "And do you think Susan knows this is just community theater?

Not Broadway?" He chuckled, glad when Simone smiled too.

"Is the pastor coming?" Susan said, standing up and looking back to the door.

"You need these for the scene," Chandler said, handing Micah a form. He looked at it, his heart pulsing around in his chest. It was a blank application for a marriage license. He looked from it to Simone, who hadn't seemed to notice Chandler handing anything out.

"Who did you pick for the pastor?" Susan asked Chandler as he joined her on the floor.

"Uh, Jason," he said. "And the actual pastor."

"Well, where is he?"

"His phone rang right when we were coming in." Chandler sat down. "Let's start with Jason as the pastor, and Chris with whoever he's partnering with."

Chris and Jason stepped forward, along with a woman named Tasha Pike. They said the lines effortlessly, complete with facial expressions and hints of humor, as they filled out the paperwork, handed it to Jason and then faced him.

He gave his few lines about love and marriage and forever, and then he married Adelaide and Jack right there on stage, like a real pastor. Micah was enthralled with their performances, and he wondered why anyone would need to go next.

Chris and Tasha kissed, and the entire crowd—Micah included—whooped and hollered as if they'd really gotten married. He looked at Susan and Chandler, and they sat with stone masks on their faces, both of them writing something on their very official clipboards.

Chris and Tasha came down the steps and found seats in the audience, and still notes were being made.

"Jerry and Ruth," Susan called a few moments later. The chatter that had broken out quieted, and the scene got acted again.

Once again, Micah thought he was way out of his league here. He was glad he hadn't had to go first, that was for sure, and he hoped he could be half as charming as Jerry was. Another I do, another pronunciation of man and wife, another kiss, and he hollered as the couple "got married."

Simone reached over and put her hand in Micah's, and he glanced at her. "I'm going to mess it up for you," he said. "You should audition with someone else."

She merely shook her head, and Chandler stood up. "Is Scott back?"

"Right here," he said from the back of the room.

"You're up," Chandler said. "With Micah and Simone."

Micah's hands broke out into a sweat, and he wiped them down his jeans as he stood up with Simone and followed her up the steps to the fake altar. He practically crushed the paper in his fingers, his muscles clenched tight too.

"If you're not going to fill that thing out, I will," Simone said, delivering the first line of the scene with flawless precision.

"I've got it, sweetheart," he said, adding his cowboy drawl to the sentence as he picked up the pen and put his name on the certificate. "You've been waiting a long time for this."

Simone linked her arm through his. "So have you."

He wrote her name too, wondering if he should've used the characters they were playing. It didn't matter; this wasn't real. He could've scribbled on it and it would've been fine. "It's been a long road home," Micah said, glancing at the script for his next line. He couldn't find it. "That's for sure. There's been ups and downs."

He knew that line wasn't right, but Simone didn't miss a beat. She reached out and pointed to the script, as if it was a line on the certificate. "Right there, dear. My birthday is March sixth."

But Micah knew her birthday was in November. He smiled, remembering what he was doing right now. The audition. "That's right. Coming up." He looked at her. "And we'll be married tonight."

She sighed, the look on her face made of absolute bliss. "Finally."

Micah signed the paper and handed the pen to Simone. "Just sign it right there, sweetheart, and let's not keep this preacher waiting any longer."

Simone signed the paper and handed it to Scott, who barely had to act to play the part. He beamed at Simone and Micah as if they were really getting married. "You two are simply perfect together. Never forget that you care about each other. It's not weakness to admit our love and concern for another human being."

He continued his short speech, and Micah reached for

Simone's hand, something none of the other couples had done. She said "I do," when it was her turn, and Micah said, "I absolutely do," when it was his.

He could hear the chuckles behind him, and he hoped Jack was meant to be a cowboy with flair.

"Then I pronounce you man and wife," Scott said. "You may kiss your bride."

Micah turned toward Simone, a smile covering his whole face. He took her into his arms and dipped her all the way down, causing a squeal to come from her mouth.

The crowd positively erupted, and Micah laughed just before he kissed her, this fake wife of his in an audition.

And what a kiss it was.

When he lifted her up, they were both laughing, and everyone in the audience had stood. Even Chandler had a smile on his face as he wrote on his clipboard.

"Too bad," Micah said. "We still didn't crack Susan." Then he led his "wife" off the stage and back to their seats.

CHAPTER EIGHT

Simone felt like she was floating on clouds as she left the theater. She'd been smiling for the past hour as the men auditioned for the roles in *A Long Way Home*. She'd done the marriage scene with Micah and then Cory, and she felt like she had a real shot of landing the lead.

"That was *amazing*," she said once she and Micah had said goodbye to everyone and were approaching his truck. A laugh filled her chest and came out of her throat, and Simone could not hold it back.

"You were great," Micah said, reaching for her hand.

Simone looked at him, wondering when this had become her life. "Did you know I did theater in high school?"

Micah shook his head. "No, ma'am, I did not."

"I was nothing special," she said, thinking of how Daddy and Gran and her sisters had come to see her in every performance. At least one of them came each night. "I was in the ensemble for *Grease*. It was fun."

"Just *Grease?*" He unlocked his truck and walked her around to the passenger side. "You just did the one play?"

"Yeah," she said, pausing in the doorway. "I was a sophomore, and Evelyn was graduating, and Callie had started doing a lot on the ranch. It was...a lot for them to support me."

Micah cocked his head. "I don't know what you mean."

Simone didn't either, and she shrugged as she got in his truck. He closed the door behind her and circled the truck. "Ice cream?"

"Yes," she said. "I want some of that raspberry sherbet from Mom and Popsicle."

"You got it." Micah put the truck in gear and pulled out of the parking lot. "Was your family too busy for you to perform in your piano recitals too?"

Simone sucked in a breath and whipped her attention to Micah. "I mean...what?"

Micah glanced over at her. "You told me that last time we dated. That you wouldn't tell them about your piano recitals because you were worried they'd be overwhelmed with everything."

Simone folded her arms and let her annoyance at the perfection of his luxury vehicle bother her. "Didn't you ever feel that way? That you were the last child, and everyone older than you was bothered by your mere existence?"

"Simone," he said, his voice very serious and very low. "Is that really what you thought?"

"Sometimes I still do," she murmured to her faint reflection in the window.

"Sweetheart." Micah reached over and tried to hold her hand. But she had her arms folded, and she was using them to hold her roller coaster emotions inside. He put both hands back on the steering wheel. "If it means anything to you, Simone, you're the only person I've spent any time thinking about in the past couple of years."

She swung her attention toward him as if in slow motion, trying to decide if he was kidding. He didn't seem to be. "You always know just what to say."

"Slide on over here and hold my hand," he said, and Simone didn't want to keep distance between them, so she did.

"Ah, that's better," he said with a smile. "And it's not just something I say, Simone. I really have thought about you more than any other person since I met you."

"Even when you were dating Ophelia?"

Micah drew in a deep breath and pushed it out. "She broke up with me, because…." He didn't finish, and Simone's curiosity rose.

"Because why?" she prompted as he pulled to the curb in front of Mom and Popsicle.

He ducked his head and tightened his grip on her fingers. "Because of you, baby. She said she knew I was still hung up on you, and she was tired of waiting for me to get over you."

Shock coated Simone's vocal cords, and she didn't know what to say.

"You still want ice cream?" He nodded toward the shop.

All she could do was nod.

He got out of the truck, and she slid over into his spot before dropping to the ground beside him. He closed the door and took her hand again. Simone needed something to fill the silence between them, but she couldn't think of anything.

Micah said nothing as well, and the bell chiming on the door of the ice cream shop made Simone flinch. Noise flowed from the inside of the shop, and several people milled around the counter and filled the tables.

The light seemed too bright, and Simone felt like everyone had turned to look at her and Micah as they entered. He certainly wasn't the only man in a cowboy hat, and in truth, no one cared that the two of them were there together.

"I think I want chocolate and bananas," he said.

"That's your favorite flavor combination," Simone said, seizing onto the conversation topic. "I need to make you those banana cream cheesecakes I told you about."

"The ones in the slow cooker?" He continued to study the menu, and Simone hated this falsely casual conversation.

"Yes," she said, and the topic had run its course. "How close are you on the house now?"

"I should be moving in about a week," he said. "Just waiting for all the deliveries."

"Are you going to finally let me in?" Simone reached up

and held his arm with her other hand, leaning into him and hoping this flirting tactic would work.

Micah looked down at her, a smile finally touching the corners of his mouth. "Maybe."

"Maybe?" She grinned at him and shook her head. "*Maybe* I'll sneak in while you're out on the ranch tomorrow morning."

"It's Sunday," he said. "I'm not going out to the ranch in the morning."

"Then after church," she said. "When you're out riding Memory."

Micah finally broke, the smile gracing his face now absolutely beautiful. Did he know how handsome he was? Had she ever told him? She didn't think she had.

"Micah," she said as they edged closer to the counter.

"Hmm?"

She balanced by holding onto his arm tighter and lifted up on her toes. "You're the best-looking cowboy in here," she whispered.

Surprise crossed his expression. "You think so?"

Simone nodded as she settled back onto her feet. "Especially when you give me that smile."

"I'll keep that in mind," he said, stepping up to the counter. "I want the banana chocolate cabana. And she wants the raspberry sherbet." He gave the sizes he wanted, paid, and they moved down while they waited for their concoctions to be scooped.

Simone got her sherbet first, and she had to let go of

Micah to eat it. "You were brilliant on the stage tonight too," she said.

"Well, look who's full of compliments tonight." Micah took his ice cream from the girl behind the counter and said, "Let's eat this in the truck."

Simone went with him, enjoying the cold, tart sherbet in her mouth as she thought about her boyfriend. Once she and Micah were back in the truck, she knew she liked this man. Really liked him. Maybe even had started to slide into loving him.

She choked on a bite of sherbet, and Micah looked at her. "You okay?"

She nodded, because while she'd confessed a few things to him tonight, she wasn't ready to drop that three-word bomb.

A WEEK LATER, SIMONE HAD SPENT A SOLID FIVE DAYS IN HER workshop, and she'd managed to get caught up on her projects for the Spring Fling. She enjoyed her regular girls' nights with her sisters, and tonight, while Micah moved into his house, Simone had invited Anita and Soren over for coffee and cake.

Anita Poulsen and Soren Hancey lived just next door to Simone, and they'd worked at the Shining Star since Callie and Liam had started improving it, a few years ago. Simone had become friends with them, and the other cowboys in the row of cabins, though she didn't have any of them over for dinner or desserts.

After her disastrous relationship with Jarrod, Simone had learned to keep the next door neighbor cowboys at arm's length.

Her doorbell rang, and Simone tossed the oven mitts on the kitchen counter to go get it. She smiled at the two women on the front step, both of them holding something that would make Simone's taste buds rejoice.

"I bought mine," Soren said, lifting what looked like carrot cake. She was tall and blonde, with freckles across her face and one of the strongest work ethics Simone had ever seen.

"I made mine." Anita stepped into the cabin and sighed. "Your place is so much better than ours."

"It's the same," Soren said.

"It is not," Anita argued as she put her pie on the counter. "She has all this nice furniture."

"Do you need new furniture?" Simone asked, stepping around the counter. "I could ask Liam about it for you."

"He won't buy anything this nice," Anita said, moving over to the couch. She sighed as she sat down and leaned back. "Ah, yes. This is amazing."

"I made that," Simone said. "But Homelife has great stuff. You could get something like it." But she knew the cowgirls wouldn't. It was Callie and Liam's job to furnish the cabins, and the house was part of their pay.

"I thought you didn't like Homelife." Soren sat at the bar while Simone poured cream into a bowl.

Simone had told them that, after running into Micah and his girlfriend there. She shrugged. "If you go during the mid-afternoon, it's not bad." She switched on the electric mixer and got her cream beating. A few minutes later, she had perfectly stiff peaks, and she pulled the chocolate sauce out of the microwave with the oven mitts.

"Okay, so I made a chocolate mousse cake," she said. "And we've got a carrot cake from the bakery." She smiled at Soren, who smiled back. "And...what kind of pie is this, Nita?"

Anita, who wore her dark hair in a braid almost every day, got up and came over to the island. "Mine is a strawberry rhubarb."

"Oh, one of my favorites," Simone said. "The cream will go well with that too." She turned and got her cake out of the fridge. "So, who has news and wants to go first?"

"That would be you," Anita said. "You're the one with the hot cowboy boyfriend."

Simone laughed, and it felt good to spend some time with her friends. She didn't do it often enough, and she set the cake on the counter and looked at Anita and Soren. "He's moving into his new house today. He still won't let me inside. I'm hoping to just stop by tomorrow after church with one of these." She indicated the cake. "He won't turn me away then, will he?"

"He better not," Anita said. "If you showed up at my house with a cake like this, I'd marry you." She laughed, and Soren and Simone joined in.

"I don't know if Micah is the marrying type," Simone

said as she cut into the mousse cake. Soren got up and took another knife from the block to cut her carrot concoction too.

"Really?" Anita asked. "All of his brothers are married."

"What makes you say that?" Soren asked.

Simone sobered as she kept her attention on the delectable cake in front of her. "I don't know. We've known each other for years. We dated before this, and it was, in my opinion, really serious. And he's...I don't know."

"Going too slow for you?" Anita asked.

"A little, yeah." Simone stopped fiddling with the cake. "It's just, I'm going to be forty soon, and I don't have a lot of time left to have kids. And I want kids."

"Have you talked to Micah about it?"

Simone remembered the night she cradled Conrad on her lap and said how badly she wanted a boy like him. "Yeah," she said. "A little anyway."

"Maybe you should make it a lot," Soren said, taking a sliver of carrot cake and a piece of pie and putting whipped cream on both. "Now, cake me. I have some news to tell."

"You do?" Simone put a slice of mousse cake on Soren's plate, her curiosity rising with every passing second while they all got their desserts. They always ate in Simone's living room, and tonight was no different.

"News," Anita said. "I think I know it." She smiled at Soren, who nodded.

She finished her bite of chocolate cake, and said, "The Shining Star is getting an agriculture award."

Simone's eyebrows shot up. "Are you kidding? Have you told Liam and Callie yet?"

Soren shook her head and forked up another bite of pie. "Not yet. I need you to help me plan an amazing surprise for them."

Simone squealed, because there was nothing she liked more than planning a surprise.

CHAPTER NINE

Skyler held Mal's hand as they waited in the sterile foyer outside the courtroom. *John's here,* he told himself over and over. All the paperwork had been submitted, and all the interviews done. He and Mal had gone in separately for questioning, and Skyler had to take a couple of sleeping pills and schedule several counseling sessions after that.

He had so many memories of the FBI questioning in Dallas, and while the ICE agents had been nicer, he still hadn't liked being contained in the tiny, windowless room while questions got fired at him.

"Our turn," John said as the courtroom doors opened and a guard came out with a clipboard.

Skyler looked at Mal. There was no way the judge could rule that their marriage wasn't real. Simply no way. It was the most real thing in Skyler's life, and he loved Mal with everything inside him.

He put his hand on the small of her back and let her go in front of him as people filled the courtroom. It wasn't the same one as last time, but close enough. A few rows for people to sit on. The huge podium that stretched across the room at the front, with the state seal and federal seal on the wall behind where the judge would sit. A feeling of anxiety, with a chill in the air. He didn't like it at all.

Last time he'd been in a place like this, he'd felt one breath away from passing out. Today was marginally better, but his nerves still felt wildly out of control. He and Mal had stayed in the apartment last night, and they'd discussed keeping it.

Skyler saw no reason to get rid of the building or the apartment on the top floor. No, they hadn't used it a whole lot in the year since they'd left Amarillo, but the point was, they could. Anyone in the family could. *Her* family could come stay there.

In the end, they'd decided to keep it. The building and the apartment weren't costing them any money or time or energy, and Skyler liked the idea of being able to stay in Amarillo any old time he wanted—like last night.

Another case went before theirs, but Skyler couldn't pay attention. He existed inside his own sphere, only coming out when Mal stood up and went up to the front table with John, their lawyer.

Then Skyler tuned in, and he looked at the man up front, praying with everything inside him that the ruling would be favorable.

"Mrs. Walker, I see you have all your paperwork in order," the judge said.

"Yes, sir," John answered for her. "And I believe the reports are all in. Mrs. Walker is thriving in a new job in Three Rivers, where she lives with her husband and all six of his brothers, as well as his parents."

"I have the reports," the judge said, a little testily too. Skyler wished John would just let him look at the stuff and make a decision. He kicked himself for not paying attention in the last case, because he would've been able to judge the official's mood.

He looked at some papers, shuffling them slowly. Every second felt like an eternity, and Skyler's patience stretched, and stretched, and stretched.

He finally looked up. "And you're expecting a baby?"

John looked at Mal, and Skyler's whole world narrowed to one pinprick of light.

"That's right," Mal said. "I'm due in September."

The words rang in Skyler's ears, and he didn't hear what the judge said after that. Mal was pregnant?

A smile started on his face, and he realized John had turned to look at him. Panic streamed through him, erasing some of the smile. "I'm sorry. What?"

"He asked if you were excited to be a father," John said almost under his breath.

"Yes, sir," Skyler said, giddiness romping through him. He wanted to whoop and throw his cowboy hat into the air. He needed to take Mal into his arms right now and tell her how much he loved her. Buzzing sang along his skin, and Skyler almost felt frantic.

"Well, the reports said the marriage was definitely real, and I have to conclude the same thing," the judge said. "You've got your conditional green card, Mrs. Walker. It's good for two years, at which time you can apply for a permanent one."

"Thank you, your honor," Mal said.

"Yeah," Skyler practically yelled. "Thank you."

John's frown silenced Skyler even as a few people in the courtroom chuckled. He couldn't get to Mal fast enough, his eyes searching hers. He had the common sense not to ask her right there if what the judge had said was true, because Mal was already crying.

Out in the foyer, they thanked John, and Skyler just stood there, kind of numb.

Mal took his hand and led him around a corner, which gave them a smidge more privacy. "Surprise," she whispered, her dark eyes looking right into his.

Skyler took her face in both of his hands, his love for her pure and growing by the moment. "I love you so much," he said back. "I can't—you didn't tell me."

"I was planning a surprise," she said. "I didn't know he was going to ask me about it."

Skyler drew her into his chest, glad when she wrapped her arms around him too. "Are you really excited?" she asked.

"Of course," he said. "Thrilled." He pulled back and looked at her. "Why wouldn't I be?"

"I don't know," she said. "I'm a little scared." A quick smile danced on her lips for a moment, and she swiped at her eyes. "I've never had a baby, and I don't know how to be a mom."

"You'll be a great mom," he said, gazing down at her as he realized with all of his cells that he was going to be a father. And no, he did not know how to do that. "We'll figure it out together."

Mal nodded and snuggled back into his chest. "What do you want? A boy or a girl?"

"I don't care," he said, still in awe that she was carrying his baby. He couldn't wait to meet the tiny human, and September seemed miles away. "What about you?"

"Doesn't matter to me," she said.

"Can I tell Momma?" he asked.

"Maybe we can use my surprise to tell your family."

He took her hand and they started toward the elevator. "What were you planning?"

"I was making a quilt, actually."

"Oh? What kind of quilt?" He never went in her sewing room in the house, and that was the perfect place for her to plan a surprise. She started telling him about the baby blanket she was putting together, but all Skyler could think was, *I'm going to be a dad.*

And that was the greatest feeling in the whole world. Well, that and that his wife would get to stay with him, hopefully forever.

CHAPTER TEN

M icah had just dozed off when his doorbell rang. He sat straight up, his eyes flying to the front door. If the person on the other side was related to him, they would've just walked in. But as it was Sunday, after church and after lunch, they were probably all ready to take their afternoon naps too.

The person there knocked, and Micah couldn't get away with ignoring them. He frowned as he crossed the living room and pulled open the door. That frown turned upside down when he saw Simone standing there with a cake in her hands.

"You were asleep, weren't you?" She grinned at him, and every part of Micah lit up.

"No," he said.

"And not a great liar." She giggled, trying to peer past him. He stood in the doorway, drinking in the sight of her. He'd really wanted to sit beside her at church, because any sermon would be better with Simone's hand in his. But she sat with her father and grandmother every week, and Micah hadn't known how to pull her from them.

"Are you going to invite me in?" she asked, cocking her eyebrows. "Or do I have to stand on your porch all afternoon?"

Micah jolted into motion, stepping back and opening the door wider. "Come in."

"Finally, I get to see the house."

Micah's nerves blitzed around his body for a reason he couldn't name. But he'd better get used to it, because he was planning on using his house as an example of the kind of work he could do for potential customers.

"Micah," she said, her voice full of awe. "This place is *gorgeous*."

"Is it?" he asked, glancing around. The exposed wood beams in the ceiling were a nice touch, he supposed. He'd had help from the woman at the furniture store to get the right rugs to go with the couches he'd bought. He'd designed and made the barstools, the cabinets, the dining room table. If it was wood, he'd touched it himself.

Simone gazed around, silent, and Micah could suddenly see all the flaws. "The blinds aren't in yet," he said. "Should be here Monday."

"Uh huh," she said.

He took the cake from her and walked around the corner to the kitchen, hoping she'd follow. She did, and he thought she'd seen something scary when she gasped.

"Oh, my goodness," she said. "Look at this place."

Micah had seen it all already. "Simone," he said. "You're being dramatic."

"Am I?" She sighed and leaned against the counter. "It's just that this is so beautiful." She ran her fingertips along the top of the counter, which was quartz, just like Micah wanted it to be.

"It's a house."

"Micah, come on."

He kept his face turned away from her as he got down plates and pulled out forks from the drawer. "This is why I haven't had anyone over."

"Because you don't want to be complimented on your superior craftsmanship?"

"It's just a house," he said again.

"This is a custom house," she argued. "And it's fantastic, and why can't you just accept my praise?"

Micah finally looked up, meeting her eye. "I don't know."

"You're going to show it to people when they want to hire you, right?"

"Yes."

"Then *I* should get to see it." She frowned at him, and Micah looked away again. He wasn't sure why he'd resisted having Simone over, only that he had.

"Okay," he finally said. "Sorry. You're right." He lifted his head and handed her the knife. "Thank you for the compliments. I'm glad you like the house." He *loved* the house. Loved it with everything inside him.

He had worked hard on it, and he'd put his whole soul into it.

Simone cut two pieces out of the cake and put one on each plate before picking one up and handing it to him. "I wanted to ask you something," she said.

"Shoot." He dipped his fork in the creamy chocolate mousse, his mouth already watering.

"It's a life question."

"All right." Micah put the cake in his mouth, the groan that came out involuntary as his eyes closed in bliss. This woman could *cook*.

"It's about marriage and family," Simone said.

Micah's eyes popped back open. "Marriage and family?"

"Yeah." She held his gaze, her cake still pristine. "Do you want those things, Micah?"

He swallowed, the rich chocolate taste still in his mouth. "Yeah, sure," he said.

Simone nodded, but she didn't seem satisfied.

"Why are you asking?" he asked. "I thought you knew I didn't want to be the only brother who was alone."

"I guess," she said. "It's just—don't you feel like we're moving sort of slow?"

"Are we?"

"You took four months to kiss me," she said, lifting her gaze to his again.

"That was because I wasn't sure what we were doing," he said.

"I'll be forty at the end of the year."

"Okay," he said, not getting it.

"Women can't have babies forever, Micah."

He just blinked at her, unsure of what to say. He wasn't

going to drop to both knees and propose right then. He'd definitely been falling in love with Simone Foster, but he wasn't sure he was all the way there yet. Was she?

"What are you saying?" he asked. Maybe if she said she loved him, Micah would know exactly how he felt.

"I'm just saying that if you want a marriage and a family, and you maybe, I don't know, want them with me, we don't have forever."

His throat was too dry to respond, so he filled his mouth with the smooth, cool mousse cake. Simone smiled at him in that gentle way she had and took her cake over to the table. "Micah, this is exquisite." She sat down. "You should put your cards in my booth for the Spring Fling. Maybe you'd get some orders."

He joined her, so many things still storming in his soul. "I don't want to just make tables," he said. "I want to build houses."

"I know," she said. "But still. People would see your work, and maybe you'd get someone looking to build."

He nodded. "All right. I'll give you some cards." They ate their cake in silence, and Micah asked her to stay for a movie. She did, and they cuddled on the couch in his living room. Micah thought he could get used to these kind of Sabbath activities, and he sighed as he closed his eyes. Simone had fallen asleep several minutes ago, and Micah took the opportunity to really examine his feelings.

And yes, he was very nearly in love with Simone. Was it possible that she loved him too? Or did she just feel her biological clock ticking, and he was the closest cowboy to her?

He felt bad even thinking that, but he couldn't help remembering how she'd kept their relationship behind closed doors for months. Months and months.

He'd just have to play things by ear and see what their next step was.

SEVERAL DAYS LATER, MICAH WAS ONCE AGAIN INTERRUPTED by a knock on the door. This time, though, Jeremiah called, "Mike?" as he walked in.

"I'm in the kitchen," he called, and a moment later, his brother came around the corner with a large envelope in his hand.

Micah put the frozen pizza he'd just pulled out of the oven on the counter. "What's that?"

"Mail for you." Jeremiah tossed the envelope on the counter. "You want to explain that?"

Micah put the oven mitts down and picked up the envelope. "Who's it from?"

"Hutchinson County," Jeremiah said, folding his arms. "The recorder's office."

Micah flipped over the envelope. "I don't get it, Jeremiah. Why are you being so weird?" He looked at his brother, wishing he'd just say what was on his mind. He'd never held back before.

"Whitney and I got an envelope like that when we got married."

"What?" Micah laughed, pulling a couple of sheets of paper out of the envelope. "I'm not married." He looked at the papers, and one of them sure was fancy. It wasn't white, but more of a buttercream, with fancy lettering on it.

"I think you are," Jeremiah said, tapping the certificate. "And this piece of paper says so."

Micah stared at it, completely confused. "But I didn't get married."

Jeremiah joined him and they both stared down at the paper. "You married Simone?"

"No," Micah said. "*No.*" He looked up. "Jeremiah, I didn't."

"Pastor Scott Daniels," he read. "He signed it. Why would he do that? When did this happen?"

Micah searched his brother's face, desperate for the same answers. His mind raced, only matched by his pulse.

And like the sky opening and the heavens falling to earth, Micah realized what had happened. "I mean, we auditioned for this play a few weeks ago…." He snatched up the paper, which had the same date on it as the audition. "But that wasn't real. That was an audition." He started for the garage door. He needed to get to Pastor Daniels now.

"Wait," Jeremiah said behind him. "Audition? What audition?"

Micah didn't stay to answer him. He needed to know if this was real or not, and how his *marriage* to Simone had come to be.

He wasn't sure how fast he drove, or if he came to complete stops at the appropriate signs. What he knew was he'd gone to the pastor's house, only to have his wife say he was at the church. So Micah pulled up to the white brick building, his heart sprinting like it was trying to flee from his body.

He half-expected the doors to be locked, but they weren't. He went inside and started down the hall toward the pastor's office, catching him just as he came out. "Oh, Micah." Pastor Daniels smiled widely at him. "What can I do for you?"

Micah had no idea what to say. He thrust the paper—the *marriage certificate* with his name and Simone's name on it—toward the preacher.

He looked at Micah and then the paper before taking it. His eyes moved side to side, the brightness in them electric. Then his whole countenance fell. "Oh, dear."

"What is that?" Micah asked. "Is it real? What happened?" He did have some questions.

Scott looked at him. "Micah, I'm so sorry. I had a bunch of papers I needed to send in, and I suppose one of them was that marriage license paper you filled out during the audition." He tried to hand the certificate back, but Micah didn't want to take it.

Or maybe he did.

The seedling of an idea started in the back of his mind, and it whispered, *All the other brothers have had a fake marriage. Maybe you could too....*

He took the paper back and looked at it again. "It's real."

The ideas and thoughts morphed now that he'd calmed down a little bit, taking on a life of their own.

"I'm sure I can do something," Scott said. "I mean, on Monday. I can make a phone call on Monday."

"It's fine," Micah said. "I can make a phone call too." He turned and started down the hall, his mind whirring. He glanced up and saw the doors to the chapel, another thought taking over. "Can I stay here for a few minutes?" he asked, glancing behind him. "Just to think and pray?"

"Sure," Scott said. "I was just headed out. I'll lock up, and if you'll just make sure the door latches completely behind you, you can stay as long as you want." He smiled at Micah, a bit of trepidation still in his expression. "Please, let me know if you need help getting that taken care of."

"I will," Micah said, reaching for the door handle. But his idea was to *not* take care of it. He entered the chapel and sat down in the back row, already voicing a prayer to the Lord. "Dear Lord, could Simone and I make this work? Like, really work? Like everyone else has?"

He took a breath and added, "I really like her. I think I'm in love with her. Just a few days ago, she said we were moving too slow. This certainly isn't slow. So what do You think? Should I ask her if she wants to give marriage a try?"

The heavens didn't open. Bright lights didn't shoot down from the ceiling. But when Micah closed his eyes and imagined what his life with Simone Foster could be like, he knew he wanted it.

So he'd just ask her if she wanted it too. Simple as that.

He basked in the silence for another moment, feeling more loved alone in the chapel than he had in a while. "Thank you," he whispered, sure he'd gotten the answer to his prayer.

Now he just needed to talk to Simone.

"Your *wife*," he amended, and that got him up and out of the chapel, the marriage certificate securely in his hand.

CHAPTER ELEVEN

Simone took a deep breath and reached for the grocery bags she'd brought with her. She'd volunteered to make breakfast for Daddy and Gran—and she'd been very specific that she wanted Belinda to be there. She hadn't questioned her father too much about his new girlfriend, and Simone supposed that their relationship wasn't that new anymore.

He'd started seeing her last summer, and that was going on nine months now. Simone took the eggs, bacon, bread, and the other ingredients she needed to make French toast and candied bacon up the sidewalk to the front door.

She entered the house, bracing herself for anything. It used to be an offending odor, or clutter on every surface. But since Belinda had been coming to the house, Simone had learned to prepare herself for anything.

"Daddy?" she called as she closed the door behind her. She stepped past the front living room, which no one used or touched, barely glancing at it. Her heart screamed at her, and she came to a full stop.

She backed up a few steps and stared at the formal living room. The very clean and nearly empty formal living room. The last time she'd been here, this room had still housed everything Daddy and Gran couldn't bear to get rid of that pertained to Simone's mother.

"Oh, my," she whispered, her mind racing as fast as her heart. Where had everything gone? Had he thrown it all away? Callie would be livid, and Evelyn would march her pregnant-with-triplets body right into Daddy's face and demand to know where it had all gone.

"Dad?" she called again, unable to look away from the room. New flooring had gone in at some point in the past week and a half, and new bookcases lined the wall to her left.

"Simone," he said, coming down the hall toward her. He joined her and looked into the room. "It looks good, doesn't it?"

"Where is it all?" Simone asked, holding her breath in anticipation of hearing the worst. How could she tell Callie and Evelyn?

"We went through it, finally," Daddy said, his voice tinged with sadness. "Belinda brought new boxes, and we packed it all up. I figured you girls would like to have your mother's things."

Relief like Simone had never known made her lean into the wall beside her. "Is it in the garage?" She'd take it with her today.

"Yes," Daddy said. "About twelve boxes or so." He finally looked at her, and Simone could tear her gaze from the newly transformed room. He smiled, and he looked so happy. Simone was glad he was happy, because it had been a while since her father had had much to smile about.

"Want me to take some of that?" he asked, leaning down to give her a kiss on the cheek. He took two of the grocery bags and preceded her into the kitchen. Simone looked for Gran in the family room, but her recliner was empty.

"Where's Gran?"

"She hasn't gotten up yet." Daddy pulled the bread and eggs out of the first bag.

"It's almost ten," Simone said, a new kind of alarm pulling through her now. She'd thought she'd been prepared for anything this morning, but she'd already endured quite the shock, and she didn't know how much more she could take.

She put her grocery bags on the counter too and turned toward the hall. "I'll go check on her."

"She's just tired," Daddy said after her. "She has a hard time falling asleep at night."

"Mm hm," Simone said, already striding toward the hall. She went down halfway and paused outside her grandmother's bedroom door. "Gran?" She knocked lightly and twisted the knob. Peering in, she could see her grandmother lying in bed. A terrifying moment passed before she saw Gran's chest rise. Simone needed to get out of her imagination—her very vivid imagination that allowed her to transform into a different character on stage—and seat herself in reality.

"Gran," she said again, entering the room and going to her grandmother's side. She looked ages old, her skin papery and pale, wrinkled and weathered. Simone barely touched her forehead as she moved back one of her curls. "Gran, can you wake up?"

Her eyes fluttered open, and she looked unfocused. A moan came out of her mouth, and Simone's worry tripled. "Are you okay, Gran?"

"What time is it?" Her voice sounded rusted into her throat.

"Time for breakfast," Simone said. "Let's get you up, okay?" She steadied her grandmother as she sat up. "You're warm, Gran." She placed the back of her hand against Gran's forehead. "You feeling okay?"

"Just tired," Gran said, but Simone thought it was more than that.

"Maybe we should go see Doctor George." She knew Gran would wave that suggestion away, but to her surprise, she didn't.

"I can manage, child," she said as she swung her legs over the side of the bed. "I'll be right out."

"Okay," Simone said doubtfully. She backed up and let Gran go in front of her to cross the hall and enter the bathroom. She went down the hall to the kitchen and organized the groceries on the counter.

"Daddy," she said, trying to be casual. "How long has Gran been sleeping late?"

"Oh, I don't know," he said from the kitchen table, where he had a puzzle book and a cup of coffee in front of him.

"When did she stop being able to sleep well?" Simone got a bowl out and started cracking eggs.

"Maybe last weekend," he said, clearly unconcerned.

"Does she seem ill?"

His book rustled, and Simone looked up, catching the annoyance on his face. "I don't know."

"Dad, she's not well," Simone said, throwing her defenses up. "You have to help me out here."

"Take her to the doctor then," he said, and Simone was not used to this level of sass from her father. She gaped at him, and the message must've been appropriately conveyed, because he held up one hand in surrender. "I'm sorry, sweetie. That was harsh."

"I will take her to the doctor," Simone said, cracking another egg a little too hard against the side of the bowl. She whisked in milk, salt, and vanilla until the batter was a little too frothy too.

Daddy got up and joined her in the kitchen, putting a pan on the stove and clicking on the flame underneath it.

"I'm candying the bacon," Simone said when he reached for the package. Her voice came out snippy too, and she pulled back on her irritation. "So if you want to lay that out on a sheet pan, you can stick it in the oven. Four hundred degrees."

"Okay," Daddy said. He turned off the stove and did what she said.

She nodded to the brown sugar. "Mound that on each piece," she said. "In the oven for fifteen minutes."

"Oh, Belinda is going to love this," he said with a smile.

"Yes, let's talk about Belinda," Simone said. "How are things going with her?"

"Great," Daddy said.

It was a strange thought for Simone to think of her nearly seventy-year-old father dating and getting married again. "That's all? Just great? That's all I get?" Simone glanced at him as she bent to get the griddle out of the cupboard.

He mounded brown sugar, keeping his eyes on the bacon. "Yeah," he finally said. "We get along real nice. She's got a couple of sons in the area. She brings food from one of their restaurants a couple of nights a week. Helps Gran go through some exercises. Walks her down the block; that kind of thing."

"Are you going to marry her?" Simone watched her father's neck turn a ruddy shade of red. A smile filled her chest, but she didn't let it out. Why shouldn't Daddy be happy? No matter how old he was, he shouldn't have to be here alone, cooped up with decades of memories, papers, and old furniture.

"Just for the record," she said, trying to keep her voice cool. "I think it's sweet that you're sweet on her, and you should marry her if you love her."

Daddy looked at her, and Simone let the smile out. He grinned too, the tension between them breaking. "I do really like her." He shook his head. "I might love her. I don't know. I just knew with your mother, and this is a little different."

"Maybe it's not a forever love," Simone said. "But it could be love nonetheless."

He nodded, finished with the bacon, and slid it in the oven. "She'll be here any minute, and I don't want you hounding her with questions."

Simone burst out laughing. She continued to do so as she dug through one of his drawers to find the cord for the griddle. "Come on, Dad," she said. "I'm not Callie."

"And don't be tellin' your sisters about this," he said.

"Well, I can't promise that," Simone said.

"Good morning," Belinda sang from the direction of the front door. Instead of spinning toward her, Daddy held Simone's gaze for an extra moment.

"All right, all right," Simone said under her breath. "I'll even look away while you go kiss her hello." She grinned at him and did not look away as her father turned and met Belinda as she entered the family room from the hallway leading to the door. He did kiss her, and then he brought her into the kitchen.

"Morning, Belinda," Simone said with a smile. "Daddy says you're a real fan of candied bacon."

"I know I am," Gran said, shuffling into the kitchen too. She wore a big, flowery blouse with a pair of denim pants that Simone knew had an elastic waistband. Her orthopedic shoes gave her a couple of extra inches, and she'd managed to tame her hair by wetting it down and then probably running a towel through it. "Is there coffee?"

"Yes," Daddy said. "Same place as always, Gran." He smiled at Belinda, but Simone watched Gran. Her hands shook as she reached for a mug. She steadied herself against the countertop, and she just did not look well.

Simone would call the doctor the moment they finished breakfast. She plugged in the griddle and got it heating up. Fifteen minutes later, they had hot French toast and perfectly candied bacon, and Simone looked at the three people waiting to eat at the kitchen table.

"So I got the part of Robyn in the play," she said, putting down the plate of bacon. "It's not the main lead, but she's still on stage a lot as one of the leads. I have one solo." She smiled around at everyone. "I hope you'll all come."

"Of course we will, dear," Belinda said, reaching over and patting her hand. "How exciting for you."

"Simone is a great actress," Daddy said, and Simone ducked her head. "Beautiful singer."

"Thanks, Daddy," she said. She couldn't help the twinge of disappointment as it cut through her. She'd been the almost-lead in a couple of plays now, and she wondered what it would take to finally get the star role. At the same time, she was grateful she got to perform in the function she did. She wasn't in the ensemble, and she would be on stage almost as much as Adelaide.

It was that dang *almost* that tripped her up. She felt like she was *almost* living her best life. *Almost* secure with Micah. *Almost* a star on stage. *Almost* to the point where she'd have everything she wanted.

"YES, THAT'S RIGHT," SHE SAID, CONFIRMING GRAN'S ADDRESS for the receptionist who'd answered the phone at Doctor George's office. She honestly didn't know why she had to go through this. Doctor George had been seeing Gran for over twenty years.

"Okay, so tomorrow at ten," the woman said, and Simone confirmed. Her morning slipped away from her again, but she reasoned that it was only early March, and she could work all day in the she-shed. Unlike summer, when she went out early-early in the morning so she didn't have to suffer in the hottest part of the day.

She had an air conditioner in the shop, but she didn't like to use it. She'd rather hold on to some of her money, thank you very much.

Someone knocked on her door as the woman kept talking about what paperwork to bring and that they needed a new copy of Gran's s Medicaid card.

"Okay," Simone said, pulling open the door to find Micah standing there. She gestured for him to come in and then indicated the phone. He wore a storm on his face, but he stepped past Simone and into her cabin.

The woman finally stopped talking, and Simone hung up. "Phew, okay. Hey." She put a smile on her face, because Micah didn't come see her during the day very often. And if he did, he texted first.

He'd gone all the way into her kitchen, where he stood at

the sink against the back wall of the cabin, staring out the window.

"Micah?" she asked, moving that way too.

He turned toward her as she neared, and he carried a lot more than thunder and lightning in those eyes.

"What's wrong?" she asked, her pulse picking up speed again. "And just say it right out, because I've had *a morning* at my daddy's house, and I can't handle any more shocks."

"You've had a morning already?" he asked, his voice emotionless and utterly calm. Which so wasn't like him and so didn't fit with the surge building on his face.

"Yes," she said. "Daddy and Belinda—that's his girlfriend, if you'll remember—went through the front room. All of my mother's things. They boxed them all up, and they're currently sitting in the back of my SUV."

"I can help you unload them."

"I can't keep them here," she said. "Out of the three of us, I definitely have the smallest house. Callie can keep them at the homestead."

He just nodded, and Simone took that as a sign to keep talking. "So that was a shock. For a moment there, I thought he'd thrown everything away." She paused, imagining that horrifying scenario for a moment. "Then Gran wasn't up yet when I got there, and Daddy gave me attitude about how she's been feeling. Then he admitted he probably maybe loves Belinda and might marry her, and then I went to get Gran, and she is *not* well." She took a deep breath and kept going. "I just got off the phone with the doctor's office. I'm taking her tomorrow."

Micah reached for her, lacing his arm around his waist. "You're a good woman," he said.

"And I need to call Callie and Evvy and let them know about Gran, but I don't want to overwhelm Evvy, who is literally about to have three babies at the same time." She nodded to the window pane. "Yep, that's it. Busy morning. Lots of revelations." She leaned into Micah's side, perpetually glad he was there. She looked up at him after several seconds of silence. "What's going on?"

He looked down at her, those dark eyes deeply concerned about something. "I'm sorry about your grandmother," he said. "I can go with you, if you want."

"Oh, it's fine," she said, though she was a bit worried about Gran. "You have work to do around the ranch."

"I'm meeting with Bear Glover tomorrow," he said. "But not until the afternoon."

"You are?" Simone grinned up at him. "That's great, Micah. The Glovers have a ton of money. Maybe he'll want you to do a new homestead."

He shook his head. "He said he wants me to look at the one he's got and see about a renovation."

"Oh, well." Simone wondered if that was what had him in this strange mood. "That's not terrible."

"I don't want to do renovations."

Simone stepped away from him, trying to find something else to say. "Then why'd you say you'd meet with him?"

"Same reason you just said. I'm hoping it'll be more." He

turned toward her and stuck his hands in his pockets. "We're still on for Denise's birthday party on Saturday?"

"Yes," Simone said. "Though she's your niece too, and we don't have to show up as a couple." She smiled at him, hoping he'd soften.

He did not. "I have to show you something. I'm afraid it's going to be a huge shock."

Simone's eyes widened, and she folded her arms to keep her heart from thrashing outside of her ribs. "Okay."

He removed a folded piece of paper from his pocket, unfolded it, and smoothed it on the counter. He nodded to it, the brim of his cowboy hat inclining down for just a moment.

Simone's mouth went dry, though she didn't know what was on the cream-colored paper. She took a step over to it, almost wanting to stay back for fear it would strike. Fancy lettering ran across the top. She read it, but her brain misfired.

"What is this?" she asked.

"That's our marriage certificate," Micah said. "And wow, I practiced saying that all morning, and it still sounds insane."

Simone laughed, because that was insane. They weren't married. She picked up the paper, and looked at it more closely. Her name sat on it. His too. The date was a few weeks ago. She frowned. "What *is* this?" she asked again.

"Pastor Daniels married us," Micah said. "I've already been over to meet with him. He had a bunch of other papers in his briefcase or whatever, and that stupid prop piece of paper we filled out got sent in with them."

Panic struck Simone right in the back of the throat. She looked up at Micah, expecting to see the same horror.

Instead, he wore a soft look now. "I want to try it."

"*Try* it?" she practically shrieked, dropping the paper. "Try *what?*"

Micah grabbed the marriage license, which was probably a good thing, because Simone had a mind to rip it to shreds. "Us, Simone," he said louder now, the real Micah Walker coming out. "The marriage thing. Me and you. The state thinks we're married. Pastor Daniels did say we were man and wife. I kissed you and there was cheering."

Simone couldn't believe what he was saying. She backed away from him one step at a time. "That's insane."

"All of my brothers have done it," he said. "Every last one of them got married under false pretenses. You know it's true. Look at Callie and Evelyn."

Well, he had an argument there. She scrambled to seize onto a reason why they'd had to say their quick I-do's.

"Evelyn needed help with her business," Simone said weakly. "And Callie was going to lose the ranch. What's our reason?"

Micah swallowed, that storm crossing his face, making him dangerous and beautiful. And what a gorgeous combination that was. Simone couldn't believe she was actually considering "trying it" with him.

"My reason is that I'm in love with you," he said. "And I

don't see the point of trying to get rid of this." He held up the paper. "Only to do it again in front of my mother."

"She should get to see at least one of her sons get married," Simone said. "And you just assume I'd say yes. That I want to marry you."

He took a step toward her. "Are you saying you don't? You wouldn't?"

Simone had no idea what she was saying. No idea.

He came all the way into her personal space, taking her easily into his arms. Simone stood stiffly, unsure how to yield on this. "Just think about it, sweetheart," he said, his voice soft as silk and oh-so-sexy. She shivered as his breath touched her neck. "You could come live at my place. We can have a life together. A good life."

Simone nodded, but it wasn't because she was saying yes. "I'll think about it," she said almost breathlessly.

"Can't ask for more than that." He tucked the marriage certificate back in his pocket and started toward the door. "You'll call me when you're ready?" He turned back, one hand on the doorknob.

All she could do was nod.

He left, and Simone slid down the wall to the floor, shaking her head. "What in the world just happened?"

We can have a life together. A good life.

She allowed herself to start daydreaming about what that "good life" would look like, and Simone lost herself in her imagination once again.

CHAPTER TWELVE

Micah stayed away from everyone for the rest of the day. He didn't want his phone to ring and have Simone be on the other end. The conversations they needed to have required privacy, something he wouldn't get with Skyler or Jeremiah or the ranch hands.

But Simone did not call that afternoon. Or that evening. In fact, Micah could absolutely consider it night time before his phone buzzed at all. Of course, he'd been inundated with texts from the family text, but he kept that string muted and he only checked it when he felt like it.

He'd just checked to make sure the doors were locked when his phone rang somewhere in the house behind him. His pulse catapulted to the back of his throat, and he jogged across the living room to grab his phone from the kitchen counter.

"Simone," he said.

"I'm not saying yes," she said. "Before we talk about a few things."

"I wouldn't expect you to."

"By 'try it,' what are you talking about?"

"Being married."

"Being married and living together? Being married and *sleeping* together? We can be married and do what we're doing now, Micah."

He closed his eyes and he could just see the look on her face. Displeasure. Challenge. Those eyes boring into his, refusing to look away though she was probably nervous inside.

He smiled and then cleared his throat. He'd beared his whole soul to the woman ten hours ago by saying *I love you.* I'm in love with you? He couldn't actually remember what order he'd put the words in. He thought he may have even blacked out.

But he knew the L-word had come up and out of his mouth.

"I need further definition on 'try it' and 'being married.'"

"All of it," Micah said. "I want all of it, Simone." He wanted to kiss her and wake up next to her, hold her close morning, noon, and night. "But if you're not ready for all of it, I get that. It's kind of…I don't know. Things have definitely sped up, and hey, you were just complaining about how slow I was going."

He knew he shouldn't have made the joke the moment it came out of his mouth. But he didn't apologize. Instead, he clenched his teeth together and mentally commanded himself to stop talking.

Simone let a healthy amount of silence bleed through the line. "Will you open your front door, please?" she asked, her voice quiet and seemingly far away.

He spun toward it, his heartbeat crashing against his lungs. "Yes." He jogged back across the room and would've ripped the door from the hinges to get to Simone. He managed to get the lock undone and the door open, and she lowered her phone from her ear.

He did too, stepping back so she could come in. She did, and he closed the door behind her. "I must be crazy," she said, continuing into his house. She wasn't gazing around and exclaiming compliments now. She turned back to him, and he got that challenge and displeasure. But underneath, he saw the softer side of Simone Foster, and for the first time, Micah thought she might be in love with him too.

"You're not ready," he said, vocalizing the truth. "It's fine. Honestly, Simone, it's okay. We can, I don't know, tell everyone we're married at the birthday party on Saturday, and go from there."

She folded her arms, the negative emotions sliding right off her face as if they were too heavy to hold for too long. "I'm not ready," she admitted. "But you're also right that it makes no sense to file for divorce—which has a waiting period. Did you know that?—only to maybe get married again after that."

"I'll take a maybe," Micah said, grinning at her. He wanted to cross the distance between them and sweep her into his arms. Kiss her until he couldn't breathe, and then take her into his bedroom.

But he knew he wouldn't be doing that, at least the last bit.

A smile cracked her face too, and Micah went to her then, wrapping her up in an embrace. This time, she hugged him back, and when he kissed her, she didn't protest.

"Okay," he said, stepping back so she wouldn't think he wasn't going to listen to her. "So I have plenty of bedrooms here. You can pick one, and maybe take the next couple of days to pack what you think you need. I have pots and pans and all of that."

He suddenly felt frantic and nervous, and it wasn't until Simone slipped her hand into his that he calmed. They looked at one another, and Micah didn't know what to say or do next.

"Move in on Sunday?" Simone asked, her voice barely audible.

Micah smiled again and nodded. "And I'll make the announcement at the birthday party."

"You better have a plan for dealing with your mother," she said, a touch of a playful smile finally reaching her mouth and eyes.

Micah's enthusiasm waned, but he covered it up quickly. "Yeah, I better."

Simone tipped up onto her toes and kissed him, and Micah liked that better than when he initiated all the kissing. She didn't stay long, and when Micah closed the door behind her, a sigh fell from his lips.

"Maybe we are crazy," he murmured to himself. But if so, he decided he didn't care. He just needed to talk to Momma and Daddy before Saturday. He lifted his phone, but it was too late to call now.

Tomorrow, he told himself as he floated around the corner and into his bedroom. He could deal with the nerves and unknowns tomorrow. Tonight, he was going to ride the high of being married to Simone and the idea of having her move in with him on Sunday.

MICAH SAT ON THE FRONT STEPS OF SKYLER'S HOUSE—CASA Skywalker—the next morning, having texted his brother earlier that day to ask what Momma's routine was. Apparently, she got up and made the coffee, which Skyler didn't drink before he went out to the ranch. Mal was working and gone to the bakery.

Momma would make breakfast for Daddy around eight or nine, and Skyler usually came back in for a little bit to eat with them. Micah had asked if he could stay out on the ranch, and Micah would eat breakfast with them, and Skyler had called.

"What is going on?" he asked.

"I just need to talk to them alone," Micah said.

Skyler had paused. "Sounds fishy."

"I'll tell you as soon as I talk to them," he said, though he wasn't sure if that was true or not. What was the point of waiting until the birthday party to make the announcement if he was going to tell individuals? Heck, he could put the news on the family text and be done with it. Most of Simone's family was on that string anyway.

One and done.

"Okay," Skyler had said. "But if you don't call me, I'm going to call you."

Micah had said he'd call just to get Skyler off the phone. It was almost nine, and he stood up and knocked on the door at the same time he opened it. "Just me, Momma," he called.

"Micah," she said from somewhere in the house. "Come in. We're just sitting down to breakfast."

Micah went through the foyer and around the corner to the kitchen. He did love this house, and Skyler and Mal obviously took care of it. Momma and Daddy sat at the table in the built-in nook, and Micah smiled at them though every cell in his body told him to flee, and flee fast.

"Mornin', Micah," Daddy said, getting up. "I'll get you a plate."

"I can get it, Dad," Micah said, but his father was already limping into the kitchen.

"He's doing great," Momma said, watching Daddy. "He should still be using the crutch though." She frowned slightly, and Micah thought he wouldn't want to use the crutch either. His father had been using it for at least four months, and his arm probably hurt.

He returned pretty quickly with a plate, and Micah started loading it with eggs and toast.

"What brings you by?" Momma asked, watching him.

Micah didn't want to lie to her. He didn't want to hurt her either. He looked right at her and employed every ounce of bravery he had. "I have to tell you guys something." He cut a glance at Daddy, who looked at him and then scooped up another bite of eggs.

"Okay," Momma said slowly. She'd stopped eating and wore that maternal worry in her eyes.

"It's nothing to worry about," Micah said. "Honest, Momma." He tried to smile, but found he was just too nervous. "Remember how I once said that I'd never been married to anyone, real or fake?"

Daddy coughed, and Micah hadn't even dropped the bomb yet.

"Micah," his mother said, her voice only air.

He watched his father as he reached for his glass of juice and then wiped his mouth. He wore an intense look in his eyes now too.

"Simone and I—"

"Dear Lord," Momma said. "Do *not* tell me this is happening again." She looked up at the ceiling. "Didn't I ask You to please *not* let this happen again? Gideon and I would like to see *one* son get married! Just *one*."

Micah sat at the table during her rant with the Lord, and when she looked at him, he just smiled. "It was an accident."

"You married a woman on accident?" Daddy asked. "Wow, Penny, I didn't know that could happen."

"For the record," Micah said, who'd never had a problem standing up for himself. With six older brothers, being loud and thinking he was right all the time came with the territory. "You saw Wyatt and Marcy get married." He looked at Daddy. "And it *was* an accident. Simone and I auditioned for a play together, and the ending scene was the marriage ceremony. Scott Daniels was auditioning too, and he took our paper—which was supposed to be a prop—and filed it with some others he had that were real."

Micah took out the marriage certificate. "I didn't even know until Jeremiah brought me this a couple of days ago." He laid the paper on the table. "I went to talk to the pastor, and it's real. I've been married to Simone for about three weeks now."

Momma sucked in a breath and picked up the marriage certificate. "I can't believe this."

"I know exactly how you feel," Micah said. "So then I went and talked to Simone, and we like each other, Momma. I love her." He cleared his throat. "I don't think she loves me—yet—but we decided we're going to try this. She's moving in with me on Sunday."

Momma lowered the certificate, her eyes wide.

"What part did you get?" Daddy asked.

Confused, Micah turned toward him. "What?"

"You said you were auditioning for a play. Did you get the part?"

Micah shook his head. "No, I got a different one. Simone too."

Daddy's dark eyes glinted like moonlight over still water. "Huh. So you guys didn't really sell the marriage ceremony."

Micah burst out laughing, beyond relieved when Daddy did too.

"I can't *believe* you two," Momma said, waving the marriage certificate at Daddy. "They're *married*, Gideon."

Daddy sobered and looked at her, taking another bite of his toast. "And they'll figure it out," he said. "Just like the other six have."

Micah's stomach roared, and he picked up his fork, bolstered by his dad's vote of confidence. He and Simone *would* figure out how to be married. They would.

He hoped they would.

SATURDAY AFTERNOON FOUND MICAH WALKING DOWN THE lane toward the Shining Star Ranch, his stomach full of stinging ants. He really needed some closure in his life. *Just one thing*, he thought, begging the Lord.

Bear Glover had called just after breakfast yesterday to postpone their meeting. Simone had not moved in yet, and they'd only spoken through text yesterday. Micah felt like he had a million doors open, and some of them needed to close before he drove himself crazy.

Simone's SUV rumbled past him as he walked along the side of the road, and he watched her pull into the driveway at the homestead and then get out to help her grandmother and father get into the house for the party.

She came back outside as Micah turned to go down the

driveway. "Hey," she said, smiling as if they hadn't agreed to move in together in less than twenty-four hours.

You're not moving in together, he told himself. *She's your wife.*

"Hi." He put a smile on his face, but he had no idea how to make this announcement. "Any chance you're feeling like spilling the beans?"

"Not even a little," she said. "Your parents really took it okay?"

He'd told her all about the breakfast conversation yesterday. "Yeah," he said. "Daddy more than Momma, and he'll keep her calm about it."

Simone ran her hands up and down her arms. "I don't feel very calm about it."

Micah's concern spiked. "We don't have to do this," he said. "I don't want you to be nervous around me. It's not worth that." In fact, she should be his only solace. His safe place. A sanctuary from the world. And he wanted to be that for her too. "In fact, Simone, I should be the opposite of that for you."

She stilled and looked at him. "You are."

"Am I? You just said you weren't feeling good about our plan."

"No, I meant I'm worried how everyone will take the announcement." She sucked her bottom lip. "Maybe I should've prepped them, like you did your parents." She looked at him for reassurance, and Micah leaned down and kissed her.

"It's going to be fine," he said. He wasn't sure if he was reassuring her or himself. "Let's go."

Inside the homestead, almost everyone had arrived, and with all the nieces and nephews, all the Walkers, and a couple of dogs, pure madness reigned. Micah didn't hate it, and he smiled as he picked up Conrad and said, "What have you got there?" The boy would be three soon, and Micah had the sudden thought that he should offer to take Conrad when Evelyn had the triplets. Momma would want him too, but she was right across the street, and they could share the cute little boy.

"Train," Conrad said, holding up the toy.

"What color is it?" Micah asked, tapping the engine. He actually had no idea if Conrad knew any colors. By the boy's silence and the way he stared at the train as he tried to figure out what Micah had asked him, Micah didn't think so.

"It's red, bud," he said. "A red train."

Conrad grinned at him and hugged him, and a powerful love moved through Micah. "Is there cake here?"

"Yep, cake," Conrad said, and he pointed to the kitchen.

"Should we go see if we can sneak some?"

"Giving my son some bad habits?" Rhett asked, grinning as he took the last step toward Micah. He chuckled as he hugged Simone and then reached for Conrad. "Come on, bud. Momma says you have to put on a bib if you want cake."

Conrad fussed and said, "No bib," but Rhett took him

from Micah anyway. Micah watched them go, then reached for Simone's hand.

"See? They made it work."

"Yeah, and they got divorced first," Simone said.

"I wasn't around for that," Micah said, taking one slow step toward the chaos. "I mean, I heard about it, but I don't really know what happened."

"My sister is a bit stubborn," Simone said. "That's what happened."

"Oh, so you mean you're not the only one?" Micah flashed her a teasing smile. She squeezed his hand quite hard, and Micah chuckled. "Okay, I take that back. You know, being stubborn can actually be a good quality."

"Good save," she said out of the corner of her mouth as they arrived in the kitchen. Callie had a gigantic birthday cake on the counter, and Mal was moving around it, adding little flourishes with a piping bag full of white icing.

Callie directed people this way and that as stacks of plates, napkins, and silverware got put out. "Where's Liam?" she called, and he raised his hand from the back of the crowd, where he'd been standing with Jeremiah and Tripp. "We're ready, baby," Callie yelled to him. "Get us started."

Liam pulled a chair out from under the table and stood on it. "All right," he called, and a couple of seconds passed before people actually quieted down. "The boss says we're ready to start. We're going to eat first and have cake second."

"No," Denise said. "Daddy, that's not right." She had the

sweetest drawl on the planet. "Mama said we could eat first and open presents second. Then cake last."

"Oh, all right," Liam said, smiling down on her. "I know we're eatin' first." He looked out at everyone. "So let's see…."

Micah's heart raced. He wasn't asking for announcements. Maybe he could just send the news on the family text.

"I have something to say," Daddy said, and Micah actually made a squeaking noise. His hand tightened on Simone's, and they exchanged a worried glance.

"We have an announcement too," Skyler said. "Can we do announcements, Callie?"

"Announce away," she said, though she didn't look particularly pleased about it.

"You go first, Daddy," Skyler said.

"My mother and father are coming to live with us in Three Rivers," Daddy said, his smile big and bold. "I'm going to need all the boys to help when we go down to the Hill Country to get them. My momma…knows how to save for a rainy day, and we're not just talking money."

"That's a nice way to say she's a hoarder, Daddy," Jeremiah said, tacking on a laugh. Several others laughed too, including Micah.

"Yes, well, maybe plan on a few days," he said. "Momma and I are going in a couple of weeks." He nodded and looked at Skyler.

"Mal's having a baby!" He lifted their joined hands as if they'd just won a gold medal.

"Oh, how wonderful," Momma said, stepping over to

Mal. All the congratulations went around, and most eyes went back to Liam. Micah saw his window to share their news dwindling, and Simone's hand in his became a vice grip.

"Okay—"

"Simone and I are married," Micah blurted out, interrupting Liam. A hush fell over everyone, and even the little children stopped playing and fussing. He took a big breath. "She's moving in with me tomorrow."

CHAPTER THIRTEEN

Momma knew Micah's news was coming, but it still stunned her how he could stand there so calmly. None of her boys seemed to understand how hard marriage was, and she knew Micah didn't.

No one does, she told herself. And besides, the rest of them had made it work. That was what marriage was—one day at a time, working through things, making it work.

"So that marriage license was real," Jeremiah said.

"It was," Micah said, and several people started talking at once. Evelyn and Callie converged on Simone, and the three of them disappeared down the hallway toward the master suite, leaving Micah to face the crowd alone. And that was saying something, as Evelyn could barely move these days. And she'd moved *fast*.

Momma stepped over to his side, and he looked down at her while questions got thrown around.

How did that happen?

You didn't invite us?

What do you mean, audition?

Momma put her hand on Micah's arm and said, "All right, now. Everyone quiet down." She had to hold up both of her hands, and Gideon whistled through his teeth before everyone stopped talking.

"He and Simone got married by accident," she said, realizing how ridiculous that sounded. "But they're going to give it a try." She glared at Rhett. Then Liam. Then Tripp. Then Jeremiah. Then Wyatt. Then Skyler. "Just like the rest of you. So leave him alone. We're here for a precious little girls' fifth birthday. Now where's Denise?"

"Right here, Gramma." She stepped out from behind her father.

"There you are." Penny's whole heart spread into a smile on her face. "Let's say grace, okay? Then we can eat."

"Let me get Callie," Liam said. "She won't want to miss this." He pushed through the others. "Okay? Just give us a minute." He gave Micah a pointed look as he dashed down the hall.

"Sorry," Micah called after him. He turned to face everyone else, and it did Penny's heart and soul some good to watch Skyler and Wyatt approach him first, the trio forming a three-way hug. Words were said that she couldn't hear. Probably didn't even want to hear.

She took Denise's hand and went back to Gideon's side. They'd been talking a lot about getting his parents up to Three Rivers so they could be looked after better. Gideon's brother still lived in Llano, but he was getting older too. He'd only made the trip up to the Texas Panhandle once while Gideon was in the hospital, but Momma didn't blame him one bit.

He was seventy-seven-years-old and still working the ranch he'd lived on for fifty years. And tending to a lot around his father's home.

In fact, Gideon was trying to get Jonas to come to Three Rivers too. Land could be sold, he said. But Jonas didn't want to lose the ranch, and he was trying to convince his daughter to take it over.

Penny didn't think that would go well, because if Jenni had wanted the ranch, she'd have taken it over a decade ago. No matter what, Jonas wasn't going to be happy. She and Gideon had told him all of this, but he simply wasn't ready to hear it.

"When are you moving back to the farmhouse?" Skyler asked, coming up beside her. "I didn't realize that was happening."

She looked at her son, seeing right past his forced casualness. "We've loved being with you and Mal," she said. "But it's been over three months. Daddy is doing really well. Rhett is only five minutes away, and the rest of you twenty."

"I'm closer than twenty minutes, Momma," Tripp said. He picked up a cup and poured some punch into it. "I'll come if you need me."

Of course he would. Any of the boys would. Their wives would too. She smiled at him. "Thank you, dear. Marcy's hired a cleaning service for us to get all the dust and cobwebs out of the house, and we're going to go down to see what Gramma and Grampa have. They really do have a ton of stuff." And Penny was actually worried about it. There was no way they could fit even a quarter of what they owned in the farmhouse.

"Once we know what will have to be sold, thrown away, or put in storage, we'll have a better idea of when they'll be ready to move."

"It's not going to be easy," Tripp said. "They've lived in that house for seventy years."

"Don't remind me," Penny said with a smile. "You'll probably find jars of homemade grape juice that old. Grandma Lucy tried to get me to take some every time we visited." She giggled at the memories she had with Gideon's parents. They'd been kind to her their entire lives, and they'd taken in Gideon and Penny—and all seven of their rambunctious sons—after Gideon's first company had failed spectacularly.

"What about Micah?" Tripp asked.

"Oh, that boy," Penny said, though. Micah was not a boy. None of them were, as Gideon liked to remind her. "I tried to tell him that marriage wasn't something you tried on like a pair of boots." She sighed. "But well, he says he loves her."

"Is that right?"

Penny turned toward Jerome, Simone's father. "Oh, dear," she said. "Did they tell you in advance?"

"No," he said, shaking his head. Penny couldn't tell if he was pleased or upset. "But Simone's always had a good head on her shoulders. They'll be okay."

Micah drifted by, and Simone and her sisters still hadn't come back down the hall. Penny did what she'd always done best—she worried about what was going on back there. "I'm sure it'll work out," she said. She'd said that a lot in the past nine months, because she didn't have anything else to say. She wanted to rely on the Lord and trust that everything would work out. But she had doubts sometimes, just as she had many nights while Gideon lay in the hospital and no one knew if he'd come out of his coma.

But he had. And he was okay. Things had worked out.

Penny also knew for every situation like Gideon's where things did work out, there was one that didn't. People died in car accidents all the time, and by all accounts, Gideon should've died. So why did God save him and not someone else?

It was questions such as those that kept Penny up some nights. They also kept her on her knees, pouring her entire thought process out to the Lord. Her reasoning was then He'd know what she wanted and how she felt. After that, He could do what He wanted.

"Okay," Callie said, and Penny turned toward her. She'd loved Callie from the moment she'd met her, as the woman possessed some of the greatest strength Penny had ever seen in a woman. She'd struggled when she first became a mother, and she didn't have one of her own to go to.

So she'd come to Penny, and it had been Penny who'd shown her how to get a fussy baby back to sleep in the middle of the night, and Penny who had taught her to give time warnings so Denise didn't have a meltdown every time they needed to go back inside the house.

She reached for her daughter-in-law, noting the pure exhaustion on Callie's face. "The cake is beautiful, love," she whispered as she hugged Callie.

"Isn't it?" Callie pulled back and smiled at the cake. "Mal is a genius."

"That she is." Penny sure did love Mal too, and she'd miss being in the same house with her and Skyler. Not only that, but Mal always brought pastries home from the bakery, and Gideon was definitely going to miss that. In fact, Penny saw trips to the bakery to appease her husband in her future.

"We're ready now," Liam said as Evelyn and Simone returned to the main part of the house. "Micah, you're the man of the hour. You get to say grace."

"All right," Micah said, not even bothered by the slightly acidic tone in Liam's voice. He swiped his cowboy hat off his head and closed his eyes. Penny usually did too, but today, she kept her eyes open and looked around at all these people she loved so fiercely.

Rhett stood with one hand on Evelyn's arm and the other holding his hat. Tripp held his son, swaying back and forth while Ivory had one of her hands twined with Oliver's. Liam had taken up a spot next to Callie, and Marcy and Wyatt stood in the back corner, Warren asleep in the swing beside them.

Skyler and Mal held hands, and Micah and Simone did too. Jeremiah and Whitney had their hands full with their two small children, but they did a spectacular job with them, keeping them quiet as Micah asked for health and safety and blessings.

Penny loved these people with her whole heart and soul. She didn't know if Micah and Simone could make their marriage experiment work, but she prayed that they could.

"And Lord," Micah said. "Thank you for everything we have. For this ranch and the one next door. For bringing Skyler and Mal to us. For saving Daddy's life. For the babies and the kids and the noise and the horses. Oh, and the dogs. Thank you for all these people here, our family. Amen."

The man seemed to be able to call down silence from the heavens above when he spoke. Several others said "Amen," after him, but for the most part, everyone took a moment to look around at the people gathered there for the birthday party.

Family.

An overwhelming sense of gratitude filled Penny, and the only way she knew how to release her emotions was through tears. She wept as the noise level picked up again, and she turned to Skyler. "Baby? Will you get me some food and bring it over to me? I'm feeling like I need to sit down."

Skyler looked at her with concern in his eyes, saw the tears, and smiled. "Sure thing, Momma."

Penny looped her arm through Evelyn's and told Rhett, "I'll take her. Come on, dear. You need to sit more than I do."

Penny pulled up to the cute little gray house with the right number on it. She reached for the gift bag on the passenger seat before getting out, and Jerome stood in the doorway on the porch before she'd made it to the bottom of the steps.

It was getting harder to lift her feet to climb steps, but with the help of the railing, Penny made it. "Good afternoon, Jerome," she said, extending the gift bag. "I hear congratulations are in order."

"Thank you." He took the bag and held the door for her as she walked inside. "At least we had the decency to tell our families about the wedding."

"*Before* it happened," Penny said with a smile. Jerome and Belinda Murphy had decided to get married, and they'd invited Penny to a small shower. "Are you going to stay here or move to Belinda's?"

"Oh, I'm movin' in here," Belinda said from the kitchen. She set down the wooden spoon she'd been using to stir the sweet tea. "Thanks for coming, Penny." Belinda had the energy Penny wished she still did, and she was just as old as Penny.

Seasoned, she liked to think of herself. She could not imagine getting married at her age, and yet there were Jerome and Belinda, getting ready to do it.

"Someone has to take care of me," a voice behind her said, and Penny turned to find Elaine Foster sitting in her recliner. She had a flash of what her life would be like once Grandma Lucy and Grandpa Jerry arrived in Three Rivers, and she told herself it could be months away still.

She put a big smile on her face and approached the elderly woman. "I feel like I need someone to come take care of me too." She patted Elaine's hand, noting how cold she was. "Do you need a blanket, dear?"

"A blanket would be lovely," Elaine said. Penny thought she could see right through her skin for a moment, and she peered at the older woman. Something was wrong; her mother heart could just tell. Just like she knew when Wyatt had contracted pneumonia as a baby. He hadn't been able to tell her what was wrong, but Penny knew.

"Let me get you one." She got up and asked Jerome where she might find a blanket.

"In the hall closet," he said. "Is she cold again?"

"She doesn't look well, Jerome."

He watched his mother and then looked at Penny. "Simone took her to the doctor. They said there was nothing wrong."

"There's something wrong." Penny went part way down the hall and got out a blanket, taking it back to Elaine. She covered her up, snug and tight, and sat on the edge of the couch next to her. "Tell me about the girls as babies," she said.

Elaine's whole countenance lit up, and Penny basked in the warmth of it. "You should've seen little Callie when she was born. She was like a kitten, with all this dark hair everywhere."

Penny smiled and let the older woman talk and talk and talk. Once the food was served and she finished eating, she fell asleep, right there in the armchair, amidst the party.

Penny watched her, unable to truly look away. Something writhed in her veins that told her Elaine Foster wasn't going to be on this earth for much longer. She'd had feelings like this before, and she'd always been right.

Her next dilemma presented itself: Tell Callie, Evelyn, and Simone? Or keep her suspicions to herself?

CHAPTER FOURTEEN

S imone absolutely had to have all of her kitchen appliances, despite what Micah said he owned. She needed her electric stand mixer, and her hand mixer, and the toaster oven. She could make the perfect avocado toast with that, and she had not seen one at Micah's.

"Is that it?" he asked after he'd carried out yet another box of kitchen equipment.

"I think so," Simone said, looking around the kitchen. She was forgetting something, but she couldn't think of what. She flinched as Micah touched her waist.

"You live half a mile from my house," he said. "Anything you've forgotten, I'll come get." He smiled at her, the gesture sweet and soft and sexy.

"You're right," she said. "It's not like I'm leaving the state."

"Can you imagine?" Micah asked, clearly joking. "I don't

feel Texan enough, because I'm the only house out here without a Texas wreath on the front door."

"I can fix that," she said. "I have at least half a dozen in my shop."

"Texas wreaths?"

"Yes," she said. "They're a big seller, cowboy."

"Huh," Micah said. "I had no idea."

"I'll pick one once I get back to the shop," she said. "Which better be soon, because I have a big event coming up."

"Yeah?" Micah turned to leave, catching Simone's hand in his. "You know, you don't have to do the events and fairs if you don't want to."

"Why wouldn't I want to?"

Micah shrugged as he walked out the front door. "I'm just saying." He turned back to her before going down the steps. "You know I have a lot of money, right? I guess we should've talked about that."

Simone swatted his chest. "Of course I know that."

He grinned at her and caught her around the waist, gazing down at her. The moment sobered and lengthened, and Simone couldn't look away. "You know I'd give you whatever you wanted, right?" Micah asked, ducking his head to nuzzle her neck.

Simone clung to his shoulders, enjoying the slip of his lips along her skin.

Someone catcalled, and Simone pulled away from Micah, who likewise jumped away from her. Anita and Soren were walking by, and Soren waved her cowgirl hat at

Simone and Micah. "Hey, y'all," she called in a high, almost singing voice.

"Hey," Simone said, waving back. "You know Soren and Anita, right?" she said to Micah, now leading him down the steps.

"Not particularly well," he said.

"Well, now's a good time to meet them." Simone took his hand and went toward her friends. "Hey, guys."

"You're moving?" Soren asked, eyeing Micah's truck with all the boxes in the back.

"Just down the road," Simone said, her chest quivering a little. "See, uh, Micah and I got married in a freaky sort of ceremony, and I'm moving into his house."

Both Anita's and Soren's eyebrows darted upward, and they looked to the tall cowboy next to Simone. "Wow," Soren said, always the more bold of the two. "Well, congratulations?"

"Yeah," Anita said, giving Soren a look. "Congratulations." She hugged Simone, adding, "We need another girls' night," in a whisper.

Simone nodded as her friend pulled back, and she said, "Anita," to Micah. "And that's Soren. They live right next door."

"Nice to meet you ladies," Micah said, extending his hand for them to shake. He was right proper with his manners, that was for sure. Simone made a mental note to tell Penny.

With the introductions done, Simone said, "Well, we have to get going."

"Yeah, we're headed out to the well this afternoon," Soren said. "We'll call you later, Simone."

"Okay." She went around to the passenger side and got in the truck. Micah unloaded everything while Simone started unboxing inside the house. A couple of hours later, it was done. She'd moved. She was living with her husband.

Not sleeping with him, she told herself as she looked around the bedroom on the other side of the house from Micah's master suite. He'd offered the suite to her, but Simone thought that was entirely too much work.

She had no idea if he'd bought the bed in the past two days or if it had been there before, as she'd had no reason to explore all the bedrooms in their entirety. The room had curtains, a rug on the floor, and a puffy comforter on the bed. And it was a big bed—bigger than hers. Simone sat down on it, wondering what alternate reality she'd entered.

She wondered if Rhett and Evelyn had shared a bedroom when they'd gotten married. Or what Callie and Liam had done. Pure foolishness hit her, and she didn't know what to do. She pulled out her phone and went to her texting app, finding the one with Callie and Evelyn in it.

I don't need details, she typed out. *But I moved in with Micah, and I feel like an idiot sleeping in a different bedroom. Is this normal?*

Of course, Simone wasn't born yesterday, and she knew none of this was normal. Absolutely none of it.

I didn't, Evelyn said. *I slept upstairs in the homestead, with three of his brothers there.*

Horror filled Simone. That was much worse than her situation.

We went straight to Hawaii, Callie said. *I was in love with him already.*

Simone didn't need more explanation than that. What she needed to figure out was whether or not she was in love with Micah Walker.

THE NEXT MORNING, SIMONE WOKE TO A TEXT FROM HER father. *I asked Belinda to marry me, and she said yes. We'd love to have you all for dinner. Evvy, I know you might not be able to make it. Tonight?*

He'd sent it before six a.m. Simone shook her head and started tapping out a response. *I can make it tonight,* she sent.

So can I, Callie said. *Congrats Daddy!*

Evelyn hadn't answered, even after Simone had showered and gotten ready for the day. She went out into the kitchen, where Micah sat on the couch, holding a bowl of cereal as he watched TV.

"Morning," he said with a smile. "How was the bed?"

"It's really great," she said, returning the smile. "My dad got engaged and wants me to go to dinner tonight."

"Am I coming?"

Simone hadn't even thought about that. "Let me find out."

She quickly tapped out the question, and Daddy said, *Of course. Spouses and families welcome.*

I need to check with Rhett, Evelyn said a moment later. *He got really sick yesterday.*

"Yes," she said. "Me and you."

"Okay," Micah said. "I'm a little scared of your father."

Simone scoffed, almost laughing. "Why?"

"If it were my daughter, and I hadn't been included in the marriage or wedding or anything…I'd be upset. I took that from him."

"So did Evelyn."

"And I'm pretty sure she apologized for it," Micah said. "And so did Rhett."

"It's an unusual circumstance."

"Doesn't mean it doesn't hurt his feelings." Micah stood up. "I'll talk to him tonight."

"Micah." She watched him take his dishes into the kitchen and put them in the sink.

Before he could answer, someone knocked on the door. Surprise darted through Simone, and she turned toward the front of the house. "Who's that?"

"I don't know," Micah said. "It's fairly early." He crossed through the house and opened the door. "Oh, Momma. Hey." He leaned down and enveloped her in a hug. "C'mon in."

His mother entered the house, and she wore a timid smile on her face. That was a sight to see, because Simone found her to be a Texan powerhouse of a woman.

"Ma'am," she said, stepping over and kissing her lightly on the cheek. Micah offered his hand, and Simone grabbed onto it.

"Oh, you don't need to call me ma'am," Penny said with a smile. "I'd hoped it wasn't too early, and it looks like you're up and ready."

"I have chores on the ranch this morning," Micah said.

Simone just watched her fiddle with her hands. "What's wrong, Penny?" she asked.

"I don't know if it's my place to say," she said. "But your father invited me and Gideon over for a little party yesterday afternoon while y'all were moving, and I went. Gideon wasn't feeling well. Anyway, I…." She looked at Micah and swallowed. "Simone, dear."

She reached out both hands and took Simone's in hers. Worry crept her through. "It's Gran, isn't it?" she whispered.

"She's not well, dear," Penny said. "I don't know how I know. I just do, and I don't think she has much time left with us." She sniffled, released one of Simone's hands and wiped her eyes. "I thought you should know. You and Callie and Evelyn should go visit her."

Simone nodded, her own emotions too volatile to speak. She cleared her throat and tried, but the words got stuck behind a ball of pain. Penny took her into a hug then, and said, "Just cry, baby. It's okay."

And though Simone was almost forty years old, she hadn't been hugged by a mother in a very, very long time. And she did allow herself to cry as Micah's petite mother held her tight. Micah put his hand on her back, and that was all she needed.

Several long seconds later, she stepped back and swiped

at her eyes. "We're going tonight," she said. "Daddy's having a dinner for us to celebrate the engagement."

"Oh, that's wonderful," Penny said. She smiled and stepped back. "Okay, will you tell the other girls?"

"I'll tell them," Simone said. "Thanks so much, Penny."

"And you and I should go to lunch," she said, more of a glint in her eyes now. "I'd love to get to know you better." She looked at Micah. "I love you already, because Micah loves you, but yeah. There's always time for a good lunch, right?"

"Always," Simone agreed.

"Marcy and I go every week," she said. "I'm sure she wouldn't mind if you tagged along."

Simone didn't know about that, and she said, "I'll ask her."

"Or I can."

"Okay." Simone watched Micah hug his mother and walk her to the front door. He turned back to her, pure compassion on his face.

"Sweetheart," he said, and Simone practically ran to him. He held her the same way Penny had, and Simone cried again, this time wetting his T-shirt with her tears.

"What will I do without her?" she asked. "She and Daddy are all I have left."

"Not true," he said, wiping her tears for her. "You have me now, and my whole, huge, crazy family."

Simone nodded, realizing in that moment that he was right. He was absolutely right. She wasn't alone anymore, and she touched her lips to his in a sweet kiss, falling a little bit more in love with him in that moment.

THAT NIGHT, SIMONE PULLED UP TO THE PERFECT WHITE house on Quail Creek Road and went up the steps. Through the closed door, she heard Conrad crying, and she didn't bother to knock. Evelyn wouldn't hear her anyway.

"Evvy," she said, finding her sitting on the couch in Rhett's office in the front of the house.

"He knows I can't get up and chase him," Evelyn said crossly. "So he hates sitting here." She gave her son a stern look. "Don't you dare move, Conrad."

The boy wailed again from the tiny chair Evelyn had set next to the desk. But he did not move.

"Rhett's too ill to stay with Conrad," Evelyn said. "And I can't handle him."

"I'll take him," Simone said, stepping toward him. "Can I?"

"Give him to me," Evelyn said, and Simone bent to pick up the little boy. She handed him to his mother, who perched him on her very pregnant belly.

"Conrad," she said. "Look at momma."

Sniffling, the little boy looked up through his long lashes.

"If ,omma says you can't have the grahams, you can't have them."

"Okay, Momma," he said, his voice straight from heaven.

"I sorry, Momma." He burst into tears again and buried his face into Evelyn's neck. How could she stay cross at him when Conrad was so contrite?

"Gramps is feeding us," Evelyn said as she stroked his hair. She didn't explain further, probably because she knew Conrad didn't get why he couldn't eat crackers just before dinner. "Now, go with Aunt Simone. She's going to take care of you tonight for Momma. Okay?"

Conrad sat up and reached for Simone, who took him. She smoothed back his hair and kissed his cheek. "Good boy, Conrad," she murmured. She set him on his feet and said, "Go find your shoes for me, okay?" He scampered off to do that, and Simone extended her hand toward Evelyn to help her off the couch.

Simone wasn't surprised when Evelyn started crying, but Simone couldn't get her arms around her sister. "I'm fine," Evelyn said. "I am. It's just I'm so big, I can't do anything. Everything hurts. I'm so ready to have these babies, but I'm also scared out of my mind."

She shook her head, and Simone didn't know how to help her. "Evvy," she said. "You'll be okay. The babies will come, and you'll have help. You won't have to do it yourself."

She nodded, and Simone put on Conrad's shoes and got them all out to the SUV. At Daddy's, they found Callie and Liam already there with their girls, and Conrad went straight over to his grandfather and gave him a hug.

Daddy loved the grandchildren, and Simone checked her phone for a message from Micah.

"Where's Micah?" Daddy asked after scooping Conrad into his arms.

"He's running late," she said. "Micah is. He had a meeting with someone today they turned into a phone call. He's almost here."

Daddy nodded and introduced Conrad to Belinda, who grinned at him like he was her grandson. Simone did really like Belinda, as she seemed to have lit a fire inside Daddy that had been out for a long, long time.

She was bright, and kind, and full of energy, and Simone stepped over to her and gave her a hug. "How's married life?" Belinda asked.

"New," Simone said, giving her a smile. A knock on the door saved her from saying anything else, and she went to get Micah from the front porch.

"Sorry," he said, and he didn't seem to be in a good mood.

"How'd it go with Bear?"

"Not great," he said. "I'll tell you about it later." He looked past her and into the house. "Did Rhett come?"

Simone shook her head, and Micah nodded just once. In the family room, Simone found Evelyn hugging Gran as they both stood up. Callie wept, and Liam steadied her with one hand while holding Ginger in the other.

Evelyn stepped back, and Simone felt like she'd missed something powerful. She glanced at Daddy, who stood in the kitchen with Belinda and Conrad still. "Dinner's ready," he said.

Micah tapped Simone on the shoulder and stepped away

from her. She heard him say something to her dad, and they both nodded. Daddy said something to Belinda, and then he and Micah went out into the garage.

"What's going on?" Callie asked, turning to Simone.

"We feel bad we got married without Daddy there," Simone said. "It really was an accident. It wasn't something we did on purpose." She rounded the couch and took Gran's hand. "It wasn't, Gran."

"I know that," she said, her voice definitely rusty and old. "I called Pastor Daniels, and he explained everything."

Surprise moved through Simone. "I explained everything, Gran. Did you think I was lying?"

"Yes," Belinda said. "She thought you were lying."

"Oh, you," Gran said, but Belinda just smiled. "And Jerome is okay. He's used to you girls doing what you want."

"Is that so?" Callie asked, her eyebrows as high as Simone's.

"I told him he should be proud of such independent, successful women," Belinda said, placing a pot of soup on a wooden trivet and looked up. "He realized he shouldn't be upset, and instead, be glad y'all have found someone who makes you happy." She grinned brightly and moved to help Gran to the table. "But she still called."

"Just for confirmation," Gran said.

Daddy and Micah came back inside, and Simone watched her father first, then her husband. "All right," Daddy said, clapping his hands together. "We're so glad you could all come tonight. Too bad Rhett is so sick."

"He feels really bad," Evelyn said.

"Tell him we love him," Daddy said, his voice choking on the last word in a rare show of his emotion. Simone's own emotions welled up for at least the umpteenth time that day, and she leaned into the man next to her. Her rock. Her anchor. Her husband. Micah.

"All right," Belinda said. "Let's eat."

Simone stepped over to her. "Thank you, Belinda," she said. "I'm just so happy for you and Daddy." She hugged the woman, who showed some surprise for the first time. She released her and hugged her father, who held her tight and whispered, "I love you, girly."

He hadn't called her by that childhood nickname for so long, and Simone sobbed into his shoulder. It seemed everyone had cried a little bit by the end of the evening, and as Simone held her grandmother one last time before she left, she hoped it wouldn't be *the* last time ever.

CHAPTER FIFTEEN

Rhett heard Evelyn groan from the other room, and he abandoned his case in the office. He knew everything forward and backward, but he liked to lay everything out in the days before court so he could see the timeline from beginning to end. Sometimes he even practiced his testimony so he could deliver his findings with a factual face and not an emotional one.

"Evvy," he said entering the hallway that led back into the main part of the house. She'd been taking a nap every afternoon with Conrad for the past few weeks, having narrowly fought off the sickness that had prevented him from going to her father's to celebrate his engagement.

She'd gone back to sit with her grandmother and share lunch with her several times since then, as Momma had told Evelyn that Gran didn't have much time left.

Momma, ran through his mind. His parents had gone to the Hill Country to assess the situation with Grandma Lucy and Grandpa Jerry, and Rhett needed them when Evelyn had the babies. *But they're not due for another three weeks.*

He entered the living room, hoping to just find his wife had groaned in her sleep, perhaps from trying to roll over. Instead, he knew in an instant that the groan was much more serious than that. She was in the process of trying to push herself up, and Rhett hurried to her side to help her.

"I think it was a contraction," she said, her eyes wide and afraid. She'd cried every day for the past couple of weeks too, and Rhett knew it wasn't all from the stress of her grandmother's illness. He understood the type of panic and fear he saw on his wife's face. He'd barely known what to do with one baby, and they were about to have three at the same time.

"I'm going to call Liam," Rhett said.

"No," Evelyn said. "Call Simone. The girls are sick, and I can't bring three babies back to an older brother who's infected."

"Okay." Rhett got up and jogged back to the office for his phone. He dialed Simone and hurried back into the living room while the line connected. "The bag is in the truck, baby. Let's go." Of course, Evelyn couldn't just jump to her feet and go. Rhett frowned as he realized the line hadn't connected to Simone, and he couldn't hold his phone and help his wife at the same time.

His heart sprinted in his chest, and he hated this out-of-control feeling. The last time he'd been this panicked had been when Tripp had called and said Daddy had been in an accident and to call everyone and get them to pray. There hadn't been much time for explanations then either.

"Okay," he said, taking a deep breath. Wife first. Conrad would be okay here—or even at the hospital—until Simone could come. He set the phone on the back of the couch and helped Evelyn to her feet. "One step at a time, sweetheart."

She actually turned toward him and gave him a smile, though it shook in the corners of her mouth. "They're coming early."

"The doctor said they might, remember?" He nodded to get her to keep moving, and they made it all the way outside and into the truck. "Stay here. I'm going to go grab my phone." He ran back inside the house, where Penny sat at the mouth of the hall. "Can you watch over Conrad for us?" he asked the dog, though of course she couldn't.

He also didn't want his son to wake up here alone. After swiping his phone back to his ear he saw that he'd missed Simone's call. Strange. He hadn't heard his phone ring. He tapped to return her call anyway, detouring down the hall to Conrad's room to check on the boy.

"Rhett," Simone said, her voice high-pitched to the point of a squeak. "Evelyn must be sleeping."

"Evelyn went into labor," Rhett said, already confused. Why was Simone crying already? "I tried to call you, but—"

"She's in labor?"

"And my parents are down at my grandparents'. Conrad is at the house, asleep, and I'm wondering if you can come sit with him. Take him back to your place. Whatever." He didn't expect her to say no, so the hesitation made him stop with his hand on his son's bedroom doorknob. "Simone?"

"Daddy just called," she said. "Gran died."

Rhett's whole soul crumpled in on itself. "Oh, no." He thought of his son here. Evelyn waiting in the car, possibly going through another contraction. "I'll call Skyler." He was close; he'd come. "Or Jeremiah."

"I'm sorry, Rhett," Simone said.

"No," Rhett said. "You do what you need to do."

"They're taking her to the Sanderson Funeral Home," Simone said. "Just so you know."

"Thank you, Simone," Rhett said. "I'll tell Evelyn."

"I can have Micah start the news around to your family about the babies," she said. "If you want."

"That would be great," Rhett said. He'd been gone from Evelyn for too long. "I have to go." The call ended, and Rhett peeked in his son's room. Conrad lay in his toddler bed, his face smashed into the pillow in such a way that Rhett was sure he couldn't even breathe. "Buddy," he said softly, rubbing his son's back. "Time to wake up, Conrad."

He quickly dialed Skyler while his son woke up and started to cry.

"What's up?" Skyler asked.

"Evelyn's gone into labor, and I'm wondering if you can come get Conrad."

"On my way," Skyler said, and relief poured through Rhett.

"He was asleep, and I didn't want him to wake up alone,

so I woke him up. I'm going to take him with us to the hospital. I know that makes your trip longer…."

"It's fine," Skyler said. "I'm literally doing nothing. I'm already in the truck. I can be to your place in ten minutes. You don't think you can wait?"

Rhett picked up Conrad, who pressed right into his shoulder, still sleepy. "Let me see how Evvy is doing." Outside, Evelyn had her eyes closed too. In the several seconds it took Rhett to get to the passenger side, he beat back the quiet panic that imagined the worst. That she'd passed out. That she wouldn't make it to the hospital. With Ivory's traumatic delivery, and Whitney's first baby delivered at home, Rhett knew they weren't immune to anything.

But her eyes fluttered open when he opened her door, and a soft smile touched her mouth. "Let me hug him," she said.

"You okay?" Rhett asked. "Skyler is on his way. We can take Conrad with us or wait for him." He passed Conrad to Evelyn, and he snuggled into her shoulder too.

"We can wait," she said. "It's okay."

"We'll wait for you, Sky," Rhett said, backing out of the way and closing the door. "Hurry, though, okay?" He knew better than most that pregnancies and deliveries were unpredictable at best.

"Be there in five," Skyler said, and Rhett hung up as he got behind the wheel and started the truck. He could go down the lane and shave a minute off of Skyler's arrival.

"Simone couldn't come?" Evelyn asked, and Rhett's

"Sweetheart," he said. "I talked to Simone, but no, she can't come."

"Oh. What's she doing?"

"She's on her way with Micah to the funeral home." He cut a look at her. "Your grandmother died."

Evelyn absorbed the news for one, two, three long seconds, and then her face fell. She sniffled and tears ran down her face. Conrad lifted his head and looked at her. "Mommy sad." He put both of his hands on either of her cheeks and looked at her.

"Yes." Her voice carried pure anguish, but she tried to smile amidst the pain and tears.

Rhett clenched his teeth together, because Gran had been a special woman. He reached over and patted Evelyn's arm, and their eyes met. She shook her head, and a whole conversation was had without either of them saying anything.

There would be time to grieve later, but right now, Rhett needed to get her and the babies to the hospital. He parked at the end of the lane, and only a few minutes later, Skyler pulled in.

"I didn't get his bag," Rhett said as he got out. He leaned into Skyler's truck as he rolled down the window. "I forgot his bag. It's in his room...somewhere."

"In the closet," Evelyn said behind him. "It's a green turtle backpack."

"Got it," Skyler said, and Rhett went to get Conrad from Evelyn.

158

"All right, bud," he said, taking him. "You're going to go with Uncle Skyler tonight, okay?"

"Mommy sad," Conrad said.

"Yeah, Mommy's going to have the babies," Rhett said. "So you do what Skyler says, ya hear? Say yes, sir."

"Yes, sir, Daddy."

Rhett loved Conrad with his whole soul, and he could not fathom there being enough room for three more babies. That was something he'd worried about the most. How could he love any of them the way they deserved to be loved? Conrad had his whole heart.

He handed Conrad to Skyler and in a desperate moment, hugged them both. He saw the surprise on Skyler's face, and then Rhett turned and got back in the truck. It was hard to be the oldest brother, something none of them would ever understand.

When Daddy had been hurt, Tripp had called Rhett. Not Jeremiah. Not his own twin. Rhett. Because as Rhett, he always had to know what to do. And the fact was, Rhett did *not* always know what to do.

"Let's go," he said, buckling his seatbelt, because he did know the way to the hospital, and he knew Doctor Johnson would know what to do from there.

ONLY A COUPLE OF HOURS LATER, DOCTOR JOHNSON SAID TO Evelyn, "Okay, Momma, it's time to push."

Rhett stood behind her, right where she'd told him to

stand, and she leaned into his body. The labor had been fairly easy so far, and he'd been praying with his whole heart and soul that the triplets would be born easily, with no complications. His heart beat a steady rhythm in his chest as Evelyn pushed.

"Here we go," Doctor Johnson said triumphantly. Rhett didn't even have time to breathe before the wail of a new baby filled the air.

A soft, "Oh," came from his mouth, and the doctor lifted the bright red infant over the drape across Evelyn's knees.

"Here's the first one, guys. He's a boy."

Rhett couldn't see Doctor Johnson's face, but his eyes crinkled up as if he were smiling big. He handed the baby to a nurse, who wiped and wrapped him before setting him right on Evelyn's chest.

Her shoulders shook as she cried. "Rhett, he's beautiful."

Rhett gazed down at his son, overcome with emotions from far and wide. "He sure is," he managed to say.

"Do you have names for them?" the nurse asked. "It'll help us keep them separated, and make sure we note the right time of birth for each of them."

"We're naming him Easton, right?" Evelyn asked Rhett, tilting her head back to look at him.

"Yes," he said. "Easton Gideon."

"Time to push again," Doctor Johnson said excitedly as the nurse lifted the baby from Evelyn's chest and took him to a warming unit. "You're going to have these babies close together."

Closer together was better than far apart in Rhett's opinion, and Evelyn pushed again. The baby didn't arrive though, and Doctor Johnson adjusted his stool. "Don't get too comfortable. And really give me a big push this time."

"I *am* giving you a big push," Evelyn said grumpily, and Rhett watched as the nurses checked on baby Easton. Only the first baby.

"Bigger then," Doctor Johnson said as Evelyn sat up, obviously ready to go. "Yes, you know when it's time."

"Of course I know when it's time," Evelyn said. "I feel like I'm going to explode." She groaned as she pushed, and Rhett hated seeing how tightly she gripped the rails on her bed.

"She's out!" Doctor Johnson exclaimed, but the baby didn't cry.

"It's a girl?" Evelyn asked, her voice raspy. They hadn't learned if the babies would be boys or girls, and Rhett knew she wanted a girl.

"It's a girl," Doctor Johnson said, passing the still silent infant to a nurse. "She's a little plugged up, Sally."

"Plugged up?" Evelyn asked, voicing Rhett's concerns. "Rhett, go see."

"If I move, there's nothing behind you," he said.

"Go see," she snapped at him, and Rhett felt like he was going to get in trouble no matter what he did.

He met Doctor Johnson's eyes, who said, "You probably have a couple of minutes before the last one will be ready."

Rhett stepped away, making sure Evelyn didn't just fall backward, and approached the warmer where the nurses had his little girl. His little girl.

His heart grew four sizes with one look at her, in less time than it took to breathe. Oh, how he loved her so much, and just like that, he had enough love and enough room in his heart for all of his children.

"She has a ton of hair, Evvy," he said over his shoulder. "It's all dark, like yours."

"Why isn't she crying?" Evelyn asked, the exhaustion plain in her voice.

He didn't want to say that the nurses had something stuck up the tiny infant's nose and were suctioning stuff out. They worked quickly, and in his opinion, roughly with the baby, and only a few seconds later, she coughed and wailed.

"There she is," Doctor Johnson said. "She just had a lot of stuff in her nose they had to get out."

The nurses wiped her quickly and wrapped her and handed her to Rhett. "Show her quickly, Mister Walker," one of them said. Rhett couldn't look away from the perfect, angelic face of his daughter. She continued to fuss, her unblemished skin crinkling like an old man's along her forehead.

He chuckled as his emotions choked him and turned to show Evelyn. "She's so perfect," he said, his voice full of awe. He passed the baby to Evelyn, who put her lips against the girls' forehead. "Can we name her after Gran?" Evelyn asked.

"Of course," Rhett said.

"Name?" the nurse wanted to know.

"Elaine Evvy," Rhett said, leaning down to kiss his wife's forehead.

"Oh, boy," Evelyn said, tensing up again.

"Last one," Doctor Johnson boomed. "Let's go."

Rhett quickly passed the baby to the nurse and stood behind Evelyn again. The last baby delivered easily, and he cried and cried, louder than the others.

"You got another boy," Doctor Johnson said. "And we won't know until we do a blood test, but he looks like he might be an identical twin." He'd been over all the scenarios for the babies Evelyn had been carrying for just over eight months. They could've all come from their own egg, or they could've come from one egg and separated. He wouldn't truly know, unless they wanted to do some in vitro testing, until birth.

And Rhett and Evelyn hadn't wanted to do any unnecessary testing. They didn't care if the babies were identical or singles.

He started massaging Evelyn's stomach, saying, "I definitely think you have two placentas in there, Evelyn. You've still got some work to do."

"Name for this last baby?" the nurse asked.

Rhett and Evelyn had talked about names for ages, it seemed. They had three girl names and three boys, since they didn't know what they'd be getting. "I like Austin more than Dallas," Evelyn said.

"Austin Foster," Rhett said, turning to the nurse.

"You can come for their baths if you want," she said. "We'll bring them to their momma in the recovery room."

"Evvy?"

"Go with the babies," she said. "I'm fine."

Rhett stepped over to her and kissed her forehead again. "You did so great. I love you."

"Love you too," she said, sighing, and Rhett went with his three new babies to get their baths. The nurses put him to work too, and he copied them as he bathed Austin and they took care of Easton and Elaine. Austin was definitely the fussiest, and the smallest, and Rhett thought he'd probably have to fight with his siblings for everything he wanted.

Pure joy filled him, because Rhett loved having a big family. Yes, they were loud, and obnoxious, and sometimes noses got bloodied over doughnuts—at least growing up. And he hoped his boys—and his one darling girl—would have the same kind of familial bond he had with his brothers and their wives.

"Okay," Sally said. "You take this one." She put tiny Elaine in Rhett's right arm. The only way Rhett knew it was Elaine was because of the pink hat the nurse had put over all that dark hair. "And this one." She put a blue-capped baby in his left arm. "That's Easton. I've got Mister Fussy here."

She beamed down at Austin, who also wore a blue hat. Neither of the boys had much hair, and Rhett did wonder if they were identical twins.

"Can we take them out to the waiting room for like, five minutes?" he asked. "Before we take them back to Evelyn?"

"She's not done," another nurse said, so Sally said, "Five

minutes. Let's go." She led the way, and Rhett kept his steps light and his eyes on the babies to make sure he wasn't jolting them. Carrying two at once wasn't the easiest thing he'd ever done, because they felt like glass, like he'd break them with his too-big cowboy hands at any moment.

Sally exited the maternity ward, and Rhett heard Wyatt whistle. "Over there," he said, nodding to his left without looking up. "There will be a ton of them. Loud. Can't miss 'em."

He looked up, a huge grin on his face, and found everyone he loved right there—except for Liam and Callie, and Micah and Simone. Evelyn's father wasn't there either, and neither were his parents, and Rhett's joy faded slightly. Skyler held Conrad, who just stared at Rhett like he was bringing him snakes instead of siblings.

Then Jeremiah whooped, and everyone broke into cheers and applause.

"Oh, you got a little girl," Marcy said, reaching for Elaine, her eyes already watering.

Rhett introduced them around, and he took Conrad from Skyler. "Those are your new brothers and sister," he said. Conrad just stared at the babies, and Rhett had to admit he could relate.

Jeremiah hugged him and said, "Jerome called, and he said he wanted to be here so badly. He said they'll come by as soon as they can, probably later tonight."

"Okay," Rhett said. "I'll tell Evelyn."

"Five minutes are up," Sally said, and Rhett took Elaine and Easton with him to truly meet their momma.

CHAPTER SIXTEEN

Liam looped his tie around his neck, knotting it quickly though everything he'd been doing for the past week felt like it had been done in slow motion. Without Jeremiah and Whitney and Mal and Skyler, he felt like he'd have left one of his girls somewhere and not remembered where.

Tripp had come over last night just to be there in the morning to help, and Liam sure did appreciate that. He found his twin in the kitchen with Denise and Ginger, all three of them eating happily. How he did that, Liam wasn't sure. Most days, he felt like he couldn't keep up with the demands of his family, his job, and the ranch.

When Daddy had been in the hospital, Liam had found the time to go visit him and read to him. He actually missed that slower pace of his day, and he really wanted to get back to it. "Morning," he said, reaching for a mug. He'd left Callie in the bathroom to get ready, and he hoped she'd be able to pull herself together for the funeral that day.

She'd been lying on the couch all week, only answering her phone if her father called. Gran had most things planned for her funeral, because she was ninety-six-years-old and knew she wouldn't live forever. But for some reason, Jerome hadn't been able to make any decisions without all three girls signing off on them, and Callie had done nothing all week but deal with funeral arrangements.

Evelyn couldn't help much, as she'd just birthed three babies, and Liam suspected a lot of the load had fallen to Simone. He'd done the dishes, and put in laundry, and put the girls in the tub at night. His mother had come to help as much as she could, but again, Evelyn had just had three babies, and she needed a lot of extra help too. He knew Mal and Marcy had been at Evelyn's every day, trying to help her establish a routine for feeding, bathing, and napping with so many new people at once. Everything took three times as long, and Liam couldn't even imagine that.

He and Callie had only ever had the one newborn, and Ginger had kept Liam awake worrying night after night. Sometimes she still did. Denise too, because Liam just didn't know if he was doing the right thing.

"Did Uncle Tripp make oatmeal?" he asked, looking into a pot on the stove.

"Cream of wheat," Tripp said. "There's tons. Come eat."

Liam dished up a bowl and said, "I'm going to go check on Callie." He went back down the hall, sniffing out the scent of eucalyptus before he reached the bedroom door. That meant she'd at least gotten in the shower. A good sign.

"Sweetheart?" he asked as he entered.

She looked up from the armchair in the corner, where she sat in her bathrobe. A soft smile touched her face, but it was clear she'd already been crying.

"I brought breakfast," he said, crossing the room to her and kneeling down in front of her. She took the bowl; Liam wiped her tears.

"I know I'm being silly," she whispered. "I mean, she was old. She lived a very good life."

Liam said nothing, just watched his wife's face as her anguish rolled across it.

"I just…." She sighed and looked up to the ceiling. "I'm the oldest. I have to pull myself together."

"No, you don't," Liam said. "You can cry all you want."

She smiled at him again. "Who's going to tell stories of my mom now?"

"You'll have to," Liam said, trying to smile in reassurance. "You know them all, Cal. You can tell them."

She nodded and dipped the spoon into the cream of wheat. One bite later, she said, "Oh, this is good."

"Tripp puts a *lot* of cream in," Liam said. "And probably a ton of sugar."

"Have him teach you how." She grinned at him then, and Liam felt like he saw a glimpse of his wife for the first time in a week.

"Let's go away after this," he said, suddenly desperate to get away from the ranch, the computer, and Three Rivers.

"The four of us. Let's go to California and Disneyland and the beach."

Callie took another bite of the hot cereal and looked at him. "Can you do that with your schedule?"

"I don't care," he said, putting both hands on her knees. "I want to. I want to get away with my family."

Callie smiled at him, and Liam loved her so. "Book it, cowboy."

"Yeah?"

"Yeah, what do I have keeping me here?"

"Well, Evelyn did just have triplets." And Callie had gone to help a couple of times, but not much more than that. She'd spent days at her father's house, cleaning out Gran's room and belongings too. He'd worked as much as he could so he didn't fall too far behind and helped at home; the girls had gone to whoever could take them for the day, usually Whitney.

Liam was thankful they had family so close to help, but he needed to get back to his core. And his core was Callie, Denise, and Ginger.

"Let's give it a week," Callie said. "I'll make sure Daddy is all set, and I'll make sure Evelyn is settled."

Liam nodded, his excitement already growing. He stood up and said, "Great. We have to leave soon."

"Yep." Callie stood up too and handed him the cereal bowl. She'd only taken five or six bites, but it was more than she'd eaten in one sitting all week. "Liam…thank you. I know this week hasn't been easy for you either."

He reached out and ran his fingers down the side of her face. "I love you, Callie."

She wrapped her arms around him, the best words in the world still, "I love you, too, Liam."

LIAM LOOKED UP AS THE STABLE DOOR OPENED. AN INSTANT smile lit his soul when his oldest brother walked in. "Rhett," he said, abandoning Pretzel to go give his brother a hug. Rhett smiled, and all the weight he carried disappeared.

"I'm last, aren't I?" he asked, clapping Liam on the back.

"Yeah, but it's fine," Liam said, stepping back. "Jeremiah took Ollie out, and Tripp and Wyatt just barely left." He hooked his thumb over to Pretzel and Memory, where Micah stood, still saddling him.

He came over and hugged Rhett too, as did Skyler, who was now ready with his horse, Red Velvet.

"Is Wyatt riding?" Rhett asked.

"He says he can," Liam said. "Says it's been over a year, but." He shrugged. "Daddy's not going to. He's stayin' here, and Wyatt said he might stay just to keep him company."

"Yeah, because he shouldn't be riding either." Rhett stepped over to the wall and pulled down his saddle.

"No argument from me," Liam said. "But he's a little sensitive about being told what to do. Says he's a grown man and all that."

"And he is," Micah said. "Let him deal with himself." He

clicked his tongue at Memory and led her down the aisle to the back door.

"You didn't bring Conrad," Skyler said.

"Not this time," Rhett said. "He's still too little."

"He's three," Skyler said. "He can start to ride, especially tethered to you, and we're just goin' slow today."

Rhett nodded and kept his head down as he saddled. Liam watched him for an extra moment, finally ready with Pretzel. "Let's go, boy," he said to the horse, and they followed Micah, leaving Skyler and Rhett to talk alone.

Liam didn't need to be in the middle of everything, though he had been the one to initiate this riding expedition. He'd taken his trip to California, and it had filed down the ragged edges of his soul. He'd wanted to spend more time with his brothers—just the brothers—and this was their first riding outing.

"Gonna be hot today," Daddy complained from where he leaned against the fence, and Liam looked up into the sky.

"Sure is." April had passed, seemingly in the blink of an eye, and Liam was ready for warmer weather.

"Are they coming?" Jeremiah asked. "Sky and I still have work to do today."

"They're coming," Micah said. "Give them a minute." He seemed happier than he'd been previously, and Liam wanted to ask him how things were going with Simone, as well as with his new business. Though he lived only a half-mile from Micah, and their wives were sisters, he felt disconnected from the youngest brother.

He swung up into the saddle and moved Pretzel over to

Micah, but he couldn't think of anything to ask him. Everything sounded too prying in his own mind, and Micah had never been super forthcoming with things.

Rhett and Skyler emerged from the stable, and with everyone in the saddle, Liam couldn't help grinning. Daddy watched them with an odd look on his face, finally saying, "Look at you boys. I wish I could come."

"I'll stay with you, Daddy," Wyatt said, moving toward him.

"No," Daddy said. "No, you go." He pulled his cell phone from his back pocket. "But everyone line up right there. All in a row. I want to get a picture of y'all." It took a couple of minutes to get the horses where they needed to go, and Daddy held up the phone. "Smile, boys."

Liam did, feeling more like a cowboy in the saddle than anywhere else. And he didn't get out to ride Pretzel as often as he'd like.

"I'll send it to ya," Daddy said, beaming down at his phone. "All my boys, riding horses." He sounded so proud, and Liam wanted to live up to that for his father.

"All right," he said. "Should we just head out to the west?"

"That's the best spot for shade," Jeremiah said, taking the lead. Liam didn't mind. It was his ranch, and he knew every square inch of it.

Liam hung near the back of the brothers, watching them as they started conversations with one another, each a good cowboy, a good brother, a good husband.

"So," he heard Skyler say to Micah. "How are things going with Simone?"

Liam inched up closer to them, because he wanted to hear this too.

"Are you asking about Simone?" Jeremiah called over his shoulder. "Hold up. I want to hear about that too."

"Come on, guys," Micah said.

"No, you come on," Rhett argued back. "It's been what? Six or seven weeks now. You admitted to everyone that you were going to try marriage and see how it went. So…how's it going?"

Micah glared at Skyler, who didn't care at all about the lasers headed his way. "I don't ask you private things about your marriage."

"I didn't ask you private things," Skyler said.

"Yeah," Tripp said. "He asked you how it was going."

Liam said nothing, and neither did Wyatt. He didn't want specifics of anyone else's marriage, and he knew his was as unconventional as they come.

Micah finally smiled, his stony exterior cracking. "It's going fine. Great. I mean, she hasn't moved out yet."

Liam held back the laugh for as long as he could. Thankfully, it was Skyler who said, "Oh, my heck," before laughing that broke the dam of tension. All the brothers laughed then, even Micah.

"I'm glad I'm not the only one who feels that way," Jeremiah said. "In fact, every day I pray Whitney won't move out."

They laughed again, and Liam settled into the saddle, enjoying the hot sunshine, the clip-clop of horse's hooves, and the time he got to spend with his brothers.

CHAPTER SEVENTEEN

"What do you mean they want us to move there?" Tripp held Isaac in his arms, trying to get the little boy to hold still so he could wipe his nose. "To Tennessee? Ivory, that's crazy." He set Isaac down with only half the job done, because his wife had just hit him with some shocking news.

"They want to see the kids more," she said, still staring at her hands as she sat at the kitchen table.

"Yeah, well, *they* can move *here*," Tripp said, feeling grumpy and unreasonable. "We live here, Ivory. Our home is here. And Daniel still has rights to see Oliver." He turned toward his son as Isaac slapped his little palms against the glass in the back door that led onto the deck. He stepped that way, trying to get his thoughts to line up.

He didn't like arguing with Ivory, and this wasn't really an argument. They'd gone to Tennessee for Thanksgiving, and the visit had been fine. Good, really. Her parents had been kind, and they'd been thrilled to meet him and Isaac, and see Oliver again. They hadn't seen their grandson for years, something Tripp couldn't fathom.

"Stay on the deck, okay?" Tripp bent down and tried to wipe Isaac's face again, but the boy whined and turned his head quickly. Tripp abandoned the idea and opened the door for him. "Stay on the deck."

Isaac took a very haphazard step down out of the house and onto the deck, going straight for the car he could sit in and pedal around. Tripp checked to make sure the gate was closed, so his son couldn't accidentally pedal down the stairs, and it was.

He left the door open a couple of inches so he could hear Isaac if he needed help, and he turned back to Ivory. She hadn't moved, and she must've had something absolutely fascinating on her hands, by the way she studied them.

Tripp sat down and took her hands in his, which brought her pretty eyes to his. He gave her a smile. "Tell me what you're thinking."

"I'm thinking I don't want them to be disappointed," she said.

"Okay," he said. "And?" He already knew what would come after the "and." Ivory wanted to do what they wanted her to, because she thought that was the only way to get them to keep talking to her. And she didn't want to be the one to say no. And she didn't want to hurt them. And she didn't want them to think she didn't want them around.

"And I don't know," she said, dropping her eyes back to their hands.

Tripp massaged her palms, trying to put the right words together. "I know what you want," he said.

"Oh?"

"Yeah." He looked at her. "You want them to be involved in our lives the way my parents are."

She lifted her chin, but she wouldn't admit it.

"I want that too," Tripp said. "But it would be much easier for them to move here. My family is here, and are you saying you want to leave Three Rivers—and them —behind?"

She shook her head.

"No," he said. "Because just last week, we were talking about buying a house closer to Seven Sons, because you feel left out of certain things the family does." It was true that most of the family lived south of town, and that yes, Tripp and Ivory weren't as involved with the happenings of the ranch. Five of Tripp's brothers lived within a fifteen-minute drive of the ranch, and so did Momma and Daddy. Only Wyatt and Marcy lived farther than Tripp and Ivory did, and Wyatt was such a dynamic force that most things revolved around him anyway.

Tripp took Oliver to the ranch at least three times a week, sometimes more. He loved riding, and Jeremiah had started to give the boy some chores so he could earn some money.

"I know," Ivory said. "You're right. Of course you're right."

LIZ ISAACSON

"Okay," Tripp said, relieved and trying not to show it. "So call them and say we just can't move there. I think they should move here."

"Daddy won't do that."

"Why not?"

"The land is my great-grandfather's. He wants to keep it in the family."

"Destiny lives there," Tripp said. "She doesn't want it?"

"Would you?" Ivory pulled one of her hands away and wiped her face as she exhaled. "It's not like my dad has taken care of the land. The house is falling apart."

"Oh, it wasn't that bad," Tripp said.

"But it wasn't good," Ivory said, shaking her head. "No, Destiny has a nicer, newer house closer to town."

Ivory's parents did live out in the middle of farmland, with sprawling horse farms that were pristine. But her parents hadn't kept up with the repairs on the land, and yeah, Tripp had seen the age of it. The wear and tear.

"So they can keep it," he said. "They don't have to sell it. They can just buy something here."

Ivory rolled her eyes and cocked her head. "I love you." She reached out and cradled his face in one hand, a smile spreading across her face. "I do, but you forget that not everyone has a bank account as big as yours." She giggled, and Tripp smiled too.

"I do not. We'll buy them a house. Heck, let's buy *us* a house down by the ranch and give them this one." Tripp liked that idea the moment he said it. Ivory looked at him again, and he'd sparked something inside her.

Just as quickly as the hope had entered her expression, it faded. "They'll never do that."

"Ask them."

"They won't let us *give* them a house."

"Then they can rent it," he said. "We'll just say the real estate market is bad here, and we can't sell it. Or that we want to keep it, and they can live in it or pay rent or whatever makes them comfortable."

Ivory's blue eyes blazed at him. "Tripp…."

"I'm going to call Fletcher right now." He got up and checked on Isaac on the deck. The little boy made race car noises with his mouth and motored around happily. He reached for his phone and started tapping.

"Tripp." But Ivory's voice had no weight behind it.

"The line is ringing," he said, lifting the phone to his ear.

"Fletcher Charles," the man said. "Tripp Walker." He laughed, and Tripp smiled. "What can I do for you?"

"We want a house," Tripp said. "Down on the southern end of town. Somewhere down there. I mean, we're open, but we want to be closer to Seven Sons."

"All righty," Fletcher said, and Ivory picked up her phone and started circling the island in the kitchen. "And are we selling your house first? You need to wait to do that before we buy?"

"Nope," Tripp said. "We're going to keep this house. We just want another one down there."

Fletcher said nothing, and that was because Tripp had surprised him. The man always had something to say, so when he didn't, Tripp knew he'd gotten him good.

"Size?"

Tripp turned toward Ivory, but she hadn't made a call yet. He put the call on speaker. "Well, this place is a little too big." He cocked his eyebrows at Ivory, and she nodded. "We just have the two kids, Fletch. I need an office. Ivory needs a craft room. It would be nice to have a guest bedroom. That's four bedrooms and an office, or five bedrooms."

"I'm sure I can find you something you'd like," he said. "When do you want to move?"

"Whenever," Tripp said, and Ivory nodded again. Tripp couldn't believe they were doing this. He had the money; that wasn't the issue. But they didn't really need two homes in Three Rivers. Most people who had more than one house had one in a place they wanted to visit. A mountain home. A summer home on the beach.

But Ivory wanted to be closer, because she'd seen the relationships Momma had with Marcy and Mal, and she wanted that too.

"I've got four I can show you whenever you're ready," Fletcher said.

"Set it up for tomorrow," Tripp said. "What time should we meet you?"

"Let's do nine-thirty," he said. "That shouldn't be too early for anyone."

"Nine-thirty it is," Tripp said. "See you then." He ended the call and looked at Ivory. "Are you going to call them?"

She held out the phone. "I want you to do it."

Surprise moved through him. He'd never talked to her

mother or father on the phone. Even when she'd been in the hospital, fighting for her life, he hadn't made the call. Rhett had.

"All right," he said, stepping toward her and taking the phone. He'd looked at her phone several times, but it was different than his, and he still struggled with it at first. He found her mother's number and tapped to get the call going. His heart thumped in a strange way, because he wasn't sure how Joan and Will would take the offer.

The phone rang, and Tripp put it on speaker again so Ivory could hear.

"Sweetie," her mother said, and Ivory held up her hand as Tripp pulled in a breath.

"Hey, Mama," Ivory said, her voice a little higher than normal. She stretched up and kissed Tripp's cheek. "I just couldn't make the call."

Tripp searched her face, warmth filling him.

"Are you there?" Joan asked.

"Yes," Ivory said. "Listen, Mama, Tripp and I were just talking, and we can't move to Tennessee."

Tripp held his breath as a pregnant pause filled the house.

"I know," Joan finally said.

Ivory exhaled at the same time Tripp did, and they looked at each other. He found strength in her he'd seen several times before. Strength he'd fallen in love with. "Instead, we want you and Daddy to move here." She pressed her lips together but didn't say anything else.

"Move there?" The shock in Joan's voice came clearly through the line.

"Yes," Tripp said when Ivory stayed silent. "Joan, we've got this big house that we're going to move out of. We'd love for you guys to live in it, or rent it from us, or whatever. We're looking for something a little smaller." There. That wasn't a lie.

"Well, I don't know. We can't just sell the land here."

"You don't need to sell it, Mama," Ivory said, and Tripp realized this was a tag-team effort. "Keep it. Have someone live on it who can take care of it. But you don't have to sell it."

"You can live here without paying rent," Tripp said. "Whatever is fine with us." He threaded his fingers through Ivory's, praying that the Lord would take the reins in this situation. If Joan and Will should be in Three Rivers, God would guide them here.

"I'll need to talk to Daddy," Joan said. "And not today."

Ivory reached for her phone and took it off speaker. "Is he not having a good day?" Around the island she went, pacing as she listened to her mother. Tripp had seen this before, and he hated the anxiety her parents brought out in her. At the same time, he knew she needed this relationship to be healed, and he'd do what he could to help do that.

"Daddy," Isaac said behind him, and Tripp turned to find the little boy trying to get in the house.

"Just a sec, son," he said, moving over to open the door. "You done outside?"

"Drink," Isaac said, and Tripp scooped him into his arms.

"Milk? Or water?"

"Juice," Isaac said, which is what he said for every drink. Tripp opened the fridge and took out his sippy cup, which he was fairly certain had milk in it, not juice. Isaac drank it, and Tripp put him back down to go play again.

Ivory said, "Okay, 'bye," and Tripp looked at her. She hung up and sighed, keeping her head down.

"Well?" he prompted.

She looked up, and he remembered why he'd been so attracted to her that first time they'd met at the post office. "She's going to talk to my dad and see what he thinks."

"Is he…?"

She nodded. "Yes, he's drinking again."

Tripp's jaw clenched.

"I know you don't want him around the kids when he does," she said. "And I know that. I don't either. I just told my mother that, actually."

"Oh, wow," he said. "What did she say?"

"She said she'd talk to him." Ivory shrugged. "That's always what Mama says. Sometimes it works, and sometimes it doesn't." She stepped over to him, and he took her into his arms. "They're my parents, Tripp."

"I know that, baby." He swayed with her as she tucked herself against his chest.

"We won't be living with them. We can keep the kids away from him if he's drinking." She ran her hands up his back, and Tripp sure did like that. "And maybe, some of your momma's faith will rub off on him."

Tripp snorted and chuckled. "Oh, boy. If we unleash Momma on him…."

Ivory laughed too, and Tripp held her close until she finally stepped back and said, "Let's see if Evelyn needs any help with dinner tonight."

"All right," Tripp said. Ivory had gone to Evelyn's and Rhett's several times over the past five or six weeks since the triplets had been born. She loved holding the babies, and rocking them, and helping Evelyn with the feeding and care of them.

She'd never said so, but he knew she wanted another baby, and if going to Evelyn's to help with the triplets helped her, he wanted Ivory to have the opportunity. So, after Oliver got home from school, they pulled onto the road where Rhett and Evelyn's white house sat, pizza and salad in the back between Oliver and Isaac.

"Look, Tripp," Ivory said, pointing further down the road. "There's a for sale sign down there."

He detoured from pulling into the driveway and continued down the road. The house sat four down from Rhett's, and it was definitely smaller than the one Tripp and Ivory lived in now. He peered at it through the windshield, waiting for Ivory's assessment first.

"I wonder if this one is on Fletcher's list," she said.

"I told him five bedrooms," Tripp said. "Do you think it's big enough?"

"I think we should ask him if we can see it," she said.

"I'll text him," Tripp said, swinging the truck around to go back to Rhett's.

"Are we moving?" Oliver asked.

"Maybe," Ivory said, though that was a definite yes if Tripp had been answering.

"Will I be able to go to the same school?" Oliver asked.

"Yes," Tripp said, glancing at Ivory. "I'm sure you'll be able to go to the same school, Ollie." They needed to talk more about things before they started telling Oliver things that would upset him. He pulled into Rhett's driveway and added, "And we're not telling anyone about moving okay, Oliver? Not to Uncle Rhett or Aunt Evelyn. And especially not to Grandma."

"Good idea," Ivory said under her breath.

"Okay?" Tripp asked again.

"Okay," Oliver said. "Can I throw a ball for Penny?" He unbuckled his seatbelt but he'd wait for permission before he'd get out.

"Yeah, sure," Tripp said. "Get the big blue one from the back deck. She loves to bop that around to herself."

Tripp went inside with the food, Ivory, and Isaac, taking his son from her as Ivory made a beeline for the newborns. He juggled the pizza and his kid, finally getting them both on the kitchen counter.

When Ivory turned back to him, she held a baby in each arm, her face alight with a glow Tripp recognized. They'd both wanted more children, but Ivory simply couldn't have them. He wished he could give her the joy seeping across her face right now, because he loved her with his whole heart, and he wanted her to have everything she wanted.

But he couldn't give her another baby. So he helped Isaac

down and said, "Go find Conrad, buddy," and then he went and picked up one of the new babies too, holding the boy close to his heart as he gazed down at his sleeping form.

"They're great," he said quietly, and he sat next to Ivory, beyond grateful for his big family and the way they selflessly shared their newborns with him and Ivory.

CHAPTER EIGHTEEN

M icah pulled off the highway after only about five minutes, the road paved for the first mile or so. The trees got thicker along both sides of the road, and Micah sure did like Bear Glover's land. He'd been out to the ranch just once previously, but Bear had encountered a problem and had cancelled their meeting. Before that, Micah had tried to talk to him over the phone, but that hadn't worked either.

So finally, weeks and weeks later, they'd managed to get their schedules aligned. Micah couldn't believe how busy he'd been in the past couple of months, but between rehearsals, the two homes he was working on, helping with the triplets, and dealing with Simone's Gran's death, he got up early and collapsed into bed late.

Alone.

Still alone.

Simone had cried in his arms for a few nights, but in the kitchen, not his bedroom. In fact, he hated that he still thought of it as his.

He'd gone horseback riding with his brothers a couple of times, and thankfully, Skyler had only asked about Simone once. Micah hadn't known what to say, because how could he tell them he and Simone were legally married but living like roommates?

His unhappiness reared its ugly head, and he tamped it down quickly as he pulled up to the homestead. He eyed it, as it could definitely use some improvements, and he hadn't even gotten out of the truck yet.

Bear came out the front door, and Micah grabbed his clipboard and got out of the truck. "Bear," he said with a smile. He was great at covering up his real feelings with a smile and a handshake. But he was tired of pretending with Simone.

He just needed to talk to her again. With everything that had been going on, he hadn't wanted to add to her burdens. But as he'd done that, the ones he'd been carrying had gotten heavier.

"Good to see you, Micah." Bear shook his hand. "I wanted to get you out here so you could see what I'm dealing with."

"All right."

"Let's start inside," Bear said, going back up the steps to the front door. He had quite a large porch that ran from corner to corner along the front of the house, and Micah looked both ways, taking it in.

"Nice doors," he said, moving through the double-wide front door and into the homestead. And…he was instantly transported back in time at least forty years.

He pulled in a breath, and Bear said, "Yeah, that's why you needed to be here."

"It's a bit…dated," Micah said.

"It's old," Bear said, not mincing words. "And it hasn't been updated since my grandmother did it fifty-five years ago."

"So you want a renovation," Micah said, glancing up at the ceiling. He saw signs of water damage where the paint had bubbled and then dried.

"I don't know what I want."

"How big is it?"

"Five thousand square feet."

"Two stories," Micah said. "Six bedrooms. Four baths?"

"Just three."

Micah nodded. "Are you looking to do the whole thing or just say, the kitchen and family room?" He finally looked at Bear. No, he did not want to do a renovation, but he hadn't signed anyone else for a new home, and his two projects would be finished in another month or so.

He didn't need the work. He just wanted it.

He got plenty of inquiries. Simone hadn't done the Spring Fling because of everything happening in the family, and Micah honestly didn't know if she had the money she needed or not. Standing there in Bear's house, he cursed himself for expecting them to be able to slip into a married life role without talking any of it through.

Suddenly, he wanted to leave. Get to Simone as quickly as he could and initiate the crucial conversation they needed to have.

"Kitchen for sure," Bear said. "And maybe more. The house is so…closed."

"Yeah, do you actually use this room?" Micah asked. "It looks like a parlor, where someone would play the piano." It was just a large rectangle, with a doorway straight back from the front door dividing the room in half.

"I think my grandmother did have a piano in here," Bear said, stepping through the doorway, his broad shoulders almost touching both sides as the narrow, old doorway. Micah followed him, feeling like he'd entered a dungeon.

The hallway was dark, with doors on both sides, and it ended in the kitchen, which was completely separated from the rest of the house. Micah hated everything about this house. "What's between this and that room out there?" he asked.

"My office," Bear said. "A bathroom. The steps go up to the right there, and my bedroom is through this door."

"Your bedroom is off the kitchen?" Micah asked.

Bear gave him a look that Micah didn't quite understand. But he definitely wasn't pleased with the question. Marcy had told Micah that Bear was a great guy—if he was in a great mood. "He can be a grizzly or a teddy," Marcy had told him. "And you best be hoping you get the Teddy Bear when you need to talk to him about something serious."

Micah thought he'd gotten Bear halfway between the

grizzly and the teddy, and he opened the door and looked in Bear's bedroom. It definitely wasn't a master suite worth telling anyone about.

"Okay." Micah drew in a deep breath. "Honest truth?"

"Lay it on me."

"It would be easier to knock this place down and build you what you want." He pushed his cowboy hat forward. "Cheaper too."

Bear let out a noise halfway between a hiss and a sigh. "I figured you'd say that."

"Sorry," Micah said. "I don't think you want me. You can hire—"

"I do want you," Bear said, his voice a bit on the growly side. "I've seen the work you do. I was hopin', though I knew it was a long shot, that you might see the potential here that I don't. But it doesn't seem like it."

"It's just an awkward layout," Micah said. "And I didn't mean to say we should raze your grandparents' house. It probably has some significance to you."

"Not to me," Bear said. "I've learned over the years that I have to adapt to the trends or I'll die."

"Yeah, but just on the ranch," Micah said, not sure why he was arguing with Bear.

"No, in everything," he said. "Will you put together a quote for me showing cost?"

Surprise moved through Micah. "To replace what you have? I can quote you now."

"Let's hear it."

"I do the design myself," Micah said. "I'll work with you on it, of course, and once we have that, we build. I contract out anything I'm not an expert in—like the plumbing, electrical, HVAC, cement work, that kind of thing."

"How long?"

"On a ready piece of land, it's about six months," Micah said. "Do you want to leave this place and build next door? Maybe this could be—I don't know. A cowboy bunkhouse or something."

"Nah, I've got cabins for my boys," Bear said.

"Family?"

"My brother and my cousin live here with me," Bear said. "Couple more Glovers out in the cowboy cabins too."

"And they're all okay with potentially getting rid of this house?"

"I own the ranch."

And therefore, Bear made the decisions.

"Okay," Micah said. "I'll be real honest, Bear. I've never torn down a house before. I don't know how long it will take or what we'll find as far as a foundation."

"I've heard good things about your skills," Bear said. "The Rhinehart's sure are happy."

"I'm glad," Micah said. "Okay, so for what you want, I'm going to quote you one-point-five million." He expected Bear to scoff and demand he leave immediately.

Instead, he said, "I can do that."

"You can?" Micah didn't mean to sound so incredulous.

Bear chuckled and said, "I was expecting it to be twice that much. Those places up in Church Ranches are twice that much. Minimum."

"And they're not even custom," Micah said, not quite daring to believe he'd just been hired by Bear Glover. He grinned at Bear, who grinned back.

"Draw it up," Bear said. "Let's get it signed and going. I'm tired of turning sideways to get in the shower."

Micah laughed, shook Bear's hand, and promised he'd be in touch with the contract, probably tomorrow.

He got behind the wheel of his truck, still shocked that a meeting that was supposed to take place two months ago had resulted in a new contract.

"Thank you," he whispered as he put the truck in gear and backed up. The Lord had been watching out for Micah, and He knew when to send him a job right when he needed it.

"Now," Micah said. "Dear Lord, let's talk about Simone…."

WHEN HE PULLED INTO THE DRIVEWAY, SIMONE'S CAR SAT there. He'd had a good, long talk with the Lord, and he drew in a deep breath for strength. One step through the door, and he knew Simone had brought home dinner.

The scent of marinara rode on the air, as did the distinct tang of chocolate. "Baking?" he asked.

She looked up from the stove where she was stirring something, her smile taking longer to come than he liked. "I brought home a big pot of spaghetti someone brought for

Evelyn. She said she was tired of spaghetti, and she has a ton of food. But she didn't want to be rude and refuse it."

"I can smell chocolate." Micah set his clipboard on the table as he passed it and joined her in the kitchen. "Ah ha."

"They're just those no-bake cookies."

"I love those." He wound his arm around her waist and pressed a kiss to her forehead. She leaned into his touch, and Micah's heart wilted.

"I know you do." She smiled at him, and Micah felt like a dozen needles had been shoved into his chest.

"Simone," he said, stepping away. "I…I don't think this is working."

She stopped stirring but didn't look at him. "What isn't working?"

"This marriage," he said, his courage growing. He'd broken up with her before when she'd just let things stall between them. He could do it again. He could. "I'm in love with you, and you've been here for over two months. I don't want this." He swallowed and kept going. "We're room-mates, and that is not what I want. It's not working for me."

She finally lifted her eyes and looked at him. "It's not working for me either."

The air left his lungs as if she'd punched it out of them. "Okay," he said. "At least we're being honest now." He took off his cowboy hat and set it on the counter. "I know I haven't done the right things. We should've talked about money. We should've talked about a lot of things, like having a family and how you were feeling about your father getting married, and Gran passing. I should've asked you out still and taken you to dinner instead of just assuming you'd fall in love with me if you lived here."

Simone clicked off the burner, and Micah said, "I'm sorry." Micah had failed at a lot of things, but this one hurt the most. A deep, stabbing pain radiated through his stomach. "I—I don't know what else to say. I've shut down a woodworking shop in Temple, and I started a business here that hasn't taken off the way I'd hoped. I'm not perfect; I know that. I guess I just…I don't know. I guess I just thought we were so perfect for each other that I wouldn't have to work so hard to get you to fall in love with me."

When she still didn't say anything, he snatched his hat back up and crammed it on his head. "I'm goin' to get something to eat in town. I really am sorry."

He'd taken enough steps to pick up his clipboard when she said, "Micah?"

He stopped, because he loved that woman, and he couldn't walk out on her when she said his name with so much trepidation. But he didn't have to speak.

"I'm sorry too," she said, and that got Micah to turn around.

"Our lives have been crazy the past couple of months," she said. "I could've brought up all those things you said. I didn't." She pressed her hands to her cheeks and when she lowered them, she was grinning for all she was worth. "And you're wrong, Micah Walker. Completely wrong."

"About what?" he asked.

"Me not loving you."

The air left his lungs again, and he could only blink at her.

She giggled and said, "Don't look so surprised, cowboy."

"I don't—what?"

"You were right. I think I fell in love with you within a week of being here. I just didn't know how to say it. There was Gran, and Evelyn, and I don't know. I let myself get swept up with helping her, and I love those babies so much."

Micah took a step toward her, just now comprehending that she'd said she'd fallen in love with him. She came around the island slowly, and then she ran toward him. "Don't go," she said as he caught her around the waist. "I love you, Micah Walker, and I don't want you to go."

Micah had no words left to say, and he wasn't going anywhere. He leaned down and kissed her, maybe a little more roughly than he normally would have. She kissed him back, just as eagerly.

"Maybe," he started, but he didn't know how to finish. He just kissed Simone again, warming from head to toe. He hadn't even fantasized that this conversation would go this way, and Micah maybe needed to stop trying to predict how his life with Simone would be.

He pulled back slightly, both of them breathing hard. "Okay," he said. "So let me just get this all lined up. I love you, and you love me."

"That's right." She smiled at him.

"And we're married."

Simone's smile drifted down, and Micah cupped her face

in his hands. "Maybe you'd like to work on getting some babies of your own."

She nodded, and Micah kissed her again, the feeling of being loved by this woman better than any fantasy he'd ever had.

CHAPTER NINETEEN

Simone woke up when Micah snapped on the light in the master bathroom. She took a moment as warmth and happiness filled her. She kept her eyes closed, and she must've dozed again, because the next thing she knew, Micah placed a kiss on her forehead and said, "Baby? We have to get going."

She moaned and drew in a deep breath of his aftershave. So she'd slept through his shower and everything. "I'm tired," she said. "You keep me up too late."

He chuckled, his hands warm on her arms. "That was Susan, sweetheart."

They'd been staying late at the theater as the date approached for their performances. Since she and Micah drove together, if Simone had to stay, Micah did too. He'd been bringing his portfolio of floor plans and sitting in the back, pouring over them while she tried to hit the right notes and get the lines right.

"Simone," he said again, and she snapped her eyes open. She reached for him, pulling him in for a kiss, which he willingly gave her. She still couldn't believe he'd been about to walk out of his own house a couple of weeks ago.

She'd almost said nothing, because talking was hard. But she loved him, and she didn't want to lose him, and his bravery to bring up the subject had inspired the courage she'd needed to confess her feelings for him. She wasn't sure why she'd caged them, and now that they were out, Simone had never been happier.

"I thought you wanted to leave by seven," he whispered against her lips. They were going to the Hill Country that day for Simone's annual loot-finding trip. He said he wasn't a big camper, and they had plenty of money for hotels. She'd finished packing everything except her toiletries last night, and she did want to get on the road by seven.

"Seven-thirty is fine," she said, tilting her head back so Micah would kiss her neck. He did, and Simone didn't care what time they left.

Micah chuckled as she slid over and made room for him in the bed, and he didn't question her further about what time they needed to leave. Simone had not doubted his love for her before they'd moved into the same bedroom, but there was a special level of adoration when he made love to her that she cherished.

An hour later, Simone tucked her deodorant and shampoo in her bag and zipped it closed. She wheeled it out into the kitchen, where Micah sat at the bar. "There's coffee," he said, getting up and looking at her. "I'll put that in the truck."

"See?" She reached for a travel mug to take her coffee with her. "We'll only be half an hour late. And we're not really late."

Micah swept one arm around her and kissed her. "You explained it to me already," he said, purring in her ear. "I'm happy with whatever, Simone." He took her bag and headed out to the truck while Simone doctored up her coffee with cream and sugar. She set a couple of pieces of bread in the toaster too, and grabbed a protein shake from the fridge. Once her toast was peanut buttered, she joined Micah in the delivery truck.

"Ready?" he asked.

"So ready."

Micah backed onto the dirt lane that ran in front of Seven Sons Ranch, and as she finished her first piece of toast, he pulled onto the highway, headed south. The radio played into the silence between them, and Simone took a deep breath, finally feeling…normal.

Life had been so hectic for so many days and weeks in a row that Simone had barely spent any time in her she-shed. And while she'd felt quite a bit of guilt about that, she now knew she didn't have to repurpose furniture at all. She and Micah had laid awake in bed one night, talking about money until well into the early morning hours.

He had a lot of it, and he didn't care if she spent it. He wanted her to be happy, and he said he'd build her a deluxe she-shed right in the backyard if she wanted him to. And she did want him to, and he'd started to design the building to go in the space they had.

Micah had about ten acres of land that extended down to the border of Seven Sons and went all the way to the highway. But it was narrow, with only about three hundred yards from the back door to the highway. He planned to fence a yard for grass, and they'd talked about adopting a dog or two.

He could put in a pasture or a corral, but he liked the land wild, and Simone saw no reason to keep horses or goats when both of their families literally owned sprawling ranches across the street.

So Simone had spent more time with her sister, helping with the triplets. And she'd gone to lunch with Micah's mother, as well as Belinda, getting to know both of them better. She'd skipped the Spring Fling completely, as she didn't have enough inventory for it, and Gran's death had put a kink in her productivity.

Micah never asked what she did with her day. He got up every morning and went across the street to Seven Sons, working there for a few hours with Skyler and Jeremiah. He owned ten percent of the ranch still, and he liked taking care of the goats and chickens. He loved horseback riding, and doing whatever else Jeremiah needed at key times around the ranch.

Then he'd work on his floor plans, his business website, take phone calls from clients or potential clients, and pick up around the house. Simone had learned that Micah was quite the neat freak, and she sure did like that. She knew only Jeremiah and Wyatt called him Mike, and that everyone else used Micah. And if he wasn't home in the afternoon, she knew she'd find him somewhere on the back of a horse.

They'd been driving for a couple of hours before her phone rang, and she picked it up from where it rested on the seat next to her. "It's Daddy."

Micah used the controls on the steering wheel to turn down the volume on the radio, and Simone braced herself. She hated that she had this anxiety inside her whenever the phone rang and one of her family members' names sat on the screen.

"Hey, Daddy," she said, infusing some false cheer into her voice.

"Sugar-bear," he said. "I have some great news."

"Great news?" Simone repeated, looking at Micah. He drove with both hands on the wheel, as if the delivery truck was hard to handle.

"Yeah," Daddy drawled. "Belinda and I have decided to get married at the end of the month."

"This month?" Simone asked.

"Yes," Daddy said. "About two weeks from now. Belinda's son will be home from North Carolina for a weekend, and then he'll be gone for nine months. So it's in two weeks or… who knows when."

"Two weeks sounds better than who knows when," Simone said.

"That's what we thought." Daddy chuckled, and Simone hadn't realized how unhappy he was until she'd seen him come alive these past few months. Now that he was happy, she recognized the unhappiness from before. She wondered if people could see the same in her. The way she'd been miserable for much of last year as Micah pursued a relationship with Ophelia, and she got passed over by men who couldn't remember her from a dance.

"I know it's short notice," Daddy said. "But we're wondering if you have anything in your workshop that would work as an altar. We're just going to get married in the backyard, and it would be a nice piece to have. Evelyn is going to do all the flowers, and Callie is going to take part of Momma's dress and make something for Belinda."

"Oh, wow," Simone said, realizing she'd gotten married in a pair of jeans. A sense of longing filled her, and she knew she wanted more than the "wedding" she'd gotten. "Yeah, sure, I'll look through my shed when I get back. Micah and I are headed to the Hill Country right now and we'll be gone a week. Maybe I'll find the perfect piece for you down there."

"Will you have time to get it ready?"

"Yes," Simone said, determined. "Whatever it takes, Daddy. I'll have something for you."

She caught Micah looking at her, but Simone kept her gaze out the windshield while her father gave her the exact date. "I'll put it in my calendar right now," she told him. "I'm so happy for you, Daddy."

"I love you, girly," he said, and Simone smiled as the call ended. "Well, they're getting married on June eleventh.

Belinda's son has a weekend away from the Army, and he'll be here."

"That's great," Micah said, clearly not understanding the time it took to get a dress, and the perfect shoes, the wedding cake, the flowers, the food, the venue…. Simone was overwhelmed with the very idea of planning a wedding, but the pricking in her chest made her clear her throat.

"Micah?"

"Hmm?"

"I want a big, fancy wedding where I get to wear part of my momma's dress and everyone we know and love is there to see us getting married."

He looked at her then, pure surprise in his eyes. "You do?"

"You're going to drive us off the road."

He jerked his attention back to the road, but he wasn't anywhere near going off the road. "I…I mean, I—we're already married."

"Yeah, but maybe we could still do a ceremony or something. I mean, Skyler can officiate, right? He married Liam and Callie."

"So it would be a show." He glanced at her again. "Unless you want…what are you saying? You want to get divorced and re-married?"

"No," she said. "Not anything that drastic. But Tripp and Ivory had a family ceremony after they'd been married for a year. Maybe we can do something like that." An idea popped into her head. "Maybe a Christmas ceremony. That's when we announced to everyone we were back together."

Micah let a few seconds pass. He opened his mouth, and then closed it. Several seconds passed, and Simone had no idea the topic of a wedding would render the cowboy mute.

"So you want to have a Christmas wedding ceremony for friends and family, where we...renew our vows?"

"I don't even think we said vows," she said. "You have to admit, our marriage was unconventional." Simone wished her lungs didn't sting quite so much. "It was barely a wedding. I want more than that."

He looked at her again, this time with acceptance in his gaze. "All right, sweetheart. You want more than that, you got it."

A smile burst onto her face. "Really?"

"Yeah, of course." He shifted in his seat. "We didn't have a wedding. There were no vows. Just a great kiss." He grinned at her, and Simone shook her head, though it had been a great kiss. "I'd like to know I'm getting married, I can admit that."

"All right, then," she said. "I'll start planning it."

"It's going to take six months to plan a wedding?"

"Yep," Simone said, her ideas already flowing through her mind.

"Oh, boy," Micah muttered, but he reached for her hand, and Simone squeezed it.

"I love you," she said, and that got him to smile and squeeze her hand back.

CHAPTER TWENTY

M icah ran his fingertips along the top of a table that had definitely seen better days. "What about that?" he asked, nodding toward a piece of furniture that looked like it needed the wall to stay standing. He'd been wandering swap meets, garage sales, and antique shows with Simone for five days. It wasn't hard work, and Micah enjoyed spending time with her away from all the regular pressures of everyday life.

If he were being honest with himself, he really liked spending time with her when they both weren't pulled in a dozen different directions by family members. Having a break from the ranch was nice too, and Micah had only taken two client calls since he'd been gone.

Maybe he just needed a vacation in general.

Simone wandered over to the counter-height table or island or cabinet and looked at it. Micah didn't know the technical name of it. Simone would, and she could see the inner soul of something that he could not. He'd tried to be helpful, but after only the first day, he realized that Simone didn't know what she was looking for.

She knew it when she saw it. She turned and gave him a soft smile that made Micah's heart thump a little harder. He stepped around a rocking chair that had definitely seen its last rock, and said, "What?"

"I think you're getting the hang of it," she said. "This is a nice credenza."

"I don't even know what a credenza is," he said, looking at the furniture. Someone had tried to paint it blue in the past, but most of that was chipped off. It rose to his waist and had doors on the front that the glass had been broken out of.

"It's a cabinet to hold dishes," she said. "You can serve food from it, just like a buffet." She looked up at him. "You have one in the house."

"Our house? Where we live right now?"

She giggled and nudged him with her hip. "Yes, silly. It's the wood cabinet on the wall behind the table. I put that picture of you and your brothers on the horses there."

"Oh," Micah said, knowing exactly what she was talking about. "I just didn't know the name of it."

"Well, this one is going to become an altar," she said, bending down to look through the holes where the glass should be. "I'll knock all these fragments out, sand it down, refinish it, and we can put flowers, trinkets, and pictures in here." She opened one of the doors, smiling. "Yep, great movement here. The hinges are all fine."

She straightened and looked around. "Now, we just need to find out how much it is...."

Micah stayed out of the way when Simone went into business mode, mostly because he sure liked watching her work. She waved over a man and asked how much the piece was. When he said a hundred dollars, she frowned.

"Fifty," she said. "There's at least four coats of paint on it."

"Fifty's fine," the man said, and Simone unzipped her hip pack and took out the appropriate number of bills with a wide smile on that mouth he liked to kiss so much. He knew that was his cue to put his muscles to work, and he waited while the man moved the lamp and what looked like some sort of modern art from the top of the credenza.

"I'm going to go down to that booth with all the fruit," Simone said.

"Okay," he said, testing the weight of the credenza. "I'll get this in the truck and come find you." He grinned at her and followed the man out of the tented booth without knocking anything over. Thankfully. Just a couple of days ago, he'd paid for a mirror he'd broken trying to get a dresser out of a booth, and while he had plenty of money, he didn't need to be paying for broken glass.

The Hill Country heat almost suffocated him as he labored with the credenza to the delivery truck, which they always parked quite a ways out in the lot. Simone knew how much she could fit into the truck, and the credenza slid right in front of the dresser. She'd also bought a couple of armchairs from the fifties, as well as four chairs she thought would go well with the barrel table she still hadn't built.

"But I'm going to," she'd said. "It's going to be a great piece. I just need to get back to a schedule."

Micah had been working on the specs for her she-shed in their backyard while he waited for her at practice, but he hadn't shown them to her yet. He wanted it to be a perfect space for her to create, and he'd spent plenty of time in the she-shed she now had. She'd converted an old barn into a work space, and while it suited her needs, he wanted more for her.

And he had the skills and money to give it to her. So why shouldn't she have it?

The shed he wanted to build for her wouldn't be able to bear the label *shed*. It would have heating and air conditioning. Finished floors, with plenty of electricity for the kiln she used. He was planning on built-in shelves for her pottery, and he'd consulted with Whitney about reserving a corner of the workshop simply for photos.

"Plenty of light," Whitney had said, and Micah had put in windows on both walls, only leaving a narrow strip of wood for the corner of the building. She worked with unfinished walls now, but he was planning to paint the she-shed, and put in a bathroom. She wouldn't have to come into the house for anything, as he was planning to put a mini fridge and microwave in her building too.

He hadn't shown her the plans yet, because he knew she'd object. The only thing he cared about was that she came in when it was time for bed. There was nothing Micah liked more than lying next to Simone in the dark. He loved reaching out and finding her right beside him. He liked listening to her breathe after she'd fallen asleep, and he liked seeing her in their bed when he came out of the bathroom after showering.

Simone wasn't a real early bird, though she'd told him she got up by six and was in the she-shed by six-thirty during the hotter months. But with her new workshop, she wouldn't have to follow the dictates of the weather as she set her schedule.

Of course, he wouldn't have it built for a few months anyway.

He locked the truck and headed back into the swap meet, stopping to buy a huge Texas boot of sweet tea before he started toward the fruit stall they'd seen earlier. One thing he'd learned about Simone on this trip was how much she liked a farmer's market. Not only that, but she had excellent people skills and could literally talk to anyone, about anything.

At least strangers. Micah had noticed that she struggled to talk with him about things near and dear to her heart, though she'd been getting better. She wasn't afraid to tell him what her schedule was for the day, or what she wanted for dinner. They got along great. It was the deeper stuff, the things that revealed what she thought and felt, that she had a hard time articulating.

After their daytime activities, he'd found her sitting on the bed in the hotel, a notebook in front of her. When he'd asked her what she was doing, she'd looked up and said, "Planning the wedding."

A twinge of regret accompanied Micah every time he thought about her planning their wedding. At the same time, it wasn't like he'd planned to get married during an audition, and all he could do was praise the Lord that she hadn't auditioned with someone else and had that paperwork sent in.

Simone wasn't in the fruit booth, but Micah went in anyway. A woman wearing a microphone stood at the back of the booth, behind a table, and she held up an apple. "This is a Pink Lady from our orchards in Medina. It's tart and sweet at the same time, and it's got a crisp bite that makes it great for snacking. At Loveland's Orchards, about a quarter of our crop each year come from our Pink Lady trees."

She put the apple down and demonstrated how to cut out the core, and then she chunked it up and started passing it around the crowd that had gathered. "This is a Gala," she said, naming one of Micah's favorite apples. "Half of our crop is Galas, and they're mild, sweet apples with a thin skin. They're great for kids, applesauce, and you don't need to worry about the yellow on the skin. Their skin is sometimes marbled, unlike some other varieties of apples where you see a solid-colored skin."

Micah wasn't sure why he was so enthralled with the apple talk. There was an apple orchard and nursery in Three Rivers that he'd visited with Ophelia. They did cider tastings and demonstrations, and they had "the cutest red barn" Ophelia had ever seen. In fact, Micah had a picture of him and Ophelia in front of the red barn. Somewhere.

Probably not anymore, he told himself. When she'd broken up with him, Micah had tried to purge everything about her from his life. It had taken longer than he'd thought it would, because they'd been dating for almost nine months, and that was a lot of intertwining that had to be unraveled.

He swiped open his phone and started looking through the pictures in his gallery. A smile touched his mouth as he saw the selfie he and Simone had taken yesterday as they'd visited the Lyndon Johnson Farm. The plane he'd fly on when he came to his Texas White House was on display, and they'd snapped a picture of themselves.

Micah loved how happy he looked as he grinned at the camera. Simone wore sunglasses, but her joy seemed to melt right into the camera's lens. Surely she was happy with him now. They weren't hiding from anyone—or each other.

And to think, Micah had thought they were going to break up only a couple of weeks ago. He'd been ready to walk out. He hadn't known what the next day would bring once he did, but he'd been willing to do it.

All he could do now was hope and pray he'd never have to make that decision again.

"OKAY," MICAH SAID A COUPLE OF DAYS LATER. THE DELIVERY truck drove differently now that it was full, and he eased up on the gas pedal and moved his foot to the brake. "This is it."

Simone peered through the windshield as he turned off the winding Hill Country road and onto a dirt lane. As did most ranches here, his grandparents' place had a gate. Brown and red bricks flanked both sides of the lane, with a black iron gate in between that, though it was open. A white W sat on the left side, and Micah freely remembered the last time he'd been here.

"I haven't been here in ages," he told Simone as they passed through the gate. "Grandma Lucy threw a big party when I graduated from high school, mostly for Momma." He chuckled as the memories ran through his mind. "I didn't want to come, because it was a long drive, and I had friends I wanted to spend time with."

"How far is it from Austin?" she asked.

"Oh, only like forty minutes," he said, laughing again. "Not long at all. But you know how everything is a lifetime when you're eighteen? It was like that. My grandmother is an excellent cook—she taught Jeremiah everything he knows—and she'd called me and asked what I wanted."

"And what was that?" Simone asked. She loved his childhood stories, and Micah had plenty, that was for sure. Growing up with six brothers gave him plenty of fodder when it came to stupid things the boys had gotten into.

"She makes this sausage and pepperoni Stromboli." Micah's mouth watered just thinking about it. "And a brownie ice cream cake." He smacked his lips. "I had a great time. Momma and Daddy were there, and Skyler. The other brothers were older, and off at college. Wyatt was already riding the rodeo circuit. So it was just the four of us. But

Grandpa has about a hundred dogs, so there was plenty of voices for the singing."

"What did you sing?"

"Grandma Lucy makes up words to whatever song she wants," Micah said as the road turned. "And the house is coming up right here." Sure enough, the ranch house came into view, and Micah's nostalgia peaked. "She really threw the party for Momma, who'd managed to get all seven sons graduated from high school, and Grandma Lucy said that took some superpowers."

"I know all of you Walkers," Simone said. "And I agree with your grandmother." She smiled at Micah, and he reached over and took her hand, lifting it to his lips to kiss her wrist.

"You're okay to visit for a bit?"

"Yeah," she said. "Our hotel is only an hour away."

Micah nodded, thinking maybe Grandma Lucy would trigger some memories for Simone of her own grand-mother, but he didn't say anything. "Oh, wow, look at that." He pulled up to the house, looking at the huge Dumpster that had been parked on the front lawn. He got out and looked inside, but the huge container was mostly empty.

Momma and Daddy wouldn't be happy about that.

"Hey-o!" someone called, and Micah turned toward the house to see his uncle coming down the steps. He raised his hand with a huge smile on his face. Simone met him at the front of the truck, and he cemented his hand in hers. "Uncle Jonas," he said, stepping into the bear of a man. He looked a lot like Daddy, though he was about five years older than

Micah's father. He laughed and clapped the older man on the back.

"It's been so long," Uncle Jonas said. "But you look just like yer daddy, so I knew it was yous."

Micah smiled at the plural of you he always used. "Simone," he said. "This is my daddy's brother. Jonas Walker."

"Nice to meet you, sir." Simone gave him her most charming smile, and Micah basked in the light it called down from heaven.

"My wife," Micah said. "Simone."

"Your mother mentioned you'd gotten married," Uncle Jonas said, leaning toward Simone and kissing both cheeks. "Nice to meet you. She sure is pretty, ain't she?"

"She sure is," Micah said, beaming at Simone. Her smile hitched, but it didn't slip off her face. He'd give her credit for that.

"Y'all come in," he said. "Momma has everything bubblin' away on the stove, and Daddy's got the dogs all lined up."

"How many dogs?" Simone asked, glancing at Micah.

"Six in the house," Uncle Jonas said. "It's pretty ridiculous, but when Momma told him he had to put them outside or train them, he started training them."

Simone and Micah followed his uncle up the steps and into the house. Micah expected to get a nose full of the same smell he'd always experienced when he came to visit his grandparents. It was somewhere between moth balls and old ice, and he could never figure out where it came from.

Today, though, roasted meat scented the air, and Micah took a deep breath of it, his stomach grumbling for food.

"They're here," Uncle Jonas called, and only a single dog barked.

He took them past the foyer and the stairs that led up to the back of the house, where the space opened up to a living room, dining room, and kitchen.

"Oh, my," Grandma Lucy said, already crying when Micah came around the corner. She seized onto him, and he had to bend down to hug her properly.

"Hey, Grandma," he said, smiling at how strong she was for how small.

"I've missed all my boys," she said. She released Micah and looked at Simone. "All those boys lived with us for a year, you know."

"I've heard," Simone said, smiling at her. "I'm Simone Fos—Walker." She glanced at Micah. "Micah's wife."

He sure did like hearing her say that, despite the stumble over her last name.

"I know just who you are," Grandma Lucy said. "Penny showed me a picture when she came a few weeks ago."

Micah looked around the house, but it sure didn't look like it had been cleaned out none. "How's the purge going?" he asked.

"Purge?"

Micah turned at the sound of his grandfather's voice, a smile lighting his whole soul.

"Grandpa." He laughed as he embraced the man, feeling the love and strength in his grandfather's grip. Grandpa

Jerry laughed too, his voice old and throaty. A dog barked again, and Micah stepped back when Grandpa did.

"Stay," he commanded, and Micah looked behind him to see a half-dozen dogs doing exactly what he said. "Look at 'em, sugar. They're doin' so good."

"Yes," Grandma said without looking. She went back into the kitchen and put some bowls on the counter. Micah exchanged a glance with Simone, wondering if they could grow old together the way his grandparents had.

They reached for each other at the same time, and Micah sure hoped so.

CHAPTER TWENTY-ONE

Whitney parked in front of her mother's house and said, "All right, JJ. Get your belt off." The little boy had to be buckled several times every time they got in the car, so he could definitely get out of his own car seat. In fact, he was like a Houdini when it came to breaking restraints.

Whitney liked to tell Jeremiah that their son was free-spirited and stubborn, just like him, but he usually tossed those characteristics back to her. She could admit she was a free-spirit and stubborn, and those qualities had served her well throughout her life. She didn't appreciate them as much in her own son, especially when he threw a temper tantrum in the middle of the grocery store that her family owned.

That wasn't cute, and Whitney hadn't been able to cure the almost-two-year-old of the habit. JJ was loud and opinionated, and he hadn't even turned two yet. She got out and opened the back door, letting the boy get down by himself before she leaned into the car and unstrapped Clara Jean.

She heard her mother talking to JJ as she straightened, and her heart warmed as she watched her mother crouch down right in front of the boy and look at something he wanted to show her. Pure joy lived on her mother's face, and a shock of guilt hit Whitney in the face like icy water.

Sometimes, she was just so tired. She couldn't deal with JJ's tantrums, and Jeremiah worked long hours on the ranch, no matter the season. "Hey, Mom," she said as she approached. Fondness filled her for her son, and she ran her fingertips along the top of his head.

She passed Clara to her mother, who cooed at the baby. The front door opened behind them, and Dalton came out of the house. "Babysitting Dalton too?" she asked.

"Funny, Aunt Whitney," Dalton said, rolling his eyes.

She grabbed onto him and laughed as she hugged him. "Ready for graduation next week?"

"He's been ready for months," Whitney's mother said, watching them.

"I'm sure he has," Whitney said. "Senior year is the worst."

"He only goes part-time."

And Whitney wasn't sure why her mom cared. "But he's graduating, and with a good GPA too." She'd always felt like Dalton's protector. "You still like it out at Three Rivers Ranch?" she asked, turning her full attention to her nephew.

"Yeah," he said with a smile. "I'm working there full-time as soon as I get back from my senior trip."

"Good for you, Dalt," Whitney said. "You know, you can come work at Seven Sons too. Jeremiah is always looking for good guys."

"Yeah, I know," Dalton said. "But I've been at Three Rivers for a couple of years now, and I like it there."

"Whitney's place is closer," her mom said.

"I get to work with the horses at Three Rivers," Dalton said. "I moved from Bowman's over to the therapy unit. Pete's been teaching me how to train the therapy horses."

Whitney's heart warmed again, and she slung her arm around Dalton's shoulders. "I'm so glad you like it."

Dalton smiled at her. "Me too."

"So are you staying here for a bit?" Whitney asked, glancing at her mom. "Maybe you can take JJ for a bike ride."

"Yeah," Dalton said. "I'm gonna be here for a couple of hours. Grandma hired me to do her yard."

"Oh, that's great," Whitney said, smiling from her mom to her nephew. Neither of them seemed to be too happy about it though. "Well." She took a deep breath. "I'm going to be late. Thanks, Mom." She kissed her mom's cheek, as well as Clara Jean's, and she got behind the wheel again.

Thankfully, her children were used to people coming and going, different people holding them at church, at home, everywhere, and they didn't cry when she left.

Penny had instituted a monthly Wives Luncheon, and Whitney needed the break. She needed the female connection with her sisters-in-law, and she craved the adult conversation that wasn't about crops, the timing of studding season, and pests in the corn. She loved her husband deeply, and Jeremiah was definitely everything she wanted in a man.

Tall, tough, rugged, but sweet, helpful, and vulnerable too. He loved her shamelessly, and Whitney loved how much he adored her. He helped with the children when he was home, and she hadn't made a meal—or a pot of coffee—for herself in years.

Sure, she missed pieces of herself, but the tradeoff was more than worth it.

She arrived at the restaurant several minutes later, seeing Penny going inside with Marcy as she searched for a parking spot. Whitney tried not to let the jealousy flood her, but it rose anyway. In a family as large as the Walkers, it was hard to stand out. Whitney didn't want to stand out. But she didn't want to be isolated either, which was very easy to do when everyone around her had such a busy life and all she did was stay home with her kids.

She hated the feelings of inadequacy. All she'd ever wanted to do was be a mother, and now that she was one, it wasn't good enough? She and Jeremiah were already trying for their third child, and Clara Jean was only nine months old. He wanted a lot of kids, and so did she. She loved taking the kids in the wagon out to the ranch to see their daddy for a quick lunch, and she loved taking care of them.

"You're just tired," she muttered to herself as she found a spot in the back of the parking lot. She didn't worry about getting a table here, as Mal worked at the bakery in town and had gotten them a table an hour ago after her shift ended.

Whitney took a moment in the car to say a prayer. "Help me to have fun," she said. "Help me to appreciate these women for who they already are, and bless them that they can accept me how I am too." She closed her eyes and pictured her beautiful children. "Thank you for Jeremiah, JJ, and Clara Jean. I don't mean to act like I don't love them or don't want them."

Like someone putting a warm blanket around her shoulders, Whitney felt wrapped in a hug from On High. Satisfied that she wasn't being ungrateful, she grabbed her phone and got out of the car. She never carried a purse anymore, because it was one more thing to keep track of when she was constantly monitoring sippy cups, diapers, shoes, and a myriad of other things.

Jeremiah had bought her a phone case that held a couple of cards and a few bills, and that was all Whitney needed when she left the house.

She entered the restaurant where the women had met twice now alone, glancing around. Her heart flipped and flopped, and she hated that she was nervous for the lunch. She wasn't nervous when Jeremiah's family came to the ranch, and she wanted to be there.

"Oh, good, I'm not the only one not at the table."

Whitney turned at the sound of Ivory's voice as she came in behind Whitney. "Hey, Ivory." She hugged the woman. "How's the packing going?"

"I had no idea we'd amassed so much stuff," she said. "I

mean, honestly. There's four of us in that house, and it's full."

"And your new place is smaller," Whitney said.

"Half the size," Ivory said with a smile. "I'm excited to move though. That place is too big for me and Tripp." She pointed to the left. "There they are. Mal's waving." Ivory stepped in front of Whitney, seemingly supremely confident as she strode through the restaurant to a huge, circular booth in the back corner.

"Hello, dears," Penny said, standing at the end of the booth seat and hugging everyone who arrived. Whitney glanced around, and she wasn't last. She slid into the booth beside Ivory and kept going to leave room for Callie, who hadn't arrived yet.

Penny sat down on the other end and beamed around at everyone.

"Callie's parking," Evelyn said. Beside her, Simone held one of the triplets, but Whitney wasn't sure which one. One of the boys, who she knew had been having some problems keeping his milk down.

Callie arrived a moment later, and Penny hugged her. They both sat, and Penny said, "Thank you girls for clearing your schedules and getting babysitters so we can be here."

Whitney once again felt like she was the only one who actually had to get a babysitter. Tripp and Liam worked from home and set their own schedules. A lunch once a month wasn't hard for them to take over the care of their children.

Skyler and Micah still worked on the ranch, but Micah

only did morning chores, and Mal's baby was still inside her. Wyatt didn't work if he didn't want to. Rhett took cases for the state if he wanted to, but Whitney knew he hadn't had one since attending court only a few days after his triplets had been born.

It was only Jeremiah who worked fifty or sixty hours each week, and Whitney wondered why. The man loved ranching, and that was a huge part of it. She couldn't imagine a Jeremiah without a task to be completed. He'd probably go mad. *Or find a way to bake brownies every day*, she thought, smiling to herself.

People started picking up menus, and Whitney did the same as conversations broke out. Mal and Marcy had become close, which made sense because their husbands were so close. Simone sat over there with them, as the three younger sons had a little clique the others weren't involved in.

Whitney had spent more time with Rhett and Evelyn in the beginning of her marriage with Jeremiah, but at the moment, Evelyn was completely overwhelmed with her kids, and Whitney could relate to that. She only had two, but they were close together and quite the handful for her.

The twins obviously had a special relationship that had carried into adulthood, and Whitney felt left out of that pairing too.

"Sometimes I feel so left out in the family," Ivory said, and Whitney whipped her attention away from the menu. She met Ivory's eyes, sure the woman had just read her mind.

She even asked, "Can you read minds?"

Ivory looked surprised too. "You too?"

"So much." Whitney suddenly felt a bond form between her and Ivory. "Is that why you're moving to the house on Quail Creek?"

"We just wanted to move closer," Ivory said. "We're really far away, and the house is too big. That house just happened to have everything we wanted."

"I'm right in the middle of it all," Whitney said. "And I still feel like an island." She had siblings too, and she talked to them. She saw them at the store from time to time. She just hadn't realized how busy she'd be with the kids, with keeping up the homestead, and with being a wife. Someone should've warned her how much time all of that took.

"So do I," Callie said. "I swear, I can't wait for this project of Liam's to be over."

Whitney almost got whiplash she twisted toward Callie so fast. "You?" She looked across the table to Evelyn and Simone. "You have sisters nearby."

"I think we all feel that way," Callie said. "It's the day-to-day details. Getting breakfast on the table. Cleaning breakfast up. Putting the kids in the tub. Cleaning up the water all over the bathroom floor. Thinking about dinner. Getting something out of the freezer. What chores need to be done? What do the kids need? Food? Clothes? A fun activity that day? Can I just take a bath?" She gave a light giggle and shook her head.

"Women have too many tasks," Whitney said. "I think

Jeremiah thinks about one thing at a time, and he never thinks about anyone's schedule but his."

"That's just how men are," Evelyn said, and Whitney hadn't even known she was listening. "I'm the one who schedules the doctor's appointments. Rhett doesn't even know the babies need them."

The talk went on for another couple of minutes, and Penny said, "Oh, our cowboys. We love 'em, but yeah, they can be a challenge sometimes."

And that about summed up Whitney's whole life. She smiled at Penny, her gaze switching to Marcy. And she knew that she belonged with these women, and they belonged to her.

The waitress arrived and took their orders, and when she left, Whitney leaned over to Callie and said, "I know your kids are a little older than mine, but we live a half-mile apart. Let's get together."

"Our sons are the same age," Ivory said. "I'd love to come over to the ranch during the day while Oliver's at school."

"Yes," Whitney said, smiling at her. "Please do. Let's set up a playgroup or something."

"I want Conrad to come," Evelyn said. "And I'm willing to host sometimes too."

Whitney watched as Marcy said she wanted to get Warren out of the house more, and though Mal and Simone didn't have children, they seemed interested in the conversation.

"Okay, so how about this?" Whitney asked. "I'll make a monthly schedule, and we can all sign up for days that work for us to host at our houses. And then whoever can come, can come?" She looked at the others. "And if you're in charge, you have activities and lunch at your house. It would be a couple of hours. Ten to noon or something, so then we can put the kids down for naps in the afternoon."

"Then I can put myself down for a nap in the afternoon," Marcy said, and everyone laughed.

"You girls are so good," Penny said, sniffling. "I just love you so much."

"I love y'all too," Mal said, smiling at them, and more of the same sentiments were echoed around the table.

Whitney said, "I love all of you. I'm so glad we're doing this. These cousins should know each other and have a safe place to come, no matter what."

"And that's family," Penny said. "Friends may come and go, but family stays forever."

"Amen," Callie said as their food arrived. Several others echoed her, and Whitney felt happier than she had in a while, especially when a plate of French fries and caramelized onion sliders was put in front of her.

CHAPTER TWENTY-TWO

Simone set the bowl of fresh guacamole on the credenza as Micah came out of the bedroom. "Look," she said. "You can put food here."

His dark eyes glinted at her as he came closer, and he finally chuckled. "I see that." He picked up a chip and swiped up some dip. "Do I really have to go?"

"Yes," she said. "You're not a girl, and it's girls' night." She gave him a smile and went back into the kitchen to stir the hot artichoke dip she'd just taken out of the oven. She hated heating up the house in the summer, but Micah's house had excellent air conditioning, unlike her cabin which seemed to leak air through the thin walls.

And it's not Micah's house, Simone told herself. *It's your house too.*

"Okay," he said. "But do we have a couple of minutes to look at the design for your workshop?"

Simone put down the spoon immediately, looking up at him as her pulse began to pound through her whole body. "You're going to finally show it to me?" She'd been begging him to see the plans since he'd mentioned them on the drive home from their Hill Country shopping trip.

"I think it's ready." Micah seemed nervous as he opened the bottom drawer in the island.

"It's been in there the whole time?" She never opened that drawer. She didn't even know there was anything in it.

"I just put it there last night," he said, grinning at her. He possessed a boyish charm that made Simone fall a little further in love with him. She smiled back at him as he said, "If there's anything you don't like, just say. It's not set in stone." He took a deep breath and spread an oversized piece of paper on the counter.

He pointed to the top corner. "It's fifteen hundred square feet, just like the barn you're in now. Fifty by thirty."

"Do we have room for that?" she asked.

"Sure," he said. "I think we put it close to the house, so we can pour a patio in the backyard and that can serve as the entrance as well." He glanced at her.

"Okay," she said, studying all the lines. "Look at those bookshelves."

"Lots of shelves," he said. "I'll build those custom, so you tell me how big you want them. The height and depth, all of that." He ran his finger along the back wall. "This is the fifty-foot wall, and I figured that would be enough shelving."

"I'll say," Simone said, thinking of the metal units she was using now. She couldn't believe this. This was a dream. This wasn't reality. No one could honestly have a workshop like this…could they?

He went on to explain how if they kept it close to the house, he could use the electricity from here for her kiln. "Which will go here," he said, pointing to the corner. "Pottery wheel here. Desk here, for all your business stuff. I can build that too and put in as many drawers as you want. File drawers, something for receipts, whatever you need."

Simone could only nod, because there were no words to say how wonderful this was.

"You need space for your bigger items," he said. "The inventory. So I didn't do a whole lot with the rest of the space." He pointed to some rectangles on the drawing. "I think some waist-high tables would be great, and I roughly sketched those in here."

He pointed in front of the bookcases. Fifty feet of them. "I thought stainless steel, because then you can paint or stain or whatever." He looked at her for approval, and Simone's eyes filled with tears. He abandoned the plans. "Hey." He took her into his arms, and Simone's emotions kept her from telling him that the tears were happy ones.

Standing there in their kitchen, Simone fought against her feelings of unworthiness. She tried to tame the storm in her chest. He just held her tight and didn't try to tell her she was being silly. She already knew she was.

"What is it?" he finally stepped back and looked at her.

He reached up and wiped her face gently, and that made Simone want to cry even harder.

"I don't know," she said, shaking her head and blinking. "It's just so wonderful. It's amazing. *You're* amazing." She gave a quick laugh and practically lunged at him to kiss him.

He chuckled and held her tight, tight for another few seconds. "Hey, you cook for me, and I'll build you what you want." He gave her a playful grin, probably trying to play off the tension she'd created.

She leaned into his bicep as he explained the rest of the drawing, finally saying, "And I know this corner looks blank. That's intentional. See the windows here and here?" He indicated the very narrow rectangles in the plan. "I talked to Whitney, and she said natural light is awesome for still photography. And this corner will be where you can pose all of your items to take pictures of them for your website."

Simone clutched his arm with both of her hands, stealing his strength from him. "I love it," she whispered.

"No changes?"

"You put a bathroom in it," she said. "If I put a bed out here, I could live in it."

He pressed a kiss to the top of her head. "No beds in the workshop, baby. I want you in here with me."

Simone looked up at him, thinking that she wanted this moment burned in her memory forever. This strong, handsome, hardworking, faithful cowboy. *Her* strong, handsome, hardworking, faithful cowboy. "I love it," she repeated. "I love you."

"I love you too." Micah leaned down and kissed her, and Simone put everything else out of her mind. She focused on kissing him and being with him and letting everything that was Micah flow over her and through her.

"Hey," a woman said. "Stop kissing." Callie laughed a moment later, and Simone broke her kiss with Micah and faced her sister. She wore a look of pure delight though, and Simone could admit she felt it moving through her. "We knocked, I swear."

"Yeah," Simone said. "We were a little busy."

"We saw," Evelyn said, coming into the kitchen from the living room. "I put Mom's dress there. We'll have to figure out what we want to do with it."

"Oh, right," Simone said. "And I have the credenza Micah and I found in his office. We'll go over what you think of my ideas, and I'll get going on it."

Evelyn sighed and looked at Simone and then Callie. "I can't believe Daddy is getting married."

Micah picked up his drawing and kissed the back of Simone's neck. "See you later, sweetheart." He slipped away, lifting his hand in a goodbye wave to her sisters as he left through the front door.

Evelyn and Callie watched him, finally facing Simone once the door had clicked closed. "So things are going well here, I see," Callie said, her smile much too big for Simone's liking.

She said nothing as she picked up the spoon and stirred the artichoke dip again.

"Obviously," Evelyn said. "She's glowing."

"I am not," Simone said. "He's building me a new workshop, and he was showing me the plans. That's all. It was exciting."

"Yeah, and that kiss looked exciting too." Evelyn cocked her eyebrow, her smile not far behind.

"We're married," Simone said. "I'm forty years old. I'm allowed to kiss him."

"You're only thirty-nine," Evelyn said as she slid onto a barstool. "And I hope there's more than just dips. I'm starving."

"Of course there's more than just dips," Simone said, though she'd never criticized what her sister had made when she hosted girls' night. No matter how old she got, she'd always be the youngest sister, and sometimes Callie and Evelyn treated her that way whether they meant to or not.

"I made mini meatloaves and saffron rice." She pulled everything out of the oven, where it had been warming for the last few minutes.

"And I'm sure there's something chocolatey in the fridge," Callie said, stepping that way. She opened the door and made a triumphant noise. "Yep. Looks like Oreo chocolate pie to me."

"It is," Simone said, smiling. "We need the pie to get through the wedding talk."

"I'm not dreading the wedding," Callie said. "Are you?"

"No, not really," Simone admitted. "It's just strange. I'm happy for them. They seem to love each other."

"They sure do," Evelyn said.

"Just like you and Micah," Callie said, beaming at Simone. "I think you two are so cute."

"Thanks." Simone gave her sister a side-hug.

"So the experiment worked," Callie said.

"I guess so," Simone said, finally leaving the artichoke dip alone. "I need to run something by you guys."

"Ooh, something," Evelyn said, smiling. Callie went around the island and sat next to Evelyn, both of them looking at her expectantly.

Simone took a breath. "I told Micah I wanted a big wedding ceremony. I mean, we got 'married' during an audition. I was wearing jeans." She looked over her sisters' shoulders to the couch, where an off-white dress had been draped. "I want to wear something of Momma's while I pledge to the man I love that I want to be with him." She looked back at her sisters. "Is that dumb? Overdramatic?"

"Of course not," Callie said. "And besides, you always have been a little overdramatic. Which is totally fine."

"I think you should," Evelyn said. "I got my wedding the second time I married Rhett. Callie got hers, even if it was a little fake in the beginning." She glanced at Callie, who nodded.

"Okay," Simone said. "I'm thinking Christmas. I've always wanted to be married at Christmastime."

"That's a long time," Callie said.

"Yeah, but...Christmas." Simone smiled, just imagining how magical it would be. "And you're going to be in the wedding too."

"We are?" Callie asked.

"Yep," Simone said. "I'm planning a big surprise, and I'm going to need everyone's help." She could barely contain her excitement. "Now let's eat. I'm starving too. Then I'll tell you all about it."

THE DAYS UNTIL JUNE ELEVENTH FLEW BY, AND BEFORE Simone knew it, she was directing Micah as he backed the delivery truck up to her workshop. "Right there," she said, holding up her palm. He stopped completely and got out of the truck.

She stood back, out of the way, while he opened the rolling door at the back of the truck and went inside her workshop. "It's just right inside the door there," she called after him.

She felt like she'd lost some of her brain cells. After girls' night a couple of nights ago, she'd worked on the wedding altar for her father and Belinda every day. The concept had come together easily, and Simone had started dreaming about building her own altar for her and Micah's wedding.

He came out with the altar in his hands. "It's gorgeous, Simone." He smiled at her and got it easily into the back of the truck. "So we're going over there to set up, then coming back here to get dressed?"

"Yes," she said. "We have plenty of time."

"Yep." He pulled the door down and faced her. "Are you okay?"

"I'm just tired," she said, though her stomach ached too. It had been for at least a week now, and no amount of peppermint oil or antacid had helped.

Micah touched her hand, and Simone looked at him. "You sure?"

"My stomach hurts," she admitted. "I just haven't eaten breakfast yet." She did always feel better after she ate. "So let's get to Daddy's and set up. Then you can buy me a pecan bun." She smiled, hoping that would erase the concern in his eyes.

They crinkled around the edges, and he said, "I like the way you think." He drove them over to her father's house and took the altar through the gate on the side of the house and into the backyard.

Simone followed, hoping Evelyn had already been there with all the flowers. Her car wasn't out front, and Simone couldn't set up the altar without them. She found Micah adjusting the altar according to her father's directions, and she paused to take in the lovely atmosphere of the backyard.

It had been completely transformed, with tea lights radiating out from the roof of the house toward an arch that had been set up. Just in front of that, Micah shifted the altar another inch before her father deemed it good.

Someone had set up chairs on the grass, creating an aisle down the middle, and there couldn't be more than thirty or forty. The coziness of it all pricked at Simone's heart, and before she knew it, she was crying again.

She swiped at her eyes before Micah could see, because

she'd been crying at the drop of a hat since they'd returned from the Hill Country.

"Are these the pictures?" she asked Belinda, who came out of the house carrying a handful of yellow bows.

"Yes," she said. "I got about ten. You use as many or as few as you want."

Simone nodded and started looking through the box that had been set on the patio table. The top of the altar would remain bare, except for a few flowers—which were not here. In the cupboards, Simone had carefully removed all the glass to make cubbies, and she wanted to put in trinkets and photos.

She didn't need ten, but three would work. Or another odd number, perhaps five. She selected them based on size and orientation, because they were all of Belinda and Daddy. Also in the box sat a few other items, and she pulled them out one by one.

"Belinda," she said, and the woman came over from where she was tying bows on the backs of the chairs. "Tell me about these things."

She took the ticket stub from Simone, a sigh coming from her mouth. "This is where your father and I met."

"Those are to my play," she said.

Belinda looked at her. "Yes, last spring. I had gone because a neighbor of mine was in it. Your dad was there for you, of course. We met in the lobby."

"And you still have the ticket stub?"

Belinda trilled out a happy laugh. "I didn't. This is your

father's. He's a bit of a hoarder, isn't he?" She handed the stub back to Simone. "But now we can display it here."

Simone looked at it too, something warm coming over her. The Lord had been aware of her father all these years, and He'd provided someone to keep him company in the later years of his life.

"These are the things we made on our first date," Belinda said. "I wanted to do one of those ceramic painting classes." She gazed fondly at the teal teapot covered in silver stars and literally the ugliest dog Simone had ever seen. "Guess which one's mine?" she asked.

"Oh, it's clear which one's yours," Simone said with a smile. "My dad never was very artistic."

"I'm here, I'm here," Evelyn said, rushing toward them with a huge box in her arms. "Sorry I'm late."

"Not at all," Belinda said, reaching to help Evelyn put the box on the table. "Thank you for coming to help." She looked from Evelyn to Simone. "I mean it. Your father is very lucky to have daughters like you." She smiled, her eyes misty, and Simone was glad she wasn't the only one prone to crying.

She hugged Belinda and said, "We're glad he found you." They gripped each other tightly for a moment, and then Simone added, "What's this last thing?"

Belinda took the small, heavy anchor. "It's a paperweight. I bought it for your father for Christmas, saying that if we anchored ourselves to the Lord and to each other, we'd be okay." She smiled at the shiny metal that had obviously been sitting on a shelf somewhere, untouched. "That no matter what storms life brought, we'd be okay."

"That's beautiful," Simone said, and she suddenly wanted an anchor on her shelf to remind herself of that. She took a deep breath. "Okay, with the pictures, I think we can only put in one piece of ceramic. I'm voting for the teapot." She looked at Belinda. "Objections?"

"Heavens, no."

They laughed together, and Simone took the pictures, the ticket stub, the teapot, and the anchor up to the altar. She arranged everything so it could be seen, and then she returned to the box on the table to pluck out a few blooms to put inside the altar and on top. She and Micah stayed to help Evelyn get the flowers where they should be, and then they all left.

Simone only ate half of her pecan bun on the way home, and once there, she barely made it to the bathroom before she brought it all back up again. Something was definitely wrong.

"Too much sugar," she said as she rinsed out her mouth. But she normally liked sugar, and it had never made her sick before.

"I think you're stressed," Micah said when she came out of the bathroom. "Could that make you sick?"

It never had before, but Simone didn't tell him that. She crawled into bed, trying to catch her breath. "I just need a minute," she murmured.

Micah's lips pressed against her forehead, and Simone's eyes shot open. "I'll come check on you in a few minutes," he said, not noticing the way she'd tensed. He left, and Simone lay in bed, her mind racing.

There wasn't anything wrong. She wasn't terribly ill.

"You might be pregnant," she whispered to herself, a slow smile crawling across her face as she placed both hands on her stomach.

CHAPTER TWENTY-THREE

Micah was melting, plain and simple. At least Simone seemed to have made a recovery from that morning. She glowed with a radiant smile, saying hello to friends and neighbors Micah had never met before. He could keep a smile on his face too, and he did, shaking hands and accepting kisses in the few minutes before the wedding began.

Simone cried through the whole thing, and Micah was seriously starting to worry about her. She'd cried when he'd shown her the design plans for her workshop too. She'd cried when she finished the altar. She'd cried during last week's sermon at church.

There was definitely something wrong with her, as she'd always been a strong, confident woman. He was fine with a little crying, he honestly was. But she seemed to break down if he mentioned he'd brought her a piece of pie from the bakery.

She's been through a lot this year already, he told himself. This marriage, for one. That was a huge change for both of them. A good change, but very big. She'd moved out of her cabin. She'd lost her grandmother. She'd watched Evelyn bring home triplets and need a lot of help. She'd found out her father was dating, and now he was getting married.

Pastor Daniels did a very nice job with the ceremony, and Micah shifted in his seat. He did feel cheated that he and Simone hadn't had the backyard wedding with the lights and flowers and friends and family. He leaned over to her and whispered, "I'm glad we're doing a wedding at Christmas. What do you need me to help you with?"

"We can talk about it after," she whispered back, tightening her hand against his arm.

Of course, now was not a great time. The preacher pronounced Jerome and Belinda husband and wife, and they kissed over the beautiful altar Simone had conceptualized and brought to life.

She'd bleached the wood, bringing out the grain and making the altar somewhat white. With the red and yellow roses and the pictures inside, it was a stunning centerpiece that complimented the simple wedding.

Jerome and Belinda walked down the aisle while everyone cheered, Micah included, and when they got to the patio, Jerome turned and said, "Lunch will be served in just a few minutes. Boys?"

Belinda's sons flew into action, setting up tables and moving the chairs around them. Simone fanned herself with the white, lacy fans they'd been handing out at the beginning of the festivities, and Micah moved her over to a chair at a table in the shade. "Sit down, baby. You feeling okay?"

She sat, a sigh coming from her mouth. "I'm okay. It's so hot, though. Isn't it?"

"It's mighty hot, yes," he said. The backyard had some shade, but not enough to cover everyone, and honestly, shade didn't do a whole lot to curb the heat of a Texas summer.

They stayed through lunch, through the cake cutting, and through the beginning of the dance, where Jerome danced with each of his daughters, and then Belinda.

After that, Simone looked like she could drop into a deep sleep from a standing position, and Micah got up to tell her they were going home. He didn't want to take her from her family party, but she looked gray and worn right to the bone.

Thankfully, she said, "I'm ready to go, Micah. Do you think we can go?"

"Yes," he said quickly. "I'll tell Callie and Liam, okay? Wait here." He ducked over to his brother and said, "We're headed out."

Liam looked at him in surprise. "Already?"

"Yeah," Micah said, glancing over to Simone, who was sipping something from a cup. Hopefully that would cool her down a little. "Simone isn't feeling well, and she needs to get home."

"She's not well?" Callie asked, concern in her voice. "What's wrong?"

"I don't know," Micah said, his own concern spiking.

"She's fine. She's been stressed about the altar, and she hasn't been eating much."

"Take her home," Liam said. "We're going to head out soon too."

Micah nodded and straightened, but Callie tapped his arm. "We're going to the cemetery tonight to visit Momma and Gran and tell them about the wedding. If she's well enough, you guys should come."

"Okay," he said. "I'll tell her." Micah hurried back to Simone, and they said a quick goodbye and congratulations to Jerome and Belinda and left.

On the way home, Micah clenched the wheel, trying to figure out what to say. "Tell me what hurts," he finally said. He'd done that a couple of times when Oliver complained of being sick, and the boy could identify what hurt. Then Micah could do something.

"I'm tired," she said. "I'm an emotional wreck. My stomach hurts. I'm throwing up."

He looked at her. "You're sweaty."

"It's hot out there."

"Do you have a fever?"

"No," she said.

"Why are you so hot then?" He was hot, but not pouring buckets of sweat hot. "Something's wrong, Simone. This is not normal for you." He turned onto the highway and pressed on the accelerator. "When we get home, you're taking painkillers and going straight to bed. Callie said they're going to visit your mom and grandmother tonight, and I'm assuming you'll want to go. So you have to rest until then."

"Nothing's wrong," Simone said quietly.

Micah looked at her again. "What do you mean?" Something was definitely wrong with her.

"When we get home, I'll go lie down," she said. "But I'm not taking any pills." She looked at him, and Micah was glad there wasn't any traffic on this lonely highway leading out of town. "Can you run back to town to the drugstore and get me something?"

"Of course," he said. "Anything."

She smiled at him and reached across the seat for his hand. "Thanks, baby."

She'd never called him baby before, and Micah did like it. "What am I getting?" he asked. "And you'll be okay alone?"

"I'm going to be fine," she said, her eyes drifting closed. "I just need you to get me a pregnancy test."

Micah's whole body jerked. "A pregnancy test?"

She giggled and squeezed his hand. "That's right, cowboy. I don't think there's anything wrong with me. I think I'm pregnant."

Stunned, Micah didn't know what to say. "Oh, wow," came out of his mouth anyway.

"That's okay, right?" she asked

"Of course it's okay," he said, realizing he needed to react appropriately. "I'm—yes. It's great." He laughed, a new kind of joy and happiness moving through him that he'd never felt before. "I'm gonna be a dad."

"We should take the test first," Simone said.

"Right." He swallowed, trying to get his thoughts in line. Everything seemed to be buzzing so quickly around him. "This is so exciting."

At the house, he helped Simone into bed, kissed her forehead, and maybe drove ten over the speed limit in his haste to get to the drugstore and back with the required test. Back in the bedroom, Simone slept, and Micah had half a mind to wake her up.

Pregnant with his baby. He couldn't believe it. He dropped to his knees right there at the side of the bed, his wife sleeping only a few inches from him. "Thank you, Dear Lord," he whispered. "Please help me be as supportive and helpful as possible." He had so much more inside him, but he couldn't articulate anything more.

He left her to sleep, going down the hall to his office, where he worked on the final plans for Bear Glover and Shiloh Ridge Ranch. They'd been back and forth a couple of times now, and with a few more tweaks, Bear would sign off on the design, and Micah would break ground.

He also needed to find a time to get back to the Hill Country to see Dwayne Carver. But with Simone possibly pregnant now, he wasn't sure he'd be able to.

"Micah?" she asked, and he looked up from his desk to find her framed beautifully in the doorway.

"Hey, sweetheart." He left his plans and went to her, taking her into his arms. "How are you feeling?"

"Better, actually." She smiled up at him. "I found the test in the bathroom." She held it up, but it was too close to

Micah's face to see. "Two lines is pregnant." She handed him the test.

Micah looked at her, but she wore a perfectly placid mask. He looked at the test.

Two lines.

He whooped, scooped her into his arms, and they laughed and laughed together. He set her on her feet, hardly able to breathe. "I love you," he said. "I love you so much."

"I love you too."

He kissed her, this beautiful, strong woman that he'd liked for so long. Now his wife. Almost the mother of his child.

Micah was reminded of God's goodness in that moment, and he never wanted to be outside the sphere of the Lord's watchful eye again.

MICAH WALKED SIDE-BY-SIDE WITH SIMONE, HIS HAND IN hers as they made their way down the lane toward the Shining Star. The sun had baked the ground until it could fry an egg, but he didn't care.

"I don't remember my mother at all," Simone said quietly.

Micah looked at her, sensing her sadness. It penetrated his heart and made him want to wrap her in a bubble that the cruel things of the world couldn't touch. "How old were you when she died?"

"Just two," she said. "I didn't know her. I never knew her."

Micah released her hand and put it around Simone. "I'm sorry."

"I don't want our baby to not know me," she said, her voice too high, which meant she was crying again. Now that Micah knew why, he didn't worry. And fine, maybe the crying had annoyed him a little bit too. Guilt zipped through him, but he pushed it away.

Their footsteps crunched over the dirt road, his mind churning for an appropriate answer. Micah finally said, "You know your mother. Callie told you stories. Your daddy did too. You have all those photo albums in the office, and you know everything about her, from what her favorite color was to what she liked for breakfast."

"Cold cereal with cream," Simone said with a smile. "I love that too."

"Even I know that," Micah said quietly.

"Promise me if I die, you'll make sure our baby knows me."

"Simone," he said, not wanting to chastise her, but he really didn't like thinking about her dying. "You're not going to die."

"I might," she said. "People do."

"How did she die?" he asked.

"She got really sick," Simone said. "Pneumonia, for weeks and weeks. She finally went to the hospital—Mama didn't like doctors or hospitals—and she had so much infection, they put her on some strong drugs." Simone reached up and wiped her eyes. "But it was too late. She had a staph infection, and it killed her."

"So we'll go to the hospital the moment you have a stuffy nose," he said.

Simone tipped her head back and laughed, and Micah enjoyed the trill of it on the air. They approached the homestead on her childhood ranch at the same moment Callie and Liam came out the front door with their girls.

"See? They're right there." She waved to Micah and Simone, who waved back. They all piled into Liam's minivan, and Micah tried not to hate riding in it. He knew Liam hated it too, and normally only Callie drove the van.

The conversation was easy between Simone and Callie, who asked her sister how she was feeling.

"Good," Simone said without even a glance in Micah's direction. "I was just tired and stressed about the wedding."

"It was a beautiful wedding," Liam said.

"Yes." Everyone agreed on that, and Micah wondered why Simone needed six months to plan a wedding when Belinda had done it in two weeks. He didn't ask though, because he wasn't the one doing the work.

They arrived at the cemetery to find Rhett and Evelyn already there. Rhett had Conrad up on his shoulders while Evelyn pushed a stroller that held all three babies. One of them was crying, but she didn't seem to mind at all.

Simone stepped over to her and peered down into the carriage. "Can I take her out?"

"Sure," Evelyn said. "She didn't sleep long enough this afternoon, that's all."

"Oh, come here," Simone said, reaching into the stroller to unbuckle the baby. "You can sleep with me, baby Elaine." She cuddled the precious girl against her chest, and the infant calmed immediately. "Yes, that's right."

She lifted her head and met Micah's eye, and she wore such a look of triumph and happiness that Micah just smiled and shook his head. They walked down the narrow lane, all of them lost in their own thoughts.

Micah had not been here before, but his brothers obviously had. He stayed near the back, Simone a few paces in front of him. He let his thoughts wander wherever they wanted to go, and when he came to a stop in front of the grave markers for Simone's mother and grandmother, he allowed his emotions to release into the sky.

Callie bent down and cleaned off a couple of weeds that had started to encroach on her mother's headstone. "There she is," she said, tucking Denise against her side. "My mama." She reached out and touched two fingers to her mother's name.

Evelyn did the same before moving over to the headstone next to Ginger Conrad Foster's, and Micah wasn't sure he knew Liam and Callie's daughter had been named after her mother. "Hey, Gran," she whispered. Rhett and Liam stayed out of the way, and Micah copied them.

Simone turned to him and handed him baby Elaine before she went up to kneel in front of her mother's grave too. Micah turned his attention back to the tiny infant in his arms. She was just over two months old now, and her skin was pearly pink, with that shock of dark hair sticking straight up all over her scalp. It was soft and feathery, and Micah loved her so very much. She wasn't even his, but in some ways, she was.

She was part of Rhett, and Rhett was part of Micah. He sniffed before he realized he'd done it. He looked up and found Rhett and Liam looking at him. "You want one of those, don't you?" Liam asked, smiling.

"I like babies," Micah said, smiling. There was so much peace in the cemetery, and Micah hadn't expected that. He hadn't spent a whole lot of time in such a place, as he hadn't been born before his grandparents on his momma's side had passed away. They'd died really young, and only Rhett claimed to have any memories of them at all.

"I like babies too," Rhett said. "But maybe try for less than three at the same time." He yawned, and Liam nodded.

"We only had the one, but Denise was only three, and she was new for us too."

Micah didn't know what to say, because he had no experience with fatherhood whatsoever. *You will soon*, he told himself, and he smiled down at baby Elaine again.

CHAPTER TWENTY-FOUR

Wyatt picked up his bag and lifted it over the tailgate of the truck before turning back to Marcy. She held Warren in her arms, and Wyatt loved the sight of them so, so much. He grinned at the little boy and took him from his mother. "You be a good boy while Daddy is gone, okay?"

Warren babbled something Wyatt couldn't understand, though he'd be a year old next month. Wait. This month. July was just a couple of days old now, and Warren would be a year old at the end of the month.

He kissed Marcy, holding her tight for an extra moment. "You're sure you'll be okay here?" He hated leaving her for any length of time. She had no other family in town besides his, and they lived so far away from everyone. Now that he had more to concern him than his latest roping score and his back, Wyatt had learned that he was quite the worrier. He didn't like Marcy flying nearly as much as she did, but she loved it with her whole heart, and it was her family business.

She'd told him a Payne should be there running it. She had hired another pilot and an office manager, and she only flew four hours a day now. She knew what she was doing in the cockpit, but Wyatt worried sometimes.

Accidents happen, he'd told her.

"I'm going to the ranch this afternoon," she said. "Whitney and I are planning a big party because all y'all will be gone." She smiled at him. "Don't worry. I'm fine."

He let his hand drift down to her belly. She wasn't showing yet, but Wyatt had found out she was expecting again last week. "And the baby?"

"Wyatt." She nudged his chest, and he fell back a step. She shook her head and laughed. "We're *fine*. Go. You're going to be late, and you don't want to deal with Jeremiah when you're late."

"I can handle Jeremiah." Wyatt kicked a grin in her direction, though she was right. He did not want to deal with the wrath of Jeremiah if he didn't have to.

"Please don't lift anything too heavy," she said, sobering. "Really, Wyatt. Stand out if you have to."

"I will, Marce."

"I mean it," she said, giving him one of her blue-eyed, piercing stares. "There are plenty of people to help. It's not the Wyatt show."

He laughed as he shook his head.

"We need you here," she said, taking Warren from him. "Whole and well, and I—"

"I'm not going to lift anything too heavy," he said, stepping up to her again. He kissed her, taking an extra moment with his lips against hers. "I love you. I'll be safe."

She nodded, and he kissed Warren quickly too. "Bye, baby. See you guys in a couple of days." He headed to his truck then, got in, and backed out. How he'd left Marcy to go on tour before, he had no idea. He didn't ever want to go anywhere without her, and this trip down to the Hill Country to get his grandparents out of their house there had brought him some anxiety.

He'd calmed by the time he arrived at Seven Sons, which was a good thing, because the intensity in the homestead would've put him over the top had he been harboring any of his own anxiety.

"What's goin' on here?" he asked Micah, who sat in the front office.

"Oh, Jeremiah found rot in some hay," he said dryly. "And he's in a bad mood and wouldn't let the kids have juice for breakfast. So the kids are crying, and Whitney's mad at him, because he snapped at them. Rhett's going to be late, and Skyler doesn't think Daddy should go at all." He looked up from a notebook he'd been sketching in. "So you know, about normal around the Walker clan."

Wyatt chuckled and looked down the hall toward the kitchen and living room. "You're smart to hide out here."

"I offered to help," Micah said, a bit defensively. "But everything I said or did earned me a glare, and well, here I am."

"So you're saying don't try." Behind Wyatt, the front

door opened, and he shifted out of the way as Momma and Daddy came in, immediately followed by Skyler.

"...that's all I'm saying," Skyler said.

"I'm going," Daddy said. "They're my parents, and I'm fine. I can ride in a car for a few hours."

"It's almost *seven* hours, Daddy," Skyler said.

"Then we'll make stops." He marched past Wyatt without looking at him, and Skyler sighed as he paused in the foyer.

"What's that about?" Wyatt asked. Since he and Marcy weren't around the ranch much, they sometimes missed out on the nitty gritty gossip. Sure, he got the family texts, and that was good enough for him.

"He has some circulation problems," Skyler said. "From the accident. His leg goes numb if he sits too long, but apparently, he can ride in a car for seven hours." He frowned, his expression made of darkness.

"That's a losing battle," Micah said from the chair in the office. "Let him do what he wants."

Down the hall, the crying stopped, and Wyatt thought it might be a good time to offer help. Instead, he said, "Well, I think I'm going with the twins and Rhett, so maybe I should head over to the Shining Star."

"Make Jeremiah go with them," Skyler said. "Then it can be us three and Daddy. I can keep an eye on him."

"And we won't have to deal with Jeremiah's bad energy," Micah muttered.

Wyatt grinned at his brothers. "I'll go see what I can do." He headed down the hall, ready to turn on the rodeo king charm if he had to. Whitney sat at the table with the kids and Momma. Daddy had taken up a spot on the couch, and Jeremiah scrubbed the kitchen sink like he needed to grind through the metal with his bare hands.

"Hey, so me, Micah, and Skyler are ready. You want to come with us, Daddy? We'll hit the road and get down there."

Jeremiah looked up, his expression filled with clouds. "I guess that leaves me with Rhett and the twins?"

"Is that okay?" Wyatt asked. "We're ready to go, and it seems like y'all might need a few more minutes is all."

"It's fine," Jeremiah said, and Wyatt stepped over to the couch to give his dad a hand up. Daddy took it, and he still had plenty of strong grip in his fingers.

Wyatt smiled at him and leaned closer, "Don't worry, Daddy. I'll keep Skyler from bugging you too much."

"That would be a miracle," Daddy grumbled. He paused next to the island where Jeremiah was now tucking cereal flaps back into place. "And Jeremiah, my son, it's just rotting hay. Don't let it ruin your life."

Jeremiah looked up, and Wyatt thought for a moment someone was about to get hit. Then his entire demeanor collapsed, and Wyatt stared at him, stunned.

Jeremiah was literally the strongest, the toughest, the most feared cowboy Wyatt knew. And he'd known some real tough cowboys on the rodeo circuit. "I just feel like a giant failure," he murmured.

"Do you remember coming to sit with me in the hospital?" Daddy asked.

Jeremiah looked at him and then Wyatt. "Yes."

"I tried to tell you then, but I couldn't talk. I could hear you though. You said you were tired, that the kids were hard, that you brought home ranch problems to Whitney." Daddy lifted his hand and put it on Jeremiah's shoulder. "And I kept telling you it was fine. That you were a good man and an excellent father."

Wyatt watched his father with an intensity he didn't understand. But when his dad spoke, Wyatt had learned to listen.

"I wanted to hug you so tight and tell you that you're just human. We're all human. Things happen. The dishes don't get done. The rain pours when we need the sun to shine. The hay rots. It doesn't matter." He looked over to the table, where Momma and Whitney sat. "*They're* what matters. So put down the washcloth and go kiss your wife. Put a smile on your face and tell your kids you love 'em."

Jeremiah stepped around the corner of the counter and embraced Daddy, closing his eyes as they hugged. "Thanks, Dad." He released him and headed over to the table.

"Wow," Wyatt said, guiding Daddy down the hall toward the front door. "I've only ever seen Momma and Whitney put Jeremiah in his place. That was incredible."

"He's a good man," Daddy said. "Thinks he's superhuman when he isn't, and it's a real let-down for a man like that." He looked at Wyatt. "You were like that when you first started riding."

"Was I?"

"Oh, yeah." Daddy chuckled. "You were so good, everything came naturally to you. You hardly had to learn anything. You could stay on a horse or a bull almost without trying. So when something happened where you actually had to *learn* something—it wasn't just a natural response— you got frustrated in about half a second."

Wyatt held his head high as he nodded at Skyler and Micah that they were ready. "I don't remember that at all."

Daddy just laughed as they went outside and down the front steps to Skyler's truck. "Y'all are just like me," he said. "Stubborn to the core. I say I'll be fine driving for seven hours, but my leg is going to hurt, and I'm going to complain and make you stop, and y'all would've been better off with Jeremiah." He climbed up into the truck, using the door and the seat for support. "But you're stuck with me now." He grinned as Wyatt closed the door and stepped to the back.

"We can handle you," Skyler said, turning the key to start the truck. "Everyone in?"

Wyatt closed his door and reached for his seatbelt. He might've ridden bulls and bucking broncos in the past but riding with Skyler behind the wheel could be a wild experience. "Yep," he said, clicking the belt into place.

"It was sudden," Micah explained as Wyatt drove him to the car rental. "I'm just going to stop off in Grape Seed Falls for a few hours. I'll be right behind you."

"But you'll have to drive alone," Wyatt said. They'd been down in the Hill Country for two days, packing and loading everything his grandparents owned. Wyatt had stuck true to his word to Marcy, and he'd only done what he could. No one asked him any questions, and he was a very good babysitter for Grandma and Grandpa when he couldn't help.

They were not good at throwing things away, and Wyatt's distractions had allowed the other brothers and Daddy and Uncle Jonas to get more into the dumpster than had been there when they arrived.

"I can't make anyone wait," Micah said. "I'll be fine."

"Okay," Wyatt said, making a turn to get into the parking lot. "The birthday party is tomorrow. You're not going to miss it, are you?"

"No," Micah said. "I'm just meeting with him for a few minutes."

"And who is this?"

"It's Dwayne Carver," Micah said. "He's Squire Ackerman's cousin. He's got quite the operation down here, and he's looking to redo the homestead and the generational house."

"Wow, that's a big project."

"So maybe it'll be more than a couple of minutes," Micah said. "But it's not going to be overnight. I won't miss the party."

"Okay, because Marcy, Whitney, and Ivory have been planning it for at least a month."

"For two-year-olds," Micah said dryly. "That seems a bit extreme, don't you think?"

Wyatt couldn't argue there, so he just laughed. "Warren

is only one. Don't you think your child's very first birthday should be celebrated?"

"Did Marcy ask you that?"

"Yep," Wyatt said. "Because we're having this family party tomorrow, and Warren gets his own bash at our house on his actual birthday. *Two* birthday parties."

"I was lucky if Momma called me the right name," Micah said, and Wyatt burst out laughing, glad when Micah did too.

"Same, brother," he said. "I got called Tripp so much, it's not even funny."

"Which makes no sense, because you're not even one of the twins."

"I think Momma lost her mind after the twins," Wyatt said. "For real. Did you know she once left me at a restaurant?"

Micah snorted, a scoff following. "She did not."

"She did," Wyatt said. "Rhett told me the story. I was a baby, in a baby seat. She went to lunch with us all, which can you imagine? It's a circus when Marcy and I go out, and we have one baby." He shook his head, thinking of all the bags and wipes and things Marcy brought to keep Warren happy.

"Anyway, when it was time to go, she got up and herded the boys out. But I was a baby, and I couldn't just go with. She left me there, in the booth. A waitress had to come running after her to say she'd left me behind." Wyatt chuckled again. "She's awesome, but yeah."

"Sounds like *you* broke her, then," Micah said, grinning. "Maybe she lost her mind after you."

"Maybe," Wyatt agreed. He loved spending time with his brothers, and he looked over at Micah. "You and Simone seem to be making the marriage work."

"Yeah," Micah said, dropping his chin to his chest as his face turned red. Wyatt knew that tactic, and he knew that look.

"You're in love with her."

"Yeah." Micah never had beat around the bush with things.

"Does she love you?"

"Yeah," he said, smiling again. "She does." He looked at Wyatt. "Can you keep a secret?"

"I'm like a vault," Wyatt said.

"She's pregnant," Micah said. "Soon enough, I'm not going to be able to leave the house without the circus too."

A grin burst onto Wyatt's face. "That's great, Micah. Congratulations."

"Yeah, thanks." Micah reached up and adjusted his cowboy hat. "I'm nervous, but excited."

"Marcy's pregnant again too," Wyatt said. "If we're sharing secrets, though we're going to announce it tomorrow at the birthday party. That's why I wondered if you'd be there."

"No way," Micah said. "That's great, Wyatt."

"Yeah," he said, smiling out the windshield like he could see his whole future in front of him. "Yeah, it is great."

CHAPTER TWENTY-FIVE

Micah turned under the arch that said Grape Seed Ranch on it, the peaches on the end obviously well-kept and well-carved. The land spread before him, and Micah liked this ranch immediately. He'd liked Dwayne Carver too, who talked like a Texan and managed to infuse kindness into not many words.

Micah scanned the roads, the buildings he could see in the distance, the fields. Dwayne obviously ran a great operation, as the ranch was pristine and the people he could see to his right went about their business as if they knew what they were doing.

He continued down the road to the homestead, which looked like it had been built many decades in the past. There was nothing wrong with old homes. Micah wanted to make sure Dwayne knew that. Not everything had to be the latest and greatest, by any means.

A man came out onto the porch as Micah eased his

rental truck to a stop, and he lifted his hand in a wave. Micah got out of the truck and called, "You must be Dwayne."

"Sure am."

"Let me grab my stuff, and I'll be right up." Micah ducked back into the truck and gathered his briefcase. Simone had been the one to suggest he keep his contracts, his clipboard, his plans, and plenty of pens in a briefcase. He felt a bit foolish using it, but the bag did keep everything he needed and wanted nice and safe, clean, and organized. And Micah liked safe, clean, and organized.

A woman joined Dwayne as Micah reached the top step. "My wife, Felicity," Dwayne said.

"Ma'am." Micah tipped his hat at her. He looked around. "This place is pretty great, Dwayne. Good bones. Huge porch." He looked back at the cowboy, who was several years older than him. At least. Maybe a decade.

"Yeah," he said. "Squire just mentioned what you do, and Felicity and I have wanted to upgrade the homestead, as well as the generational house. My father just passed away, and it's just my mother now. She's going to go live in town with my sister, and it felt like a good time to do it." He took a step toward the front door, and Micah went with him.

"Sorry about your father," Micah said. He hadn't lost his, but when he'd gotten the call about Daddy's accident, Micah's whole world had come to a stop right then and there.

"Thank you," Dwayne said. He opened the door and they

went inside. "So Felicity and I live here now, but we'll move into the generational house at some point."

"You have kids?"

"Two sons," Felicity said, reaching for Dwayne's hand. Micah sure liked both of them; they projected a really good air about them, and he looked back and forth between them.

"Okay," he said. "Why don't you walk me through the place and tell me what you're thinking." He put his briefcase on the couch. "Can I leave this here?"

"Sure," Dwayne said.

"Great." Micah took out the clipboard and a pen. "Ready whenever you are." He smiled at the two of them, and they smiled back.

"All right," Dwayne said. "I hate how this front room is separated from the back of the house. We never use it, because the kitchen is back there." He started toward the kitchen, which was under an arched doorway and down a short hall.

"What's this?" Micah asked, pointing to the door in the hallway.

"The half bath," Felicity said.

Micah made a note and kept walking.

"And back here, we have a tiny living room, but this is where we all end up," Dwayne said. "Because this is where the kitchen is, and where everyone wants to be."

Micah entered the space, and he saw immediately what Dwayne wanted. He held up his phone and took a measurement. "I'm going to measure some things," he said. "Then I can give you a more detailed idea of what you can do." He stepped around and took several measurements with the app he'd bought just for such a thing. "It saves it all for me, so I can import it into my computer and see your floor plan with just a few clicks."

"Wow," Dwayne said. "That's pretty cool."

"It is," Micah said, because it was. He smiled at them again. "What's here?" He indicated the wall they'd had to pass by to get from the front to the back, opposite of the bathroom.

"That's the pantry for the kitchen," Dwayne said, stepping around the corner and opening some folded closet doors.

"Oh, we can fix that," Micah said, making a note. He followed Dwayne and Felicity through the rest of the house, which was pretty big. Plenty big for two children. Plenty big for six children.

He did the same thing as they walked through the second house in the backyard, and Micah's head felt full to bursting by the time they were done. "Okay," he said. "And we have a budget?"

"No," Dwayne said. "I just want you to operate as if we don't have a budget." He exchanged a glance with Felicity, who nodded.

"All right," Micah said, his stomach growling. Grandma Lucy had fed them breakfast a mighty long time ago.

"You should stay for dinner," Felicity said, having clearly heard him.

"Oh, I'm fine," Micah said. "I have a long drive back to Three Rivers today." He smiled at them.

"Kurt has food," Dwayne said. "We can eat now, and you can go."

Micah didn't want to say no. He liked this ranch, the vibe here, these people. "Who's Kurt?" he asked.

Dwayne smiled. "My foreman. He lives out in the cabin community. Come see." He stepped over to the back door, and Micah went with him. As he ate with a whole crew of cowboys, wives, and children, Micah thought Grape Seed Ranch was a lot like Seven Sons.

When he got back in the rental truck, he took a moment to put his clipboard away and bow his head. "Thank you, Lord," he whispered. "Help me get home safely, and bless me that I can work on this ranch."

You should fly home. The thought popped into his head, and Micah tried to push it away. But it wouldn't go, even when he'd left the ranch and started down the highway that led north, back toward the Texas Panhandle.

He saw a sign for Austin, and without second guessing himself again, he veered toward the road that went that way. If he had the impression he was supposed to fly home, he should fly home.

It seemed to take forever to get to Austin, and he hurried to buy a ticket for the last plane leaving for Amarillo that day. Finally on the airplane, Micah sighed and texted Simone. *I'm flying to Amarillo instead of driving. Do you think you could come pick me up?*

His phone rang, and since they hadn't pushed back from the gate yet, he answered the phone.

"You're on a plane?" she demanded, her voice shrill.

"Yes," he said. "Is that okay? I can ask Skyler to come get me."

"No, it's fine," she said, sobbing in the next moment. "He's on a plane. He's not on the road."

"Simone?" Micah didn't know what was going on or who she was talking to.

"There's been a huge accident on the road about fifty miles north of Grape Seed Falls," she said, sniffling. "I called you, but you didn't answer, and I was scared."

"I was on some back road between there and Austin," he said. "Maybe I lost service."

"You're okay," she said. "That's all that matters."

"Yeah," he said, thinking of the thought to fly instead of drive. "I should be home in an hour or so." The plane moved, and he added, "I love you, baby, but I have to go. We're taking off."

"Okay, love you. I'll send Skyler to the airport. I've had a rough day."

"Oh, I'm sorry," he said. "And okay." He hated hanging up while his wife was crying, but the flight attendant said, "Sir."

He held up his hand and said, "Love you," and hung up. He couldn't wait to get home to Simone, and he leaned his head back and offered up a prayer that she'd be feeling better when he arrived.

"THIS PLACE IS GREAT," SIMONE SAID AS THEY ENTERED

Tripp's new house. "Look at these old floors, Micah. They're beautiful."

"They are," he said, studying everything in the older, two-story home his brother had bought on the same lane where Rhett and Evelyn lived. He knew he was more interested than most men, so when Ivory volunteered to take everyone around on a house tour, he went with. He wanted to see the wainscoting in the dining room, the ceiling fans in the bedroom, the crown molding in the kitchen.

"It's smaller," Ivory said, bringing them all back into the family room. "But it's good for us. And look, there's room for everyone."

Micah sat in a straight-backed chair someone had brought in from the kitchen table, so he wasn't sure about that. But the seating arrangements were doable for a birthday party that would likely break up and expand into the kitchen, and then outside to the huge deck at the back of the house.

"Welcome, everyone," Tripp said, beaming out at them all. "First, we want to say welcome to Grandma Lucy and Grandpa Jerry. It's your first family party."

"Probably be their last," someone said.

"Nah," Liam said. "They'll just turn down their hearing aids and they'll be good."

"Wish I had hearing aids," Skyler said, grinning. Several people laughed then, and Tripp held up his hand to stop the group from snowballing into chaos.

"We have a lot of July birthdays, and we're going to sing to Isaac, JJ, and Warren. Then we have a picnic planned, and we can hang out here, over in the kitchen, or outside. We have the shade up, and the house came with misters, so it's not terrible out there."

Micah thought it would still be terrible, but he didn't say so. He sang happy birthday to the little ones and watched as they each opened a few presents. Conrad tried to take one of Isaac's toy cars from him, and a small scuffle ensued, which ended in Rhett getting up and taking his son away from the party for a minute.

"He's gotten bad about grabbing things," he explained from the mouth of the hallway, where he'd sat the boy further down and told him to stay.

"Oh, he's just a baby himself," Momma said. "I can't stand to hear him cry."

"He's fine, Momma," Rhett said, folding his arms and looking down the hallway. Momma's anxiety touched Micah's heart, but she didn't get up and go try to rescue Conrad. A few minutes later, Rhett went to get him, and he brought the tearful boy back to the party and made him apologize to Isaac.

Isaac didn't even seem to know what had happened, but Conrad hugged him—nearly choking him—and asked, "I play cars?" He squatted down right in front of Isaac, both hands on his knees, his want for that toy car palpable. Micah wanted to get up and get it for him. Heck, he'd buy him a whole chest of them, because Conrad was the cutest little boy on the planet.

Ivory said, "Isaac, you say 'yes.' We share." She gently took the car from him and gave it to Conrad. Isaac looked at the car, and looked at Conrad, and looked at his mother. Ivory smiled and nodded and said, "Yes. You play with Conrad. Share with him."

"Share," Isaac said, and he picked up another toy, this one a truck.

"I've got hamburgers and hot dogs ready to go," Tripp said, and Micah got up.

"That's my cue," he said. "Who wants to eat with Uncle Micah?"

"I do!" Denise cried out, scrambling to get to her feet. "Can I have a hot dog, Uncle Micah?"

"Sure thing, sweets." He grinned at her and extended his hand for her to take.

"Come with me, Mom," Momma said, helping Grandma Lucy to her feet. "You have to get in the front of the line with these boys or there won't be any food left."

"You can go in front of me, Grandma," Micah said, smiling at her.

"Wait," Wyatt roared. "We're not doing announcements?"

"We don't need to do announcements at every blasted family function," Jeremiah said.

"Yeah, but we should," Skyler said. "There's a lot of us."

"Send a text," Jeremiah argued back.

"You think I should've just texted y'all that I'd gotten married?"

"Boys," Momma said.

"I'm just saying the announcements have gotten out of hand."

"I agree with Jeremiah," Liam said.

Micah didn't care much. If someone had an announcement they wanted to make, why couldn't they?

"The food is hot now," Liam continued. "If we do announcements, then there's all this congratulating."

"Oh, heaven forbid we celebrate something," Whitney said. "Life is hard enough. Shouldn't we be glad we can congratulate someone on something?"

"Boys," Momma said again.

"I agree with Whitney," Ivory said. She stood up and got up on one of the chairs. "Okay, enough." She waved her hands, and everyone quieted down. "It's our house, and our rules. Who has an announcement?" She scanned the crowd, and Micah met Simone's eye. She shook her head, and he casually looked away. She was still very early in her pregnancy, and he understood her desire to wait.

"Wyatt?"

"Yeah, but now I feel stupid," he said, glancing around.

"Just say it," Jeremiah said. "Or I will, because I bet we all know what it is."

"You know what?" Wyatt asked, clearly angry now. "You're being a jerk." He bent and picked up Warren. "I can get a hamburger on the way back to my place."

"Wyatt," Marcy said after him, but Wyatt started for the front door and left. Actually left. Marcy looked like she might cry, and Mal stepped over to her and put her arm around her. "Sorry," Marcy said, her bottom lip quivering. "It was a great party, Ivory." She picked up her diaper bag and purse and followed her husband.

"Jeremiah," Whitney said, her face growing redder by the second. "You go apologize right now."

Jeremiah had the decency to look ashamed. He stood up and held up both hands. "I'm sorry, everyone. He's right." He went after Marcy and Wyatt too, and Micah didn't think he'd ever heard his family be so quiet and so still—at least outside of a church.

"What's going on?" Grandpa Jerry asked, turning to face everyone. "I turned down my hearing aids, and I think I missed something."

Micah tried to hold back the laughter, but he couldn't. It came out, first as a snort and then as a big, full, belly laugh. Others joined in, and the tension in the house broke. He took Denise to get her hot dog, and he kept a close eye on the front door. Neither Wyatt nor Jeremiah ever did come back to the party, and Micah worried about both of them.

He finally decided to text Wyatt. *Hey, can I come sit with you in the hot tub this week?*

His brother didn't answer for the longest time, and that only made Micah's stomach squirm even more. When he was full of cake, and Simone looked like she might fall asleep right there on Ivory's couch, he said, "Let's go, sweetheart. I'm going to take you home, and then I'm going to go visit Wyatt."

They said their goodbyes, and there were a lot of people to hug and thank. Finally outside, Micah helped Simone into the truck and took her home. He'd just kissed her on the forehead as she lay in bed, her eyes already closed, when his phone chimed.

His heart leapt as he read Wyatt's text. *I'm okay*, he'd said. *Sorry I got mad and made everything awkward.*

Not on you, bro, Micah sent back. *Jeremiah was being a jerk.*

He carries a lot of responsibility, Wyatt sent back.

So do all of us. Micah wasn't going to let his brother off that easy. Heck, Rhett had four children under the age of three. Jeremiah and Whitney had two kids—and they'd chosen to have them close together. Micah was supposed to just give him a pass because he was tired? Because he had the wife and family he'd always wanted?

Micah was tired too. So was Wyatt. They could all name something plaguing them, and none of them had practically made an announcement that wasn't theirs to make.

I embarrassed Marcy, Wyatt said. *I feel so stupid.*

Micah didn't know how to make this better for his brother. Out of all of them, Wyatt was the biggest, the strongest, the best. He always had been. But he'd also come with the biggest, strongest, and best heart. He didn't deserve to be belittled and made to feel stupid.

He tapped the phone icon and lifted his phone to his ear. "Hey," Wyatt said, and the word dripped with misery.

"Hey," Micah said, realizing he still hadn't left the bedroom. He glanced at Simone and hurried out, closing the door behind him. "Tell Marcy congratulations. You don't need to make a big announcement for it to be big news."

Wyatt didn't say anything, and Micah just nodded to himself. "Love you, brother. I can come sit with you if you want. Grab a dog from the ranch and come up."

"Nah," Wyatt said, his voice a bit thick. "I'm okay. Marcy's asleep with her head in my lap, and...I'm okay."

"Okay," Micah said. "I'm a text away."

"Thank you, Micah." Wyatt almost whispered the words, and the call ended. Micah stood still for a moment, trying to find that inner voice that told him what to do. Go talk to Jeremiah? Find out why he was so angry again? Or leave it alone?

Leave it alone.

Satisfied, Micah went down the opposite hall to his office, where he could work on the plans for Grape Seed Ranch.

CHAPTER TWENTY-SIX

Jeremiah knew he'd messed up. Regret lanced through him with the strength and pain of a white-hot blade, and he wished he could go back in time and fix things. Whitney rode in the truck with him, her silence the worst of all.

He'd apologized to Wyatt as the man sat in his truck in Tripp's driveway. He wouldn't get out, and Jeremiah understood why. He and Marcy had left a few minutes later, and Jeremiah couldn't face the family again. So Whitney had brought the kids out, and they were almost back to the ranch.

Jeremiah wanted to disappear out to the stables, where he could gripe to the horses, and they wouldn't judge him. But he knew that wasn't helpful. He'd been doing it for months, and while he loved his equines, they weren't the kind of therapy he needed.

His stomach clenched, which caused his throat to tighten, which made his fingers strangle the steering wheel. He'd felt like this before in his life, and he could pinpoint exactly when.

When Laura Ann had left him at the altar.

He wasn't sure why he had to deal with these feelings of failure and anger again. They felt like a curse from God Jeremiah would have to wrestle with for his entire life.

Start the match then, he told himself.

"I'm sorry," Jeremiah said, glancing at Whitney. "Talk to me, please. I'm sorry."

She turned her head toward him, and it seemed to happen in slow motion. He loved her so much, and he could not lose her. But the truth was, they'd been drifting apart for months now—since his anger and personal failings had started to infect him again.

"I'm sorry," he said again. "I feel like I'm doing the best I can, but I know it's not good enough. I'm…angry. I'm *angry* all the time. Something easy like a rope being hung on the peg the wrong way sends me into a rage." His throat closed, and he shook his head. She deserved so much better than him.

He'd *been* better in the past.

"What are you mad about?" she asked.

"I don't know," he said. "It makes no sense. I don't have anything to be angry about. It's stupid. I know it is." He turned onto the road that led back to Seven Sons. "I need to go back to therapy."

"I think that's a good first step," she said as he reached to press the button to open the garage door. It started to lift at the same time Clara Jean started to fuss. Whitney turned to look at her, and Jeremiah knew something else he could do.

"Will you go out with me?" he asked. Whitney looked at him, surprise on her face.

"What?"

"Without the kids," he said. "Just me and you, the way we used to. Let's take the dogs hiking. Or go to Wilde & Organic and you can pick out random ingredients and I'll see what I can make for dinner." He smiled at her as he came to a stop in the garage. "Remember how that used to be one of our date nights?"

Whitney smiled, and though it was slow as it spread her lips, it was there. "Yeah," she said. "That was fun."

"I love the kids," Jeremiah said. "I really love them. I feel guilty leaving you home with them all day. And then when I'm home, I'm tired and stressed, and I'm annoyed at them for being kids." The words just streamed from him now. "And then I feel guilty that I'm not enjoying them for who they are, and for how old they are. I know I'm not paying attention to you enough, and I know I don't provide the adult conversation you need."

He pressed his lips together and switched his gaze out the windshield, because he was about to cry. And Jeremiah Walker did not cry. He worked through the problem. He made things right. He got the help he needed.

Get the help you need.

"I want to hire a foreman," he said to the cabinets in the back of the garage. "I don't want to run the ranch anymore." When the thoughts came into his mind, he said them. "I want to be a father and husband. I want to take the kids to the zoo with you. You're more important than the haying or the branding. So are they."

"Go," JJ said from the backseat, but both Jeremiah and Whitney ignored him. Whit slid across the seat and put her hand on the side of Jeremiah's face, gently making him look at her.

"I love you, Jeremiah Walker," she said. "The best thing about you is you're not afraid to fail. You're not afraid to admit it when you're wrong. You're willing to change and be better."

He blinked at her, sure he hadn't managed to rope this angel into his life. "I'm going to do better."

"I know you are." She kissed him, and Jeremiah hadn't actually been kissed like that for a while. She told him how she felt without words, and he kissed her back, hoping she knew how much he appreciated her for her good heart and bright spirit.

"Go!" JJ yelled, pulling on the door handle now. He'd already gotten himself out of the car seat, which he sometimes did while Jeremiah drove.

Jeremiah pulled away and ducked his head. "All right, Jay," he said. "Daddy will get you out." He glanced at Whitney again and got out of the truck, stepping to the back door to get JJ out. "You can't yell at Daddy, though, okay? You have to be nice."

"Nice," JJ said, stuffing his chubby fingers in his mouth immediately afterward.

"Yes," Jeremiah said. He loved his son, but JJ was a bit of a devil. "Strong willed," Momma called him. And while he drove Jeremiah to frustration most days, he wanted time to enjoy his son too.

"Let's go get the dogs, okay?"

JJ grinned, and Jeremiah checked on Whitney to make sure she was okay getting Clara, and she was.

"I'm going to put her down for a nap," Whitney said.

"We're going to go throw a ball for the dogs," he said. "Okay?"

She nodded, and they went inside the homestead. Jeremiah knew he wasn't out of the weeds yet. Whitney would forgive him, because she'd been living with him and loved him. But Wyatt could literally never talk to him again.

And Jeremiah couldn't stand that. He didn't want family functions to be awkward, and he'd made them that way. Foolishness filled him as he got out the dog treats and the ball. Winston had his front paws on the window by the time Jeremiah had everything ready, and he pushed the dog back, chuckling. "Let me open the door."

He did, and the dogs ran outside, Willow barking in her excitement. He loaded up the ball in the thrower and launched it from the deck, sending both dogs after it.

JJ toddled after him, and Jeremiah watched him navigate the steps. "Good job, Jay," he said. "You want to give them a treat?" He handed his son a beef bit as Willow got to the ball first, and the two dogs started back toward them. Willow dropped it, but Winston immediately lunged for the ball again, as if he'd brought it the whole way back.

"Drop it," Jeremiah said. "Give her the treat, Jay."

JJ did, and Willow sat back, ready for the ball to be thrown again. Winston still had it in his mouth, though. "Drop it," he said again, holding up the treat. That got the dog to release the ball, and Jeremiah treated him, picked up the ball, and launched it again.

Willow was simply faster than Winston, and the only time he got the ball before her was when she bobbled it and it went bouncing off in a different direction. After only a few throws, JJ lost interest and went over to the sandbox Micah had built when the boy was born. He had trucks and cars there, and he could play happily in the sand for hours.

Jeremiah kept throwing the ball until he couldn't put off calling Wyatt for another minute. And he'd probably need to call his mother too. And then send a family text, begging everyone for forgiveness.

You're a good man and an excellent father. His father's words from a few days ago meant the world to Jeremiah. All he'd wanted was for his parents to be proud of him. He did sometimes try to be superhuman.

He'd made a mistake today. Everyone made mistakes, and he cast a look at JJ to make sure the boy was still playing nearby, and then he bowed his head and prayed. *Dear Lord, I'm so sorry for letting the anger inside me come out. Wyatt didn't deserve that. Help me to find a way to make it right. Help him to forgive me.*

He took a breath and paused, taking a moment to listen.

He just heard the wind, but his thoughts also quieted. *Help me manage this anger. I want to do better. With Thy help, I know I can do and be better.*

"Daddy," JJ said, and Jeremiah looked up, his prayer over.

"What, buddy?"

"Cow." He pointed, and Jeremiah got up and looked around the corner of the deck. Sure enough, a cow stood there—exactly where it shouldn't be.

Instant irritation bloomed inside him, and he had to pull back on it. "Come over here, Jay," he said, walking toward his son with sure steps. His beef cows weren't exactly dangerous, but they were unpredictable if they got spooked. He picked up JJ in one arm and pulled out his phone with his other hand.

"Orion," he said when the man answered. "We've got at least one cow out. It's in the backyard of the homestead."

"I'll grab Wallace. He's out with the goats, and I just finished with the horses."

"Great," Jeremiah said. "Thank you, Orion."

"Yep," the cowboy said, and that was it. He didn't know Jeremiah had belittled his brother in front of everyone, ruining the announcement Wyatt had probably been excited to say.

"Let's go in and get lunch," he said to JJ, because they'd left the party before Tripp had served the hamburgers and hot dogs. Inside, he found Whitney in the kitchen, stirring something in a pot.

"Mac and cheese," she said as Jeremiah set JJ down.

"I'm going to call Wyatt," he said. "Okay?"

She met his eye and nodded. "You can go up there if you need to."

"I'm going to see if he'll talk to me first." Jeremiah's heart beat in a strange rhythm, and he sent up another prayer that Wyatt would answer his phone.

CHAPTER TWENTY-SEVEN

W yatt looked at his phone when it lit up on the table beside him. He knew Jeremiah would call, but his first instinct was to ignore him. He'd already apologized once. He didn't need to drag things out.

"You're not going to answer it?" Marcy asked.

Wyatt forked up another bite of spaghetti. Since he'd stormed out of the party, they hadn't eaten, and Marcy had whipped up pasta for them. He'd apologized at least a dozen times to her. He'd forced her to choose between him and the birthday party for their son, and she'd chosen him.

"Not right now," he said. "I already snapped once when I was annoyed, and I don't want to do it again."

"Okay." Marcy pushed another piece of garlic bread onto Warren's tray. "It's smart not to talk until you're ready."

Wyatt watched the phone darken again, and a slip of disappointment pulled through him. He didn't want to have contention between him and Jeremiah. He usually got along well with everyone, and he knew that if he were on Jeremiah's side of the equation, he'd want to clear the air as quickly as possible.

Warren let out a screech, pushing his hands through the food on his tray, sending some of it flying.

"Okay, buddy," Marcy said. "You're done." She got up and unbuckled him from the high chair. "I'm going to get him cleaned up and put him down for a nap. Want to watch a movie with me?"

"Always," Wyatt said, realizing he was done with his lunch too. "Thanks for lunch, sugar." He picked up his bowl and took it into the kitchen, where she stood at the sink, wrestling with their boy to try to get the sauce off his hands and face.

Wyatt put his hand on her lower back and said, "I'm real sorry. I didn't mean to embarrass you."

"I know." She smiled at him, and Wyatt's heart started beating normally again. "It'll only be awkward for like, a second, Wyatt. It'll be fine. I'm okay."

"Everyone's going to be checking on us all day."

"Good," Marcy said. "You need that."

Wyatt searched her face. "I do?"

"Yes, Wyatt," she said. "You're so used to being loved, and I think Jeremiah doing what he did today knocked you back into reality." She smiled at him and made one more swipe at Warren's face. "And it's okay to be reminded that your family cares about you." She hitched the baby higher on her hip. "Okay, Mister. Time for a nap."

Wyatt watched her leave the kitchen, thinking about

what she'd said. He knew his family cared about him. Didn't he?

"Of course I do," he said to himself. But yeah, Jeremiah's behavior had made him wonder why he'd been so excited to share their pregnancy with the family.

Feeling calm and like he could talk to Jeremiah now, Wyatt called him back.

"Wyatt," Jeremiah said after only one ring. "I'm—do you have a minute to talk? I can come up there too."

"You don't need to make the drive," Wyatt said, feeling his chest tighten and then loosen. "Listen, I'm sorry I got all worked up and walked out. That was a bit dramatic."

Jeremiah said nothing, and Wyatt pulled the phone away from his ear to make sure the call was still connected. It was. "Jeremiah?"

"You're apologizing to me?"

"I didn't have to react that way," Wyatt said. "So…yeah. I'm sorry I let my irritation shoot to the top of my head and come out of my mouth." He knew better, that was for sure. His public relations manager would've been mortified.

"I know I already said it back at Tripp's, but *I* wanted to apologize again."

"Then do it."

"I'm sorry," Jeremiah said. "I'm…struggling right now."

"Yeah." Wyatt started nodding as he moved over to the couch in the living room. "Gonna get some help for that?"

"I am," he said. "I do too much around the ranch, and I'm going to do something about that. I'm going to go back to therapy too. And I'm going to get out to Three Rivers and do some equine therapy too."

Wyatt couldn't help smiling, because Jeremiah knew how to root the darkness out of his soul, and Wyatt had no doubt he'd do it. "I'd like to do the equine therapy too," he said. "Could we go together?"

"I'd like that," Jeremiah said.

"I'll call Pete," Wyatt said. "I know they book pretty far in advance, but I'll see if he can get us in."

"Wyatt," Jeremiah said, his voice coming through the line a little strangely. "You're a good man," he finally said, the words rough around the edges now. "A good brother. I love you, and I'm real sorry I upset you."

"I love you, too," Wyatt said, because he did love all of his brothers. Jeremiah was intense, sure. But he was a good human, and he did amazing things with his life.

"Okay." Jeremiah cleared his throat. "Well, let me know about the equines. I can get away any time."

"Yeah? You really can?"

"I'll make it work."

"I'll let you know."

Jeremiah cleared his throat again and said, "Thank you, Wyatt," in the softest, gentlest voice Wyatt had heard him use in at least six months.

"Yep," he said, because his own chest and voice had grown tight too. "Talk to you soon." He hung up before his own emotions could overflow, and he pressed his eyes closed. He didn't want animosity between him and Jeremiah. Between him and anyone, and he said, "Thank you, Lord."

"Okay," Marcy said, coming back into the room. "What are we watching?"

"You pick," he said. "I'll probably fall asleep."

"Nope," she said, grinning at him. "*I'm* going to fall asleep. You pick."

CHAPTER TWENTY-EIGHT

I vory hadn't felt this sick since she'd been throwing up every morning while she was pregnant with Isaac. She glanced at the little boy buckled in the back seat of the car. "You're going to see Gramma again, sweetheart," she said to the two-year-old.

Which meant Ivory would have to face her mother too. "It's going to be so fun," she said, and that was definitely to psyche herself up. Tripp had taken Oliver to school, as he normally did, because her parents had done what they normally did—picked the worst time for Ivory and the others to do anything.

School had just started up again, and Oliver didn't want to miss his first day at the junior high. Ivory didn't blame him, and she wasn't going to make him miss it so he could see his grandparents' reaction to the house.

Tripp had promised to get doughnuts and meet her at the house, and Ivory had left ten minutes late on purpose in the hopes that he'd get there first. Sure enough, when she rounded the corner and the house where she'd lived for a few years came into view, Tripp's giant black truck sat in the driveway.

So did a huge moving van and her mother's bright red sedan. Ivory's palms were suddenly slick, and she wiped them on her jean shorts, one at a time. She probably should've worn pants to move boxes, but she couldn't go home and change now.

She pulled into the driveway, which had plenty of room for all the vehicles, and got Isaac out of the back seat. He babbled to himself as he walked along, seemingly one step away from falling. His language wasn't as developed as JJ's, something Ivory had worried about as she spent more time with Whitney, Marcy, Callie, and Evelyn. Simone and Mal came to the girls' days too, and Ivory had done her best to include them though they didn't have children. She'd want to be included if she didn't, and when she'd hosted last month's get-together, she'd had everything ready for bunko, as well as plenty to do for the kids so they kept busy in the living room while the ladies played in the dining area.

Penny brought a new Texas treat every time, and Ivory had really enjoyed getting to know her better. She went to lunch with Penny, just the two of them, too, and Ivory loved how open and warm her mother-in-law was. She'd determined that she wanted to be like that for her kids, no matter who they married, because she certainly hadn't received such treatment from her parents—and they were *her* parents.

Bless Tripp, she prayed as she went up the steps and opened the door. "Mom?" she called. "I'm here." Her husband was a saint, and Ivory thanked the Lord every day for him. She knew she was lucky to have him, though he was the one who claimed to have hit the lottery the day he met her.

Tripp appeared back in the kitchen and gestured to her. "Come here, babe," he said.

Ivory looked at Isaac. "There's Daddy. Can you say daddy?"

"Dad," Isaac said, reaching for his father. Tripp grinned at the boy and took him from Ivory. He plunked a kiss on the baby's head and then kissed Ivory real quick.

"How long have you been here?" she hissed out of the corner of her mouth. Her mother stood in the kitchen, opening drawers as if she expected rats to come springing out of them.

"Five minutes," he said. "Your dad is in the bathroom."

So he'd been alone with her mother. Great. "Mom," Ivory said. "What do you think?"

Her mom looked up, and Ivory recalled every negative thought she'd had that day. Her mother's eyes shone with tears, and she broke down crying as she rushed at Ivory.

"Oh, uh, okay," Ivory said, holding onto her. Then, as if God Himself had opened a bottle of magic and poured it out, everything inside Ivory softened. She closed her eyes and drew in a deep breath of her mother's scent.

This was her mother. The woman who'd given her life. She had been difficult to live with sometimes. She made mistakes, like everyone else. But Ivory could forgive her. She could.

"It's wonderful," she said. "And I've only been in here. But it's just wonderful. Thank you, Ivory." She sniffed and pulled back, keeping her head low as she wiped her eyes. "We'll definitely pay you rent."

"You don't need to, ma'am," Tripp said, meeting Ivory's eye. They'd discussed at length whether or not to tell her parents about his money. Their money. All the money.

Ivory nodded, and Tripp looked back at her mom. "We have plenty of money. We bought the house with cash, and we don't have a payment. So...we don't need you to pay rent."

Her mom looked at Ivory, who just nodded. She wasn't an overly emotional person, but her throat felt like a straw, hardly able to get enough air down it.

"Don't say anything to your dad," she said. "But thank you."

Tripp stepped over to her and hugged her. "We're glad you're here, Joan. Tell us what to do, and we'll do it. You've got us for a few hours, and my brothers should be here soon."

Ivory's dad came out of the hallway that led back into the master suite. "This house is amazing," he said, smiling at Ivory. He hugged her, but it wasn't the same soft, forgiving hug Ivory had experienced with her mother. "Are we unloading?"

"Yes," Ivory's mom said. "Let's start unloading, at least the boxes and little things. The brothers can get the bigger items." She exchanged another glance with Ivory, who reached for her mom's hand. They walked out to the driveway together while Tripp opened the garage door and her dad went to turn around the moving truck so the back faced the house.

"What are you going to do here?" Ivory asked.

"Oh, I don't know," her mother said, sighing. "I'll probably look for a secretarial job. Your dad will do what he's always done."

Nothing, Ivory thought, watching him. He'd get a job probably, but he'd only keep it for a while. Sometimes six months. Sometimes a year. By the time Ivory was old enough to realize that her dad had a new job all the time, she'd also discovered how very poor her family was. Her mother did the best she could, and she'd retired from the doctor's office where she'd worked for two decades a year or so ago.

"You should look at the hospital," Ivory said. "A friend of mine says they're always needing people."

Her mom smiled at Ivory. "I will." Her eyes burned bright, and she hugged Ivory again. "I'm so glad we're here."

"Me too," Ivory said, and for the first time, she meant it. She didn't expect things to be perfect, because families weren't perfect. The little tiff between Wyatt and Jeremiah from a few weeks ago proved that.

But they tried. They forgave. They included, and they loved each other. So Ivory would try. She would figure out how to forgive. She'd include her parents in as much as she could, and she'd love them.

Tripp came toward her and said, "He needs to be changed, and then why don't you see if you can put a movie on for him or something? Maybe your mom can watch him and you can help me out here?" He looked at her, and Ivory reached for Isaac.

"I'll take him," her mom said. "You're definitely stronger than I am, Ivory."

"Wyatt is five minutes away," Tripp said. "And Skyler and Micah will be here in ten."

Ivory grinned at her husband and linked her arm through his. "I guess I can help for ten minutes."

CHAPTER TWENTY-NINE

S imone stepped into the pair of pantyhose, pulling to get them all the way up. Her baby belly wasn't showing yet, but she could feel it. She was only three and a half months along, and she hadn't told anyone but Micah yet. He'd confessed that he'd told Wyatt, but the secret was safely in his brother's vault.

"Do you have the flowers?" someone asked her, and Simone glanced up. The activity backstage made her dizzy, but she managed to nod to the prop sitting on the table beside her.

"Right there." She hurried to reach for the barrettes to hold her hair back. Her character wore them all the time, as the play made sure to point out, and she couldn't go on stage without them.

Tonight was the last night of *A Long Way Home*, and Simone would honestly be relieved when it was over. Attending rehearsals the past few months had been difficult, and she'd almost quit a few times. Micah had encouraged her to continue, and she'd only kept going because he had to go too.

She loved acting, but it meant long hours after the work day was supposed to be done, and she didn't love this role. But she'd do it one more time, because the entire Walker family should be in attendance tonight.

That only made her nerves buzz even louder, and she stepped up to a mirror and pressed her lips together, deciding she needed more lipstick. Definitely more. Her father and Belinda had come last night, but they'd be there again tonight. Ivory's parents were coming.

Simone's stomach lurched, and she froze. Could that be the baby?

Impossible, she told herself. She'd spent plenty of time researching pregnancy and what to expect over the past couple of months and she was only fourteen weeks along. It was too soon to feel the baby.

She was just nervous. And tired.

Micah had been gone a lot in the past six weeks, and Simone had spent her days and nights alone—any that she wasn't here at the theater with him. He worked all day long out at Shiloh Ridge, and then he'd come home and get on the phone with Dwayne Carver down in Grape Seed Falls, or another client, or he'd go across the street to Skyler's, or up to Church Ranches to see Wyatt, or he'd fall asleep on the couch the moment he finished eating.

He hadn't even started her she-shed in the backyard, and Simone wasn't going to ask him about it. She had her workshop a half-mile down the road, and it still served her just fine.

She did miss Micah though, and she hoped that once… she didn't even know what. Maybe this was just her life now. Working in the she-shed at the Shining Star. Coming home alone to the big house while Micah worked and visited his brothers.

Sourness filled her mouth, along with a strange sense of unhappiness. She'd seen Callie weather a storm exactly like this, as Liam still worked a very demanding job. Whitney had cried about it at one of their girls' gatherings after the birthday party, but she'd only broken down for sixty seconds.

Then she'd wiped her beautiful eyes and said Jeremiah was going back to counseling and that he was going to hire a foreman.

Evelyn had asked, "Why do these Walkers think they have to work twenty-four hours a day? Don't they know they're already rich?"

Because Wyatt still worked at Bowman's Breeds, though he had more money than Micah and Skyler combined. Skyler worked on the ranch and in the office until at least six, Mal said. Rhett had just taken another case, even though he wasn't going to.

Only Ivory reported that Tripp worked less than full-time, and Simone had kept quiet. She didn't want to say anything bad about Micah, because she wanted him to achieve all of his dreams. And she knew better than most that achieving dreams took a lot of time, effort, and energy.

"Ready?" Susan asked. "You should be in place."

"Right." Simone said, putting down the lipstick container without using it. She hurried out of the dressing room, her skirts swishing against her legs. The shoes pinched, but she'd performed in them about a dozen times now. She could do it one more time.

She approached Kelly, the woman playing Adelaide, and put a smile on her face. "Ready?"

"Last time," Kelly said, smiling.

"Are you sad?" Simone asked.

"A little, yeah." Kelly took her hand and squeezed it. "I have loved performing with you. You are so talented."

"Thank you, Kelly," Simone said, her heart warming with the compliment. "You are as well. Just a gorgeous singer."

"Thank you."

The opening notes of the first song started from the live orchestra, and Simone nodded to her. She'd be on stage in just a minute, and she closed her eyes and took a deep breath. She knew Micah had stepped beside her before she opened her eyes.

"Hey," he whispered. "Last time. You're going to kill it."

She smiled her acting smile at him too, loving how he looked in all the stage makeup and that fake beard. He could grow one, but he said it itched too much, and he hated that. So he glued one to his face to perform every night.

"They're going to be loud," he said.

"Who?" she asked.

"My brothers." He grinned. "Good luck."

With that, her note sounded, and Simone had to step

away from him. Out onto the stage, under the lights. Simone loved it out here, and everything else disappeared. There was no audience. No one else on the stage at all. Just her, and everyone could see her.

She stepped right up to Kelly's side, linking her arm through the other woman's. Then she turned her head toward the audience and sang her first line, nearly getting knocked back by the cheering that definitely had the Walker tones all over it.

They were so loud, she could barely hear herself sing. Heat filled her face, but she finished her part of the song, and Kelly sang her part. They ended the song in harmony, one of Simone's favorite parts of the whole show, right there in the first five minutes.

The note ended, and the orchestra kept playing as normal. There was usually applause for the opening number, of course, but tonight, the whooping and hollering was downright deafening. She heard her name more than once, and she knew then that she should've given those Walker brothers a lesson in theater etiquette.

At the same time, she also knew in that moment that she belonged to them. They belonged to her. So they were loud. She better get used to it, she supposed, and the orchestra started the transition piece again, only moving on once the crowd—the Walkers, really—had quieted down.

A couple of hours later, she took Micah's hand and went out into the hall to see his family. They weren't hard to spot, as every Walker male seemed to be taller than everyone else in Three Rivers.

"There they are," someone said, and another cheer went up. Simone had thought they'd been loud for her, but when Micah had come out and done his minor part, they'd nearly brought the roof crashing down.

Simone and Micah started hugging everyone, and people started talking about ice cream and doughnuts, and Simone kept the smile on her face. She couldn't be lonely while in such a big group of people, could she?

But yes, she could. She had been before. And tonight, that bitter loneliness stayed with her though she wasn't alone until much later, behind the bathroom door in her house, brushing her teeth while Micah checked on something for Bear.

———

"BUT THEY'RE GOING TO BE HERE IN FIVE MINUTES," SIMONE said.

"I know," Micah said. "You go with them and tell them."

"I want to tell your parents together," she said, frustrated beyond belief. She'd managed to stop working in time to get home and wash the black paint from her hands. She'd showered, checked on the roast she'd put in the slow cooker that morning, and made coffee, all in anticipation of Penny and Gideon's arrival. They were supposed to go over to the Shining Star to visit Gideon's miniature horses, who still lived there, and have dinner together.

She and Micah had planned to tell his parents about

their new grandbaby coming in February, and she couldn't believe Micah wouldn't be there.

"I'm sorry," Micah said, but he sounded distracted already. He said something else, clearly not for her, which meant he was having this conversation in front of other people. Simone wanted to throw the phone across the room. But that would break something, and then his mother would know how frustrated she was.

"I'll let you go then," Simone said, ending the call though Micah started to say something. She half-expected him to call back, but he didn't, and that only made her angrier.

The play had ended a week ago. September was almost upon them. Mal was due any day now, and Simone thought Micah would be around more now that the construction at Shiloh Ridge was entering its third month and the play was over.

But he'd actually signed a new client on Wednesday, and she'd smiled though she'd wanted to scream. He'd been *so happy*, and she couldn't burst that.

A knock sounded on the door, and Simone's gaze flew to it. She couldn't ignore it, though that urge was powerful. Instead, she pretended she was in another play, this one where she had to act pleasant and delighted to see her in-laws.

"Hello, dear," Penny said when she opened the door. She hugged her, Penny's standard greeting for most people.

"Hey, Simone," Gideon said, not quite as tough as he'd been before the car accident, over a year ago now. He was softer somehow, and Simone sure did love him. She hugged him too, eliciting an "Oh," from him.

"Should we go over to the ranch?" she asked, stepping back quickly. She'd gotten better control of her emotions, and she hadn't teared up in days.

"Sure," he said. "Where's Micah?"

"He's still out at Shiloh Ridge," Simone said, turning away from them so they wouldn't be able to see the displeasure on her face. "Let me grab a couple bottles of water, and we can go." She'd already gotten them out and set them on the counter. She retrieved them, and followed them out the front door to Gideon's truck.

He drove now, but he didn't go fast, not that he could on the dirt road anyway. He went past the homestead and turned to go along the road that led back to the barns and stables. He parked there, and they all got out.

No one spoke, and Simone loved the silence out on the ranch. The way the wind whispered through the tall grass and tried to play games by ducking around the corners of buildings. She loved the evening sky as the sun started to go down on another day.

She drew in a deep breath and sighed.

"Everything okay?" Penny asked, looking at her. She held her husband's hand, and Simone's chest tightened. She wanted to be Penny and Gideon, strolling along when she was old and gray, Micah's hand in hers. But at the moment, she couldn't see that future for them.

"Micah and I invited you out to spend time with you," she said. "I'm sorry he's stuck at work."

Penny's eyes sharpened, and Simone regretted saying anything. "I still have dinner at the house for when we get back," she hurried to add. "He said he'd probably make it for that." He hadn't said that, but Simone started praying that he'd get the nudge to finish up at Shiloh Ridge and get home.

They reached the fence, and Gideon clicked with his mouth. The closest horses lifted their heads and immediately started toward him.

"We wanted to tell you something," Simone said, focusing on one of the gray miniature horses. She did like them, as they possessed a charm in their smaller bodies and hooves. "I'm expecting a baby in February."

Penny sucked in a breath and then let out a squeal. "Oh, Simone, I'm so happy for you." She didn't hold back her tears as she hugged Simone tightly.

"Thanks," she said. She'd wanted to be a mom for as long as she could remember. "I hope I know how to raise a baby."

"Of course you do," Penny said, stepping back.

"Congratulations, Simone," Gideon said warmly, hugging her again. "You and Micah will be wonderful parents."

She nodded, her eyes going back to that gray horse. This should be one of the happiest, most content moments of her life. But it wasn't, because Micah wasn't there.

CHAPTER THIRTY

Micah knew he was in trouble the moment he stepped into the house. Number one, all the lights were off. Completely off. Simone always left two lights on for him—the one over the stove in the kitchen, and the lamp on the end table next to the hall that led down to their bedroom.

Everything hurt, from his feet to his head, and Micah needed painkillers and his bed. He fumbled his way into the kitchen, finally reaching a light switch. He pushed it, only to have the garbage disposal start grinding. The loud noise startled him, and he muttered under his breath as he turned it off. The switch next to it got the light above the sink on, and he got the painkillers out of the cabinet next to the sink.

With four of those downed, he turned around to see Simone standing there. She wore those sexy, silky black pajamas he liked, but he didn't move. "Sorry," he said.

"What kept you?" she asked, her voice like ice.

He had promised to be home in time for dinner tonight. After he'd missed dinner with his parents last week, she'd sat him down and told him he worked too much. He hadn't been able to disagree, and he'd promised to cut back. Work less. Be home—and present—at night.

He wasn't keeping track, but he knew Simone was. And he knew he'd only been home on time once since making the promise.

"They poured the foundation while the ground was too wet," he said. "So we had to get an emergency crew out to the ranch, and it took forever."

"And I suppose you didn't have service?"

"It was spotty," he hedged. The truth was, he'd signed a new client, who had hired another builder who had flaked on them. And Micah didn't want to give them the same experience. He wanted them to have the complete opposite experience, in fact. The Thompson twins had plenty of money, and they wanted their ranch on the southeast side of Three Rivers to be ready to pass down to their kids. Mary and Amy Thompson were tough old birds, that was for sure, and Micah hadn't been able to tell them he had to leave because his wife would be mad if he wasn't home for dinner.

"Mary sent a loaf of her Amish bread," he said weakly. "I left it in my truck. I'll go get it."

"It's fine," Simone said, still glaring at him. "Micah, I can't keep living like this."

"I know things are crazy right now," he said. "They won't—"

"It's been crazy for months," she said. "You don't have to work fifteen hours a day. You don't even have to work at all."

He sighed, because they'd had this conversation twice now, and he was not in the mood to have it again. "It's late, Simone," he said. "And I have to leave for Grape Seed Falls in the morning." He didn't move, though. He couldn't get past his wife, who stood like a sentinel guarding the way to the bedroom.

"I want you to stay home from Grape Seed Falls," she said. "And come to the doctor with me."

He frowned, his exhaustion only growing. "You said you didn't need me to come."

"I know what I said," she said. "Now I want you to come."

She couldn't just change the rules of the game like that. "I have to go to Grape Seed," he said. "I can't cancel on Dwayne." He was supposed to be there for two weeks, too. He'd hired a professional demolition crew, and Micah planned to work as many hours as possible while at Grape Seed to get Dwayne's house as close to livable as he could. He and Felicity had moved into the generational house while the work was being done on the homestead, and Micah had promised he wouldn't keep them displaced for too long.

He silently begged Simone to understand.

"I don't want you to go," she said. "But you're a grown man. You make your own choices." She turned and walked away—down the wrong hall. Micah stared after her, and the house was so quiet, he could hear the bedroom door in the wrong wing of the house click closed.

Honestly, it would've been better had she slammed it. Hard. Yelled at him and called him names. Given him an ultimatum. She hadn't, but he knew there would be consequences if he chose to go to Grape Seed Falls in the morning.

"There will be huge consequences if you don't," he said to himself. He'd felt trapped like this before, in Temple, and it was not a pleasant feeling. No matter what he did, someone would be upset with him. How had he gotten in this position again?

And even more importantly, how did he get out?

His alarm went off before the sun had even thought about rising. Micah pulled himself from bed and into the shower, his mind sluggish but getting started. By the time he'd shaved and put the razor in his bag, he was having third and fourth doubts.

But he couldn't cancel on Dwayne. There was no one else to do the work, and Micah didn't know anyone down in Grape Seed Falls he could call for a last-minute build. Besides, Dwayne and Felicity had paid *him* for *his* custom cabinets. The custom dining room table. The custom fireplace mantel.

He was Micah Walker, and they'd paid for and wanted *his* craftsmanship.

He had to go.

Please help Simone understand, he prayed. He hadn't been able to make her understand, but he was only a man. Surely the Lord could soften her heart. Help her see that he hadn't meant to get himself into such a tight spot, especially with her.

He knew he didn't need to work, but he sure did like it. Especially this new venture he'd started, because every job was different. He got to work with people and make their dreams come true, and he found joy and fulfillment in a way he hadn't had before.

So he finished packing, zipped his bag closed, and headed out to the kitchen. Part of him thought he'd find Simone waiting for him again, but she wasn't there. The light he'd left on over the sink still shone into the darkness, and Micah decided to forgo making coffee and drive through somewhere.

He pulled open a drawer and took out a notebook, quickly scrawling a note for Simone and leaving it on the counter next to the coffee maker, where she'd surely see it. He looked over to the hallway she'd disappeared down last night, half a mind to go wake her and make her understand.

She'd said the Walker men had a stubborn streak that couldn't be budged, but he could say the same for her. He couldn't handle the confrontation this early in the morning, so he left the house and went into the garage. He felt like a rebellious teenager, trying to sneak out of the house. Skyler had done that numerous times growing up, but Micah had used the front door. His parents had probably given up on policing his schedule by the time he was old enough to want to sneak out to see the girl he liked.

He started his truck, cringing at how loud it was in this early morning hour. As he backed onto the dirt road and looked at the house, he once again said, "*Please* help her understand."

LATER THAT DAY, HE'D ARRIVED AT GRAPE SEED RANCH. HE'D met with Dwayne and Felicity, and he'd started on the accent wall, which was getting covered in barn wood from the oldest barn on the property. Dwayne had decided it was too unsafe to use, but he'd reclaimed the wood, and Micah was fitting it together on the short wall next to the back door. The room behind him was huge now, with the kitchen tucked into the corner, the bathroom behind that, and the stairs going up from there. But the pantry was gone, which left the view all the way to the front windows wide open.

Micah had repurposed the space, and he had painters coming in the morning, with flooring a few days after that. He was building new pantry doors, new cabinets, and a new island for a more functional—and beautiful kitchen.

He'd ordered new appliances as well, and the interior designer he'd found online would be here at the end of the week to go over colors for rugs, curtains, and furniture. Then Felicity and Dwayne would order what they wanted to complete the new house.

He'd texted Simone twice, with no response. His

thoughts weren't completely dominated by the task at hand, and he found himself wandering toward her with every board he tried, cut, and nailed into place.

Determined to call her later until she picked up, Micah kept up the pace around the house. He didn't have a moment to spare if he wanted this job done in two weeks. And he did, because he couldn't imagine telling Simone he had to come back here to finish the job. This was it. He got the two weeks, and all he could do was pray his wife would forgive him when he got back to Three Rivers.

CHAPTER THIRTY-ONE

"Look, Aunt Simone," Denise said, pointing down the row of pumpkins and sunflowers in the field where they walked "There's a rabbit."

Simone found the animal as it hopped. "There sure is," she said, smiling at such a simple gesture from nature. She kept hold of the girls' hand, because Simone needed an anchor right now.

Micah had only been gone for four days, and she missed him with the force of gravity. Still, she had been strong, and she hadn't answered any of his texts or calls. His last voice-mail had been, "Is this it then? You're just never going to talk to me again?"

There had been plenty of frustration in his voice. Simone had actually felt bad when she listened to it. Even now, she could hear the words echoing in her ears.

"Simone," Callie called, and Simone turned toward her. She pushed the flatbed cart, and it was nearly full.

"Looks like your mama has everything she needs," Simone said, tugging on Denise's hand. "Let's go." They left the field surrounding the nursery, joining Callie and Evelyn, who had come out to buy shrubs and trees and flower bulbs for the Shining Star with all four kids, by herself.

She had a new stroller that allowed her to put the babies in forward-facing seats, and had a little seat for Conrad, facing her. He loved it, as he could ride standing up, and Evelyn could get out of the house without relying on anyone else.

"Let's go start loading up," Simone said, taking Ginger from Callie so her sister could pay. "Stay right by me, Deni, okay?" They left the nursery with Evelyn, and Simone heard the distinct cry of a puppy to her right, and she looked that way.

"Oh, look at them," she said, detouring instantly. The white pups in the double-wide apple crate couldn't have been bigger than the palm of her hand, and she smiled widely at them as she looked at the two girls standing by the crate. "What kind are they?"

"Western terriers," one of the girls said. She didn't look older than twelve or thirteen. "They'll get to be about fifteen pounds."

Ginger weighed more than that, and Simone could carry her. "How much?" she asked.

"Five hundred," the girl answered.

"I want one," she said at the same time Evelyn said, "Simone, don't you dare."

The girls looked from Evelyn to Simone, who nodded at

them. "Let me go grab my checkbook and get my sister's kids buckled up. You'll take a check?"

"Simone," Evelyn said again.

Simone glared at her sister, because she wasn't a child. She'd be forty in just a few months, and she'd wanted a dog for a long time. Life the past several months had been trying and difficult and busy, but her days had gone back to normal the last few weeks. She was ready for a dog, and she liked Western terriers as much as anything else.

"Yes, ma'am," one of the girls said, and Simone smiled at her.

"I'll be right back."

She continued out to Callie's minivan and strapped Ginger into her seat while Denise climbed into the bucket seat. Evelyn had parked right next to her, and Simone turned and said, "Come on, Conrad. Time to get in the car. Evelyn had one baby in, and she was working on the second one.

Conrad jumped down from the step and got in the van, climbing all the way to the back row seat. She put one knee on the floor and leaned back to help him, but he said, "I do it," and she let him try to buckle his own seatbelt.

He did it too, and Simone's pride soared. "Nice job, Conrad," she said, and the little boy rewarded her with a grin.

She turned to get the last baby out of the stroller, and she got to put Easton in his car seat. He was the biggest of the babies, and he'd really chubbed out in the past month or so. They were five months old now, and no one would've ever guessed that they'd been born three weeks premature. Simone put his pacifier in his mouth while Evelyn wrestled with the stroller and got it in the back.

"Okay," she said. "Lunch?"

"I'm going to buy a puppy," Simone said. "I'll have Callie drop me off at home."

"Simone," Evelyn said. "Are you really going to buy a puppy? What about Micah?"

"What about Micah?" she asked, her breath coming shortly at the mention of his name.

"Aren't you going to talk to him about it?"

"We've talked about it," she said. Briefly. Once or twice. But she wasn't lying. As if bidden by the sisters saying his name, her phone lit up with his name on the screen. And Evelyn saw it while Simone swiped it to voicemail.

"I don't think you've talked to him about a puppy," she said with a smile.

"I'm not talking to him right now at all," Simone said coolly.

Evelyn's joviality dried up. "What? Why not?"

Simone's chin started to tremble. "Because," she said. "He chose a job over me and the baby." She shrugged, though there was nothing blasé about what she'd said.

She'd ridden with Callie, so her purse sat on the floor of the passenger side up front, and she grabbed it and then started the van so Denise and Ginger wouldn't roast in the van. She pulled their side door closed and faced Evelyn again.

Evelyn's eyes had filled with tears. "You're going to have a baby?" she whispered.

Simone nodded, her own tears spilling down her cheeks. Evelyn shrieked and grabbed onto her, and Simone half-laughed and half-cried right there in the parking lot at the nursery.

Callie said, "Hey. I thought you were going to pull the van up."

Simone looked at her, and she did not look happy. Evelyn released her so fast, Simone almost lost her balance. "She's pregnant!" She danced over to Callie and grabbed her in a hug too.

Callie's mouth dropped open, and though Evelyn was hugging her like a maniac, Callie didn't look away from Simone.

"Oh." Evelyn stepped back, going from hot to cold and back in under a second. "And she's not talking to Micah."

"Pregnant and fighting with my husband," Simone said. "What a loser, right?"

"Of course not," Callie said. "We've all been there, right, Evvy?"

Simone had always felt third-best in her family. Callie always knew what to do, and Evelyn had a special way of questioning her about her choices that made her feel two inches tall. But right now, they both just wore identical expressions of compassion.

"Of course," Evelyn said. "You should've heard Rhett and I, um, discussing why he needed to take on another case. He seems to think he's the only forensic veterinarian in the state. I practically threw the computer at him as I showed him the long list of others that could take this case."

Callie left the trees and shrubs and bulbs on the flatbed and came toward her. "I'm sorry, Simone. What did he say?"

"He's apologized a bunch of times," Simone said, feeling guilty that she hadn't forgiven him instantly. "But he still went, even when I asked him—twice—not to." She pulled in a breath and pushed it back out again. "I just…he seems to pick everyone and everything over me, and I'm maybe wondering if that's just how it's going to be forever."

She looked at Callie, wanting her to say that *of course not. That's not how it will be forever.* Desperate to hear it. She didn't say it. Instead, she looked at Evelyn.

"Simone," Evelyn said, and she now wished they had gone to lunch so they didn't have to stand in the September heat to have this conversation. "Here's what I think. You've always known exactly who you like, and exactly how you want to be treated. You deserve to have a man who thinks you're a queen. So I say, you stick to your guns. You tell him how you want him to treat you, and if he can't…."

"He can," Simone said. "He has in the past. He's just busy with his houses." She realized as she finished speaking that she'd just made an excuse for him.

"Yeah, and Liam is busy with his movies," Callie said.

"And Rhett is busy with his cases," Evelyn said. "But when I need him, he's there."

"Liam has already turned down the next job. He's done in December. We're going to take the girls and travel all over the country for a while."

"You are?" Evelyn's eyebrows shot to her hairline.

"Yeah." Callie smiled. "Surprise. We need time together as a family, and I've barely left the state of Texas."

"So I just need to tell Micah what I need and see if he can do it."

"You can compromise," Evelyn said. "Finally, I told Rhett he could take the case if he worked less than four hours a day on it. And he has."

Simone thought of Micah's broken promises about being home for dinner. Maybe he just needed to be trained up a little bit. "I do love him," she said. "I don't want to be alone, and I don't want to have a baby alone."

"When is he coming home?" Callie asked.

"Not for another ten days," Simone said.

"Then you go down there," Evelyn said. "Go down there and be with him where he is. What's keeping you here?"

That was a great question, and Simone couldn't answer it. Well, she could. "Nothing," she said. "Nothing is keeping me here." An idea began to form in her mind, and it included seeing Micah tomorrow morning, stealing him away from his work for just a few minutes, and begging him to choose her.

No, she told herself. She would not beg. She would wait and see what his reaction was to her showing up at Grape Seed Ranch.

With a Western terrier puppy.

Before she could move to get her checkbook out of her purse, all three of their phones went off, each making a different noise as they got simultaneous texts.

"Mal," Evelyn said, pulling hers from her back pocket. "I bet it's Mal."

Simone looked at her phone, and sure enough, Penny had texted. "It's Mal." She tore right down the middle. She wanted to be here for Mal, as all of the women had grown closer over the past couple of months as they spent more time together with their kids—and with Penny.

But she wanted to get to Micah as fast as possible too.

Maybe she could call him. Tell him she was coming. But the dramatic side of her wanted to show up unannounced and see what he did.

"What are you going to do?" Callie asked, reaching for the door handle. "Should we head to the hospital?"

"Penny says she's been there a couple of hours," Evelyn said, reading from her phone. "We can come wait, or she'll text when the baby is born."

"Let's go wait," Simone said. "I like being there when they bring the baby out, only hours old." She smiled to herself and unconsciously put her hand on her stomach, imagining she could feel the life there. "Then I'll go see Micah."

CHAPTER THIRTY-TWO

Mal opened her eyes and turned toward the door as it opened. Her handsome cowboy billionaire husband came through the door, his smile so wide it barely fit. He carried a tiny, wrapped baby in his arms, the girl wearing the purple hat she'd knitted for her.

They were back, and all was right in the world.

Mal shivered, because she still wasn't quite warm enough. The nurse noticed, and she said, "I'm going to get you another blanket. You should be warm enough soon." She ducked out of the room as Skyler arrived at the bedrail. "She's so perfect, Mal," he whispered, and Mal couldn't imagine talking in louder than a whisper either. Being in the presence of one who had just been with God seemed to require some reverence.

She reached up, and Skyler passed their little girl to her. Mal had only seen her for a few seconds before they'd whisked her off to have a bath and get checked. She'd made Skyler go with her so she wouldn't have to be alone, but that had left Mal alone.

She felt so tired, and like her brain wasn't quite connected to her body the way it should be. "What are we going to name her?" she asked.

"I liked Camila," he said, pulling up a chair. "And do you want me to take her out to meet the family, or can they come in?" He reached over and brushed her hair off her forehead. Mal loved him so much, and she could hardly believe this life she had now. From the grandeur of the house she lived in, to the man she slept beside, to this tiny human who had carved out a place in her heart in only a moment. A breath. A wisp of time.

She looked down at the snoozing baby. "Camila Rose," she said. "They can come in."

The nurse returned with two heated blankets, and she laid one across Mal's legs and feet, and one across her torso. She checked the monitor that displayed Mal's vitals. "If you're not warmer in the next ten minutes, I'm calling the doctor."

Alarm crossed Skyler's face. "Is she not warm enough?"

"Not quite yet," the nurse said. "She could be in shock, or she could have some internal bleeding." She looked sternly at him. "I'll be back in ten minutes."

"Have them come say hello to her now," Mal said, watching the nurse leave. "Then they can all go home. They won't have to wait."

He stood and bent down to kiss her and then Camila. He left, his boots making too much noise against the floor for Mal. "Just you wait until all the uncles come in," she whispered to her daughter. "They are so loud." She smiled fondly at the baby, who seemed to snuggle closer to her. Mal had read that babies knew their mother's voices, and she hummed as she waited for Skyler to return.

It felt like a long time had passed before the door opened again, and Penny entered first. She cried as she hugged Mal and took the baby from her. Mal smiled at everyone as they filed in. The noise level went up, but certainly not as much as it could have.

Simone wept as she bent over Mal and hugged her. "Congratulations, my friend," she whispered. Mal held a special place in her heart for all of the women in the room, as well as everyone with Walker DNA. They had all rescued her. Literally rescued her.

She hadn't even realized she'd started crying until Skyler took her hand and pressed a kiss to her wrist. "What's wrong, baby?"

"Nothing," she said, her voice weak. She shook her head. "This is just amazing to watch."

The love hanging in the air could be felt, and Mal wanted to rake her fingers through it. Wyatt and Jeremiah stood next to one another, and there was absolutely no animosity between them.

"Can we have a family prayer real quick?" Gideon asked, and everyone nodded.

Baby Camila got passed back to Mal, who cradled her against her chest. They took hands or put their hands on one another's shoulders, and Gideon closed his eyes. Mal's burned as she closed hers too, though her tears had come from only the happiest of things.

"Dear Lord," Gideon said, his voice unlike anything Mal had heard before. He did not continue, and she wasn't the only one in the room crying.

"We thank Thee for family," Gideon finally said. "Bless Micah, who is not here with us. We are grateful for the land where we live. We love Texas, and the ranches Thou hast provided for us. We love our spouses and our children and our grandchildren, and are especially grateful for Camila, this new addition to our family. Bless us not to take each other for granted, and bless us to forgive one another if we do wrong. Bless any here with exactly what they need, if it be Thy will. Amen."

"Amen," over a dozen voices said, and Mal opened her eyes and smiled. Gideon pressed a kiss to her forehead, his dark eyes absolutely glittering with emotion.

"Okay," Skyler said. Camila jerked, her face crumpling as she started to cry.

"You woke her up," someone said.

"Good job, Dad," another brother teased.

"Everyone out," Skyler said. "Mal's tired, and you've all seen her now."

Mal shushed the baby back to sleep while everyone left, and when she looked up at Skyler again, she could only smile and sigh.

"Love you, Mal," he whispered.

"And I love you." Mal didn't know how many children she'd be blessed with, but in that moment, her life felt absolutely complete with just her, Sky, and Camila.

Her last thought before she drifted to sleep was, *Thank you, Lord. Thank you.*

CHAPTER THIRTY-THREE

Micah lowered the saw, the feel of it in his hand as familiar as breathing. He loved working with wood. Measuring it, marking it, envisioning what he could sculpt out of it. He loved the smell of it, the way it got caught in his hair and eyelashes, the taste of it on his tongue though he wore a mask over his nose and mouth.

Wood didn't give him any trouble, as it seemed to want to be transformed under his careful and talented hands, and he'd made great progress on Dwayne's house. The paint looked amazing with the floors going in that day, and most importantly, Dwayne and Felicity were happy.

Micah worked outside in the yard, under a tent he'd set up. He'd finished the mantel a few days ago, and it was ready to install once the flooring was finished. He'd kept the original fireplace for a sense of home and heart and nostalgia, but the modern mantel would be a centerpiece all its own.

He'd finished the new doors for the new pantry, and he'd pieced together the countertop for the island in the kitchen. That slab wasn't quite done yet, as he had to sand it and sculpt it and stain it.

Sand, sculpt, stain. Micah loved doing those things with his whole soul, and Simone's words swirled around in his mind. *You don't have to work at all.*

No, he didn't. But he was only thirty-four years old. What was he supposed to do with his life? He didn't think God would want him to sit idle all the time, and Micah knew he'd go nuts within a week.

He hadn't even started Simone's workshop, and guilt tugged at the edges of his conscience. He probably shouldn't have signed Mary and Amy Thompson and their abandoned, poorly poured foundation.

He should've rented an excavator and dug the foundation for his wife's she-shed. He should've called the cement mixers and scheduled a time for them to come pour that foundation.

He should've been working on the foundation of his marriage. He should've been home on time for dinner when he'd said he would be. He shouldn't have missed dinner with his parents. His mother had told him congratulations about his baby—his first-born child—via text.

Micah frowned, though the work was going well. His thoughts moved to Jeremiah, and how his brother had started working on things again. He'd hired Orion as the ranch foreman, and he'd gone back to therapy. Micah knew, because he owned part of the ranch, and Jeremiah had called an owner's meeting to discuss hiring a foreman.

He wanted to be more present in his family's life, and Micah hadn't even realized he'd stepped back from the life he and Simone were building. *Should've* been building.

He'd called her every day since he'd left Three Rivers, and she hadn't picked up once. He'd been in a situation like this with her before, and it was as miserable now as it had been then. He also knew the stakes were higher. They were married, with a baby on the way. He couldn't just walk away, meet another woman at church, and start dating her.

At the same time, he couldn't abandon the responsibilities he'd committed to. He saw no way out of his situation, other than time. So after he finished this cabinet, he'd call Simone again and beg her for more time.

Just a little more time.

He wouldn't take another client. He'd finish what he'd started, and he'd put his focus where it should've been all these months.

The frame of the cabinet went together nicely, and Micah sculpted the door from a piece of wood he'd planed yesterday. The trim came next, and Micah ran the wood through a molding machine he'd customized to ensure that Dwayne and Felicity's cabinets were unlike any others. The special molding would go around the top of this piece of cabinet, as it would sit atop the pantry and connect to the ceiling.

With that done, he stepped away from the machines. He'd kept them going from as early in the morning as he dared to as late as he dared. Tonight, he had enough pieces to glue and nail as the last of the sunshine seeped away into darkness.

With four more cabinets built, he took them into the house and set them on the plastic that had been spread across the new floor. The blessed air conditioning made him sigh, and he swiped the face mask off his nose and mouth to look at what had been accomplished inside today while he'd been outside, crafting, cutting, and cabinet-making.

The light gray paint on the walls looked fresh and inviting. The baseboards had been taken out to be sprayed, but they were back in today, making the house feel more complete. At least where the floor had gone in. Dwayne had chosen a dark, rich wood that had a lot of brown and black in it, and it contrasted nicely with the walls.

As Micah walked forward, he could see there was still a section of the floor that hadn't been finished. "Tomorrow," he said, his voice echoing a bit in the house. Where the floor had been done, the baseboards had been put back. The interior designer would be here tomorrow, and Micah would start putting in the cabinets he had built in the afternoon and evening. Then it was just more of the same. Build the cabinets. Hang the cabinets. The last thing he'd do was paint or stain them. Dwayne and Felicity hadn't decided on that yet, as they were waiting to meet with Hailey.

But all in all, the house was coming together nicely, and Micah was right on schedule. He went upstairs, where he was staying in one of the spare bedrooms, and showered the sawdust out of his hair and off his skin. When he couldn't put off calling Simone any longer, he sat on the bed and picked up his phone.

Before he could even take a breath, it rang. His heart leapt into the back of his throat in the split second before Dwayne's name came up on the screen. He sighed, because he wanted to hear Simone's voice so badly.

He didn't want to talk, but he swiped on the call anyway, reminding himself that Dwayne had paid him a lot of money to answer his phone when he called. "Hey," he said.

"Just wondering if you've had dinner," he said.

"I had a protein bar," Micah said, though his stomach growled as if it had ears.

"Well, we've got pizza over here," he said. "And you're welcome to it. We'd love an update on the house too, if you're not too tired."

Micah was, and he wasn't. "Sure," he said. "I'll be over in a few minutes, okay?"

"Take your time. The boys are out tonight, and we have to wait up for them anyway." The call ended, and Micah let his phone drop back to his lap. He'd been eating with Dwayne's family for a few nights now, and it wouldn't be awkward in the generational house. And he'd leave with a full stomach.

But he didn't want to talk to Dwayne and Felicity. He wanted to talk to Simone.

First, though, he slid off the bed, twisting to face it as he landed on his knees. He pressed his forehead to the comforter, trying to find the right words to beg the Lord for help. Such desperation flowed through him that Micah felt like the very gates of Hell were only moments behind him, about to claim him as theirs.

In the end, he said nothing. The panic and vibrating fear left him, and Micah drew in a long, calming breath.

He got to his feet, and he went downstairs, past all the construction, and out the back door. The generational house sat down a sidewalk in the back corner of the yard, and Micah reached it in only seconds.

He knocked, and Dwayne opened the door as if he'd been standing right beside it. He wore a grin the size of Texas, and Micah sensed something was off. He tried to see past Dwayne, but he'd filled the doorway with those shoulders and that smile.

"C'mon in," he boomed, and Micah hesitated.

"Are you okay?" he asked.

Felicity arrived, and she glared at her husband. "He's acting weird, isn't he?"

"A little," Micah admitted, glad he wasn't the only one who could see it. He didn't know Dwayne all that well, but he'd never seen him smile like that. He'd never seen *anyone* smile like that.

Felicity pushed against Dwayne's chest, backing him into the house. "Come in, Micah."

He wasn't so sure he wanted to anymore, but he stepped up to enter the house. The scent of marinara mixed with something else. Something inedible but that he liked a whole lot. Something he'd smelled before.

Felicity finally succeeded in getting Dwayne into the

living room off to the right of the door, and Micah looked back toward the kitchen, which sat against the far wall of the house.

Everything froze, from his feet to his heartbeat.

"Simone," fell from his lips as he drank in the beautiful, dark-haired woman standing near the corner of the kitchen table.

In the next moment, his grin felt like it was the size of Texas and he was moving fast toward his wife. He reached her, barely noticing her smile as he swept her off her feet. "You're here," he said, taking a deep breath of her. "Oh, I love you, and I'm so sorry, and—" He set her down and stepped back. "Why are you here?"

Everything seemed to be happening so fast, his heart beating double-time, and the seconds racing by.

Simone giggled and tucked her hair, which had grown out a lot in the last year or so. "I think that was the perfect reaction." She turned her attention to Felicity and Dwayne. "Don't you?"

Felicity had one palm pressed to her chest. "Absolutely perfect," she agreed.

"What's—?" Micah started to ask, but Simone turned to him and entered his personal space at the same time. Her mouth touched his, silencing his question as she kissed him.

Micah's desperation and worry, his fear and panic, his exhaustion and need to please vanished. Simone possessed magic that made him whole in a way nothing else ever had and ever could.

She didn't kiss him long, and Micah looked at her. Those

bright, shining eyes the color of midnight. That mouth. Oh, that mouth. "What are you doing here?" he asked, easily settling his hand on her hip. "Are you okay?" He leaned closer to her and lowered his voice. "Is the baby okay?"

He shouldn't have come to Grape Seed Falls. Why had he come? How was this job more important than his pregnant wife and child?

"I'm okay," she said, alleviating some of his fears. "The baby's fine."

She wasn't saying enough, and Micah's frustration grew.

"I wanted to see you," she said. "I thought if I could see your reaction to seeing me, I'd know how you felt." She smiled and took both of his hands. "And I did. I do."

"I love you," he said simply, still trying to process what was going on. Behind her, he saw Dwayne and Felicity leave the house, carefully and quietly bringing the door closed behind them.

"And I love you," she said. "I'm sorry I didn't take your calls. It took me some time to forgive you."

"I'm sorry I left. I hope you understand. I've been begging God to help you understand."

"I do," she said. "And Dwayne and Felicity are wonderful people."

Micah nodded, wanting to tell her everything he'd been thinking the past few days. "I'm not going to take any more jobs for a while," he said. "I'm going to be home on time. I'm going to finish your workshop for you."

"Mal had the baby," she said.

Micah blinked at the topic change. "Yeah, Skyler's been

texting me. He sent pictures." He cocked his head at her. "Did you hear what I said?"

"Yeah," she said, smiling, inching closer. "You said I love you. And that encompasses everything else."

"You don't care if I don't make it home for dinner?"

"Oh, if you're late again, you'll be sleeping outside." She tipped her head back and laughed, but Micah wasn't sure she was kidding.

He took her fully into his arms, holding her close to his body, just where he wanted her. "I'm not going to be late." He looked at her as she sobered. Right down deep into her eyes. "I hate that I didn't make you my top priority."

"I know why you didn't," she said, wrapping her hands around the back of his neck. He leaned down and touched his forehead to hers as they swayed.

"Yeah? Why didn't I?"

"Because it takes a lot of time and energy to make dreams come true," she whispered, her lips dangerously close to his. "And you're making your dreams come true, and Dwayne's and Felicity's."

His eyes drifted closed, which heightened every other sense. "Yeah," he said. "But baby, I want your dreams to come true."

"They are," she said. "With you, Micah Walker, my husband, they are."

He kissed her, really taking his time to commit the feel of this amazing woman in his arms. He wanted her forever, and he promised himself—and God—that he would not let anything come between them again.

Simone broke the kiss several long seconds later. "Now," she said, stepping back and lacing her fingers through his. "Come show me this house you've dreamed up. And show me where I'm sleeping." She smiled at him, and Micah's pulse pounced in his chest.

He knew where she was sleeping—within the safety of his arms—and he couldn't wait to show her what he'd been doing here for the past four days.

CHAPTER THIRTY-FOUR

Jeremiah brushed down the pale, cream-colored horse. Peony's light brown eyes with the long, light lashes, closed in bliss, and he smiled at her. "You like that, don't you?" he asked her. "Don't get too comfortable. Daddy's going to try to ride you today."

He glanced over to his father, who was working with a tall, dark mare named Red Velvet. And in the stall past him, Wyatt shared all his secrets with Mountain High, a brown and white horse that made Jeremiah smile every time he saw him.

He, his father, and his brother didn't need to learn to take care of the horses, but Pete Marshall said it was part of the therapy, even for experienced horsemen. Jeremiah had been annoyed at first, but he now enjoyed the slower start to the riding sessions. He liked taking time to connect with the horse—and with himself.

He'd been coming out to Courage Reins for a couple of

months now. He'd just moved to visiting with Dr. Wagstaff every other week instead of every week. He'd passed a lot of responsibility around the ranch to Orion and Wallace, and he'd actually gone with Whitney and the kids to the Fall Festival, watched them paint pumpkins, shared a pumpkin spice funnel cake with them, and strolled through the glimmering pumpkin walk after dark, all the candles throwing light into the night in the spookiest of ways.

JJ hadn't liked that much, and when Jeremiah had asked him what he'd liked best that day, he'd said riding the ponies. He was still too young to really start to ride with Jeremiah, but once the New Year came, Jeremiah was going to buy the boy a saddle and find him a calm, quiet horse like Peony to learn to ride with.

Rhett had already started with Conrad, and Jeremiah loved watching Rhett tie the two horses together and go riding with his son.

"All right, boys," someone said, and Jeremiah looked away from Peony. "We're riding today, so lead your horses out to the arena. We'll help anyone who needs help getting on."

Jeremiah switched places with Daddy, so he could take Peony, and they followed Wyatt and two others out to the arena. Jeremiah didn't need help mounting a horse, and he swung into the saddle like he'd been born to do it. He was, but so was Wyatt and so was Daddy, and they both needed help.

Wyatt exhaled heavily, and Jeremiah wondered if he had any pain in his body. He didn't want to ask though. He wouldn't want Wyatt to bug him about his back. Wyatt was a grown man, and he knew what he could handle and what he couldn't.

His brother shifted in the saddle and then twisted. "All right, Jeremiah?"

"All right."

Wyatt brought Mountain High around, and Jeremiah turned to watch Daddy get in the saddle. His right leg had been injured pretty badly in the accident almost sixteen months ago, and to Jeremiah's knowledge, he had not been in the saddle since.

"I'm gonna have to try the other side," Daddy said, a frown etched between his eyes. Jeremiah's heart squeezed watching his father try to do something that had come naturally to him for so many years of his life. "This leg just isn't strong enough to get me up there."

"We've got a stool, if that would help," one of the cowboys said. Karl, Jeremiah thought his name was.

"Try 'im on the left side," Pete said, holding Peony steady, though she didn't need it.

Daddy limped around the other side and put his left foot in the stirrup. His hands shook. His right leg trembled, and Karl stepped right next to him, bracing that side. "Up you go," he said, and Daddy did it.

Push, lift, throw, and he sat in the saddle. He grunted, keeping his eyes down as he situated himself in the seat, with the reins in the right hand. He looked up, and Jeremiah grinned at him while Wyatt whistled between his teeth.

"Thatta boy, Daddy," Wyatt said, smiling too. "Hold

there. I want to text Momma." He held up his phone and snapped a picture of Daddy, who seemed to think smiling was against his religion.

"Come on, Dad," Jeremiah said, chuckling. "Could you look like maybe you don't want to die?"

"Yeah," Wyatt said. "Smile, Daddy." He smiled widely, as if demonstrating for a small child.

Daddy smiled, and Wyatt snapped, and Pete called, "We're headed out. It's a forty-minute ride today, and we'll be out in the wilds of the ranch. You're free to go wherever you want, but if you see a blue rope, that's the limit. Come on back the way you went if you see that." He led them out of the arena, and Jeremiah, Wyatt, and Daddy fell into line behind each other.

Outside, Jeremiah looked up into the blue, blue sky and let the weak November sunlight wash over his face. "What a time to be alive," he said, meaning the words just for himself.

But Wyatt said, "Amen, brother," as he waited for Jeremiah to catch him. The three of them walked in a row, side by side, saying nothing.

Jeremiah wasn't sure what was so soothing about horseback riding in Texas, but he knew it definitely smoothed the ragged edges of his soul. "I feel so much better," he said.

"I'm glad," Daddy said.

"Me too," Wyatt said.

"And look at Daddy, gettin' back in the saddle," Jeremiah said, looking to his left just in time to catch his dad's proud smile for himself.

"It's been a long road, boys," he said. "And I don't just mean since the accident."

"Ah, life lesson," Wyatt said, a teasing quality in his voice. He too looked forward though, same as Jeremiah and Daddy.

"A good road," Jeremiah said a few minutes later, as if no silence had passed between them.

Daddy nodded, and Wyatt added, "A blessed road."

Jeremiah couldn't argue with that, and while he'd spent some years of his life in a boxing match with the Lord, he now knew not to fight Him but to work with Him. He was the Master, and while Jeremiah didn't necessarily like being pulled and shaped and formed, he truly believed God knew what He was doing.

He had to, because he'd created horses and the good state of Texas, and Jeremiah was sure those had been done just for him. A smile touched his soul, and he finally felt like he was back in God's good graces.

Thank you for the gift of forgiveness, he thought, knowing he'd probably need it again in this lifetime. And that was perfectly okay.

Jeremiah was okay.

CHAPTER THIRTY-FIVE

S imone couldn't suck in her stomach, so she stood there and waited while the dress attendant tried to get the zipper to go up. "I don't think this is the one," she said.

"Maybe just one size up," the woman said.

Simone met her eye in the mirror and smiled. "I'm pregnant, and there's no way one size up is staying on my shoulders." She did like this dress, but not if she couldn't zip it. And there was still three weeks until the wedding.

She was only going to get bigger.

"Let me talk to Angela," she said. "I know we have some maternity dresses." She waited while Simone stepped out of the wedding dress and then she took it with her.

Simone sat on the bench in the dressing room in her slip, her sisters' voices beyond the door filtering back to her. This dress was the last thing Simone needed for the perfect Christmas wedding.

She had the cake. The flowers. The tables and chairs

rented. She'd held all the Walker brothers and their wives as she hosted a special family meeting at their house, and there would be all the wedding essentials—arches, lights, altars, candles, lanterns, ornaments, and plenty of mistletoe.

Simone and Micah were getting married at night, under the vast, starry sky of Texas, and she sighed, seeing the event in her mind's eye in all its glory.

But she couldn't show up in her slip and shoes. And she supposed she still had to get those too, because she hadn't wanted to buy them before the dress in case they didn't match.

Several minutes later, a blonde woman with a faux hawk entered the dressing room. With such short hair and such bright lipstick, Angela's beauty struck Simone right in the throat. Maybe she should cut her hair like that, and she eyed the shaved sides of Angela's head.

After the wedding, she told herself. She didn't want to make any drastic changes this close to the ceremony. No need to be too dramatic.

"Simone?"

"Yes." She stood up and shook Angela's hand.

"Can I take your measurements? Then we can pull a few things from the back."

"Of course." Simone stood straight and tall and let Angela measure her bust, around her baby belly, her hips, and from shoulder to shoulder.

"I know we have a beautiful dress for you," she said. "I saw it come in last week."

"For someone five months pregnant?" Almost six, actually.

Angela smiled as if they had pregnant brides in Three Rivers every day. "Yes," she said. "I even said I wished I was pregnant so I could wear it." Her eyes sparkled with truth, and Simone actually believed her. "Be right back."

She hadn't written anything down, and Simone caught the door as she left, gesturing for Evelyn and Callie to come into the dressing room with her.

"What are they doing?" Evelyn asked.

"Finding a dress for a six-month pregnant woman," Simone said. "I told them I was pregnant when I called."

"It's fine," Callie said, sitting on the bench. "Liam has the kids today. I'm good for forever."

"Same," Evelyn said.

"You're going to be home when I have the baby, right?" Simone asked Callie. She'd asked her a handful of times already, but she needed the reassurance.

Callie smiled, always so patient. "Yes, Simone. We've scheduled to be here for three weeks starting a week before you're due. I'm going to be here."

"Where are you going first?" Evelyn asked. "Have you decided?"

"Yes," Callie said. "I booked a house for a week in Oklahoma City."

"Oklahoma City? What on Earth are you going to do there?"

"Explore," Callie said. "Then we're going to Bentonville,

Arkansas. They have fun biking trails there, and I can't remember the last time I rode a bike."

"Those are mountain biking trails," Evelyn said. "You know you're not just going to be riding down the street, right?"

"Thank goodness I have you to tell me," Callie said, rolling her eyes.

Simone burst out laughing, because Evelyn was not handling Callie's travelogue very well. Simone suspected Evelyn would like to be the one moving from vacation house to vacation house every week or two or three, seeing the country and exploring with her kids.

"I'm just saying," Evelyn said.

"Yes, I know," Callie said. "But I have the Internet, and I did research. We're going to stick down here until Simone has the baby, and then we're going to go west to the coast and the beach."

"Sounds amazing," Simone said, her own jealousy spiraling a bit. But she knew that if she wanted to travel, Micah would make it happen. Micah could make anything happen, and he'd done exactly what he'd pledged to do. He'd been home for dinner every night on time. He hadn't taken on any new clients.

He'd finished the homestead at Shiloh Ridge Ranch, and he'd gotten the Thompson ladies all squared away too. He'd been steadily working on her workshop, and he'd gone into secret mode, not letting her come in and see the progress he made each day.

He claimed it would be ready any day now, and she'd

just have to wait to see the final product. Simone smiled just thinking about him and the workshop, because it was a physical representation of how much he loved her.

And it felt so nice to be loved by a good cowboy.

"All right," Angela said, opening the door again. "Oh, we have a crowd."

"Can they stay?" Simone asked. The dressing room could easily fit them, and Angela hung up the dress she carried as she nodded.

"Sure. Come in, Taylor." The woman who'd been helping Simone earlier, entered with two more dresses. There seemed to be entirely too much lace, too many poofs, and an abundance of layers.

"Let's try the Marion Smith first," Angela said.

"Marion Smith?" Simone asked, her eyes meeting Angela's in the mirror. "She has maternity dresses?"

"It's not exactly a maternity dress," Angela said as she removed the hanger from a pair of straps that looked like they could hold Simone together properly. "But she's got a unique design that allows the dress to be tailored in specific spots—like the midsection—and I think it's going to be fabulous." She smiled like she really believed herself too, and Simone looked at the dress.

It was pure white, like driven snow untouched by humans, protected by angels themselves. It was made of ruffles, and Angela said, "It's got a ridged design that hides a lot." She stooped and Simone stepped into the dress.

"Oh, it's nice," she said, as the fabric kissed her skin like cold water in a desert. She closed her eyes and added, "I'm not going to look. Tell me when I can open my eyes."

Angela laughed as she pulled the dress over Simone's hips, belly, and bust and started doing something in the back. "Can you pull it on the sides, Taylor?" she asked, and Simone sensed the other attendant moving around her.

"Like this?" She tugged on the sides, and Angela did something to hold the dress in place. Simone wasn't sure how she would get herself into this thing for the wedding, but she knew Evelyn and Callie would help. Penny, and Mal, and Whitney too. And Marcy and Ivory. She had plenty of help, she realized.

"It's gorgeous," Evelyn said.

"Absolutely stunning," Callie added.

"I'm not looking," Simone said, smiling and working hard to keep her eyes shut. "Stop trying to entice me to look."

"Almost got it," Angela said, and she and Taylor kept working together until she finally said, "All right. Open your eyes."

She took a deep breath, preparing herself to see something hideous. But this was Marion Smith. Nothing the designer did was hideous.

She opened her eyes, and the perfect picture of a bride looked back at her. "Oh," came out of her mouth.

Behind her, one of her sisters sniffled, but Simone could not look away from herself. They had not hidden the baby, but the dress bumped out where her body did, and she loved that. The fabric clung to her chest too, the wide straps tasteful and wide enough to keep everything lifted where it should be.

The skirt drifted down from the bottom curve of her baby bump, ending in a puddle on the floor.

"I love this," she said, twisting to see the back. Angela had been tying back there, as well as threading dozens and dozens of little cords through tiny eyelets that allowed them to pull more where she needed it and leave room where she did too.

The cords then created a beautiful waterfall down her back that Simone absolutely loved. "Wow."

"It's lovely," Callie said.

Yes, the dress was perfect. Simone smiled as she put one hand on her baby and one on the strap on her left shoulder.

In that moment, the baby kicked, and she looked down, giggling. "He likes it."

"Is he kicking?" Evelyn stepped around her and put her hand on Simone's stomach too. "Oh, he is." She grinned and leaned against Simone in a half hug. "I love you," she said.

Surprise moved through her. They weren't a terribly sentimental family, and while they'd always gotten along, looked out for each other, and worked together, they didn't often express their love for one another.

"I love you too, Evvy." Simone's excuse for her tears was the pregnancy hormones. Callie wept as she joined them, and they hugged.

"I love you both," she murmured, and they repeated the sentiment back to her. Simone thought of Gran, and then her mother, and they were suddenly both with her and Evelyn and Callie in the dressing room.

———

LATER THAT DAY, SIMONE HAD BARELY HUNG THE DRESS IN the closet in the spare bedroom when she heard Micah enter the house. "I'm home," he called, and Simone hurried out of the room, taking a moment to close the door behind her.

"Hey," she said, arriving in the main area of the house a little out of breath.

He eyed her. "What were you doing?"

She smiled as she approached him, putting both hands around his neck and tipping up on her toes to kiss him. "I found a dress today."

"Is that right?" He held onto her waist and leaned down to meet her halfway. She kissed him hello, though he'd just been working in the backyard.

"Yes, that's right," she said.

"And I don't get to see it."

"Not before the wedding," she said. "It's bad luck."

Micah chuckled as he released her. "Simone, you know everything about our wedding is whack, right?"

"Whack?"

"Weird," he said, tossing his wallet on the counter and stepping over to the sink to wash his hands. "Unconventional. We're already married."

"Yeah, I know," she said.

"So maybe I can see the dress."

"I need a lot of help getting into it," she said.

"I can help." He finished washing and grabbed a towel hanging from the handle of the oven. He faced her, that trademark smirk on his face.

Simone toyed with the idea, because he was right. They were already married. The whole ceremony was unconventional. "Fine," she said. "You can see it."

"I can?" He laughed and put the towel back. "I wasn't really expecting that to work." He started toward the front hallway, and Simone went with him. In the few seconds it took to go into the bedroom, she oscillated back and forth about this decision.

But then Micah pulled open the closet, and he saw the dress. So it was done. "Wow," he said, reaching for it. Simone nearly darted in front of him, narrowly reminding herself that he'd just washed his hands.

He held it lovingly and looked up at her. "This is going to be so much better than the first time."

"Yeah," she said. "Because this time, we'll both know it's happening."

"There's that too," he said. "It won't be this mock matrimony thing we didn't even know about."

"Exactly."

Micah grinned and said, "All right, my bride. Get those clothes off and let's get you into this."

CHAPTER THIRTY-SIX

Micah held tight to Simone's hand, hoping she didn't stumble down the steps that led to the back patio. "Keep your eyes closed," he said. "We're going down the three steps from the kitchen to the patio."

"Okay," she said, one hand in his and the other thrown out in front of her. He smiled to himself as he took her down the stairs. His heart beat like a big, Hawaiian drum, loud in his ears and chest and the back of his throat.

He'd been working on her she-shed for a couple of months now—maybe longer—and it was time to reveal it to her. After making her wait for an hour while he made sure every little thing was in the just-right place, adjusting the pictures on the wall a thousand times before taking a deep breath and standing back.

"Okay," he said, reaching for the doorknob. "I'm going to take you all the way in, and you don't open your eyes until I say, okay?"

"Okay," she said again, her smile permanently on her face. He opened the door, and the softly blowing warm air brushed his face. "The heater's been on for a couple of hours. Don't worry, I didn't set it too high."

"Sixty-eight," she said, and he echoed it.

"A small step over the doorframe," he said, easing her over it. He shuffled her inside and closed the door behind her. "I think I'm more nervous than you are." He took a deep breath, admiring the corner directly in front of them. It was the photo corner, with huge windows shining pure light down on the white table he'd put there. Simone could eat there too, and that was the corner he'd decorated with a letter board already set up for the month of December, a picture of them she'd snapped at Thanksgiving dinner, and the poster he'd made her for her birthday.

"All right," he drawled. "You can open your eyes." He knew what the she-shed looked like. He'd spent the better part of the last three days moving everything from the workspace at the Shining Star to her new location, and he wanted to see her reaction to what he'd done for her.

"Oh, my goodness." She sucked in a breath and covered her mouth with both hands. Tears filled her eyes, but she blinked them back. "Look at that table."

"That's the picture nook," he said.

She nodded, taking a delicate step forward. She gasped. "My birthday poster. That's what you did with it." She turned toward him, letting the tears flow down her face now. "I love you so much."

"I know, baby." He took her into his arms and hugged

her, their baby between them. He'd made her a big poster for her birthday that said 40 things he loved about her. She'd turned forty last month, and they'd celebrated with cake every day for a week, a quick trip to a luxury lodge near San Antonio, and he'd made the poster for her.

He'd taken it a couple of weeks ago, claiming to have a plan for it, and he'd mounted it to a thin piece of sheet metal and hung it in her shed. Now, every time she came out here to work, she'd remember how much he adored her.

"You have so much more to see," he said, stepping back and wiping her face. He smiled down at her gently. "Come on, I'll take you on a tour." He fixed his hand in hers and indicated the corner. "You'll notice that the doorway is set back from the shop. I thought it would be a box, but it's not really. This wall is only twenty feet, instead of thirty, but I wanted the windows."

"It's amazing," Simone said. "Look at all those shelves."

"Built-in," Micah said. "Fifty feet of them." He looked down the length of the wall. "Varying heights, according to your specifications. You can remove some of them to adjust them and fit in larger items." He took her to the left. "Work tables here. Thirty feet of those, with a shelving unit underneath, and two of them have those mesh drawers for brushes, buttons, bobbles, you know. All that stuff you said you wanted."

Simone reached out and pulled open one of the mesh drawers, which contained segmented compartments of various sizes inside. "This is perfect. They really will hold buttons or pins or knobs."

"Yep." He nodded straight ahead as they walked. "Your kiln is right there. A desk next to it so you can do your administrative stuff. That's the wall by the house, so there's electricity for your computer, the kiln, the fridge, and the microwave."

"Micah." She froze, and he knew she'd seen the desk. Really seen it. She looked at him, pure shock in her eyes. "Is that—?"

"Yes," he said. "That's your mother's desk. I managed to whine enough to get it away from Callie. And really, it was Liam who made it happen. He said she got to have the whole ranch, the house, the wedding dress. You could have the desk. You'd take good care of it." He beamed at her. "You're impressed with my bargaining skills, aren't you?"

"I'm impressed with everything," she said, giggling. "But that one hadn't crossed my mind."

"Anyway, one of the drawers was broken, so I fixed it up, and it's all yours now."

She stepped over to it and ran both hands along the top of the nearly black antique. "My mother used to sit here and write letters to my father while they were dating," she said. "At least that's what Daddy told me. She brought it with her when she came to Three Rivers to marry him. She brought this one piece of furniture and three suitcases. Nothing else."

"It must've been very special to her," Micah said.

"It was her grandmother's." Simone smiled as if she could look back through the generations and see her mother, her grandmother, and her great-grandmother. She took his hand again and said, "I'm going to eat so much popcorn out here while I work. That microwave is seriously the best part."

"The microwave?" Micah asked, shaking his head. He laughed, the sound flying up to the ceiling where it bounced around.

"Well, and that wall of shelves," she said. "Or that perfectly cute little table where I can take pictures of my vases and lamps."

"And this is your stock back here," he said. "See how it's around the corner so you can keep the more unsightly things away from the door?"

"Or the really awesome things," she said. "I don't want anyone to see when they come to the door."

"Both, yes," Micah said. "I just know you used to keep your unfinished or un-started stuff out of sight in the other shed."

Simone nodded at all the things she had in the she-shed. The barrels, the old wood, the frame of a chair that had a cushion with stuffing spilling out of the top and bottom of it. She could see beauty where he saw trash, and he loved that about her.

"Merry Christmas," he said. "And I'm counting this as a wedding gift too."

She turned toward him, her smile big and beautiful. "You still want to marry me?"

"Simone," he said, deadly serious. "I've wanted to marry you since nearly the day I met you."

Tears filled her eyes again, and she shook her head. "We've had quite the road, then, haven't we?"

It had been quite a wild year, with a lot going on. Micah felt more mature than he had twelve months ago. He felt more grounded in his faith. He wasn't afraid of his emotions anymore.

"Yeah," he said. "And hopefully, a lot more to come." He leaned down and kissed his wife, whom he would exchange real vows with tomorrow night. He couldn't wait, and he hoped he'd always be as happy to be with her as he was in that moment.

"Thank you, Micah," she whispered.

"Anything for you."

Simone drew in a long breath, her chest pressing against Micah's. "All right. Let's get back inside and get ready for one last practice. They'll be here soon."

"I really think everyone's got it," Micah said, threading his fingers through his wife's as they started back through her she-shed.

"But it has to be *perfect*," Simone said. "It's for your mother, Micah. Don't you want it to be perfect?"

He kinda did, and he couldn't deny it. So he said, "Yeah, Simone, I want it to be perfect."

"She's going to love it," Simone said, clearly excited. And Micah got excited about anything she did. He had to admit, what she'd planned for Momma was pretty awesome, and he couldn't wait until tomorrow night to walk down the aisle with Simone and give her the wedding she'd always wanted.

WALKER FAMILY EPILOGUE

Momma drove down the highway, the night already starting to turn the day into twilight. She hummed as Gideon rode beside her, still fiddling with his bow tie. They'd spent a long time on their knees that morning, thanking the Lord for all of His blessings.

Seven sons.

Seven daughters-in-law, each of them perfectly suited for the son they'd chosen and married. Momma couldn't tell a lie and for a while there, while the boys entered their teens, stayed for a bit, and then left, she wondered if she'd ever be able to marry them off.

Who would want one of her boys? A loud, broad, stinky man who only wore cowboy boots and barely took off his cowboy hat? When she'd say such things to Gideon, he'd remind her that she'd wanted him, and Momma would laugh and say, "I guess that's true."

"It's been quite the year," Gideon said, and Momma glanced over to him.

"It sure has." Babies being born. More coming. Death. Grief. Healing. Hope. They'd managed to get his parents to move out of their house, and while that had been painful for a few months as they had to purge so much of what they'd been holding onto for years, they'd done it.

"Your parents are getting a ride with Tripp, right?" she asked. In her older age, she was forgetting more and more.

"That's what he said."

Momma nodded. She hadn't forgotten to get them, because Tripp was picking them up. Ivory's parents would be at the wedding too, along with Jerome and Belinda. Momma had cooked for them a couple of times, and she did like spending time with the Foster girls' father and step-mother.

She turned onto the road that led to the ranch, a sigh coming from her lips as she saw the Christmas lights. "This ranch is beautiful," she said.

"The boys sure do out-do themselves year after year," Gideon said. "Look at the stars on the fence this year. They have the grandkids' names on them."

Momma had seen them before, but she looked again anyway. Five girls. Seven boys, with two more on the way. Both Simone and Marcy were expecting baby boys very soon, and Momma couldn't wait to hold them and whisper how much she loved them.

There was no greater joy than that of being a grandparent, and she basked in the glow of the all-white lights on the huge oak tree between Skyler's and Jeremiah's homes. She was so glad four of her boys lived right here on this land, because she believed that they needed each other.

She worried about Wyatt up in the hills alone, but he'd bounced back just fine after the incident with Jeremiah.

"We're goin' to Micah's," Gideon said when Momma started to turn into the homestead.

"Oops," she said, jerking the wheel the other way. "You're right." She parked in his driveway, beside a couple of other trucks, and she and Gideon got out.

Music filtered into the air from the direction of the backyard, and she took her husband's hand and they walked toward the corner of the garage where a bunch of white balloons fluttered in the evening breeze, illuminated by a beautiful white light atop a decorative pole. Another cluster of balloons sat at the next corner, and they made their way there.

Turning the corner, Momma's excitement grew. She paused to take in the wonder that existed back here. Simone had planned everything right down to the very last jar of fireflies sitting on the tables on the massive patio Micah had put in their backyard.

The rows of chairs faced away from the house, and on the edge of the patio, an arch had been set up. The altar waited beneath it, and several more jars of buzzing fireflies sat there, waiting for the bride and groom.

"Rhett's here," Gideon said. "I see Jeremiah. Tripp. Liam…."

Momma saw them all too, and her lungs seized. Her

heart scrunched against itself. Her boys. Her grown men, all wearing suits and ties and matching cowboy hats. They were so handsome, and each of them seemed to turn toward her at the same time.

"Momma," Rhett said, coming over with Austin in his arms. "I was just gonna call you."

"We're not late, are we?" she asked, accepting his hug.

"Nope. And not last either. Skyler lives across the street and isn't here yet."

"Hey, Momma." Liam hugged her, and she clung to him. Her dear Liam, who had a heart of gold.

"How are the girls?"

"Good," he said, smiling. "We're getting packed up. Excited for our new adventure."

"I want to hear all about it," she said. "Every night."

"Momma," Jeremiah said, stealing her attention from Liam. He held her tight, whispering, "Whitney's going to have another baby."

"Oh," Momma said, patting him on the back. Her smile seemed permanently etched on her face. "That's great news."

"I'm not going to make an announcement, though," he said with a smile.

"Is Wyatt here?"

"Yeah, he's back with Micah. Skyler too."

"So Skyler's not late." Momma shot a glance at Rhett, who shrugged. The three younger boys had often banded together, and she was glad someone was in with Micah. She'd heard Simone's dress was a showstopper, and

Momma had half a mind to go inside and see it before the ceremony started.

Before she could, Tripp came over and said, "Hey, Daddy. Hey, Momma." He hugged her and added, "Can you sit by Joan and Will? I think they feel lost."

"Sure," Momma said, stepping around him to see where Ivory's parents were. "Oh, they're by Jerome and Belinda." She reached for Gideon's hand. "Let's go sit by them."

She made her way past the long dessert table, which had all the signs set up but none of the treats. Yet. Micah and Simone were feeding everyone too.

"Gramma," Conrad said coming toward her, and Momma scooped him right into her arms.

"Hello, my boy," she said, giving him a kiss on the cheek. "How are you?"

"Good," he said, sitting happily with her as she sat next to Joan.

"It's nice of you to come." Momma smiled at Ivory's mother.

"This is wonderful," Joan said, bouncing Isaac on her knee. "I can't even imagine what it took to do this." She gazed up at the tea lights hanging everywhere, and Momma had to agree. "It's so beautiful. I've never thought of doing a night wedding."

"Simone is a creative woman," Momma said with as much love as she had. She sensed something happening behind her, and she turned to see Skyler and Wyatt coming out of the house. Behind them came Evelyn and Callie, and Momma took a few seconds to get to her feet.

She thought the other boys and their wives would come sit down, and then Micah would come out and stand at the altar, leaving Simone to parade to his side alone. Gideon had offered to walk her down the aisle, but she'd said she wasn't going to have an escort. She was definitely unconventional, but Momma supposed that even having this ceremony wasn't traditional.

But the boys stayed by the steps, lining up in age order. The music that had been playing stopped, and a moment later, the wedding march began.

Oliver sat with Rhett and Evelyn's triplets. Denise sat next to Ginger. Whitney's parents had Jeremiah's two kids with them.

Rhett took a step forward from his side of the aisle, and Evelyn from hers, the two of them meeting in the middle. They smiled at each other, leaned forward and kissed, and then linked arms.

"I love you, Evvy," Rhett said, beaming at her as if they were the couple getting married that night.

"I love you too, Rhett Walker." They turned and walked down the aisle.

Momma's soul lit up, watching them. Rhett and Evelyn. The perfect couple. They went all the way to the front row and down to where Oliver sat with their triplets.

Jeremiah stepped to the middle and offered his arm to Whitney. She looked like she might not take it, then burst into a laugh, tipped up on her toes to kiss him, and said, "I'm so glad you asked me to marry you."

"Sometimes I still wonder how I got so lucky to have

you." He grinned at her, and they walked toward Momma too.

She'd known she was going to cry, and she decided not to hold it back. She touched two fingers to her lips and threw the kiss to Jeremiah and Whitney. How well-suited they were for one another. They went down the row where her parents sat with their kids.

Liam, the oldest of the twins, stepped forward and took Callie into his arms, dipping her back and kissing her while the other boys whooped. They came up laughing, the two of them, but Momma couldn't stop weeping.

"Love you, sweetheart," Liam said, grinning at her.

"Love you too, Mister Walker."

As they walked past Momma, she felt sure she was looking at angels. They went down the row and sat beside their girls, Callie putting her arm around Denise, and Liam settling Ginger on his lap.

Tripp met Ivory at the bottom of the steps, and it was in that moment that Momma finally realized all the women were wearing a version of the same dress. It was white and long, dragging slightly on the ground. The fabric flowed around them, and seemed to be made of gauze.

It was a wedding dress.

That Simone sure was a clever woman, and downright amazing too.

Ivory wasn't as much for show as some of the other women, but she kissed Tripp while she held his face in both of her hands.

"I've been so happy since I met you," Tripp said.

"You're my whole world," Ivory replied.

They walked to the spot next to Momma, and she could only smile at them, despite her tears.

Wyatt stepped forward and cocked his elbow for Marcy to take. Marcy carried Warren, sported her baby bump, and wore a cowboy hat. One of Wyatt's for sure.

They both took off their hats and waved to the crowd, and everyone already in their seats—and those who hadn't made it there yet—took theirs off and waved back.

Beside her, Gideon sniffled, and she was glad the old, tough cowboy still had the ability to cry.

"I love you," they said in tandem, and Wyatt kissed Marcy as if he'd forgotten they weren't alone, They walked toward a couple of empty seats in the front row, but Wyatt had to stop to engulf Momma in a tight hug before he made it to his seat.

Skyler extended his hand to Mal, who also carried their baby in her arms. She put her hand in his and twirled into his side, both of them laughing. He kissed her, and Momma saw the joy on both of their faces. Skyler reseated his cowboy hat and walked toward them, saying, "I love you, Mal."

"And I love you, Sky."

He nodded to Momma, like, *There you go, Momma.*

She knew this entire show was for her.

She'd missed a lot of the weddings. In fact, she'd only been to Wyatt's wedding, and that had been fake.

Nothing she'd just seen had been fake. Her sons loved their wives. Their wives loved her sons. And Momma's love for Simone doubled and then tripled. She knew Momma had wanted to be there for all of her sons' weddings, and she'd planned this just for her.

Her tears flowed faster now, and Momma wiped at her eyes furiously so she didn't miss her youngest son's promises to his wife.

Micah came outside, his smile absolutely blinding. He waited at the bottom of the steps, finally turning around and extending his hand toward the gorgeous bride that emerged from the house like a butterfly breaking free of her cocoon.

They held hands and looked at one another before walking forward. No kiss, Momma noticed. Neither of them spoke, but Micah stopped in front of Momma and reached for her.

"I love you, Momma," he whispered, and his joy seeped from him and into her. She could tell and taste how much he loved Simone, even if he had wanted to "try the marriage thing."

She released him so he could step over to Daddy, and Momma immediately took Simone into her arms. "You precious woman," she said. She pulled back and looked into Simone's eyes. "I sure do love you."

"Are you surprised?" Simone asked, her eyes twinkling. They seemed a bit shinier too, and Momma supposed they should be. After all, it was Simone's wedding day.

"So surprised," Momma said. "And I love it. You got everyone to go along."

"I fed them a bunch of times," Simone said with a laugh.

She too stepped over to Daddy and hugged him, and then Micah led her to the next row, and they hugged Jerome and Belinda too.

Simone took several long seconds with her father, and she did swipe at her eyes just once before securing her hand in Micah's and going back to the aisle with him.

They continued to the altar, where Skyler joined them, and Momma was glad she wasn't the only one weeping.

The music stopped, and Skyler invited everyone to sit down. After several seconds where everyone got settled, he looked out at everyone.

"We hope our mother and father enjoyed the six weddings they just watched," he began. He smiled, but Momma had looked into that face so many times, and she saw the wobble in her son's bottom lip. "All of us sons love our parents very much, and they didn't get to see very many of us enter into this illustrious thing we call matrimony."

"Oh, boy," Tripp said under his breath. "Who let him get up there again?"

Momma ignored him and kept her eyes on Skyler, even as Conrad tried to get down. "Stay here, buddy," she whispered.

"Daddy," he said, and Rhett turned around. Momma let the boy go, and he went up the aisle to his father.

"I'm not going to say anything today," Skyler said. "Micah and Simone have vows they want to say as part of their ceremony, so I'm going to turn it over to them." He went to sit beside Mal, and Micah and Simone turned toward each other and faced the crowd too.

"Micah," Simone said, looking at him. "We've had our fair share of ups and downs, over what felt like a long time. I know life can be bumpy, and scary, and hard sometimes. And there's no one else in the whole world I want to be with through all the speed bumps, anything that scares me, and all the hard times than you. I love you." She paused and swallowed. "I love you with all I have." She nodded, a final punctuation mark to what she'd said, which was simple and beautiful and pure.

"Simone," Micah said. "I've painted your house. Snuck into your workshop. Spent days mourning that I couldn't text you or talk to you. Begged you to go out with me. Talked to you on the porch when I was dating someone else. Mourned with you. Laughed with you. But the best thing I've ever done is allow myself to fall completely in love with you." He reached for her hands and held them in both of his. "I love you, love you, love you, and I will do everything in my power to make sure you're the happiest woman in the world." He dropped one of her hands and lifted the other one into the air.

Everyone started cheering, as if they'd been given instructions to do so. Obviously, they had. Momma pressed her hands to her chest, because her husband and boys could make plenty of noise without her.

As they cheered, Micah kissed Simone, his very real wife.

Momma looked around at the crowd of people there. They were her world. They epitomized love and forgiveness. She felt removed from them, basking in their warmth, their life, their love.

Gideon took her hand and said, "Look what they've become, Penny. Aren't they wonderful?"

"Yes," she said, coming back to the moment, back to her precious Gideon, to their family. "They're all so wonderful."

Keep reading to find out who my favorite Walker brother is - maybe we'll have the same one?

Also, I have a brand-new family of cowboy brothers running to Whiskey Mountain Lodge from their high-profile family in Colorado...read on to meet Colton Hammond in **HER COWBOY BILLIONAIRE BIRTHDAY WISH**, which is coming soon!

I love how Micah wants to try on marriage like a pair of cowboy boots - and that he and Simone got their real wedding, and that Momma and Daddy got to see ALL of their sons walk down the aisle with the woman they love. **If you liked this book, please leave a review now.**

Join Liz's newsletter for deals, sneak peeks, and more.

AUTHOR'S NOTE

To my dear friends and readers,

Wow! What an amazing journey we've had with the Walkers. Hopefully, you've seen yourself in one or more of the people in this series. I know I have. I've poured my heart and soul into this series in a way I've never done before.

I've never written more of a family saga than just a straight romance, but that's what Seven Sons turned out to be. It's part women's fiction, part family drama, and part romance. I love all of those things, and I love that we got to spend time with the individual family members for longer than we normally do.

I love Rhett's strength and family loyalty. I love his drive to be the best big brother he can be, and the best father to those three boys and one little girl. I love that the other brothers look up to him, and that he doesn't know any better than them. Don't we all feel like that sometimes? I

AUTHOR'S NOTE

know I do. People looking at me like I know what to do, and I'm really making things up as I go.

I love the twins. They formed early in my mind, and I love that we see them start out as a bit more fun-loving. Quipping with each other and the other brothers. But as they face serious things in their lives, they grab them by the horns and hold on.

I love love love Liam's devotion to Callie. When I wrote him wandering out by the fence between their two properties, just hoping to catch a glimpse of her...that sums up Liam for me. He's loud but quiet. Strong yet soft. Serious, with a quick laugh.

And Tripp is different in some ways, and identical in others. He knew from very close to the beginning that he wanted Ivory to be happy and that he'd do whatever he had to do to make it so. He reminds me so much of my husband, who also deals with difficult in-laws, children who are quite far apart, and concern for those around him. Tripp is helpful and present, and I love that about him.

You'll notice I skipped Jeremiah. I know that. In thinking about who my favorite brother is, I decided it was Jeremiah. Then I thought Rhett. Then I was like, "No way. It's Wyatt."

Or maybe it's Skyler, with his depth, his growth in his faith, in accepting who he is. He didn't only accept it, he embraced himself. And I love that so much about him.

And now that I've written Micah's book, I actually considered Micah for my favorite brother. In writing this book, I had to go back to several of the others and read

376

sections of them, and every time I did, I fell in love with that brother.

So my favorite is definitely Liam.

Okay, it's not. It's Tripp. I mean, I just said he was like my husband in a lot of ways!

I love Micah because he dreams big dreams, and he's not afraid to go after them. I have no doubt we'll get to see him in future books I write in Three Rivers, because he's going to be the best premium builder and cabinet maker in the county. (And yes, there is another series coming to Three Rivers. It's the Shiloh Ridge Ranch series, and Bear Glover will get his happily-ever-after! So don't fret that you didn't get to see Micah's creation for Bear and Shiloh Ridge. You will!)

And now I'm down to the two brothers I think I connected to the most, personally. Jeremiah and Wyatt. In this book, they get in a little argument, and that was such an important part of the family saga for me. I wanted to show that even the best families have problems they have to deal with. They have misunderstandings. They say things to hurt each other, sometimes unintentionally, sometimes on purpose.

But the Walkers have learned to forgive one another, and that is admirable to me.

I love Wyatt with my whole heart. His book was completely the love affair that had started a few books before. I love that he was this big, tall, ultra-rich and ultra-popular man, but he didn't have what he wanted most.

Love. A wife. A family. He was not complete just because

his bank account was big, or that a lot of people knew his name. I loved creating his hat wave for his daddy, his family, and his fans. It was *my* love story with my readers, and Wyatt to me just flows from me as if he is part of me.

And you know who else does? Jeremiah. I understand Jeremiah on such a deep level. He is perceived as superhuman, and he likes it. He *wants* to be seen that way, and he works hard to know what he knows and do what he does.

At the same time, he has a lot of insecurities. He has a deep fear of failure and abandonment. He struggles beneath the tough surface. That speaks to his need to take care of other people, feed them, and welcome them to the ranch he's spent years turning into the type of ranch that wins Ranch of the Year.

I honestly wish he could feed me!

And let's not forget about the Foster sisters. How much do we love them? And Marcy? Mal? Ivory? Whitney?

Did you notice I brought all these strong, smart, and yes, sexy women into the fold, and all of them needed exactly one thing: a family.

Mal has no one in the country. Marcy has lost both of her parents by the time her book begins. Ivory has parents she hasn't spoken to in years, and she's under the threat of losing her son. The Foster sisters haven't had a mother for decades. Whitney has family in Three Rivers, and she might be the outlier here, though she still needed somewhere safe to belong.

And I gave them this loud, obnoxious family of all boys. Haha.

And then, I gave them Momma. (Cue crying here.)

I actually think Momma is my favorite member of this family. She is everything I hope and wish to be one day. Patient with her adult children, prayerful, loving, accepting, and faithful. I love her relationship with Gideon, and her relationship with all of her sons as individuals, that she brings the women together and helps them see how they each have the exact spot in the family they're meant to have.

I gave them Daddy, complete with his love of miniature horses and his incredible faith.

I did this, because I believe everyone needs a Momma and Daddy in their lives, and I wanted these women to integrate into the family, find a place to belong within their core families, within the larger family, and ultimately, with each other.

Ah, the Walkers.

I am now a Walker. You are too.

Welcome to the family.

~Liz

PS. Read on to see Micah and Simone and their baby boy in the first two chapters of **THE MECHANICS OF MISTLETOE**, the next Three Rivers Romance, coming in October. **You can preorder it now on any retailer.**

The End

SNEAK PEEK! HER COWBOY
BILLIONAIRE BIRTHDAY WISH
CHAPTER ONE

T he life and energy of Whiskey Mountain Lodge
pulsed through Annie Pruitt as she climbed the steps
from the basement to the kitchen. The door at the top of the
steps had been slid closed, but as the family gathered in the
kitchen burst into laughter, no barrier could contain the
sound.

Annie smiled, because she loved the Whittaker family,
and all those that had come to be included in that family.
Herself and her girls included.

She paused on the top stair, her fingers scrambling for
the divot to latch onto so she could slide open the door. It
moved easily, because everything at Whiskey Mountain
Lodge now ran like a well-oiled machine. Not that it hadn't
before, but Graham and Beau had worked together over the
course of eight months to bring the lodge out of retirement
and back into a full luxury vacation destination in the beautiful Teton Mountains.

They'd hired four more people to work at the lodge, increased Annie's hours to full-time, and made every room available for nightly stays, even the master suite. Beau and Lily had moved down the canyon to the town of Coral Canyon, and the brothers had built a cabin on the hill in the backyard for the manager who now ran this place.

Annie liked Patsy Foxhill a lot, and she ran a very tight ship for someone so petite and a decade younger than Annie.

"There she is," Graham practically yelled as Annie entered the kitchen. "Celia was just suggesting we come down and get you." He grinned at her, his eyes bright and glinting.

Annie shook her head. "You said dinner was at six. It's quarter till." She glanced around at everyone gathered at the table. Tonight was the first night they'd all gathered to the lodge for their annual family Christmas celebration.

Over the course of the next six days, they'd transform the lodge into Holiday Central, with a tree-cutting expedition planned for the day after tomorrow.

For starting tonight and continuing for at least the next twenty-four hours, Mother Nature would be dumping snow. At least according to the forecast and the National Weather Service. In fact, the family wasn't supposed to gather to the lodge until tomorrow night, but they'd come early to avoid the weather.

All of the guests had left that morning, and Annie was supposed to have two days to clean the lodge from top to bottom before the Whittakers and Everetts arrived. She'd had four hours.

As Eli and Meg arrived, then Andrew and Becca, then Beau and Lily, they'd simply put their bags in the rooms where they'd be staying, and Annie had stripped beds and scrubbed tubs around the luggage.

Lily's sisters and parents had become an integral part of the Christmas traditions at the lodge too, and Vi and Todd and Rose and Liam had arrived that day as well. Fran and Jack Everett had come after Annie had finished the upstairs rooms, as had Amanda and Finn, her new husband, and Celia and Zach.

Annie's thoughts lingered on Amanda and Celia the most these days. She'd watched them find their second chance at happily-ever-after, and she wanted it for herself. She'd been out with a couple of men in the past couple of years as the lodge went through the changes, but neither of them had panned out.

She found herself stuck in the middle of her life, taking each day one at a time the way she'd learned to do after her husband's death, alone. She didn't want to be alone forever, and she certainly didn't want to be a burden to anyone.

"Where's Bree?" she asked. "Everyone's not even here yet."

"Happy birthday," Amanda said, appearing in front of her and hugging her.

Annie giggled as she hugged the woman a couple of decades older than her. "Thank you."

"I know it was a couple of weeks ago," she continued.

"But Finn and I haven't been down to the lodge in that long." She extended an envelope toward Annie, who looked at it with love and appreciation for Amanda and Finn streaming through her.

"You didn't have to get me anything." She glanced to the table, where several others still loitered. A couple of kids ran into the kitchen, excitedly asking Celia for just a pinch of the chocolate bread she'd made that day. She shooed them out, and Annie still hadn't taken the envelope from Amanda.

"We got you something too," Graham said, setting a bright red package on the counter that separated the large kitchen from the dining area, where most people sat to visit. More gifts appeared, and Annie pressed her hand against her heart. Tears threatened to spill down her face, but she pushed them back.

Maybe she was simply closer to fifty than forty now, and her emotions couldn't be controlled as easily, because one tear managed to slip out of the corner of her eye. She swiped at it, and said, "You guys. You didn't have to."

"But we wanted to," Eli said, standing up as he picked up the slim, blue package someone with less clumsy hands than his cowboy fingers had wrapped. He nearly shoved the gift at her, and Annie finally took it and the envelope.

"Well, I appreciate it," she said.

"You don't turn forty-six every day," Amanda said. "It's a good year. One of my best." She smiled, and it sat beautifully on her face. Annie would've never guessed she had turned seventy years old that year, and she could only hope she looked as good as Amanda in twenty-four more years.

The thought made her stomach clench. Twenty-four more years. Would she have to spend all of those days with a sponge in her hand, her two cats the only living things waiting for her at home?

She reminded herself that both Emily and Eden still lived at home, though they were both adults, as she looked down at the envelope. Before she could open it or the gift, a child screamed from somewhere in the house, and someone came through the back door, yelling the words, "The storm is starting already."

Bree poked her head around the corner as she removed her hat, which bore enough snow to shake to the floor and gather into a fist-sized ball. Annie frowned at it, because she knew she'd be the one to clean it up.

"It's coming down out there," she said. "We barely made it up the path."

"Good thing we're all staying here tonight," Celia said, and Bree ducked back around the corner to hang her winter gear in the mudroom off the back entrance. The chatter picked up again; Rose left to discover the source of the screaming, assuming it to be one of her triplets. She and Liam had two boys and a girl that had just entered their terrible two's, and they all possessed a healthy set of lungs.

Bree and Elise entered the fray of people, and Annie felt less alone. They didn't have boyfriends or husbands either, and she suddenly wasn't the only one.

"Everything's ready," Sophia said, putting a large pot on

the counter. She'd been hired as the full-time cook at the lodge, which offered breakfast and dinner to its guests. Celia worked weekends now, when they only offered a brunch, choosing to spend the rest of her time in Dog Valley, on Zach's farm with him.

Annie wondered what that life would be like. Working a few hours a day, and living in a beautiful, modern home with the man she loved. Her chest tightened again, and she gathered the gifts from everyone, keeping her smile cemented in place.

Annie had learned long ago to smile, to find the silver lining in any situation, to make the best of what she'd been given.

But would it be so hard to give me someone to grow old with? she wondered, directing her question up. Up through the ceiling. Up through the storm. Up, up, up and hopefully, all the way to the Lord's ears.

"Thank you," she said to everyone, nodding and smiling. "Thank you so much." She hurried into the family room and put the gifts in a pile on the armchair there, reaching for the two tweens sitting on the couch. "Come on, guys. It's time for dinner."

Bailey and Stockton were the oldest of the Whittaker children, with mostly children under the age of six to play with. So they tended to stick together, talking about their friends or looking at things on their phones.

They got up and Bailey wrapped her arms around Annie. "Oh," she said, patting the girls' head. "What's that for?"

"Happy birthday," she said, smiling up at her. Bailey had

always been a sober child, and she'd matured into a four-teen-year-old with the same calm demeanor as her mother.

"Thank you," she said.

"Stockton and I helped Sophia and Celia with the cake," she said. "I think you're going to like it."

"I'm sure I will," Annie said, further relaxing. "In fact, do you think we could have cake first?'

Stockton said, "I'm going to go ask Celia," and ran ahead of them.

"I don't think we can have cake first," Bailey said.

"Why not?" Annie asked. "I hate waiting until after dinner to eat dessert. I'm always too full then."

"Good point," Bailey said, and Annie giggled again.

They stepped through the doorway, a wall in front of them forcing them left or right. To the left and through that doorway was the main kitchen. To the right was the dining area, and Annie stepped that way, very aware that for the number of people in the house, it was entirely too quiet.

And she knew from experience that silence meant nothing good. In fact, when children were quiet, that spelled trouble. Emily and Eden had drawn all over one of Annie's walls during one of their silent bouts.

So something was definitely happening in the dining room. Annie rounded the corner behind Bailey, trying to see into the kitchen and left and right and back to everything in the dining room at the same time.

A loud blast of singing hit her, and she couldn't help grinning as everyone who'd gathered for their second annual family Christmas party started wishing her a happy birthday. Those darn tears came again, and Annie didn't even try to swipe them away this time.

Celia lit the candles on a massive chocolate cake that had been set on the edge of the table, and Annie led them with both hands as the song wrapped up.

She stepped forward to blow out the candles, and someone called, "Make a wish!"

Annie closed her eyes, wondering what a forty-six-year-old widow should wish for.

I wish...I wish...I wish for a cowboy billionaire of my own to fall madly in love with.

She giggled at the ridiculous thought, opened her eyes, and blew out the candles. Thankfully, Celia had not put on forty-six, but just a four and a six, and she only had to get out two flames.

"Thank you, everyone," she said when the last bits of applause stopped.

Celia gestured to the kitchen, where Sophia came out with a stack of plates and Stockton followed with forks. "And because I've known Annie since she moved to town, I know she likes her sweets first. So we'll be having cake first."

Annie grinned at Stockton, who wore a look on his face like Christmas had come six days early. "Did you ask?"

"She already had the cake out," the boy said. "Honest."

"Hello?"

Annie turned toward the unfamiliar male voice as others started to look past her and the cake.

A tall man stood there, wearing cowboy boots, jeans, the

biggest, puffiest coat Annie ever did see, and a deliciously white cowboy hat without a speck of snow on it.

"I knocked," he said. "But you must not have heard me." He put a smile on his face, and Annie darn near swooned on the spot. He had a handsome smile, perfectly framed by a dark beard with more salt than pepper. She sure did like that silver hair on a man, and her heart shot out several extra beats.

"I can see I'm interrupting," he said. "I was just…hoping you'd have an open room tonight. See, my brother stayed here once with his son, and he said it was a great place, and—"

"I'm sure we have a room," Lily said, one of the closest ones to Celia and this new man crashing the party. "And you can stay for cake and dinner too."

"I can pay," he said.

"Oh, the lodge is booked," Patsy said, glancing at Lily and then Graham, who'd also come forward. "But I think we can manage to have you for one night." She gave him a tight smile, but Annie honestly couldn't look away from him. She needed to know his name, and where he was from, and how long he was going to be in town.

One night, rang in her ears, and she started desperately praying that God would send more snow. So much snow that none of them would even be able to leave the lodge for days.

"Okay," the man said, peeling off that huge coat. "I'm much obliged." He stuck out his hand for Patsy to shake. "You seem like you're in charge. I'm Colton Hammond."

Colton Hammond. It was the type of name Annie could float away on as she tried to drift to sleep, and she caught herself sighing before she jolted to attention and turned back to the cake. Chocolate. Yes, all she needed was chocolate to get herself back into the right mindset.

A lot of chocolate.

Colton Hammond faced the group of people, picking out the ones who belonged together. There were couples here, and single women. A few women with very similar hair. Generations of people, with grandmothers, mothers, and children. Cowboys who looked a whole lot alike. Colton knew all about families like that, as he had four brothers, which included a set of twins.

He didn't much care who was with who and how they all connected. He needed a place to stay, and Gray had texted him the name of this lodge as Colton put the town of Ivory Peaks, and then the entire state of Colorado, in his rear-view mirror.

And it would be just fine with him if he never went back.

A couple of people turned and looked at him, and he moved further into the expansive area at the back of this building. No wonder they hadn't heard him knock. The noise level here was enough to make Colton think that perhaps the back seat of his truck would make a nice bed after all.

Only the temperatures and the threat of being buried under several feet of snow kept him standing in that kitchen. He reached up and adjusted his white cowboy hat, at least feeling like he belonged here, with all these other men wearing practically the same thing as him.

"Cake," a woman said, handing him a plate with a thick slab of chocolate cake on it.

"Thank you, ma'am," he said, but she'd already moved on. The blonde who'd spoken earlier edged over, and Colton got the hint that he could take a spot at the table next to her. Another woman sat right in front of the cake, and he glanced at her.

"Is it your birthday?" he asked.

"Kind of," she said.

Colton reached for a fork, taking one from the pile several inches in front of him. "How do you have a kind of birthday?"

She smiled, and Colton sure liked the way her face lit up. She had a spattering of freckles across her nose and cheeks that spoke to Colton. But he would not be getting trapped by a pretty face with freckles.

Been there, done that.

"My birthday was a couple of weeks ago," she said. "But we decided to celebrate it at the lodge this year." She gave him that smile again, and he noticed her straight, white teeth this time, framed by those pretty pink lips.

His face heated and he focused on his cake. His heartbeat

screamed through his bloodstream, and Colton tried to mentally reassure himself that he didn't need to run. This woman wasn't a threat to him. She wasn't.

"What's your name?" he asked.

"Annie," she said.

"Like, the sun will come out…tomorrow?"

She blinked at him, and Colton realized how he'd sounded. "I mean, it's a nice name."

"Thanks." She took another bite of cake, and Colton took his first. His taste buds told him to take another bite. Then another.

"This is the best chocolate cake I've ever had," he said. And he'd eaten at dozens of high-end restaurants in his life.

"Celia's doing," Annie said, pointing with her fork. "She's the one who gave you the cake. She's been the chef up here for years."

Colton found her talking to a cowboy in the kitchen and enjoying her own cake.

"Sophia is a chef here too," Annie continued. "She works full time during the week. Celia's just here on the weekends."

"And you're all up here right now," he said.

"Yes." Annie tucked her shoulder-length hair behind her ear, shooting a glance at him before looking away again. "The Whittakers own the lodge, right?" She nodded to the man who'd emerged from the back of the crowd. "Graham bought it several years ago. He hired me to clean, Celia to cook, and Bree to do décor and grounds. Each of the four brothers lived in the lodge at some point, but they've all got other houses now. They turned the lodge back into a mountain resort about eighteen months ago."

Colton liked listening to her voice, though he didn't much care about the family history lesson. He nodded though, wondering if he could simply serve himself another piece of cake once he'd finished this one.

"Anyway," Annie said. "They hired a bunch more people, rent out all thirteen rooms—except from December twentieth to January fifth. Or so. That's when they all gather here for their holiday family traditions and to spend time together."

"It's only the nineteenth," Colton said.

"Yeah, we came up a day early, because of the storm." She flashed him another smile, and Colton wondered what it would be like to be able to do that. He hadn't had a reason to smile at will for a couple of months now, and it felt like six years instead of six weeks.

"So," a man said, pulling out the chair the blonde woman had vacated at some point. "What brings you to Coral Canyon?"

Colton looked at the guy, his defenses already in place. He hadn't anticipated having to talk to anyone for longer than a few minutes. Just his luck that he'd walk in during a family party.

"Just getting out of town for the holidays," he said coolly. He hadn't fooled the other cowboy for a moment, though.

"Well, I'm Graham Whittaker, and you're welcome to stay as long as you like." He glanced up as someone said his name. "I'll have Patsy find you a room."

"Thanks," Colton said, finishing his last bite of cake.

Graham got up and clapped Colton on the shoulder, which sent a physical vibration through his arm as well as a buzz of annoyance. He was forty-two-years-old, and he didn't need to be talked down to like a thirty-year-old.

He'd started businesses and sold them. He'd been part of the biggest genetic achievement of the last century. He'd gotten an MBA while working at the family company as the executive marketing director. He hated to admit it, but Colton had drank in the whole lodge in a single look, and he knew exactly what he'd do to ger more people staying here. Not to say that the lodge didn't already have every night booked for the next year, but if he worked for them, they would.

"You might be here more than one night," Annie said on his left, and Colton was starting to get whiplash from looking left and right, right and left.

"Yeah, the snow is supposed to be bad," he said. If the weather had been clear, Colton would still be in the truck, aiming himself for the Canadian border. Frustration built in his chest, and he pushed against it. Pushed hard.

"Time to eat." Celia got up on a chair and held up both arms. Everyone settled down, and Colton basked in the relative silence. This place had great energy though, and Colton did like that. Compared to the farmhouse on the eastern edge of Ivory Peaks, where Colton had escaped after the failed attempt to get married, had only offered sadness and the ability to completely overwhelm a man in a single moment.

His father had just turned seventy-eight, and he couldn't keep up with the chores around the farm. His mother hadn't done anything on a farm, ever, and most of her time was spent taking care of Dad's mother, keeping them all fed and wearing clean clothes.

Colton had thought he might be able to lie low there for a month or two. Through the New Year. Then he could return to the high-rise building in downtown Denver where HMC operated their global office.

Then the article detailing his humiliation had been leaked to the media, complete with cellphone photos. Colton wasn't new to dealing with the fallout of bad press. Heck, he'd done it for a living for HMC—Hammond Manufacturing Corporation—for a decade.

But the fact that Priscilla, the woman he'd invested five years of his life into, had left him standing in the doorway of his dressing room, half ready for a wedding that had never happened. An event he'd endured by himself and that had destroyed his confidence. He didn't know how to put together a media package to dispute the photos. He couldn't write a statement to read to the microphones thrust in his face.

Well, he did know how to dispute the photos, and how to write and deliver the official HMC statement.

He didn't *want* to. Not anymore.

So after six-week hiatus at the family farm, he'd taken a security team to his condo on the north side of the city and snuck into his own house to quickly pack a couple of bags. He'd put them in the back seat of his truck, gassed up while the security guards watched, and tipped his cowboy hat to them.

He'd been driving all day by the time the National Weather Service alert had come on the radio station he'd put on but hadn't really been listening to. And he'd immediately called Gray to help him find somewhere to stay.

"Whiskey Mountain Lodge," his brother had said without a single beat of hesitation.

And now Colton sat at the table while a petite woman controlled a room full of adults and children.

"We have barbecue pork sandwiches," she said, and Colton's stomach growled. "Plenty of chips and dips. Vegetable tray. Tomato basil soup. Chicken noodle soup. Cheese biscuits. There's plenty of everything, so come eat."

Another man stood up before Celia could get off the chair. He said nothing, but he swiped his cowboy hat off his head and folded his arms. To Colton's great surprise, everyone else in the room did the same, and Colton hurried to remove his hat before anyone saw his shock.

This man—clearly one of Graham's brothers—said, "Dear Lord, we thank Thee for this bounty in front of us today. We're grateful for our daddy, who worked and built a bright future for us. We're thankful for all who work here at the lodge and provide such an amazing family experience for us. Bless them in their individual lives, and help us to remember who we are, where we came from, and who we represent. Oh, and we're grateful for Colton and that he arrived safely. Amen."

"Amen," everyone chorused, and a wave of noise rolled

through the room as everyone stood up, gathered their children to them, and started filling plates with food.

Colton got up and got out of the way, his heart touched by the prayer. *We're grateful for Colton.*

He didn't even know that man's name. He now held a little boy in his arms that looked to be two or three. He asked the child if he wanted every item, finally putting him in a highchair in the corner and returning to the line.

"Come get something to eat," a woman said, and Colton turned toward Patsy.

He gave her a smile, but he secretly wanted to escape. His stomach growled at him to stay put, so he did. "Thank you."

"I'm going to put you in room three," she said, extending a white card toward him. "Annie will go down with you. She's right next door in room four." Patsy gave him a professional smile and joined the fray of bodies in the kitchen.

He made it through the line with a smile on his face, talking to anyone who spoke to him. He'd seen a couple of people leave the kitchen, and he followed them, as there was no room at the table.

He found them in the living room, sitting on the couch with their food balanced on TV trays in front of them. "Room for one more?"

A dark-haired woman looked at him and smiled. "Sure," she said. "There are trays beside the fireplace."

Colton grabbed one with one hand as he passed the fireplace and set up his dinner in front of the loveseat, as three women had taken the spots on the couch.

"I'm Bree," the dark-haired woman said. "I do all the room decorating, as well as events here at the lodge."

He nodded at her, and she turned to the woman next to her. "This is Elise. She does all the groundskeeping."

"So you're part of the family?" he asked.

"No," Elise said, her long, blonde hair swinging as she shook her head.

"Yes," Bree said, correcting her. She shot her a look and then faced Colton. "Yes, we're part of the family. I've worked her for eight years, and yes, when you work for the Whittakers, you become a Whittaker."

Colton switched his gaze to Elise, who clearly hadn't worked for the Whittakers long enough. He could tell she didn't feel like a Whittaker.

He moved his gaze to the last woman on the couch, and she said, "I'm Rose. I'm out here, because I have three two-year-olds, and I need fifteen minutes to eat a full meal." She smiled and started slowly buttering her roll.

"Wow," Colton said, unsure of what else to say. "Three two-year-olds?"

"That's right," she said. "I'm sick of eating my meals one bite at a time over the course of an hour while I chase them."

Colton wondered who was chasing them if Rose sat out here slathering a rich, orange jam on her roll now. But he didn't ask.

Another woman came into the living room, and Annie paused as she assessed the situation.

"There's room by Colton," Bree said, and Annie looked like she might kill the woman later. But when Annie looked at him, she had that gorgeous smile on her face. She got her tray too, and she perched on the love seat as far from him as possible.

Colton knew he didn't smell; he'd showered that morning. She hadn't had a problem talking to him in the kitchen, and his mind went round and round about what he'd done to cause a change in her.

He finished eating while the four women chatted with each other about familiar things to them that made no sense to him. When he pushed his tray back so he could stand up, Annie asked, "Would you like me to take you down to your room right now?"

"I'm sure I can find it," he said. How hard could it be?

"I want to check it anyway," she said. "Since we came up early, I cleaned the rooms in the order they were getting used. It might not be ready for you." She left the remains of her food on her tray and joined him. "This way."

She led him back toward the kitchen, to the right down the hall past it to a pocket door that slid into the wall. She went first, saying, "Slide that closed behind you, would you?" as she started down a flight of steps.

Colton did as she asked, the noise level almost disappearing behind the closed door. By the time he reached the bottom of the steps and turned to go down a few more, he couldn't hear the zoo in the kitchen.

"This is a big common area," Annie said, indicating the two couches in the room. "There's a theater room there. Someone will put up a schedule for the holidays, and there's usually food down here too."

He noticed the kitchen built into two walls of the room, directly across from the theater room. Annie went past the theater room down a wide hall. "These are rooms one, two, three, and four." She held out her hand. "Do you have your key?"

He handed it to her, and she went to the room in the back left corner and flashed the card in front of the sensored lock. With the green light on, she opened the door and pushed her way inside.

"Thanks." She handed the key back to him, and he stood in the doorway instead of squeezing in behind her. The scent of her floral perfume tickled his nose, and his male side once again told him how attractive Annie was.

He shut down the feelings fast, because he was not interested in another relationship. Not now, and not ever.

The sigh Annie let out wasn't lost on Colton, and he took a step into the room then, easily able to peer over her shoulder. "What's wrong?" He saw the unmade bed, as well as the overflowing trash can next to the desk in front of the window.

Annie turned to face him, and they suddenly found themselves face-to-face, only a few inches separating them. "Do you mind…?" She stared at him, and Colton tried to back up, but the door had started to close, and he hit his elbow on the door.

"We could just switch rooms," she said. "I know mine is clean."

"No," Colton said instantly. "I'm not going to make you do that." It did seem like she'd have to clean a room no matter what, and he hadn't meant for that to happen.

"It's your party," he added. "I can empty trash and make a bed if you'll point me to the sheets and garbage bags." Yes, he had a housecleaner for his condo in Denver, but that didn't mean he didn't know how to clean up after himself. Or, apparently, other people.

"If you'll help me," Annie said. "We can get it done in fifteen minutes and both go to bed."

"Deal," Colton said, finally smiling for the first time since the day he was supposed to get married but hadn't. Fifteen more minutes until he could be alone. They couldn't pass fast enough.

Bear Glover stood in the equipment warehouse, his mood growing darker by the moment. Bishop and Ranger both lay on the ground, and Bear could only just see the tips of Bishop's boots. Ranger wasn't underneath the tractor nearly as far, but if it suddenly started, he'd lose plenty of skin.

Bear felt himself transforming into the grizzly some of his friends and family members often told him he could become. He worked against the instinct, but he honestly didn't have time for a downed tractor. They had field prep to do, and it if didn't get done on time, crops didn't get put in on time, and then the ranch was behind for an entire year.

He really didn't want to wear the grizzly skin for a year, though he'd done it in the past. He finally entered the warehouse, trying to tamp down the temper he'd been graced with. As the oldest of the Glover family, he'd been running the ranch since his daddy had fallen ill, almost fourteen years ago.

Truth be told, he'd probably been too young to take over, but sometimes a man had to do what needed to be done, and Daddy couldn't be out in the fields, with the cattle, or on the horses anymore.

Several dogs entered the warehouse with Bear, most of them never getting too far from him. Bishop liked to tease him about that too, claiming Bear even let one canine sleep in the house with him every night. That he'd made a rotating schedule for their cattle dogs.

None of it was true. The last thing Bear wanted was another heat source in the bed with him. He blew a fan all night as it was, even in the winter.

"Ranger," he said, and his cousin pulled himself out from underneath the tractor. "Where we at?" Bear tried to act like he didn't care. No one in the family would buy it, but Bear had managed to keep several cowboy employed for years now by acting like he didn't care. His falsely calm demeanor in the face of trouble had also kept Samantha Branton coming to fix his equipment when it broke down.

Except she couldn't come for another couple of days, which was why Ranger and Bishop had grease all over their hands.

Bear's pulse kicked out an extra beat at the simple thought of Sammy. He'd wanted her to move onto the ranch and work for him full-time, but she wouldn't. She had good reasons, he supposed, but that didn't make Bear any less of a well, bear about having to wait for her services.

Truth be told, he'd harbored a crush on the woman for three solid years now, and he should just ask her out. She seemed settled with her new responsibilities as a single mom, and her shop hummed along without her there twenty-four-seven.

"You're not even listening to me," Ranger said, and Bear blinked out of his own mind. He could sometimes get caught in there, especially once he started thinking about Sammy and all that dark hair she had, with a reddish-purple tint.

"I am," Bear said. "You said you can't get it to start."

"I said," Ranger said with a growl in his voice. "It won't start, and Bishop thinks it needs new spark plugs. So we went to town and got some. He's puttin' 'em in now, and then we'll see." Ranger wiped his hands on a dirty towel and turned back to the tractor. "Sammy can't come till when?"

"Friday," Bear said, another dose of darkness filling his soul. He should just replace all the equipment when it broke down. He had plenty of money. But that wasn't the Glover way, and Bear had been raised to repair rather than replace.

"Start 'er up," Bishop said, sliding out from under the tractor.

"Moment of truth," Ranger said. He came from Bear's uncle Bull, but he had the same brown hair as all the Glovers did. Before Bear's grandmother had passed away, she'd called it "earthy." The color of good, rich soil that had just been overturned. Bear just used the word "brown."

Ranger climbed up into the cockpit of the tractor and yelled, "Clear."

Bear and Bishop backed up a couple more feet, because who knew what could come spewing out of an engine once it started. The tractor grumbled, then growled, finally roaring to life and chugging along in an irregular pattern.

"That's not right," Bishop said over the noise. He waved both hands over his head to get Ranger to shut the tractor off. "I know we need this fixed," he said to Bear. "Don't worry, Boss. I'll get it." He grinned at Bear and dove under the tractor again.

Oh, to be in his thirties again. Bear wished he had half the energy his brother did, but as the oldest, and comparing himself to the youngest, he didn't.

He also didn't want to stand there, growing ever more impatient while Ranger and Bishop fiddled with settings and trims and the seating of the spark plugs. Everyone on the ranch knew the fields had to be ready by next weekend, and they'd get it done. He himself had worked through the night once to make sure the crops got put in on time.

He left the equipment shed in favor of the corral, where his team led over the horses had let all the equines out today as he worked to get the stables cleaned. Bear's family was a traditional ranching family, doing everything from horseback, with dogs and men. None of the fancy ATVs and helicopters some ranches used. He was never as comfortable as he was in the saddle, with a few dogs streaking along beside him as they moved cattle.

Therefore, the horse care at Shiloh Ridge Ranch was crucial, and Bear kept his finger on the pulse of all of it. He stroked the nose of one horse, stealing some of the calm energy, and saying, "You don't think I'm a grizzly, do ya?"

The horse didn't answer, and Bear wasn't sure he'd have wanted to hear the animal disagree anyway. His phone rang, and Bear didn't even want to look at it. Tuesdays weren't usually this rough.

Evelyn Walker's name sat on the screen, and Bear's mood changed instantly. He connected the call with his rough rancher's fingers, nearly knocking the phone out of his own hand. "Hey," he said easily, actually smiling while he did it.

"Bear," Evelyn said. "Sammy is at Micah's, fixing Simone's kiln."

His heart started dancing in his chest. "How long will she be there?"

"She just arrived," Evelyn said. "It's impossible to know, but Simone said the kiln has been acting up for a few weeks now. Could be a while."

"Thanks, Evelyn." Bear normally didn't waste words, especially when he didn't have much time. A sliver of humiliation went with him as he turned from the horses in the corral and strode toward his truck.

He could get to Seven Sons Ranch, where Micah lived and his wife did her antiques restoration, in fifteen minutes. Fine, the drive was usually twenty, but Bear was unusually motivated today.

He hadn't been able to figure out how to ask Sammy out on a date. He'd been the nicest to her out of anyone who set foot on Shiloh Ridge property, that was for sure. And he wasn't the only one who'd noticed.

His brothers—and he had plenty of them—had been teasing him for months and months, but he didn't see any of them dating anyone.

He drove down the dirt road as fast as he dared. He didn't need anyone asking questions later, and if he didn't kick up too much dust, no one would even know he'd left the ranch.

Several months ago, he'd had the thought that he just needed the right situation to present itself for him to ask Sammy to dinner. Nothing ever had. No amount of prayer had produced a different result than Bear giving her tasks around the ranch, Sammy completing them, and him paying her for a job well done.

He needed a matchmaker. And that was when he remembered a small town scandal from several years ago, when Evelyn had married Rhett Walker to prove her worth as a matchmaker.

It had taken Bear four more months to get up the nerve to call her, and he never would've done that had Micah not encouraged him. He said Rhett and Evelyn were real happy in their marriage, even if it had started out fake.

Micah was a good man, and his wife was Evelyn's sister. So Bear had made the call.

Evelyn had said it would take some serious planning to get Sammy in a situation where Bear would just happen to show up. She'd said they'd have to be patient and wait. She'd never called before.

Bear's mind blanked as he turned onto the asphalt and started down out of the foothills. Sammy was working on a kiln. He was just stopping by to see Micah's…something.

Bear frowned at himself. This was going to fail spectacularly.

And yet, he kept driving.

He turned onto the main highway and really got his truck going now, arriving at Seven Sons only a few minutes later. Sure enough, Sammy's rickety, old red and brown truck sat in Micah's driveway.

Bear parked right behind it, his heart thumping out a strange rhythm in his chest. He sat in the cab of his truck— much nicer and newer than Sammy's—for a few minutes, trying to convince himself to get out.

He didn't want to be made the fool. At forty-five years old, he didn't need to feel like such a spectacular failure.

Micah came out onto the front porch, and Bear couldn't just leave now. So he got out of his truck too, trying to remember the scenarios Evelyn had created for him.

"Bear," Micah said with a big grin. And why shouldn't he be smiling? He had a beautiful wife now too. A baby boy born last month. In fact, Simone came outside too, that little infant in her arms with a shock of dark hair.

"He wants you," she said, passing the baby to Micah. She gazed at her son for a moment, and Bear thought he was made of all head. Though he supposed all newborns were. "Afternoon, Bear."

"Ma'am." He touched the brim of his cowboy hat. "Micah, I was wondering if you'd show me that wall of bookcases." He met Simone's eye, and she grinned widely at him. Micah simply looked confused.

"In Simone's she-shed?"

"Yeah," Bear said. "I want to get some pictures of them for my brother. He's going to be doing some remodeling, and he's got it in his head that his house needs a library."

"All right," Micah said. Of course the man wouldn't suspect anything about Bear's story was off. He did have a brother that definitely leaned toward the eccentric side. Simone certainly knew though, and Micah had been the one to suggest Evelyn's services in the first place. Maybe he'd just forgotten, because it had been months since Bear had talked to Evelyn, and longer since Micah had mentioned the possibility of having Evelyn create a situation for Bear and Sammy that would get them out of the friend zone.

But Bear followed Micah through his house silently, grateful he'd hired the man to design and build his new homestead too. Yes, it had been outdated. No one could argue with that. No one in the family had protested when Bear had torn down the old homestead and put up another one. He lived there with two of his brothers now, and his place was as amazing as this one.

Micah went out the back door and down the steps to an expansive patio. "It's just over here," he said, as if Bear couldn't see the huge shed to the left. The baby in Micah's arms fussed, and Micah bounced the little boy, shushing him.

"What did you name him again?" Bear asked.

"Travis," Micah said. "We call him Trap, though."

"You'd fit right in my family," Bear said with a chuckle. His real name wasn't Bear, of course, but Bartholomew, after his father. Bear had never been called anything but Bear, at least in his memory. Once or twice, his momma had called him Teddy, but that went with Bear.

Just like Grizzly does, he thought as Micah stepped to the door. Bear's heart throbbed against the back of his throat, filling his mouth and rendering him mute.

Trap continued to fuss, breaking into a wail that said he wasn't more than a few weeks old, as Micah went into the she-shed. "I don't know why she said he wanted me," Micah said. "He's clearly hungry."

Bear just followed Micah inside, automatically looking around for Sammy. He didn't see her immediately, and then she poked her head up from where she knelt next to the kiln in the far corner.

His heart thrashed now, part of it telling him to do something. Ask her something. The other half warned him against doing anything, saying anything, just in case they got broken again.

"I have to take him inside," Micah said over his baby's wails. "I'll be back in a minute." He looked at Sammy and back to Bear, and Bear saw all the dots connect in Micah's mind. A slow smile crossed the man's face, and Bear almost growled at him to get him to leave.

But he didn't want Sammy to see him act like that, especially toward a friend. And if there was someone outside of Bear's family he considered a friend, it was Micah Walker.

All the Walkers really, as he knew Jeremiah quite well from their ranch owners meetings too.

"Take your time," Bear said, and Micah's grin only grew. He thankfully ducked out of the she-shed a moment later, leaving Bear alone with Sammy.

Finally.

Alone with Sammy, away from his own ranch. Outside of anything that had to do with their professional, working relationship.

In Bear's fantasies, he wanted a completely different kind of relationship with the woman, and he managed to smile at her as she stood up. She wore a dark blue tank top and jeans, both of which had plenty of dirt and grime on them.

Bear absolutely loved that about her. She was strong and sexy and not afraid to get dirty. She shook her hair over her shoulders and smiled back. "Hey, Bear," she said easily, like she didn't think about him in her quiet moments.

Panic reared inside Bear, and he couldn't say anything back.

She looked down at her tools, which she'd spread over a nearby counter, flicking her gaze back to his a moment later. "What are you doing here?"

Ah, it was a great question. And Bear had no idea how to answer it.

Samantha Benton picked up another wrench, though it was the wrong size. Bear Glover had been touched by God Himself when he was created—at least in Sammy's opinion. He exuded power, and he was easily the most handsome man Sammy had ever laid eyes on. With hair the color of fresh motor oil and those bright, bright blue eyes.

Yes, the Lord had definitely carved Bear out of a special piece of cloth. Very special indeed.

Sammy could feel those eyes on her, though the man said nothing. She put down the wrong wrench and picked up the flat-head screwdriver. She was of the opinion that almost any problem could be fixed with a wrench and a flat-head screwdriver, and while she'd only spent twenty minutes with the kiln, she knew the exhaust fan just needed to be cleaned or replaced.

She'd try to clean it first, and if that didn't work, she'd order a new fan for the unit. Things with moving parts spoke to her, and Sammy could diagnose almost any machine within the first hour of meeting it.

If only Bear Glover had cogs and wheels and screws inside him. Then maybe she'd be able to figure him out too.

"Sammy," he said, and she nearly fell to her knees when he said her name. Down she went, all the same, and he didn't need to know it was because of the care he put into the two syllables of her name.

"Yeah?" She got right back into the side panel of the kiln. The man had serious pull over her, and everything would be easier if she just focused on her work. That was what had gotten her through going out to Shiloh Ridge for the past three years. That, and the excellent money he paid for the work she did. And yes, he was easy to look at and made her feel like the young woman she'd once been.

The woman she'd been before she'd had to become a mother overnight, grieve the loss of her sister and brother-in-law, and hold the remaining members of her family together.

Sammy's dating life had dried up when she'd gotten custody of Lincoln. It was already on the decline, because she'd opened her mechanic shop six months before the terrible accident that had claimed her sister's life.

She kept telling herself that she'd go on a date when Lincoln started school. Then it was when he could read by himself. Then when he could tie his shoes without help. Then when he knew how to ride a bike.

The truth was, no one was asking, and Sammy didn't have time to find someone herself. She felt perpetually surrounded by men—at the shop, at the ranch—but none of them interested her half as much as Bear.

She looked up again to find he'd moved closer. He ran his fingertips along some of her tools, and she said, "Did you say something? Sorry, I got lost inside this thing for a second."

He looked at her, those eyes overpowering her in less than a breath. "I was just going to ask you—" He pulled his hand back from her tools. She kept them in a bag she'd bought online that was made for chefs to carry their knives.

And it went with Bear's hand, her tools clattering all over the cement floor in the she-shed. The noise was absolutely astronomical, and she clapped both hands over her ears as the metal bounced on the cement.

"I'm sorry," Bear said while her ears were still ringing. He got down on the ground and started picking up the pliers, the wrenches, the screwdrivers.

"It's fine," Sammy said, finally getting her senses back. She reached for a ratchet at the same time Bear did, and they froze, their hands touching.

"Listen," Bear said, maybe a little roughly. He turned his hand, and slipped his fingers between hers. "Would you go to dinner with me?"

Sammy's world turned white for a moment. "What?" she asked, out of instinct and nothing else. A light giggle followed, one she'd never made before and would likely never make again.

Bear released her hand and stood, seemingly in one

motion. For a big, tall cowboy, he could move really well. He laid her bag out on the countertop and said, "Forget it."

Forget what? her mind asked, and Sammy looked down at her hand. Her skin tingled for some reason, and she could still feel Bear's fingers between hers.

Dinner, her brain whispered. *He asked you to dinner!*

But Bear had already started walking away.

Wait, she called to him in her mind.

He opened the door and walked out, leaving Sammy mute and alone on the floor. Everything that had happened in the last thirty seconds rushed at her, and Sammy groaned as she realized she'd laughed when Bear had asked her out.

Legit *laughed* at him. At the idea of going out with him.

"Why did I do that?" she asked, looking up at the ceiling. "Dear Lord, can't anything go right for me? Would it have been so hard to make me loquacious for that one moment?" She felt like crying, but the door opened again, and Sammy spun onto her hip and hid her face from whoever came into the shop.

"Hey," Simone said. "How's it going? Did Bear get his pictures?"

"Pictures?" Sammy asked, glancing over her shoulder. "I have no idea."

Simone frowned as she bounced her baby in her arms. "What do you think?"

"I think you need a new exhaust fan," Sammy said, deciding on the spot not to try to clean the one inside the kiln. "I'm just getting the serial number and make and model so I can get one ordered for you."

"Oh, that sounds easy," Simone said.

"It should be," Sammy said, standing up. Her tools were an absolute mess, but she needed to get out of this shop and away from this ranch. She folded them up to deal with later and practically ran from the she-shed with, "I'll call you when it comes in, okay?"

"Oh, okay," Simone said behind her, and Sammy knew she'd have to answer the woman's questions later.

Right now, that didn't matter. Right now, she needed to get back to the shop, because Clayton would be there with Lincoln in less than thirty minutes. She didn't like leaving Lincoln alone for any amount of time, though he'd turned eight last fall and could certainly go inside and get a snack by himself.

She lived next door to the bus driver who brought the kids home from the elementary school, and Clayton had agreed to bring Lincoln to her mechanic shop every after-noon after the regular run. The system had been working for three years now, and Sammy always made sure she was in the shop at three-forty-five.

Sure, Lincoln could stay with the other mechanics there, and he'd probably prefer it. But Sammy carried a great burden to care for her nephew according to her sister's wishes, and she was going to do that the best way she knew how.

Sammy practically flew through the garage, only to find Bear's big, black truck parked behind hers, blocking her escape. He sat behind the wheel, looking down at something in his hand. Probably his phone.

He'll move, Sammy told herself as she opened the passenger door and tossed in her tools. She walked around the back of her truck so he'd see her, but she didn't look directly at him. Looking directly at a man like Bear Glover was like looking into the sun, and she'd already made a big enough fool of herself for one day. For a whole month, in fact.

"Sammy," Bear said, getting out of the truck.

"Hmm?" She didn't turn fully toward him as she put her hand on the door handle of her beat-up pickup. It had been her brother-in-law's, and it was familiar to Lincoln, so Sami kept fixing it when it broke down, and she kept driving it to keep something of Lincoln's father's in their lives.

Bear said nothing, forcing Sammy to look at him. He commanded every room he stepped into, and she wondered what it was like to hold that much power in the palm of one's hand.

"Look," he finally said. "I'm a real idiot, and I've gone about this all wrong." He held up his phone. "I've got a whole script, and I can't say it." He sighed like his ranch had been infested with tens of thousands of grasshoppers, as it had been in the past.

"I like you," he said, sort of yelling the words at her. "I like, you know, *like* you, and I wondered if maybe you'd go to dinner with me, so we can get to know each other on a personal level, not just a ranch level."

Sammy's brain threatened to shut down again, but she steadfastly refused to let it. "I'd have to get a babysitter," she said.

"And…you don't want to?" He looked absolutely miserable, but he was still standing there. Still looking at her, even as a flush colored his neck and stained his cheeks. Oh, that wasn't fair. Seeing him in a vulnerable state only made him more attractive than he already was.

"I can ask around," she said.

"We'll take Lincoln," Simone called from the porch, and Sami spun that way. She didn't know they'd had an audience.

"We've got older nieces and nephews," Micah added. "He'll love it out here."

They both beamed like this was the solution to world peace or something equally as great. Sammy looked at Bear; Bear looked back at Sammy.

Together, they burst out laughing, and he took another step closer to her. "Just one dinner," he murmured so Simone and Micah couldn't overhear. "If it doesn't go well, at least it'll be free."

"Why wouldn't it go well?" she asked.

"Well, I mean, I've already thrown your tools all around and stomped out of the room like a grizzly. So dinner can't be as bad as that, right?" He grinned, one side of his mouth pulling up higher than the other. So adorable, and she never thought she'd use that word to describe a man like Bear Glover.

Of course, she'd never seen him smile much around the ranch either.

"All right," she said. "I'll go to dinner with you."

"Yeehaw!" Micah yelled from the porch, and Sammy's face heated with embarrassment too.

She looked at Bear, who had glared Micah into silence. "And I'm expecting to hear about this script at dinner. Tonight?" She looked back to the porch. "Does tonight work for you guys?"

"Tonight is fine," Simone said, completely unashamed to be standing there, intruding on this private conversation. Or what Sammy wished was a private conversation.

"I'll pick you up at seven," Bear said. "Does that work? We can bring Lincoln out here together, and then go grab something to eat."

"Sounds like a date," Sammy said. She finally opened the door and got in her truck, glad when Bear waved to the porch and did the same. He backed out first, and she expected him to trundle on down the lane. He didn't, but waited for her to leave.

She did, watching in her rear-view mirror as he pulled back into Micah and Simone's driveway and got back out of his truck. She finally had to look away as the road curved toward the highway, but she acknowledged the jittery feeling in her stomach as she came to a stop and looked both ways.

She wasn't sure if it was because of what Micah, Simone, and Bear might be saying about her, or because she'd finally accepted a date and would be leaving Lincoln with someone besides his teacher.

"Or because the best-looking man in the state asked you out," Sammy said as she turned onto the highway and pressed on the gas pedal to get the truck going. It shuddered in protest, its acceleration not very good.

"And you said yes." A smile curved Sammy's mouth, and she enjoyed the excitement until she pulled up to the mechanic shop on the south side of town. Then she realized she'd need to pick out something to wear and put on makeup without her sister's help.

That's right! There's more ranch romance and another amazing family — the Glover's of Shiloh Ridge Ranch — to meet in beloved Three Rivers, Texas! Get ready for heartwarming Christmas traditions, true-to-life family drama, Christian cowboy romance, and strong women in unconventional occupations in the Shiloh Ridge Ranch in Three Rivers Romance series.

THE MECHANICS OF MISTLETOE is coming soon - to all retailers.

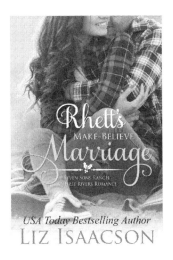

Tripp's Trivial Tie (Book 2): She needs a husband to keep her son. He's wanted to take their relationship to the next level, but she's always pushing him away. Will their trivial tie take them all the way to happily-ever-after?

USA Today Bestselling Author
LIZ ISAACSON

Liam's Invented I-Do (Book 3): She needs a husband to be credible as a matchmaker. He wants to help a neighbor. Will their fake marriage take them out of the friend zone?

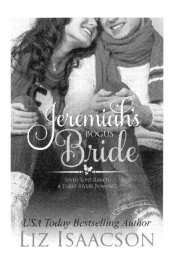

Jeremiah's Bogus Bride (Book 4): He wants to prove to his brothers that he's not broken. She just wants him. Will a fake marriage heal him or push her further away?

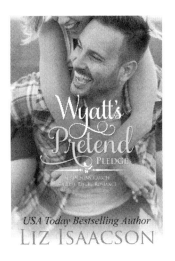

Wyatt's Pretend Pledge (Book 5): To get her inheritance, she needs a husband. He's wanted to fly with her for ages. Can their pretend pledge turn into something real?

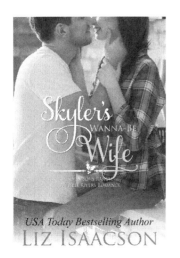

Skyler's Wanna-Be Wife (Book 6): She needs a new last name to stay in school. He's willing to help a fellow student. Can this wanna-be wife show the playboy that some things should be taken seriously?

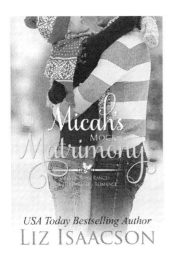

USA Today Bestselling Author
LIZ ISAACSON

Micah's Mock Matrimony (Book 7): They were just actors in a play. The marriage was just for the crowd – until a clerical error results in a legal marriage. Can these two neighbors negotiate this new ground between them and achieve new roles in each other's lives?

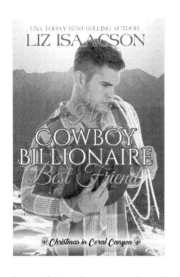

Her Cowboy Billionaire Best Friend (Book 1): Graham Whittaker returns to Coral Canyon a few days after Christmas—after the death of his father. He takes over the energy company his dad built from the ground up and buys a high-end lodge to live in—only a mile from the home of his once-best friend, Laney McAllister. They were best friends once, but Laney's always entertained feelings for him, and spending so much time with him while they make Christmas memories puts her heart in danger of getting broken again…

Her Cowboy Billionaire Boss (Book 2): Since the death of his wife a few years ago, Eli Whittaker has been running from one job to another, unable to find somewhere for him and his son to settle. Meg Palmer is Stockton's nanny, and she comes with her boss, Eli, to the lodge, her long-time crush on the man no different in Wyoming than it was on the beach. When she confesses her feelings for him and gets nothing in return, she's crushed, embarrassed, and unsure if she can stay in Coral Canyon for Christmas. Then Eli starts to show some feelings for her too...

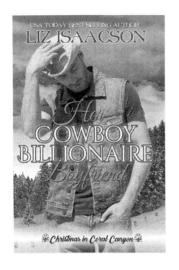

Her Cowboy Billionaire Boyfriend (Book 3): Andrew Whittaker is the public face for the Whittaker Brothers' family energy company, and with his older brother's robot about to be announced, he needs a press secretary to help him get everything ready and tour the state to make the announcements. When he's hit by a protest sign being carried by the company's biggest opponent, Rebecca Collings, he learns with a few clicks that she has the background they need. He offers her the job of press secretary when she thought she was going to be arrested, and not only because the spark between them in so hot Andrew can't see straight.

Can Becca and Andrew work together and keep their relationship a secret? Or will hearts break in this classic romance retelling reminiscent of *Two Weeks Notice*?

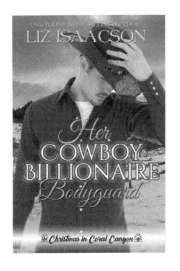

Her Cowboy Billionaire Bodyguard (Book 4): Beau Whittaker has watched his brothers find love one by one, but every attempt he's made has ended in disaster. Lily Everett has been in the spotlight since childhood and has half a dozen platinum records with her two sisters. She's taking a break from the brutal music industry and hiding out in Wyoming while her ex-husband continues to cause trouble for her. When she hears of Beau Whittaker and what he offers his clients, she wants to meet him. Beau is instantly attracted to Lily, but he tried a relationship with his last client that left a scar that still hasn't healed...

Can Lily use the spirit of Christmas to discover what matters most? Will Beau open his heart to the possibility of love with someone so different from him?

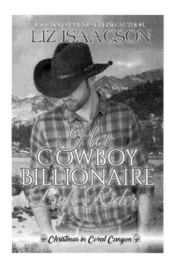

Her Cowboy Billionaire Bull Rider (Book 5): Todd Christopherson has just retired from the professional rodeo circuit and returned to his hometown of Coral Canyon. Problem is, he's got no family there anymore, no land, and no job. Not that he needs a job--he's got plenty of money from his illustrious career riding bulls.

Then Todd gets thrown during a routine horseback ride up the canyon, and his only support as he recovers physically is the beautiful Violet Everett. She's no nurse, but she does the best she can for the handsome cowboy. **Will she lose her heart to the billionaire bull rider? Can Todd trust that God led him to Coral Canyon...and Vi?**

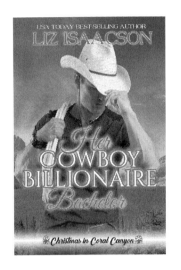

Her Cowboy Billionaire Bachelor (Book 6): Rose Everett isn't sure what to do with her life now that her country music career is on hold. After all, with both of her sisters in Coral Canyon, and one about to have a baby, they're not making albums anymore.

Liam Murphy has been working for Doctors Without Borders, but he's back in the US now, and looking to start a new clinic in Coral Canyon, where he spent his summers.

When Rose wins a date with Liam in a bachelor auction, their relationship blooms and grows quickly. **Can Liam and Rose find a solution to their problems that doesn't involve one of them leaving Coral Canyon with a broken heart?**

Her Cowboy Billionaire Blind Date (Book 7): Her sons want her to be happy, but she's too old to be set up on a blind date...isn't she?

Amanda Whittaker has been looking for a second chance at love since the death of her husband several years ago. Finley Barber is a cowboy in every sense of the word. Born and raised on a racehorse farm in Kentucky, he's since moved to Dog Valley and started his own breeding stable for champion horses. He hasn't dated in years, and everything about Amanda makes him nervous.

Will Amanda take the leap of faith required to be with Finn? Or will he become just another boyfriend who doesn't make the cut?

Her Cowboy Billionaire Best Man (Book 8): When Celia Abbott-Armstrong runs into a gorgeous cowboy at her best friend's wedding, she decides she's ready to start dating again.

But the cowboy is Zach Zuckerman, and the Zuckermans and Abbotts have been at war for generations.

Can Zach and Celia find a way to reconcile their family's differences so they can have a future together?

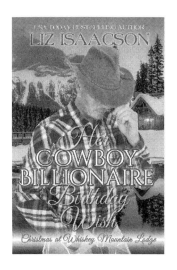

Her Cowboy Billionaire Birthday Wish (Book 9): All the maid at Whiskey Mountain Lodge wants for her birthday is a handsome cowboy billionaire. And Colton can make that wish come true—if only he hadn't escaped to Coral Canyon after being left at the altar...

BOOKS IN THE LAST CHANCE RANCH
ROMANCE SERIES

Her Last First Kiss (Book 1): A cowgirl down on her luck hires a man who's good with horses and under the hood of a car. Can Hudson fine tune Scarlett's heart as they work together? Or will things backfire and make everything worse at Last Chance Ranch?

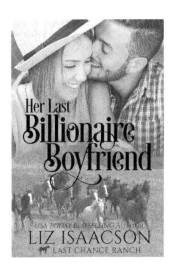

Her Last Billionaire Boyfriend (Book 2): A billionaire cowboy without a home meets a woman who secretly makes food videos to pay her debts...Can Carson and Adele do more than fight in the kitchens at Last Chance Ranch?

Her Last Make-Believe Marriage (Book 3): A female carpenter needs a husband just for a few days... Can Jeri and Sawyer navigate the minefield of a pretend marriage before their feelings become real?

Her Last Second Chance (Book 4): An Army cowboy, the woman he dated years ago, and their last chance at Last Chance Ranch... Can Dave and Sissy put aside hurt feelings and make their second chance romance work?

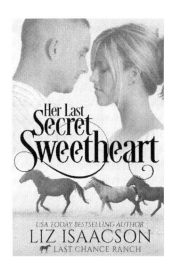

Her Last Secret Sweetheart (Book 5): A former dairy farmer and the marketing director on the ranch have to work together to make the cow cuddling program a success. But can Karla let Cache into her life? Or will she keep all her secrets from him - and keep *him* a secret too?

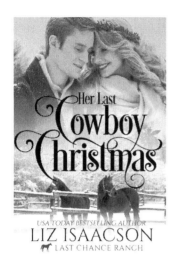

Her Last Cowboy Christmas (Book 6): She's tired of having her heart broken by cowboys. He waited too long to ask her out. Can Lance fix things quickly, or will Amber leave Last Chance Ranch before he can tell her how he feels?

Her Cowboy Billionaire Best Friend (Book 1): Graham Whittaker returns to Coral Canyon a few days after Christmas—after the death of his father. He takes over the energy company his dad built from the ground up and buys a high-end lodge to live in—only a mile from the home of his once-best friend, Laney McAllister. They were best friends once, but Laney's always entertained feelings for him, and spending so much time with him while they make Christmas memories puts her heart in danger of getting broken again...

Her Cowboy Billionaire Boss (Book 2): Since the death of his wife a few years ago, Eli Whittaker has been running from one job to another, unable to find somewhere for him and his son to settle. Meg Palmer is Stockton's nanny, and she comes with her boss, Eli, to the lodge, her long-time crush on the man no different in Wyoming than it was on the beach. When she confesses her feelings for him and gets nothing in return, she's crushed, embarrassed, and unsure if she can stay in Coral Canyon for Christmas. Then Eli starts to show some feelings for her too…

Her Cowboy Billionaire Boyfriend (Book 3): Andrew Whittaker is the public face for the Whittaker Brothers' family energy company, and with his older brother's robot about to be announced, he needs a press secretary to help him get everything ready and tour the state to make the announcements. When he's hit by a protest sign being carried by the company's biggest opponent, Rebecca Collings, he learns with a few clicks that she has the background they need. He offers her the job of press secretary when she thought she was going to be arrested, and not only because the spark between them in so hot Andrew can't see straight.

Can Becca and Andrew work together and keep their relationship a secret? Or will hearts break in this classic romance retelling reminiscent of _Two Weeks Notice_?

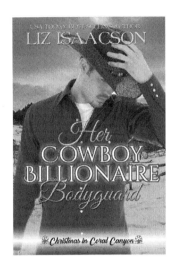

Her Cowboy Billionaire Bodyguard (Book 4): Beau Whittaker has watched his brothers find love one by one, but every attempt he's made has ended in disaster. Lily Everett has been in the spotlight since childhood and has half a dozen platinum records with her two sisters. She's taking a break from the brutal music industry and hiding out in Wyoming while her ex-husband continues to cause trouble for her. When she hears of Beau Whittaker and what he offers his clients, she wants to meet him. Beau is instantly attracted to Lily, but he tried a relationship with his last client that left a scar that still hasn't healed...

Can Lily use the spirit of Christmas to discover what matters most? Will Beau open his heart to the possibility of love with someone so different from him?

Her Cowboy Billionaire Bull Rider (Book 5): Todd Christopherson has just retired from the professional rodeo circuit and returned to his hometown of Coral Canyon. Problem is, he's got no family there anymore, no land, and no job. Not that he needs a job--he's got plenty of money from his illustrious career riding bulls.

Then Todd gets thrown during a routine horseback ride up the canyon, and his only support as he recovers physically is the beautiful Violet Everett. She's no nurse, but she does the best she can for the handsome cowboy. **Will she lose her heart to the billionaire bull rider? Can Todd trust that God led him to Coral Canyon...and Vi?**

Her Cowboy Billionaire Bachelor (Book 6): Rose Everett isn't sure what to do with her life now that her country music career is on hold. After all, with both of her sisters in Coral Canyon, and one about to have a baby, they're not making albums anymore.

Liam Murphy has been working for Doctors Without Borders, but he's back in the US now, and looking to start a new clinic in Coral Canyon, where he spent his summers.

When Rose wins a date with Liam in a bachelor auction, their relationship blooms and grows quickly. **Can Liam and Rose find a solution to their problems that doesn't involve one of them leaving Coral Canyon with a broken heart?**

Her Cowboy Billionaire Blind Date (Book 7): Her sons want her to be happy, but she's too old to be set up on a blind date...isn't she?

Amanda Whittaker has been looking for a second chance at love since the death of her husband several years ago. Finley Barber is a cowboy in every sense of the word. Born and raised on a racehorse farm in Kentucky, he's since moved to Dog Valley and started his own breeding stable for champion horses. He hasn't dated in years, and everything about Amanda makes him nervous.

Will Amanda take the leap of faith required to be with Finn? Or will he become just another boyfriend who doesn't make the cut?

Her Cowboy Billionaire Best Man (Book 8): When Celia Abbott-Armstrong runs into a gorgeous cowboy at her best friend's wedding, she decides she's ready to start dating again.

But the cowboy is Zach Zuckerman, and the Zuckermans and Abbotts have been at war for generations.

Can Zach and Celia find a way to reconcile their family's differences so they can have a future together?

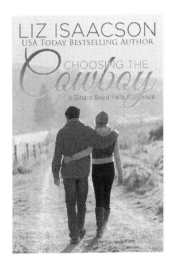

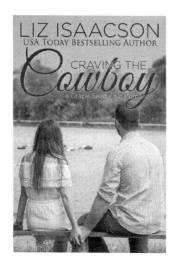

Craving the Cowboy (Book 2):
Dwayne Carver is set to inherit his family's ranch in the heart of Texas Hill Country, and in order to keep up with his ranch duties and fulfill his dreams of owning a horse farm, he hires top trainer Felicity Lightburne. They get along great, and she can envision herself on this new farm—at least until her mother falls ill and she has to return to help her. Can Dwayne and Felicity work through their differences to find their happily-ever-after?

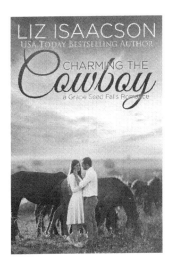

Charming the Cowboy (Book 3): Third grade teacher Heather Carver has had her eye on Levi Rhodes for a couple of years now, but he seems to be blind to her attempts to charm him. When she breaks her arm while on his horse ranch, Heather infiltrates Levi's life in ways he's never thought of, and his strict anti-female stance slips. Will Heather heal his emotional scars and he care for her physical ones so they can have a real relationship?

Courting the Cowboy (Book 4): Frustrated with the cowboy-only dating scene in Grape Seed Falls, May Sotheby joins Texas-Faithful.com, hoping to find her soul mate without having to relocate--or deal with cowboy hats and boots. She has no idea that Kurt Pemberton, foreman at Grape Seed Ranch, is the man she starts communicating with... Will May be able to follow her heart and get Kurt to forgive her so they can be together?

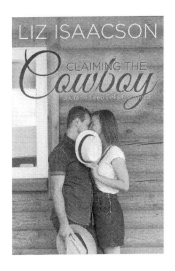

Claiming the Cowboy, Royal Brothers Book 1 (Grape Seed Falls Romance Book 5): Unwilling to be tied down, farrier Robin Cook has managed to pack her entire life into a two-hundred-and-eighty square-foot house, and that includes her Yorkie. Cowboy and co-foreman, Shane Royal has had his heart set on Robin for three years, even though she flat-out turned him down the last time he asked her to dinner. But she's back at Grape Seed Ranch for five weeks as she works her horseshoeing magic, and he's still interested, despite a bitter life lesson that left a bad taste for marriage in his mouth.

Robin's interested in him too. But can she find room for Shane in her tiny house--and can he take a chance on her with his tired heart?

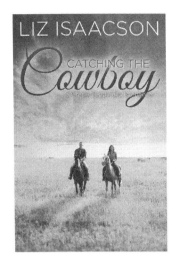

Catching the Cowboy, Royal Brothers Book 2 (Grape Seed Falls Romance Book 6): Dylan Royal is good at two things: whistling and caring for cattle. When his cows are being attacked by an unknown wild animal, he calls Texas Parks & Wildlife for help. He wasn't expecting a beautiful mammologist to show up, all flirty and fun and everything Dylan didn't know he wanted in his life.

Hazel Brewster has gone on more first dates than anyone in Grape Seed Falls, and she thinks maybe Dylan deserves a second... Can they find their way through wild animals, huge life changes, and their emotional pasts to find their forever future?

Cheering the Cowboy, Royal Brothers Book 3 (Grape Seed Falls Romance Book 7): Austin Royal loves his life on his new ranch with his brothers. But he doesn't love that Shayleigh Hatch came with the property, nor that he has to take the blame for the fact that he now owns her childhood ranch. They rarely have a conversation that doesn't leave him furious and frustrated--and yet he's still attracted to Shay in a strange, new way.

Shay inexplicably likes him too, which utterly confuses and angers her. As they work to make this Christmas the best the Triple Towers Ranch has ever seen, can they also navigate through their rocky relationship to smoother waters?

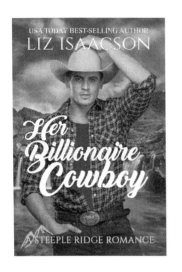

Her Billionaire Cowboy (Book 1): Tucker Jenkins has had enough of tall buildings, traffic, and has traded in his technology firm in New York City for Steeple Ridge Horse Farm in rural Vermont. Missy Marino has worked at the farm since she was a teen, and she's always dreamed of owning it. But her ex-husband left her with a truckload of debt, making her fantasies of owning the farm unfulfilled. Tucker didn't come to the country to find a new wife, but he supposes a woman could help him start over in Steeple Ridge. Will Tucker and Missy be able to navigate the shaky ground between them to find a new beginning?

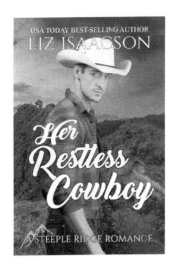

Her Restless Cowboy (Book 2): Ben Buttars is the youngest of the four Buttars brothers who come to Steeple Ridge Farm, and he finally feels like he's landed somewhere he can make a life for himself. Reagan Cantwell is a decade older than Ben and the recreational direction for the town of Island Park. Though Ben is young, he knows what he wants—and that's Rae. Can she figure out how to put what matters most in her life—family and faith—above her job before she loses Ben?

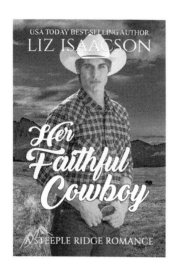

Her Faithful Cowboy (Book 3): Sam Buttars has spent the last decade making sure he and his brothers stay together. They've been at Steeple Ridge for a while now, but with the youngest married and happy, the siren's call to return to his parents' farm in Wyoming is loud in Sam's ears. He'd just go if it weren't for beautiful Bonnie Sherman, who roped his heart the first time he saw her. Do Sam and Bonnie have the faith to find comfort in each other instead of in the people who've already passed?

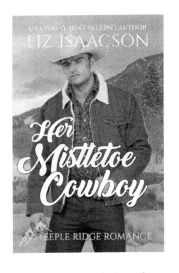

Her Mistletoe Cowboy (Book 4): Logan Buttars has always been good-natured and happy-go-lucky. After watching two of his brothers settle down, he recognizes a void in his life he didn't know about. Veterinarian Layla Guyman has appreciated Logan's friendship and easy way with animals when he comes into the clinic to get the service dogs. But with his future at Steeple Ridge in the balance, she's not sure a relationship with him is worth the risk. Can she rely on her faith and employ patience to tame Logan's wild heart?

Her Patient Cowboy (Book 5):
Darren Buttars is cool, collected, and quiet—and utterly devastated when his girl-friend of nine months, Farrah Irvine, breaks up with him because he wanted her to ride her horse in a parade. But Farrah doesn't ride anymore, a fact she made very clear to Darren. She returned to her childhood home with so much baggage, she doesn't know where to start with the unpacking. Darren's the only Buttars brother who isn't married, and he wants to make Island Park his permanent home—with Farrah. Can they find their way through the heartache to achieve a happily-ever-after together?

Falling for Her Boss: A Horseshoe Home Ranch Romance (Book 1): Jace Lovell only has one thing left after his fiancé abandons him at the altar: his job at Horseshoe Home Ranch. Belle Edmunds is back in Gold Valley and she's desperate to build a portfolio that she can use to start her own firm in Montana. Jace isn't anywhere near forgiving his fiancé, and he's not sure he's ready for a new relationship with someone as fiery and beautiful as Belle. Can she employ her patience while he figures out how to forgive so they can find their own brand of happily-ever-after?

Falling for Her Roommate: A Horseshoe Home Ranch Romance (Book 2): Professional snowboarder Sterling Maughan has sequestered himself in his family's cabin in the exclusive mountain community above Gold Valley, Montana after a devastating fall that ended his career. Norah Watson cleans Sterling's cabin and the more time they spend together, the more Sterling is interested in all things Norah. As his body heals, so does his faith. Will Norah be able to trust Sterling so they can have a chance at true love?

Falling for His Best Friend: A Horseshoe Home Ranch Romance (Book 3): Landon Edmunds has been a cowboy his whole life. An accident five years ago ended his successful rodeo career, and now he's looking to start a horse ranch-- and he's looking outside of Montana. Which would be great if God hadn't brought Megan Palmer back to Gold Valley right when Landon is looking to leave. Megan and Landon work together well, and as sparks fly, she's sure God brought her back to Gold Valley so she could find her happily ever after. Through serious discussion and prayer, can Landon and Megan find their future together?

Be sure to check out the spinoff series, the Brush Creek Brides romances after you read FALLING FOR HIS BEST FRIEND. Start with A WEDDING FOR THE WIDOWER.

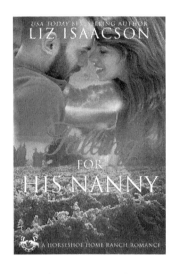

Falling for His Nanny: A Horseshoe Home Ranch Romance (Book 4): Twelve years ago, Owen Carr left Gold Valley—and his long-time girl-friend—in favor of a country music career in Nashville. Married and divorced, Natalie teaches ballet at the dance studio in Gold Valley, but she never auditioned for the professional company the way she dreamed of doing. With Owen back, she realizes all the opportunities she missed out on when he left all those years ago—including a future with him. Can they mend broken bridges in order to have a second chance at love?

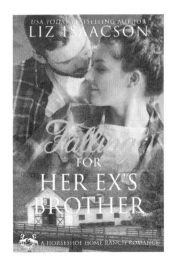

Falling for Her Ex's Brother: A Horseshoe Home Ranch Romance (Book 5): Caleb Chamberlain has spent the last five years recovering from a horrible breakup, his alcoholism that stemmed from it, and the car accident that left him hospitalized. He's finally on the right track in his life—until Holly Gray, his twin brother's ex-fiance mistakes him for Nathan. Holly's back in Gold Valley to get the required veterinarian hours to apply for her graduate program. When the herd at Horseshoe Home comes down with pneumonia, Caleb and Holly are forced to work together in close quarters. Holly's over Nathan, but she hasn't forgiven him—or the woman she believes broke up their relationship. Can Caleb and Holly navigate such a rough past to find their happily-ever-after?

Journey to Steeple Ridge Farm with Holly—and fall in love with the cowboys there in the Steeple Ridge Romance series! Start with STARTING OVER AT STEEPLE RIDGE.

Falling for Her Old Boyfriend: A Horseshoe Home Ranch Romance (Book 6): Ty Barker has been dancing through the last thirty years of his life--and he's suddenly realized he's alone. River Lee Whitely is back in Gold Valley with her two little girls after a divorce that's left deep scars. She has a job at Silver Creek that requires her to be able to ride a horse, and she nearly tramples Ty at her first lesson. That's just fine by him, because River Lee is the girl Ty has never gotten over. Ty realizes River Lee needs time to settle into her new job, her new home, her new life as a single parent, but going slow has never been his style. But for River Lee, can Ty take the necessary steps to keep her in his life?

Falling for His Next Door Neighbor: A Horseshoe Home Ranch Romance (Book 7): Archer Bailey has already lost one job to Emersyn Enders, so he deliberately doesn't tell her about the cowhand job up at Horseshoe Home Ranch. Emery's temporary job is ending, but her obligations to her physically disabled sister aren't. As Archer and Emery work together, its clear that the sparks flying between them aren't all from their friendly competition over a job. Will Emery and Archer be able to navigate the ranch, their close quarters, and their individual circumstances to find love this holiday season?

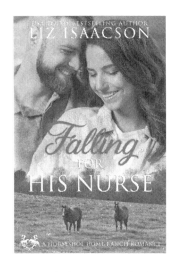

Falling for His Nurse: A Horseshoe Home Ranch Romance (Book 8): Cowboy Elliott Hawthorne has just lost his best friend and cabin mate to the worst thing imaginable—marriage. When his brother calls about an accident with their father, Elliott rushes down to Gold Valley from the ranch only to be met with the most beautiful woman he's ever seen. His father's new physical therapist, London Marsh, likes the handsome face and gentle spirit she sees in Elliott too. Can Elliott and London navigate difficult family situations to find a happily-ever-after?

Second Chance Ranch: A Three Rivers Ranch Romance (Book 1): After his deployment, injured and discharged Major Squire Ackerman returns to Three Rivers Ranch, wanting to forgive Kelly for ignoring him a decade ago. He'd like to provide the stable life she needs, but with old wounds opening and a ranch on the brink of financial collapse, it will take patience and faith to make their second chance possible.

Third Time's the Charm: A Three Rivers Ranch Romance (Book 2): First Lieutenant Peter Marshall has a truckload of debt and no way to provide for a family, but Chelsea helps him see past all the obstacles, all the scars. With so many unknowns, can Pete and Chelsea develop the love, acceptance, and faith needed to find their happily ever after?

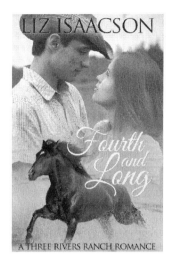

Fourth and Long: A Three Rivers Ranch Romance (Book 3): Commander Brett Murphy goes to Three Rivers Ranch to find some rest and relaxation with his Army buddies. Having his ex-wife show up with a seven-year-old she claims is his son is anything but the R&R he craves. Kate needs to make amends, and Brett needs to find forgiveness, but are they too late to find their happily ever after?

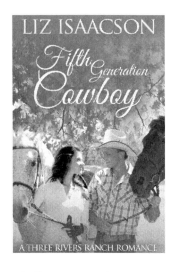

Fifth Generation Cowboy: A Three Rivers Ranch Romance (Book 4): Tom Lovell has watched his friends find their true happiness on Three Rivers Ranch, but everywhere he looks, he only sees friends. Rose Reyes has been bringing her daughter out to the ranch for equine therapy for months, but it doesn't seem to be working. Her challenges with Mari are just as frustrating as ever. Could Tom be exactly what Rose needs? Can he remove his friendship blinders and find love with someone who's been right in front of him all this time?

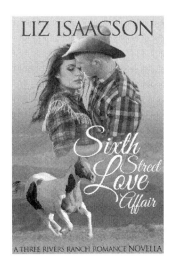

Sixth Street Love Affair: A Three Rivers Ranch Romance (Book 5): After losing his wife a few years back, Garth Ahlstrom thinks he's ready for a second chance at love. But Juliette Thompson has a secret that could destroy their budding relationship. Can they find the strength, patience, and faith to make things work?

LIZ ISAACSON

A THREE RIVERS RANCH ROMANCE

The Seventh Sergeant: A Three Rivers Ranch Romance (Book 6): Life has finally started to settle down for Sergeant Reese Sanders after his devastating injury overseas. Discharged from the Army and now with a good job at Courage Reins, he's finally found happiness—until a horrific fall puts him right back where he was years ago: Injured and depressed. Carly Watters, Reese's new veteran care coordinator, dislikes small towns almost as much as she loathes cowboys. But she finds herself faced with both when she gets assigned to Reese's case. Do they have the humility and faith to make their relationship more than professional?

Eight Second Ride: A Three Rivers Ranch Romance (Book 7): Ethan Greene loves his work at Three Rivers Ranch, but he can't seem to find the right woman to settle down with. When sassy yet vulnerable Brynn Bowman shows up at the ranch to recruit him back to the rodeo circuit, he takes a different approach with the barrel racing champion. His patience and newfound faith pay off when a friendship--and more--starts with Brynn. But she wants out of the rodeo circuit right when Ethan wants to rejoin. Can they find the path God wants them to take and still stay together?

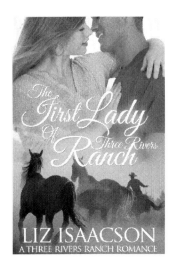

The First Lady of Three Rivers Ranch: A Three Rivers Ranch Romance (Book 8): Heidi Duffin has been dreaming about opening her own bakery since she was thirteen years old. She scrimped and saved for years to afford baking and pastry school in San Francisco. And now she only has one year left before she's a certified pastry chef. Frank Ackerman's father has recently retired, and he's taken over the largest cattle ranch in the Texas Panhandle. A horseman through and through, he's also nearing thirty-one and looking for someone to bring love and joy to a homestead that's been dominated by men for a decade. But when he convinces Heidi to come clean the cowboy cabins, she changes all that. But the siren's call of a bakery is still loud in Heidi's ears, even if she's also seeing a future with Frank. Can she rely on her faith in ways she's never had to before or will their relationship end when summer does?

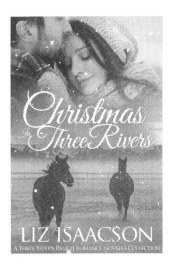

Christmas in Three Rivers: A Three Rivers Ranch Romance (Book 9): Isn't Christmas the best time to fall in love? The cowboys of Three Rivers Ranch think so. Join four of them as they journey toward their path to happily ever after in four, all-new novellas in the Amazon #1 Bestselling Three Rivers Ranch Romance series.

THE NINTH INNING: The Christmas season has never felt like such a burden to boutique owner Andrea Larsen. But with Mama gone and the holidays upon her, Andy finds herself wishing she hadn't been so quick to judge her former boyfriend, cowboy Lawrence Collins. Well, Lawrence hasn't forgotten about Andy either, and he devises a plan to get her out to the ranch so they can reconnect. Do they have the faith and humility to patch things up and start a new relationship?

TEN DAYS IN TOWN: Sandy Keller is tired of the dating scene in Three Rivers. Though she owns the pancake house, she's looking for a fresh start, which means an escape from the town where she grew up. When her older brother's best friend, Tad Jorgensen, comes to town for the holidays, it is a balm to his weary soul. A helicopter tour guide who experienced a near-death experience, he's looking to start over too--but in Three Rivers. Can Sandy and Tad navigate their troubles to find the path God wants them to take--and discover true love--in only ten days?

ELEVEN YEAR REUNION: Pastry chef extraordinaire, Grace Lewis has moved to Three Rivers to help Heidi Ackerman open a bakery in Three Rivers. Grace relishes the idea of starting over in a town where no one knows about her failed cupcakery. She doesn't expect to run into her old high school boyfriend, Jonathan Carver. A carpenter working at Three Rivers Ranch, Jon's in town against his will. But with Grace now on the scene, Jon's thinking life in Three Rivers is suddenly looking up. But with her focus on baking and his disdain for small towns, can they make their eleven year reunion stick?

THE TWELFTH TOWN: Newscaster Taryn Tucker has had enough of life on-screen. She's bounced from town to town before arriving in Three Rivers, completely alone and completely anonymous--just the way she now likes it. She takes a job cleaning at Three Rivers Ranch, hoping for a chance to figure out who she is and where God wants her. When she meets happy-go-lucky cowhand Kenny Stockton, she doesn't expect sparks to fly. Kenny's always been "the best friend" for his female friends, but the pull between him and Taryn can't be denied. Will they have the courage and faith necessary to make their opposite worlds mesh?

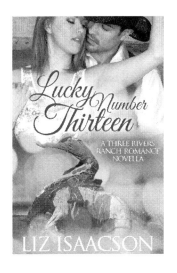

Lucky Number Thirteen: A Three Rivers Ranch Romance (Book 10): Tanner Wolf, a rodeo champion ten times over, is excited to be riding in Three Rivers for the first time since he left his philandering ways and found religion. Seeing his old friends Ethan and Brynn is therapuetic--until a terrible accident lands him in the hospi-tal. With his rodeo career over, Tanner thinks maybe he'll stay in town--and it's not just because his nurse, Summer Hamblin, is the prettiest woman he's ever met. But Summer's the queen of first dates, and as she looks for a way to make a relationship with the transient rodeo star work Summer's not sure she has the fortitude to go on a second date. Can they find love among the tragedy?

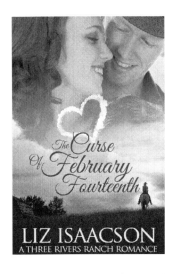

The Curse of February Fourteenth: A Three Rivers Ranch Romance (Book 11): Cal Hodgkins, cowboy veterinarian at Bowman's Breeds, isn't planning to meet anyone at the masked dance in small-town Three Rivers. He just wants to get his bachelor friends off his back and sit on the sidelines to drink his punch. But when he sees a woman dressed in gorgeous butterfly wings and cowgirl boots with blue stitching, he's smitten. Too bad she runs away from the dance before he can get her name, leaving only her boot behind...

Fifteen Minutes of Fame: A Three Rivers Ranch Romance (Book 12): Navy Richards is thirty-five years of tired—tired of dating the same men, working a demanding job, and getting her heart broken over and over again. Her aunt has always spoken highly of the matchmaker in Three Rivers, Texas, so she takes a six-month sabbatical from her high-stress job as a pediatric nurse, hops on a bus, and meets with the matchmaker. Then she meets Gavin Redd. He's handsome, he's hardworking, and he's a cowboy. But is he an Aquarius too? Navy's not making a move until she knows for sure...

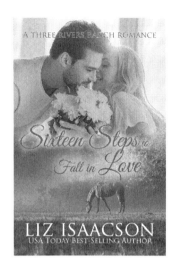

Sixteen Steps to Fall in Love: A Three Rivers Ranch Romance (Book 13): A chance encounter at a dog park sheds new light on the tall, talented Boone that Nicole can't ignore. As they get to know each other better and start to dig into each other's past, Nicole is the one who wants to run. This time from her growing admiration and attachment to Boone. From her aging parents. From herself.

But Boone feels the attraction between them too, and he decides he's tired of running and ready to make Three Rivers his permanent home. **Can Boone and Nicole use their faith to overcome their differences and find a happily-ever-after together?**

The Sleigh on Seventeenth Street: A Three Rivers Ranch Romance (Book 14): A cowboy with skills as an electrician tries a relationship with a down-on-her luck plumber. Can Dylan and Camila make water and electricity play nicely together this Christmas season? Or will they get shocked as they try to make their relationship work?

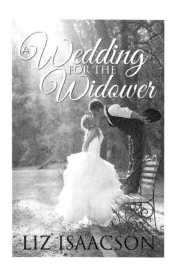

A Wedding for the Widower: Brush Creek Brides Romance (Book 1): Former rodeo champion and cowboy Walker Thompson trains horses at Brush Creek Horse Ranch, where he lives a simple life in his cabin with his ten-year-old son. A widower of six years, he's worked with Tess Wagner, a widow who came to Brush Creek to escape the turmoil of her life to give her seven-year-old son a slower pace of life. But Tess's breast cancer is back...

Walker will have to decide if he'd rather spend even a short time with Tess than not have her in his life at all. Tess wants to feel God's love and power, but can she discover and accept God's will in order to find her happy ending?

A Companion for the Cowboy: Brush Creek Brides Romance (Book 2): Cowboy and professional roper Justin Jackman has found solitude at Brush Creek Horse Ranch, preferring his time with the animals he trains over dating. With two failed engagements in his past, he's not really interested in getting his heart stomped on again. But

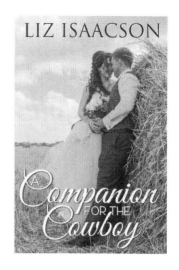

when flirty and fun Renee Martin picks him up at a church ice cream bar--on a bet, no less--he finds himself more than just a little interested. His Gen-X attitudes are attractive to her; her Millennial behaviors drive him nuts. Can Justin look past their differences and take a chance on another engagement?

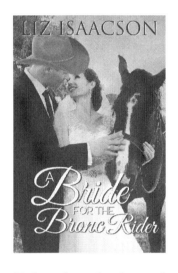

A Bride for the Bronc Rider: Brush Creek Brides Romance (Book 3): Ted Caldwell has been a retired bronc rider for years, and he thought he was perfectly happy training horses to buck at Brush Creek Ranch. He was wrong. When he meets April Nox, who comes to the ranch to hide her pregnancy from all her friends back in Jackson Hole, Ted realizes he has a huge family-shaped hole in his life. April is embarrassed, heartbroken, and trying to find her extinguished faith. She's never ridden a horse and wants nothing to do with a cowboy ever again. Can Ted and April create a family of happiness and love from a tragedy?

A Family for the Farmer: Brush Creek Brides Romance (Book 4): Blake Gibbons oversees all the agriculture at Brush Creek Horse Ranch, sometimes moonlighting as a general contractor. When he meets Erin Shields, new in town, at her aunt's bakery, he's instantly smitten. Erin moved to Brush Creek after a divorce that left  her penniless, homeless, and a single mother of three children under age eight. She's nowhere near ready to start dating again, but the longer Blake hangs around the bakery, the more she starts to like him. Can Blake and Erin find a way to blend their lifestyles and become a family?

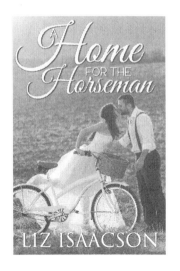

A Home for the Horseman: Brush Creek Brides Romance (Book 5): Emmett Graves has always had a positive outlook on life. He adores training horses to become barrel racing champions during the day and cuddling with his cat at night. Fresh off her professional rodeo retirement, Molly Brady comes to Brush Creek Horse Ranch as Emmett's protege. He's not thrilled, and she's allergic to cats. Oh, and she'd like to stay cowboy-free, thank you very much. But Emmett's about as cowboy as they come.... Can Emmett and Molly work together without falling in love?

A Refuge for the Rancher: Brush Creek Brides Romance (Book 6): Grant Ford spends his days training cattle—when he's not camped out at the elementary school hoping to catch a glimpse of his ex-girlfriend. When principal Shannon Sharpe confronts him and asks him to stay away from the school, the spark between them 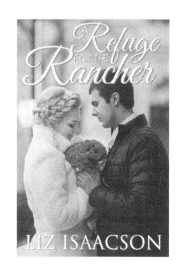 is instant and hot. Shannon's expecting a transfer very soon, but she also needs a summer outdoor coordinator—and Grant fits the bill. Just because he's handsome and everything Shannon's ever wanted in a cowboy husband means nothing. Will Grant and Shannon be able to survive the summer or will the Utah heat be too much for them to handle?

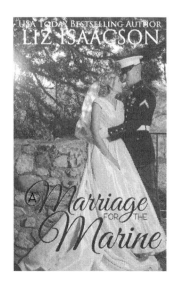

A Marriage for the Marine: A Fuller Family Novel - Brush Creek Brides Romance (Book 7): Tate Benson can't believe he's come to Nowhere, Utah, to fix up a house that hasn't been inhabited in years. But he has. Because he's retired from the Marines and looking to start a life as a police officer in small-town Brush Creek. Wren Fuller has her hands full most days running her family's company. When Tate calls and demands a maid for that morning, she decides to have the calls forwarded to her cell and go help him out. She didn't know he was moving in next door, and she's completely unprepared for his handsomeness, his kind heart, and his wounded soul.Can Tate and Wren weather a relationship when they're also next-door neighbors?

A Fiancé for the Firefighter: A Fuller Family Novel - Brush Creek Brides Romance (Book 8): Cora Wesley comes to Brush Creek, hoping to get some in-the-wild firefighting training as she prepares to put in her application to be a hotshot. When she meets Brennan Fuller, the spark between them is hot and instant. As they get to know each other, her deadline is  constantly looming over them, and Brennan starts to wonder if he can break ranks in the family business. He's okay mowing lawns and hanging out with his brothers, but he dreams of being able to go to college and become a landscape architect, but he's just not sure it can be done. Will Cora and Brennan be able to endure their trials to find true love?

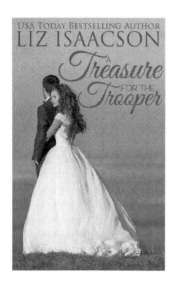

A Treasure for the Trooper: A Fuller Family Novel - Brush Creek Brides Romance (Book 9): Dawn Fuller has made some mistakes in her life, and she's not proud of the way McDermott Boyd found her off the road one day last year. She's spent a hard year wrestling with her choices and trying to fix them, glad for McDermott's acceptance and friendship. He lost his wife years ago, done his best with his daughter, and now he's ready to move on. Can McDermott help Dawn find a way past her former mistakes and down a path that leads to love, family, and happiness?

A Date for the Detective: A Fuller Family Novel - Brush Creek Brides Romance (Book 10): Dahlia Reid is one of the best detectives Brush Creek and the surrounding towns has ever had. She's given up on the idea of marriage—and pleasing her mother—and has dedicated herself fully to her job. Which is great, since one of the most perplexing cases of her career

has come to town. Kyler Fuller thinks he's finally ready to move past the woman who ghosted him years ago. He's cut his hair, and he's ready to start dating. Too bad every woman he's been out with is about as interesting as a lamppost—until Dahlia. He finds her beautiful, her quick wit a breath of fresh air, and her intelligence sexy. Can Kyler and Dahlia use their faith to find a way through the obstacles threatening to keep them apart?

A Partner for the Paramedic: A Fuller Family Novel - Brush Creek Brides Romance (Book 11): Jazzy Fuller has always been overshadowed by her prettier, more popular twin, Fabiana. Fabi meets paramedic Max Robinson at the park and sets a date with him only to come down with the flu. So she convinces Jazzy to cut her hair and take her place on the date. And the spark between Jazzy and Max is hot and instant...if only he knew she wasn't her sister, Fabi.

Max drives the ambulance for the town of Brush Creek with is partner Ed Moon, and neither of them have been all that lucky in love. Until Max suggests to who he thinks is Fabi that they should double with Ed and Jazzy. They do, and Fabi is smitten with the steady, strong Ed Moon. As each twin falls further and further in love with their respective paramedic, it becomes obvious they'll need to come clean about the switcheroo sooner rather than later...or risk losing their hearts.

A Catch for the Chief: A Fuller Family Novel - Brush Creek Brides Romance (Book 12): Berlin Fuller has struck out with the dating scene in Brush Creek more times than she cares to admit. When she makes a deal with her friends that they can choose the next man she goes out with, she didn't dream they'd pick surly Cole Fairbanks, the new Chief of Police.

His friends call him the Beast and challenge him to complete ten dates that summer or give up his bonus check. When Berlin approaches him, stuttering about the deal with her friends and claiming they don't actually have to go out, he's intrigued. As the summer passes, Cole finds himself burning both ends of the candle to keep up with his job and his new relationship. When he unleashes the Beast one time too many, Berlin will have to decide if she can tame him or if she should walk away.

ABOUT LIZ

Liz Isaacson writes inspirational romance, usually set in Texas, or Montana, or anywhere else horses and cowboys exist. She lives in Utah, where she teaches elementary school, taxis her daughter to dance several times a week, and eats a lot of Ferrero Rocher while writing. Find her on her website at lizisaacson.com.

Printed in Great Britain
by Amazon